Selkie Cove

Book Five of the Ingenious Mechanical Devices

Kara Jorgensen

Fox Collie Publishing

Copyright © 2017 by Kara Jorgensen
Cover Design © 2017 Lou Harper

First Edition, 2017
Paperback ISBN: 978-0-9905022-8-9
Ebook ISBN: 978-0-9905022-9-6

To Javier,
For never telling me to make my own
coffee.

ACT ONE

"We must believe that we are gifted for something, and that this thing, at whatever cost, must be attained."
-Marie Curie

Chapter One
A Confirmed Bachelor

Adam Fenice resisted the urge to turn around and check the clock again for fear of drawing the attention of the other clerks and accountants. Keeping his back to them, he took a quick glance at his pocket watch. He smothered his anticipation beneath a veneer of practiced nonchalance. In a little over an hour, he and Immanuel would be having lunch. No matter how often they saw each other, knowing that he and Immanuel would be in public together sent a thrill through his breast. It didn't matter if they were pretending to merely be flat mates, they were out. For the past few weeks Immanuel had been busy running errands for the Natural History Museum and the British Museum, and between the late nights, the impromptu meetings with the heads of the museums, and the nightmares and insomnia from the added stress, they had barely spent a peaceful day—or night—together. Today would be different. Immanuel said everything had been taken care of, and now things would go back to normal.

Adam scoffed at the thought. *Normal.* Nothing about his life was ever normal. Instead of dealing with Hadley's toy business or his brother's consumption, he had Immanuel's magic to enliven his humdrum life. His time spent at the office puzzling out inconsistencies was a welcome relief from coming home to find Immanuel experimenting with new sigils that sent things crashing across the room or turned his tea to dingy brown ice. Between magic and Percy, their *cat*—if one could call him that when he was solely comprised of bones and mischief—Adam was happy to come to work and deal with facts and figures, where things were certain no matter what happened outside the office walls.

"Fenice, can you come here a moment?" Mr. Bodkin called from his office.

Rising from his desk, Adam stretched and glanced at the clock one more time. He silently sighed, hoping this wouldn't turn into an hour long conversation on Sarah Bernhardt's latest exploit. He had promised Immanuel he would get to the museum promptly to prevent Sir William Henry Flower from commandeering him. If he played his cards right, he could distract Bodkin with a question or two and return to his work. As Adam pushed open the door to the dim cubby of an office, he knew something was wrong. His supervisor sat with his hands folded on his blotter, his thumbs twitching in time with his beady eyes, which ran over everything but Adam's face. Adam stiffly sat in the leather-backed chair before his desk, resisting the urge to scratch his wrist.

"Sir, is there anything—?"

"You've been dismissed," Bodkin blurted.

For a moment, Adam merely stared at him, unsure if his ears had played a trick on him, but when Bodkin's eyes never wavered and his lips twitched into a regretful frown, he knew he had heard correctly. The saliva dried in his throat as he strained to speak.

"I beg your pardon, sir, but may I ask why? Have I made an error?" Adam asked, his mind churning over the numbers he had tabulated and double-checked over the past few weeks.

"Oh, heavens no. You're one of my best workers."

"Then, why am I being let go?"

Mr. Bodkin released a tired breath, his rounded shoulders slumping in agreement. In the dim light with his face more pensive than Adam had ever seen, he seemed so much older. Adam had liked him best of all his employers. The man had given him his extra tickets to the theatre and chatted with him about novels and society page gossip, but as he tented his meaty, ringed hands and met Adam's gaze, the fissure of rank widened into a chasm. It had been foolish to ever assume they were friends.

"You must understand, this isn't my doing, Fenice," Bodkin said, dropping his voice. "It was Mr. Ellis. His eldest is to marry soon, and he needs to secure a proper position for him."

"I see," he spat, his chest tight with a raw resentment he hadn't felt since his older brother was alive. Adam's jaw tightened as he pictured that miser Ellis's lout of a son sitting at his desk. He eyed Bodkin. How long would it be before the boss's son was out of his desk and in Bodkin's chair? "And what about Penn or Weiland? They have been here less than a year. I've been here for *four*. This isn't fair."

"Trust me, I agree with you. You know you're one of my favorites." For a moment, he looked as if he might reach out and touch Adam's arm, but upon seeing the blue fire in Adam's eyes, he thought the better of it. "It's just that— that— you aren't the *image* Mr. Ellis wants for his business. You know, you go to the theatre, you're an Aesthete who openly supports Wilde's crowd, you dress flamboyantly—"

Adam glanced down at his silk paisley waistcoat as if seeing it for the first time before crossing his arms over it.

"And you're a bachelor."

A derisive laugh escaped his lips. "What does my marital status have to do with my work? If anything, I should have less distractions."

Mr. Bodkin swallowed hard, his shiny black eyes darting for an answer. "A bachelor could pick up and leave at any moment, but a man with a wife and children has an anchor. You're sharing your flat with another bachelor, aren't you?"

Adam froze. Something lurked beneath the question, plunging his anger into something far colder. Bodkin of all people should have known the significance of Ellis's decree. Then again, he had a ring on his finger and a brood at home.

"Yes, sir, I am."

"I have no problems with it, but Mr. Ellis…"

"Dashwood shares a flat with another bookkeeper. Many young men have roommates."

"Yes, I know, but do you perhaps have a lady friend you—?"

"No," Adam replied, his voice sharper than he intended.

"I figured as much." Pulling an envelope from his desk, Bodkin held it out for Adam to take. "I was able to convince him to give you an extra week's wages for the inconvenience. I really am sorry about this, Fenice, but there was nothing I could do to change his mind."

As he reached to take the money, Adam steadied his hand, stifling the urge to snatch it from his grasp. It was Ellis' fault, he reminded himself. Bodkin was merely a mole forced to do his bidding. A man who, like him, had kept his head down and tried not to make trouble for anyone. Only he had succeeded.

"Thank you for your generosity," Adam murmured, his voice quavering against his will.

He didn't try to suppress it. The rage would come out one way or another, and a little edge was far better than the venom creeping up his throat. Adam swallowed and dug his nail into his wrist as he turned, pushing in until he regained control. That was his whole life, wasn't it? Maintaining an air of control. As he stood to leave, Bodkin's eyes bored into his back, but before he could look away, Adam whipped around in time to see the man jump back.

A smug, unkind smile crossed his lips as he stuffed the envelope of money into his breast pocket. "I appreciate all you have done for me, Horace. I just hope Ellis can see past our shared faults when he inevitably decides to promote his son. Good day, sir."

Without looking back, Adam marched into the office with his back rigid and his face a mask of hauteur. His heart pounded as the junior accountants and clerks raised their gazes from their papers in unison to watch him pass while the only other senior accountant kept his eyes buried in his work. Adam stared ahead as he silently walked to his desk near the window despite half a dozen pairs of eyes pressing into his form. How much had they heard? He couldn't look at them. He didn't want to know what they thought of his sudden fall. All he wanted was to get out with some semblance of dignity.

His eyes traveled over the contents of his desk, lingering on the ledgers he had been perusing for a suspected embezzlement case. The figures he had toiled over for days were meaningless now. Some other man would finish his work and take the credit for the case he had built. Adam drew in a constrained breath. Unlike the other men in the office, he had no pictures of his pretty wife or handsome children to show to clients or Mr. Ellis when they came to call. Sitting on a stack of papers by the window was an ammonite fossil Immanuel had given to him when they stayed at his brother-in-law's estate in Dorset that summer. It was the only bit of his life he had allowed to bleed into his work. He could still remember the thrill of danger at having a token of Immanuel's love in plain view. That was all he would take with him. Adam snatched the fossil, ignoring the slap of paper and the startled cries of his coworkers as the wind scattered the stack. As he slipped on his coat and top hat, he felt the weight of the ammonite in his hand and saw himself hurl it through the windowpane in his mind's eye. Dropping it into his pocket, he kept his gaze forward, his mouth neutral, and passed down the familiar creaking steps to Lombard Street.

The bitter October cold pawed at his cheeks and tousled the edge of his pomaded henna hair as he slipped out the door. With his hand tightly around the ammonite in his pocket, Adam walked blindly and tried to keep his pace casual. He up the rent, the cost to bring in a housekeeper, their monthly expenses, and how much the washerwoman charged against Immanuel's salary and what Adam remembered to be inscribed in his bankbook. How long would it last? He had only been temporarily out of work once during his career and money had been the least of his concerns then. Bodkin had refused his resignation and given him time off to put his mind to rights, citing his brother's recent passing. No one would come through for him now.

Men clad in dark wool and brushed top hats pushed passed him on their way to banks and solicitors' offices just like his. One man tipped his hat to Adam. Recognizing him from their business dealings only a month before, Adam gave him a nod but kept his eyes ahead. How long would it take for news of his dismissal to reach the other accountants or the clients he regularly worked for? He had spent his whole life avoiding becoming the subject of gossip, and now, it had been thrust upon him.

When Adam stopped moving long enough to surface from his thoughts, he found his hand on the iron railing of the Met station that would take him home. *Home.* The word caught in Adam's throat in a wet knot. He swallowed it down and hardened his jaw. He wouldn't lose it. It had been his family's home for as long as he had been alive and now it belonged to him and Immanuel. There was no way he would let someone like Ellis take that from him, but the idea of sitting alone with his thoughts until Immanuel came home was more than he could bear. Without someone there to temper his emotions, he could only imagine the destruction he might wreak, and that would be far worse than holding it in a while longer. That was simple. After all, he had choked down the same bitter pill for nearly twenty years.

Glancing at his watch, Adam took the stairs into the labyrinth of brick and wood two at a time. The stench of urine and feculence burned his nose as he listened for the distant rumble of the electric train. He could take the train to Greenwich and vent to Hadley about what had happened. His sister would understand. She would rail against the injustice of it as only she could, but then, she would have solutions. Hadley would have half a dozen thought up in an instant, most of which would inevitably be tied to her husband, the Earl of Dorset. The thought sent a wave of nausea gurgling through Adam's gut.

No, Immanuel was waiting for him, and he wouldn't disappoint him twice in one day. Before he could change his mind, the train barreled into the station. Straightening, Adam slipped into the crowded car. All he needed was to pretend everything was all right. Perhaps if he simply didn't acknowledge it, then he wouldn't be a disappoint to Immanuel, too. If it had worked for most of his life, then surely it could work for another hour.

Chapter Two
Sigils and Seals

Immanuel closed his eyes, drinking in the crisp autumnal air as it ruffled his sigil for conjuring wind. For most of the morning, he had barely gotten a stir of air. It wasn't until he stopped picturing hurricanes and replaced them with birds soaring and the smell of rain that he felt the kiss of Hyde Park's earthen perfume brush his cheek. Opening his eyes, Immanuel found a loose Celtic knot beneath the nib of his pen. A smile flashed across his lips as he quickly jotted down his thoughts and results before they could sink beneath the sea of the research piled on his desk. For most of the morning, he had been gathering information on Arctic mammals out of half a dozen books from the museum's library, but he desperately needed a break from penguins and whales. Immanuel shuddered at the thought of having to dissect the latter beast and studied the new sigil's form. While magic had only been part of his life a short while, it was proving to be as interesting a discipline as science.

Immanuel eyed the tea cup resting at the edge of his blotter and chewed his lip in thought. He had at least fifteen minutes before Sir William Henry Flower finished his weekly meeting with the heads of the museum's departments. Anyone with any authority would be in the Shaw Room, which meant there would be time to practice a trick he had been working on. Placing the cup before him, Immanuel drew in a slow, steady breath. With his eyes locked on the cold tea, his finger traced a whirl that grew into a deformed star on the tabletop. For a moment, nothing happened. He pictured water rolling over his back, the sensation of water dripping across his skin, the call of the ocean lapping against the shore. A ripple passed from his mind to the tea's surface. The harder he stared, the rougher the waves became until the tea nearly sloshed over the edge of the china. When it reached a peak in the center, Immanuel's mind snagged it. The sigil evolved beneath his hand, twisting into a lattice of peaks and valleys as the surface rose high above the cup.

"What the devil do you think you're doing!"

Immanuel jumped and the liquid plummeted into the cup, splashing tea across his blotter and papers. Scrambling to keep the ink from bleeding into an indecipherable blur, Immanuel looked up to find Peregrine Nichols glaring back at him from the doorway. The junior botany curator's sharp brown brows furrowed as he kicked the door shut and stood at the end of Immanuel's desk. Despite being over a head shorter than Immanuel, Peregrine had a commanding air he couldn't hope to emulate. He had seen Peregrine take down a revenant with a pry bar and an incantation when Immanuel could scarcely will his fear-frozen body to move. Carefully mopping his notes with a handkerchief, Immanuel avoided Peregrine's gaze.

"Are you out of your bloody mind, Winter?" Peregrine hissed. "What if someone saw you? How would you have explained your levitating tea?"

"It wasn't levitating, I was merely experimenting with— with— I didn't think anyone would barge in." Immanuel's face reddened against his will as he held the handkerchief over his paper and hoped he hadn't ruined the wind sigil. "Sir William always knocks."

"But not everyone does. That's the point. If you're looking for a way to get on Elliott's bad side, provoking a modern Inquisition by being careless is a good way to start."

"I didn't mean any harm."

"It doesn't matter. One slip up and we're all pyre fodder." Running out of steam, Peregrine deflated and rested on his heels. "So, have you decided yet? She's been nagging me to find out."

A wave of guilt rippled through him as he broke from Peregrine's hard gaze to shut the window and put the wet pages on the radiator to dry. He still didn't have an answer. After discovering he had extranormal abilities and helping to foil a witch hell-bent on bringing an otherworldly creature to London, he had been offered the chance to join Her Majesty's Interceptors, a sort of Home Office to deal with England's overlooked world of magic. It had been tempting, but— Immanuel wasn't certain what the "but" was. With all that transpired since he had been given a second chance at life, he was tired, and he savored the peace that had finally fallen over his life. His job as a junior curator and his relationship with Adam were all he could have wanted. Becoming an Interceptor would change all of that.

"I will get back to her soon. What is it you need?"

"For you stop doing magic at work," Peregrine snapped, keeping his voice low. Releasing a sigh, the impish curator stepped around Immanuel's desk to inspect the drowsy pink orchid blooming on his shelf between an ammonite and a sea urchin's shell. "This is *Hexalectris colemanii*. Where did you get it? They're exceptionally rare. I tried to get one, but it arrived dead."

Immanuel met Peregrine's umber eyes before quickly averting his gaze back to his papers. "I— I didn't think you wanted it anymore."

"So you fished it out of my rubbish bin?"

"I... Well, yes. I thought it might be pretty, and I wanted to see if I could revive it. It was an experiment, really. You can have it back if you want."

"Thanks," he replied tartly as he stood on tiptoe to pull the plant down. Hugging the orchid to his chest, he turned on heel at the door.

"Oh, Sir William wants to see you in the loading dock, and may I suggest you put your papers away before you go."

The moment Peregrine shut the door behind him, Immanuel released a slow breath. Carefully moving the drying pages behind his desk, he blocked them from sight with a stack of books and darted down the hall, hoping to god Sir William hadn't been waiting long. The last time he did, he became the liaison between the director and the British Museum, which really meant a month of being a glorified errand boy. At the bottom of the steps, Immanuel nodded to the archivists at the front desk before slipping into the storeroom's maze of dusty wooden shelves. His heart thundered in his throat as he crossed the boards, focusing his attention on the shelves of specimens and bones. It had been months since he was attacked between the stacks by Lord Rose, but each time he ventured into the vast storeroom alone, he found his mind grasping to relive those dark moments. More than anything, Immanuel wished he knew how to make it stop.

Near the loading docks, an unintelligible mix of accented voices rose through the stillness. Ahead, a crane swung, dangling a long box the size of a coffin. Sir William stood near the controls, watching the crate with an eagle eye as he fed its operator directions. As Immanuel stepped from the shadows, Sir William stared down his patrician nose at the lanky young man, his gaze lingering on Immanuel's scar and blotted eye. Immanuel shifted beneath his gaze before clasping his hands behind his back to stop from fidgeting.

"I beg your pardon, sir. I got caught up helping Peregrine."

Without a word, Sir William turned and gestured for Immanuel to follow him the he way came. "A specimen has arrived that I need you to examine. I know it to be the work of a mountebank, but it came from a well-respected benefactor who claims it to be genuine. I will not tolerate forgeries in the collection, which is why I would like you to give it the time and attention it deserves. Very little. But make the report detailed, so I can present it to them with little conflict. Do you understand what I'm asking of you, Winter?"

"Yes, sir. I believe so, but what is it?"

"A charlatan's creation." Stopping beside a man-sized crate hidden beneath a canvas sheet, Sir William scowled. "Here it is. Put the report on my desk when you're finished, so I can review it. No matter how foolish this is, we must take care not to offend our donors."

The breath hitched in Immanuel's throat as the director tossed back the sheet. Floating within the glass-walled case was a seal-like beast. While the skin retained the smooth, grey speckled fur of a harbor seal, the face and body had the unmistakable profile of the human form. Its arms were short, as if stunted, and ended in a webbed hand tipped with sharp claws. Spotted, hooded lids covered the creature's large eyes, which peeked out beneath long lashes. A twang of recognition rang through him, touching the deepest parts of his mind. All thoughts escaped him as he took in the creature's bisected tail and elongated human torso. With a tut, Sir William tossed the sheet back over the glass coffin, hiding the creature from view as a dockhand passed.

"Take this up to Mr. Winter's office and let no one else see it."

Before Immanuel could speak, the director snapped his fingers for one of the men to fetch a cart. Whatever the creature was, Immanuel had the sinking feeling it wasn't as unbelievable as Sir William thought. The director turned and headed back to the dock, leaving Immanuel standing mute as two rough dockhands tromped in. The wooden dolly yawned beneath the weight of the beast and the gallons of fluid surrounding it. Immanuel flinched as the gruff men rammed the cart into the doorframe on their way to the upper floor before shoving the corner further into the elevator with their scuffed boots. Following close behind them, Immanuel stood silently in front of the elevator doors, staring down at the shoes Adam had polished for him the previous night. The men beside him spoke of a new freak show opening in Piccadilly. Immanuel's scarred eye burned as he clasped his nervous hands behind his back. Would they call him a freak if they knew what he truly was? That with a touch of his hand, he could see the last moments of the creature at their feet's life, *if* it really was a creature at all and not some amalgamation of body parts. Would they

18

call for his demise if they knew all the ways he went against nature?

With a thud, the elevator doors opened, and the men rolled the box down the hall to Immanuel's office. Immanuel inwardly sighed, standing out of the way until, with a few more bangs, they left him alone with the veiled creature. Ignoring the glass box monopolizing the space between his desk and door, Immanuel shimmied behind his desk to gather up the papers and fallen books the men had scattered in their wake. His eyes roamed over the sigils and notes. The ink had bled in a few places, but overall, his work appeared to still be legible. He carefully tucked the papers into his notebook and turned his attention to the pile of letters sitting on his blotter. As he turned over the first envelope, his eyes lit up; the seal was from the Royal Zoological Society. Immanuel's hands shook as he ripped open the wax and pulled out the letter.

⊱⊰

Adam watched from the threshold as Immanuel read the letter. His bichrome eyes widened, and a smile brightened his features. Immanuel bit his lip and reread the letter again, the look of glee refusing to leave his face. Swallowing hard, Adam lightly wrapped on the door with his knuckles. Immanuel jumped, but upon seeing Adam, relief washed across his face only to be replaced with unbridled joy.

"Adam, I got in," Immanuel said, beaming. Standing, he held the letter out for Adam to take, but his companion didn't move from his place near the door. "Look! I got into the Zoological Society. Read it. Tell me I'm not imagining this."

"Congratulations. I'm very proud of you," Adam replied, his voice tight.

"I can't believe it. I was certain my paper wasn't good enough. Walrus evolution isn't exactly interesting, but—" Glancing at the clock above his door, Immanuel paused as he stuffed the letter back into the envelope with trembling hands. "You got here quickly. I wasn't expecting you for another few minutes."

"Mr. Bodkin let me go early."

Immanuel's gaze drifted to the letter again but he caught himself. "That was very nice of him."

Adam kept his eyes locked on the knotty floorboards. How could Immanuel not notice the strain in his voice or the tightness in his features? Immanuel walked toward the door but returned to grab the letter off his desk. Adam drew in a breath and steeled himself. Happiness could blind as much as anger, and it wasn't his place to ruin Immanuel's day. It wasn't his place to ruin anything for anyone. Clearing his throat, Adam turned to the cloaked crate at his ankle.

"What's this?" he asked, nudging the box with his foot.

Immanuel glanced toward the window for any sign of rain before grabbing his top hat. "A specimen Sir William wants me to take a look at after lunch. A seal of some sort."

"Great. The flat will stink like dead fish."

Adam turned at a gentle squeeze of his arm. Immanuel let his hand linger as he met Adam's gaze, a fleeting embrace before they had to pretend they were nothing more than friends. Most days Adam would have relished such an allowance in public, but today he wanted nothing more than to peel his lover's fingers off his coat.

Staring into Adam's eyes, Immanuel whispered, "It's nothing a bath for two can't fix."

He should have smiled, he should have done something, but all Adam felt was the gnaw of dread hollowing his chest.

⚬ᘎᘙᘎ⚬

Immanuel wouldn't stop rambling. It was a habit Adam normally found endearing, that his enthusiasm could send his mouth and mind spinning out of control, but after the day he had, Adam wished he would shut up. Sitting in a leather-backed booth at Benekey's, Adam rubbed his brow as Immanuel prattled on about walrus anatomy between bites of fried fish. His head pounded with the clank of glasses and silverware, the din of voices all around them, and the stink of cigarette smoke drifting in despite the high walls of the booth. A plate of roast beef sat untouched beside a glass of wine he hadn't intended to order. It would turn his face red, if it wasn't already, but perhaps it would make denial that much easier.

Adam snapped out of his thoughts as Immanuel's hand brushed against his under the guise of chasing a loose chip.

"What's wrong? You're very quiet today," Immanuel said softly, his mismatched eyes intent with concern. "Tell me about your office. Any interesting clients?"

Resisting the urge to scratch his wrist, Adam tapped his nails on the base of the glass and kept his gaze on the merlot within. *Ruin it*, his mind whispered. "I was sacked today."

"You were wha—?" Immanuel's mouth wordlessly opened twice before he shook his head and put his hand over Adam's. "Why didn't you say anything? I'm so sorry, Adam. If I had known, I wouldn't have—"

Adam ripped his hand away and picked up his knife. "It's fine. I don't want to make a thing of it."

"Can you fix it? Can you prove to Mr. Bodkin that whatever it was, was an accident? You always seemed to get on so well, so maybe he would listen after given the chance to rethink his decision."

He swallowed against the knot in his throat and tried to keep his voice level. "It wasn't due to a mistake. They needed to make room for Mr. Ellis's son, so they gave me the ax."

"Oh." Immanuel's expression lightened as he leaned back in his seat. "Then, it shouldn't be too hard to find new employment. You didn't do anything to deserve it. There must be other offices looking for accountants."

"Yes, but Ellis… Ellis has a hand in half of them. The others are either friends of his or they wouldn't hire me because I don't think he will give me a reference. Bodkin never mentioned it and I forgot to ask. That's what happened when Reynolds was dismissed last year. He was blackballed. Last I heard, he had to take a position in Edinburgh," Adam replied, his voice alien, tighter but calmer than he anticipated.

"But— but why wouldn't they give you a reference if you were let go due to nepotism?"

"Because I don't 'fit their aesthetic,'" he spat as he turned to watch his reflection in the smoked glass mirror hanging beside them.

"What do you mean by aesthetic?"

His henna-red hair and blue eyes flared, taking on an otherworldly hue under the dim electric lights. "I think you know what I mean."

Dropping his voice, Immanuel pushed aside his plate and leaned closer. "That you're— you're," the word escaped him, "*schwul?* There's no way for them to know that for certain. You're so careful."

Ignoring Immanuel's imploring stare, Adam ground his jaw and hacked his meat into cubes. "Apparently, they suspect it. It seems no matter what I do, people still see through me."

"Even so, I'm sure you'll get a new position before you know it. You're pretty perfect to me."

"Unfortunately your opinion matters very little."

Adam looked up from his blood-ringed plate to find Immanuel glaring at him. His blotted blue eye glistened with moisture while his lips sealed in a hard line. On the table beside his fork, Immanuel's finger twitched with the urge to draw a sigil. For a moment they merely stared at each other as Adam waited for something on his side of the table to go flying with a twist of his lover's finger. *Let him*, he thought bitterly.

"I understand that you have had a very trying day, but could you please not take it out on me? I have done nothing to you, Adam."

"My apologies. It's just that while I was on the train, I realized I can only be without work for two months before we're in the red. My sister's toy business has been slow since she married and I only have a little over a month's worth of pay in reserve."

When Adam's gaze returned to his plate, Immanuel asked, "Have you spoken to Lord or Lady Dorset? I'm certain they—"

"I'm certain they would too, but I'm not going to sponge off my brother-in-law for the rest of my life," he snapped.

"It would only be for a little while."

"I said, no."

"Then, what do you plan to do? You act like you won't be able to find work as an accountant, but then you say you couldn't possibly ask your sister for help when you need it. If your fears are correct, you may not have an income. Then what will we do? My wages at the museum…" Immanuel drew in a tremulous breath. He liked living on Baker Street in their own flat where they could do as they please without fear. A boarding house could ruin all of that. "I suppose I could ask Sir William for a raise or an advance. If I tell him the circumstances, then—"

"Don't you dare. I don't need everyone knowing my business." No one would discuss how far the countess's brother had fallen behind his back.

"Adam," Immanuel pleaded, shaking his head, "what do you expect me to do? You act like you won't be able to get work, but you act like we should do nothing to stay afloat. I'm certain Hadley—"

"Don't bring up my sister. I don't need her help."

Immanuel sat back, watching Adam stab a piece of beef and twirl it on the tip of his fork without bringing it to his lips. "Are you really going to let your pride sink us? This doesn't only affect you, Adam."

For a moment, Adam merely scowled at him, but in an instant, his hand was on his coat and his hat was on his head. Immanuel scooted out of the booth after him, calling his name as Adam cast a burning glance over his shoulder. Standing next to their table, Immanuel watched Adam cut through the crowded restaurant and disappear onto the street. Tears burned the backs of Immanuel's eyes at the sudden sensation of falling. He blinked until his clouded eye cleared, stuffing his hand into his pocket for coins. The cool metal with its familiar striations and reliefs brought his mind back to the clatter of the smoke-hazed room. Drawing in a long slow breath, Immanuel released it as the panic momentarily receded.

Paying their bill, Immanuel slipped onto the street hoping to see Adam leaning against the brick façade waiting for him, but when he reached the corner, he knew for certain he was gone. Fear welled in his breast, compelling him to run home to make certain his lover was all right. Immanuel stood very still until, with each breath and droplet of rain pattering against his face, the feeling finally relinquished its hold. Adam would be fine. He was a reasonable man, who had shown no sign of wanting to hurt himself. He would be fine. Pulling out his pocket watch, Immanuel clicked open the cold brass face. Even if he wanted to, there was no way he could make it to the house and return to the museum without arousing suspicion at his tardiness. There was only one thing he could do. He had to go back to the museum and carry on as if Adam Fenice's troubles weren't his own.

Chapter Three
A Foot in Both Worlds

On the walk back to the museum, Immanuel replayed what had happened at Benekey's over and over, searching for any way he could have made Adam stay. Reaching the museum's familiar Gothic façade, Immanuel stared at the masses of people tittering within. All week he had been looking forward to having lunch with Adam, and he ruined it. He swallowed against the tightness working its way from his throat to his chest and ducked around the side to take the servants' entrance in. As he climbed the back stairs up to his office, he dreaded running into another curator as much as he dreaded what awaited him at home. Adam was angry, and rightly so, yet the thought of wrangling with Adam's vile stubbornness was more than Immanuel could bear. Whatever the solution, it would have to be Adam's idea. That much was clear.

At the top of the stairs, Immanuel froze with his hand on the worn door. Someone was in his office. A shadow passed behind the mottled glass, disappearing near his desk. Immanuel's heart pounded in his temples as the urge to run tensed his muscles and set every hair on end. Drawing in a steadying breath, he tried to banish all thoughts of Lord Rose. It had been months since he was attacked and Lord Rose's soul was sealed in a lead tomb in the bowels of Interceptor Headquarters. Lady Rose supposedly shared a similar fate, but as the shadow paced past the glass again, Immanuel caught the unmistakable shape of a corseted waist. Could she have gotten free and come after him?

Slowly ducking back into the stairway, Immanuel fumbled through his leather satchel for the vivalabe. The moment his fingers brushed its cool, brassy surface, a wave of calm passed over him. The brass ball was the size of a compass and weighed twice as much. If he took it out at night, he could hear the steady cadence of its clockwork heart, ticking in time with his own. With two clicks of the hidden button, the ball's lid fell back to reveal an etched face lined with minute chips of colored stone. In an instant, the marbles scattered like billiard balls, leaving only three clustered together: a white, a green, and an amber. Immanuel exhaled, letting his head fall back against the cold wall in relief that Lady Rose's red stone was nowhere to be seen. He stared at the amber stone and chewed his lip. Had Peregrine already reported his transgression to Judith Elliott?

Stuffing the vivalabe back into his bag, Immanuel smoothed his rumpled coat and pushed a wet blonde curl from his forehead. Even if Judith would ultimately discern something was amiss, he didn't want her to read it on his face. If she wanted to know, she would have to work for it. In three long strides with his eyes cast to the floor, Immanuel reached his office and slipped inside. Judith looked up from behind his desk, her hazel eyes meeting his without hesitation. With a knowing smile, she studied his latest sigils with a gold magnifying glass hanging from a chain around her regal neck. No matter where he saw her, Judith Elliott was unabashedly American. Where the British embraced etiquette to the point of meekness or passive aggression, her intentions were always as straight and loud as a gunshot. If he hadn't known any better, he would have assumed it was her office by the glint her eye and the self-assured way she stayed rooted in his seat even as he hung up his bag and coat.

"Your sigils are quite interesting, Winter. Very complex for someone who has only begun their studies. Did you know no two sigils are exactly the same? Every practioner leaves their mark, their own image, so to speak. Did the books I lent you help any?" Judith asked, her blonde hair glinting in the electric lamps as Immanuel switched them back on.

"Somewhat," he replied, shifting uncomfortably beside the veiled specimen. "I've been trying to expand my knowledge outside of life and death magic, and it's given me plenty of ideas there. But some of the books... some I can barely read. It doesn't seem to click no matter how hard I try."

"Too many archaic rules?" A smile quirked across her lips as she looked from the water-stained paper to Immanuel's downcast brows. "Don't be sheepish. It happens more often than most of us would care to admit, especially in the beginning. Some things won't work for you. You'll find magic is more of an art than a science."

"The strange thing is, the techniques... It felt like a lot didn't apply."

"You're an evolutionist, right? Think of it this way, magic has evolved over the centuries with human need and understanding. It morphs with geography, time, beliefs, and of course, the practioner. What worked then, doesn't necessarily work now, and plenty of practioners make rules to prevent novices from getting any farther than the basics. I know some of the writings are dense, but I thought they might, inspire your work rather than serve as a guide. Stop by Interceptor headquarters and I'll have the librarians give you some texts more suited to your interests."

Immanuel stood at the end of his desk, watching Judith study his work. "I don't mean to be rude, Miss Elliott, but what are you doing in my office? Does the director know you're here?"

"Sir William was more than willing to let me speak to the curator who will be handling my prized specimen," she replied with a flourish of her magnifying glass toward the creature.

His eyes widened. "That was you?"

"Technically yes, though it actually belongs to the Interceptors. We heard from our sources off the coast of an interesting specimen that was to be sent to the Royal Zoological Society. The box mysteriously disappeared and ended up at the museum with special instructions to have their resident seal expert examine it."

"Fantastic."

Judith chuckled at Immanuel's grimace. "Finding a scientist who has a foot in both worlds is incredibly difficult. You should be flattered that we chose you, especially when you don't officially work for us. I had to fill out a lot of paperwork to get an exception to involve you."

"You think the thing is real?"

"Despite what Sir William told you, there is more in this world than what your books lead you to believe. You of all people should understand that. What we need you to do is study the specimen, analyze it, dissect it, and tell us how it died. The latter may require you to use *unconventional* means. Before I leave you to it, I need you to sign a contract promising that you won't divulge what you find to anyone outside of the Interceptors, including Sir William."

"Don't worry, I have no intention of telling him any more than I have to." Being the laughing stock of the department was the last thing he wanted to be if the *thing* turned out to be genuine.

Reaching into her reticule, Judith retrieved a folded wad of parchment and smoothed it across the desk. She handed him the pen from his blotter and pointed to each place he should sign. Immanuel released a soundless sigh at the magazine-thick stack. He should have read it, but he had neither the time nor the patience on a good day. Near the bottom of the fifth page, Immanuel paused. *Any party involved may be recalled to carry out a further investigation on behalf of Her Majesty's Interceptors if they see fit.* As he reread the minute type, Immanuel felt the nudge of Judith's energy caressing his mind like the invisible arm of a jellyfish. If he let her, she would slip in, waltzing through his thoughts until she found what she sought.

"You could have asked first," he replied, ripping his mind away from her grasp with a turn of his head. Hastily signing the last of the documents, Immanuel pushed them back to her and dropped his pen into his top drawer. "Will that be all?"

"My apologies, Winter," she said, her eyes traveling over his scar before lingering on his crooked frown and faraway gaze. "I didn't mean to offend you, but you don't seem yourself. Have I come at a bad time?"

"I received some bad news at lunch, but I will have my report to you about," he paused, trying to picture the creature trapped within the glass coffin, "whatever that is, by the weekend."

With a nod, Judith tucked the contract into her bag and slipped past him. At the door, she stopped to watch Immanuel collapse into his chair. "There's one thing I have been meaning to ask since we last spoke. Have you given any thought to becoming an Interceptor? You never gave me an answer."

Immanuel stared at the pages of sigils littering his desk alongside his acceptance letter into the Royal Zoological Society. His nights were spent trying to manipulate cups of tea when he should have been knee-deep in research. He had a career now, one that he was actually decent at, and yet... He frowned, averting his eyes from Judith's. Yet he still felt out of place at the museum. Every day he feared that he would be unmasked for the imposter he was. Something was missing. At times he wondered if it was the absence of fear now that Lord and Lady Rose were gone, but there was a bigger void that research and recitation, or even Adam, couldn't hope to fill. And that terrified him.

"I fear I still don't have an answer for you, Miss Elliott. I haven't ruled it out, but I don't know if I'm ready to take that step."

"Fair enough. If you should change your mind, you and Mr. Fenice know where you can find me."

Immanuel tidied his papers and hesitantly asked, "Your... Your offer is still open to both of us?"

"Of course. Your earnest relationship makes you stronger than the sum of your parts." She flashed a measured smile even as her power pried at his mind once more. "Good day, Mr. Winter, and give Mr. Fenice my regards."

When the door closed behind her, Immanuel melted deeper into his chair, letting his head fall over the low wooden back. As his chair lazily spun, his eyes fell upon the dirty sheet covering the crate. Peace had sounded like a wonderful thing to have, but like most of his life, peace was fleeting. It had been foolish of him to expect that Judith Elliott wouldn't come barging back into his life after all that had happened. But did it even matter now that Adam lost his job? Equilibrium had been destroyed by the time the creature reached his office.

Tucking the sigils back into his desk drawer, Immanuel tugged on the pair of elbow-length leather gloves he kept tucked beside his sigil journal. Immanuel drew in a long breath, steeling himself against whatever nightmare he was about to uncover. In one swift motion, he ripped off the canvas and tossed it aside.

Staring back at him from beneath the bath of embalming liquid was a seal with a not quite human face. For a moment he merely stared at it, unable to grasp how the mismatched pieces fit together so seamlessly. While the body retained the shape and grey spotted fur of a seal, the creature's face appeared out of place with its sharp cheekbones and Cupid's bow lips, but what held him wholly were the creature's eyes. They were wide and round like the seals he had studied, yet they retained the colored iris of a human. Hers were the steely blue of tossing waves, now unnerving in their stillness. Immanuel lowered his gaze, following the curve of the creature's body until he reached its hands. Hands. Where there should have been bow-legged fins, there were fine fingers jutting from a meaty furred palm. Backing up, Immanuel looked at her feet to find a tail and nothing more.

Carefully opening the lid of the steel and glass box, Immanuel leaned closer until the embalming fluid bit at his eyes and left the unforgettable tang of death and alcohol on his tongue. With his nose scarcely a breath above the surface, Immanuel probed the monster's fur for any sign of stitches or manipulation from a charlatan. The Fiji

Mermaid had been the talk of the scientific community until they realized Barnum had sewn a fish to a monkey in an attempt to dupe the public and scientists alike, but this was different. No matter what Sir William thought, his wasn't some poorly crafted hybrid freak. Gathering his tools, Immanuel draped tubes into the glass case, letting the preservative fluid drain into a large bucket until the creature beneath was laid bare. He locked eyes with the creature as he hesitantly squatted at its side. At any moment, he feared it would turn toward him with its sightless eyes and release some ungodly sound he only knew in nightmares. Carefully removing his gloves, Immanuel let his hand hover over the beast's brow. He bit his lip, knowing that he would see the last moments of a seal or a human or some strange life form in between. Sucking in a breath, skin and fur met.

Water flooded every orifice, filling them with the cold salty murk of the sea as he hung weightless. His mind fought the unnatural sensation, but the body whose eyes he saw through merely twisted toward a dull hum thrumming somewhere nearby. He and the creature effortlessly glided through the forest of waving kelp toward the vibration. In the distance five massive brown contraptions rose through the silt. He thought it could have been a sunken ship or the remains of some ill-fated dirigible from its steel frame and the wire umbilical cords running up to the surface. As they grew closer, fear bubbled in her breast. Someone was supposed to be there. She had sworn she heard the call crying out to her beneath the waves with its hypnotic resonance. Watching the swirls of silt, a soft note wrapped around their mind. It spoke to a part of her so deep she felt it in her core and drew closer to the hunks of churning metal.

Immanuel felt it before they saw it: the thrust of water crashing into them followed by the sudden bolt of pain that started at their armpit and spread to every cell in their body. They thrashed, catching sight of a long pole and the faceless brown beast at the end of it, its face caked with mud and weeds. An indescribable feeling pass through their body. Something beneath the surface peeled away as pain tore through their arms and crept into every bone until their body screamed once more. In an instant, where there had been grey flippers upon the pole, now there were hands, but before Immanuel could stop them, they tore the blade out. Blood drifted out, flooding their vision as a weight fell over them. Their mind reeled at the disorienting constriction of the net as they sank beneath the mass of their misshapen body. Their heart sputtered and their vision spotted. He was coming. The brown beast was coming for them, looming over them with its hooded, faceless head and hook at the ready. They drew in a breath, lungs convulsing against the alien burning of salt water. *The others,* she cried as the world darkened to a pinpoint of dim light.

Immanuel fell back, landing hard on his side as he gagged and wheezed. His lungs tightened as he released another tearing dry heave despite tasting the brine of the ocean on his lips and deep in his throat. His stomach and lungs spasmed while his mind sought to save him from drowning on land. Resting his head against the cold planks of his office floor, Immanuel swallowed and fought to slow his breathing until the urge to vomit passed and he curled in on himself. He shuddered; the strength had been sapped from his body as if he had spent the entire day fighting the tide. Raising his gaze to the door, he made certain no one was coming before closing his eyes. His hands shook as he rubbed his forearms to silence the burn that had flooded his bones accompanied with the deep cracks of tissue restructuring. He was fine, he reminded himself over and over until his body quieted enough that his mind could believe that what he had seen had happened to someone—something—far from himself. It had seemed so human. The thoughts felt more like his own than animal's ever did.

Immanuel slowly climbed to his knees, fighting his trembling limbs as he used the desk for support. Squeezing his eyes shut, Immanuel wished Adam was there to anchor him to reality, to rub his back and make him tea to help the shakes subside, but then he heard the chatter of the other curators outside his door and remembered there were hours to go before he could see Adam again. He staggered forward and knocked the lid of the glass coffin closed with the back of his hand before tossing the sheet over it to hide the creature's lifeless features. Sinking into his chair, Immanuel grabbed his pen and quickly sketched out the details of his vision.

Chapter Four
Postmortem Examinations

The house stood dark when Immanuel arrived home. The only sounds were his grunts and strained breathes as he struggled to push the creature in its glass coffin over the threshold. Kicking the door shut behind him, he straightened and wiped the hair and sweat from his forehead. For a moment, he merely listened for any sign of Adam, but all he could hear was the sound of blood rushing through his ears.

"Adam! Adam, if you're home, I could really use your help for a minute."

When no answer came, Immanuel sighed and pushed the veiled crate onto the carpet runner and shoved it with all of his strength. His ribs and back cried in protest while the box barely budged apart from the slosh of liquid within. It had been surprisingly easy to get Sir William to consent to letting him study it in the seclusion of his home, but it had taken several men and a cart to get it out of his office and into the backseat of a steamer cab. The driver had looked at him like he was a madman and nearly pulled away from the pavement upon seeing his cargo. It was only at the promise of a generous tip that the driver hopped out to help him. Immanuel hoped the specimen was a fake just so he wouldn't have to take it back again; he didn't know how many more times he could afford to pay for an expensive cab ride.

Once the coffin hit the bare wood floor of the hallway, it picked up speed and Immanuel pushed it the rest of the way to the workroom. Even though Hadley had been married months ago, remnants of her life at Baker Street remained in disarticulated automatons and boxes of spare parts stashed in the corner behind her battered work table and stool. Adam had told him to throw it all away, but having remnants of someone else in the room made it feel less vacuous when he was still tentatively curating his new life. Immanuel shoved the creature all the way to the cast iron slop sink on the far wall. Leaning against the sink to catch his breath, Immanuel's eyes trailed to the cloaked specimen.

What was he going to tell Sir William? If he told him that the beast was closer to human than he cared to admit, he would be laughed out of the zoology department even with the body as evidence. Pulling the gloves from his pocket, Immanuel carefully removed the box's fragile lid and averted his gaze from the seal-like creature's vacant eyes. At Oxford, he had been forced to debone a walrus and a Caspian seal for the university's museum, and even when he was in better health and shape, the corpses had been impossibly heavy. He couldn't imagine how bad it would be now with his misshapen ribs and miserable constitution. Immanuel reached into the shallow layer of alcohol and was about to slip his arms beneath her neck and tailfin when a shadow fell across the doorway.

The breath caught in Immanuel's throat as he stood. Adam leaned against the door with his shirt open far enough to expose the henna hair dusting the firm planes of his torso. His carefully pomaded coiffure hung askew in a wayward wave that made him look like some debouched Brontëan rogue. Immanuel would have abandoned the creature in an instant if it hadn't been for the glazed look in his lover's eyes and the red flush that hid his faint freckles. It was only then that he spotted the glass in his hand and the clear liquid within.

"Bringing your work home with you again?" Adam asked, his voice uncharacteristically languid as he drew closer. Leaning in with his drink clutched close, he wrinkled his nose and tapped the box with the end of his boot. "What is that thing?"

"I'm not certain yet."

Before Adam could straighten, Immanuel snatched the glass from his hand and dashed it into the sink. The sweet, acidic tang of gin burned his nose as it splashed up.

"Hey! What's wrong with you?"

Immanuel's body shook against his will. "You don't need it. How much have you had?"

"What do you care?" Adam cried as he pulled the glass from Immanuel's hand but refused to meet his gaze.

"Adam, just tell me."

"I don't need your permission to have a drink. I'm bloody old enough to make my own decisions. I did so for quite some time before you got here."

As Adam turned to leave, Immanuel whipped off his gloves and cut in front of him. He blocked the door with his body, knowing his thin form would do nothing to stop Adam if he wanted to leave. "Is this what you have been doing all day? Drinking yourself into a stupor? I thought you were going to look for employment."

For a long moment, Adam merely stared at him. His lips nearly disappeared into a tight line as he glowered at Immanuel with an intensity he had never seen. His blue eyes flared with fury, and for an instant, Immanuel feared Adam would shove him or strike him. His hands twitched at his side, but he quickly folded his arms over his chest and rested on his heels, waiting. Immanuel stepped out of the way to let Adam storm past him. The redhead clomped up the stairs with Immanuel a step behind him. When Adam reached their bedroom, Immanuel expected him to slam the door in his face, but instead, he walked over to his desk near the window and grabbed his journal. Flipping through the pages, he turned to the last one and shoved the it at Immanuel's face. The page had begun with a list of law offices, accounting firms, and various banks before becoming jumbled with row upon row of numbers.

"This is what I've been doing all day," Adam spat, shoving the book into Immanuel's hand. "I have been all over town speaking to anyone I thought could help me. I went to a dozen places, and you know what I found? One position. One! And it was for a clerk. *A clerk.* I have been an accountant for *four* years. I can't be a clerk again. I can't afford to be a clerk."

"But at least it would be money. We wouldn't have to—"

"No." Grabbing the open bottle of gin from his desk, Adam poured another glass to the brim. "Let me have some semblance of pride, Immanuel. I have worked far too hard to settle for a position I had when I was seventeen, but you wouldn't understand, would you? Uncle Elijah handed you a lovely position at the museum the moment you were out of Oxford. Well, some of us aren't Oxford boys with connections and privileged lives."

Adam's mouth hung open, as his hand came to his lips. Slowly, he raised his gaze to Immanuel's face, which had blanched apart from his reddening eyes.

"Oh, Immanuel, I didn't mean it. I…"

"You have had enough," Immanuel rasped, his voice tight. Without waiting for a response, he took the glass and bottle from Adam's hands and set them down on the dresser. "You're done."

Blinking, Adam stared at his feet and rubbed his wrist. He winced as his nail dug into the leaking wound that had grown to the size of a coat toggle. "It used to help. Before you— before Hadley found out, it worked."

He wanted to say something. Words should have been easier, as they had been a moment before, but they never were when he needed them. Secrets stayed secret when they could be drowned, but much like Immanuel, they always managed to rise and beg for life.

⋅ඏ⋅ ⋅ඏ⋅

Hunched at the window, Adam seemed so small. Usually, he was larger than life, a handsome face in a suit made to draw the eye to the beauty of the fabric and flesh beneath, but as he stood staring ahead with his blue eyes dark, it dawned on Immanuel just how young they both were. After all they had been through, it felt as if years had passed, and while they had been together less than a year, Adam had been there for the entirety of his new life. Immanuel drew closer, gently stroking Adam's flushed cheeks until the redheaded man slowly met his gaze.

"I love you, but gin won't help anything," Immanuel whispered.

"It might make me forget. I don't know what else to do to make it easier."

The words died in Adam's throat. He wanted to snatch the gin and down it until the tears looming behind his lids dried. Alcohol fed the fire, and as long as he kept it stoked, it was impossible to feel anything more. That was one of the things he admired about Immanuel, he faced his problems. He wasn't a coward, like him.

"Let me make you some tea, and we can talk about it," Immanuel said with a faint smile as he brushed the hair from Adam's face. "How does that sound?"

Crossing his arms, he nodded, refusing to meet his lover's gaze

Gently kissing Adam's forehead, Immanuel snatched the leftover glass and gin. Halfway down the hall, he ducked into the bathroom and dumped the remaining liquor down the drain. In the kitchen, after filling the kettle, he rooted through the cabinets until he found every bottle of champagne, sherry, and cognac he could lay his hands on. One by one he emptied them into the sink, listening for the satisfying glug as the last of it swept away. He loved Adam, but he didn't need this. If Adam wanted to drink himself to death, he would have to leave the house to do so. Sinking into one of the kitchen chairs, Immanuel's eyes trailed down the hall to where the light from the workroom spilled into the hall in a golden pool. As the kettle whistled and his mind returned to the creature in the tank, Immanuel wished he could hop into the nearest steamer and drive to Greenwich or Folkesbury or even back to his office at the museum. He would go anywhere if he thought he could have some semblance of peace for a while. After everything that had happened with Lady Rose and the late Lord Hale, getting entangled with the Interceptors once again and Sir William running him ragged, this was the last thing he needed.

With a pit growing in his gut, he loaded a tray with biscuits and tea and mounted the steps, but when he reached their room, his frustration quickly sank to guilt. Adam sat upright in bed with his head resting against the headboard and his face lax. Leaving the tray on the nightstand, Immanuel perched on the edge of the mattress and watched Adam's chest rise and fall in a sleepy rhythm. He planted a kiss on his gin-tainted lips, but he never stirred. Careful not to disturb him, Immanuel padded across the room and shut off the light. Lingering at the threshold, he waited a moment to see if Adam would call out to him. When he didn't stir, Immanuel snuck downstairs.

⁕⁕⁕

Dragging the stool to the workroom sink, Immanuel stared down at the creature—the woman—lying prone before him. Even though the visions had never occurred twice, Immanuel kept his gloves on as he hesitantly reached for the scalpel in his dissection kit. No matter how many times he had participated in autopsies and dissections, it never got easier. People like Dr. Hawthorne or his mentor at Oxford, Dr. Martin, were able to separate the body from the person, but once Immanuel saw their last moments, that became nearly impossible. As he pulled the stool closer with his foot, he heard the gentle tap of cat claws.

Percy bounded in, his boney tail swishing as he surveyed the room until his eyeless sockets fell upon Immanuel. A small smile crossed the scientist's lips as the cat rubbed his nose and back against the hem of his trousers. With a twitch of his hips, he was in Immanuel's lap with his feet resting on the lip of the sink.

"No. Not for you, you greedy bugger," Immanuel said, watching Percy sniff the air. Holding him to his chest, Immanuel scratched the

39

cat's neck and gave him a kiss on the head before putting him outside the workroom door. "Go find Adam, Percy. Go ask him for pets."

Shutting the door, Immanuel returned to the creature. How could he pretend she wasn't a person? Perhaps he shouldn't. "My apologies, he doesn't know better. You aren't food, and you certainly didn't deserve this." Immanuel paused, his chest tightening at the phantom sensation of drowning. "I don't know what you are, but you didn't deserve the agony you suffered."

As expected, the woman never stirred.

"Unfortunately, I need to do worse than he did. Perhaps not worse, but I don't like doing it."

Immanuel carefully parted the fur near the creature's armpit, and after a moment, he found what he was looking for: a gash that went down to the muscle and bone beneath. The wound was an inch long, and as expected, there was no healing or indication that she had been given aid. Immanuel drew back, biting his lip as he stared down at the lethal blow. It had taken so little to end her life. Raising the scalpel, Immanuel murmured an oath under his breath as he did before every dissection and carefully cut from neck to tail. He winced as the reek of alcohol, fish, and the coppery stench of cadaver wafted out with each inch he cut through her thick, blubbery hide. Immanuel glanced over his shoulder at the door and hoped Adam wouldn't come down. There was nothing he wanted to do less than clean up gin-laced vomit. Making a cut across the midline, Immanuel grabbed a handful of pins to hold back the creature's flesh and expose the organs.

The moment he pulled back the skin, the breath hitched in his throat. Shaking his head, he counted her limbs before turning his gaze back to the thoracic cavity where two elbows rested on either side of her ribcage. Immanuel grabbed the scissors from his kit and cut along the creature's arms until he reached her shoulders. It was as if the outer seal-like hide had grown over a set of gracile human arms. Peeling back the skin of her tail, he found a pair of human legs, folded under her as if she had been kneeling in prayer.

Immanuel's heart pounded in his throat as he pulled off his gloves and grabbed his sketchpad from the work table. With an artist's skill and a scientist's eye, Immanuel sketched every detail of her form, carefully labeling each bone and ligament he could identify. Most were clearly human and instantly recognizable, but as he delved into the layers of organs, it was clear that evolution had taken a strange turn back to the sea.

Chapter Five
Evolution

When Immanuel surfaced from the creature's corpse, the blackbirds and robins outside the alley window had begun their morning trills despite the brumous day. Squirming on the narrow stool, Immanuel cracked his back and neck as he leaned back to examine the creature, which now lay in pieces. She was real. At lunch the day before, he never would have thought it possible. Even after seeing her final moments, he was hesitant to believe it hadn't been a hallucination, but after working on the dissection all night and carefully documenting the anatomy of her organs, he knew he had found a human-pinniped hybrid. If only he had a microscope and supplies at home, then he could prepare slides and study the creature's microanatomy. He had only studied human tissue under a microscope, but if he could get his hands on some seal samples, then he could—

"There you are!" Adam called as he threw open the workroom door but immediately brought his hand to his eyes. "Dear Lord, it's bright in here."

A weary smile spread across Immanuel's features as he watched his companion grimace and squint. *Serves him right*, he thought, eyeing him warily for any sign of drink. Beneath Adam's blue silk robe, he still wore his shirt from the previous night, but now, it had been buttoned to his collar. His hair had been brushed down, and without pomade to keep it in place, it stood out in floppy waves around his bloodshot eyes. As Adam took a step forward, he yelped a curse as Percy darted in, nearly knocking him over as he flew past. At the edge of the worktable, the cat wiggled his hips and flipped his tail. Adam reached for him as the cat dove for the liver sitting in the nearest metal tray.

"No! Don't you dare!" Immanuel cried as he swatted at the skeleton cat.

The cat's eyes locked on the liver as he took a slow step back. His tail wiggled and snapped, but when he pounced, Immanuel caught him, the scalpel clattering to the floor. Grimacing at the cat's claws sinking into his wrists, Immanuel shoved him into Adam's waiting arms.

"Take him, please. I'm not finished yet."

"Fine, fine. Just stop yelling. My head is killing me," Adam grumbled as he held Percy at arm's length. "Ugh, he smells like a corpse."

"I'll bathe him later. Just put him in the kitchen."

Tossing the cat into the other room, Adam shut the door and stood at Immanuel's shoulder as he settled back into his work. Adam's eyes flitted over organs he vaguely recognized before landing on the nearly empty cadaver. He had hoped that what he had seen the day before had been a nightmare from far too much gin, but even disarticulated, he recognized its mermaid-like form. While its hands still reached for something unseen, Immanuel had cut along its forehead and peeled the skin back to reveal a nearly empty human skull, its sightless eyes hidden beneath the flap. Adam shuddered at the thought that this nightmarish being lived inside of him, and one day, it would live on without him. Averting his gaze, he meandered around the room, looking through Hadley's remaining tools and bobbles before turning to the gleaming wall of windows.

When his eyes started to burn and his head pulsed in time with his heart, he sat at the work table and began picking through the pages littering the table. Immanuel's notes ranged from drawings as detailed as Da Vinci's notebooks to page upon page of observations written in tight lines of German and English. Pushing through his hazy mind, Adam calculated the time he thought he fell asleep to when he came downstairs and divided it by the speed of dissection with pauses for reflection and study.

"Have you been at this all night?"

Immanuel continued working with his head down.

Adam frowned. "Why didn't you go to bed? You have to go to work soon, don't you?"

"I told Sir William I would be working from home today," Immanuel replied, his accent formal and clipped. "He agreed, so long as I have a report on the deceased by this afternoon. If you don't mind, I must get back to work."

"I see."

Pinching the bridge of his nose, Adam tried to remember what had happened the night before, but it only came in smatterings and blurs. He remembered the creature, he couldn't forget that even if he wanted to, but what had happened to make Immanuel cross with him? It wasn't like him to be so curt. He had awoken with the taste of stale gin on his lips, a splitting headache, and the only body in his bed an undead cat nestled on Immanuel's pillow. As he stared at Immanuel's notes, a pit formed in his stomach at a vision of Immanuel's face breaking with hurt. Adam tried to remember what exactly he said, yet all he could see was Immanuel. What had he done?

"I made an ass of myself last night, didn't I?"

"You could say that."

Adam drew in a slow breath and winced as he scratched his wrist. Blood coated his nails, but he tucked his injured arm out of sight before Immanuel could notice. "I don't remember what I did or said, but I am sorry I took it out on you, Immanuel. You must believe me. I would never try to wound you."

Immanuel paused, his pencil hovering above a sketch of the creature's lungs. "I know, but you did."

Putting his work aside, he swiveled to face Adam. Their gazes locked, and the silent regrets snapped between them like a tether. In that moment, Immanuel wanted nothing more than to take Adam into his arms and kiss him until they both forgot the previous day's trials, but he couldn't do it. There had been a moment of alcohol-induced abandon when Immanuel felt the threat of impending violence. He swore Adam might hit him, and he couldn't live with that fear. He refused to.

"Promise you will never do that to me again," Immanuel said, keeping his damaged eye locked on Adam's face even as it clouded. "I have to be able to trust you, Adam. I have been able to count on you thus far, but I can't live with uncertainty when it comes to you. If you're going to drink like that…" He shook his head. "I'm not trying to be dramatic. I just can't do it after all that's happened."

Even if it means losing you. The words hung in his throat, but Adam knew they were there. He lowered his eyes to the floor and fingered the loosened scab on his wrist.

"I don't know what to say, except that I will try not to do it again. I didn't think it would upset you so. I thought it would take the edge off. It's what I've always done." He closed his eyes as Immanuel stroked his cheek. A little voice told him to tear his face away. He didn't deserve it. "Anyway, after I get cleaned up, I'm planning to visit Hadley. I don't want a position out of pity or loyalty, but the earl has connections and it would be foolish not to use them."

Immanuel nodded, but as he turned back to his work, Adam put his hand on his arm and carefully turned him until they were face-to-face again.

"Immanuel, please trust me. I'm going to try to make things right. I promise I'm not going to let us sink."

Drawing closer, Adam gently pressed his lips to Immanuel's, his fingers sweeping his lover's hair from his brow. Adam pulled him in deeper with the touch of his tongue upon his lips and a hand on his back. Entering his mouth, Immanuel could taste the tang of last night's gin, and he wondered if Adam noticed the salt of the sea clinging to his teeth, a remnant of the dead woman's final moments. Adam leaned between Immanuel's legs, brushing his thighs as they parted. Heat sparked in Immanuel's core as he rose upon feeling his lover's hands squeeze his shoulders and slip along his side in time with their lips. He wanted to hate him, he wanted to be angry, but it seemed impossible to sustain.

"Am I forgiven?" Adam asked between kisses.

"We'll see."

Adam's arms closed around him, hugging him closer until their bodies were flush. Stumbling back, Immanuel braced himself against the workbench as Adam's lips skimmed the delicate flesh of his neck, sending a shudder through his form. As his palm brushed a metal dissecting tray, Immanuel stepped away and carefully guided Adam back toward the empty wall where crates of finished automatons had once sat. His lover's hands kneaded Immanuel's sides and back, cupping his buttock as his back collided with the wall. Immanuel lightly ran his tongue along Adam's lip, eliciting a rough laugh from his companion as he tugged Immanuel's shirt from his trousers. Before he could reach for his belt, Immanuel gripped Adam's arm and slowly pulled it away. He stared at him through hooded eyes, his breath coming in heavy puffs as he steadied himself.

"We can't," Immanuel said, his voice hoarse with desire. "After, we will, but I need to finish this first."

Disappointment flashed across Adam's features, disappearing as quickly as it materialized beneath a concessionary nod.

"And I stink like a fishmonger. Please, Adam, I promise we can, but later." Immanuel kissed him again until the tension released from Adam's arms. "Later."

Clearing his throat, Adam looked around the workroom as if seeing it for the first time. "I guess I'll leave you to it, then. I'm going to take the train to Greenwich. Hopefully I can catch Hadley before she goes out for the day. Would you like to come? I could wait for you to clean up."

"I would love to, but...," he gestured to the glistening organs littering the table. "Send Hadley and Lord Dorset my love."

Wiping his lips and straightening his clothing, Adam slipped out of the room. As the door shut behind him, a knot twisted in Immanuel's stomach. Even if Adam had kept his head out of his cups long enough to think straight, there was something Immanuel still had to do. Reaching into a cabinet, he hefted a typewriter onto the only clean corner left on the workbench, a gift from Adam's cousin and her husband upon his graduation. Carefully arranging his notes, he pecked out a report that would hopefully satisfy Sir William Henry Flower. He stared down at the page, rereading his half-truths and outright lies until he steeled himself against the knot in his stomach. If this plan was to work, he would need enough room to weave his story. There was only one missing component.

Reloading the typewriter with paper, Immanuel pulled his notes closer and hammered them out word-for-word. Judith Elliott asked for a comprehensive report, and he wasn't going to fail his first mission as one of Her Majesty's Interceptors.

⁊ଓ ଓ⁊

Standing outside Miss Elliott's door, Immanuel's hand hovered, poised to knock. For a long moment, he merely stood in the hall, trying desperately to remember if he had brought everything he might need. During the entire journey to the Inner Temple Gardens, Immanuel had rehearsed all that he wanted to say, but the moment he reached the main hall with its sundial floor and practioners rushing between destinations like a swarm, his mind seized. What was he doing here?

After being attacked by Lord Rose in its courtyard and returning after the disastrous affair involving Lord Hale, he told himself that he never wanted to step foot there again, yet every few weeks he managed to slip in during his lunch break to exchange books with Judith Elliott. As he wove between Interceptors and made his way up the iron steps, he felt the deep resonance of magic reverberate through his bones like the hum of a hundred tuning forks. There was a whole building of people who in some way were just like him. He bit his lip to suppress a smile at the thought. Even after working at the museum for months, he still felt the distance of being an outsider. He was younger, quieter, less charismatic, less sure of his convictions, less accomplished, and certainly less English than any of the other curators. From what he had seen of the Interceptor Headquarters, there were plenty of young people and even those with darker complexions and accents that betrayed their origins. When he left Germany, a little part of him thought it would be a grand adventure. Maybe he needed to listen to that voice more. Immanuel tugged at his collar and straightened the strap of his leather satchel before knocking.

"Come in, Mr. Winter."

Immanuel froze with a frown. Pushing open the door, he found Judith with her head bowed and her eyes on the paper in front of her. "How did you know it was me?"

"I could see you through the glass. Besides, no one who works here waits or even knocks. If you don't barge right in, you aren't an Interceptor."

Barely raising her gaze, she motioned to the seat in front of her. Immanuel sank into the chair, clutching his bag as his eyes ran over the whitewashed cabinets lining the walls. Judith Elliott always seemed at odds with her surroundings. Her dark blonde hair had been expertly pinned and tightly bound in an elaborate chignon that hovered above the mandarin collar of her military-style jacket. Lining the perimeter of her office were display cases and art nouveau wallpaper that led the eye from shelf to shelf. Sunlight from the tall window behind her desk glinted off the crystals and artifacts locked within the cases. He wished he could borrow her powers just for a moment to understand how such a martial woman could own such a feminine space.

Finally surfacing from her work, Judith gave him a slight smile. "So how may I help you, Mr. Winter? Come to trade books?"

"No, I— I finished the report you wanted." Immanuel reached

into his bag and pulled out his sketch pad along with the packet of typed pages. "I tried to be very thorough, as you asked."

"I can see that."

Taking the papers from his outstretched hand, Judith flipped through them. Immanuel watched, holding his breath as her eyes skimmed over his notes before traveling to the black sketchpad between them. She returned back to the page, but every so often her gaze flickered from the rickety type to Immanuel's face. After a moment, she cleared her throat and set the papers aside.

Folding her hands on the desk, she said, "This is all rather technical for me. Tell me, what did you find regarding our dead selkie?"

"Selkie?"

"My apologies, I meant to tell you, but I didn't want to influence your findings. Selkie is the common name for what she was. Sometimes the Scottish call them *maighdeann-mhara*. I did some research on our friend after she arrived. According to several legends, selkies are creatures with the ability to take on two forms: one human and the other seal. I'm sure you've heard of sirens or mermaids in fairytales. Much like them, selkies are often described as beautiful women who lure men to their deaths or fall in love with humans and shun their true, animal form. Some folklore talks about how their magic resides in their pelts, which allow them to slip between forms or, like werewolves, they may be merely shapeshifters. It's still unknown."

"Did— did you say werewolves? Are they real, too?"

"Don't fret about them, Mr. Winter. They are of little consequence at the moment." Leaning forward, she tented her fingers and focused on Immanuel's bisected eye, her mind's probing tentacle nudging at Immanuel's thoughts. "So how did the selkie die?"

"She was murdered." Immanuel fought his mind as it threatened to travel back to that awful moment under the silty green water. "She saw something. I'm not certain what it was, a sunken ship or a foundation, but as she approached it, she was attacked by someone."

"Was it another selkie?"

"No, I'm certain it was a human or at least close to it. I didn't feel the same sensation I felt when I saw her for the first time."

"A sensation?"

Immanuel chewed on his lip and watched Judith warily. Something about her made him nervous. Even if he was telling the truth, he still felt as if she might uncover a secret he never intended to hide. It made it harder to think, to find the words he needed to make sense.

"It's like what Nichols described to me when he talked about meeting another person with magical abilities. It's like an itch or a frequency resonating in my bones. I felt it at the museum when Sir William showed her to me."

"Interesting. Tell me more about the murder and the murderer. Thus far, we know the perpetrator isn't a selkie nor a practioner. Even so, we could still have an incident on our hands that could result in an uprising. These situations are touchy. Go on."

Immanuel swallowed hard. He rested his hands on the cool wood of the chair, fighting back the sensation of water burning his throat. Closing his eyes, he rubbed his brow as pain constricted his temples. "She was stabbed, but when she tried to fight back, I think— I think she began to transform into a human. Then, she pulled the blade out. I don't know what kind of blade it was, but it was long and thin, on a handle. It only took a few seconds for her to begin to bleed out. When I examined her, I found a tear in her heart and a matching wound on her chest. I couldn't tell whether she bled out or drowned first due to the preservation fluid." As he released a tremulous breath, he bit down on his lip until the pain blossomed anew. "Her thoughts… They were so human. She was scared in her last moments for the others. Does that mean there are others of her kind?"

"Oh certainly," Judith responded as she flipped through the collection of sketches. Her mouth parted in surprise as she turned to the two page sketch of the selkie's body exposed for examination. "She was mid transformation. Do you realize how rare this is, Winter? To see a selkie transform is a once in a lifetime opportunity. They don't change in front of humans, that's why there's pelt versus shapeshifter confusion. A selkie mid transformation," she repeated, turning the page to study her organs and bone structure, "what luck. The cryptozoologists will be beside themselves at the news."

A pang of guilt rang through Immanuel's gut. "Is this really something to celebrate? She's dead, and it felt like my body was ripping in half when she transformed. Changing like that—"

Immanuel rubbed his arm where pain had radiated from the marrow as every bone broke and regrew in an instant.

"You felt it?" she asked, the joy sapped from her voice.

He released a tremulous breath and squeezed his arm to remind his mind that the visions of her underwater tomb were only a memory. "I feel and see everything they do as if I were in their bodies. It was excruciating. Her transformation, her fear, her death. Please understand that seeing their last moments is rarely a cause for celebration."

"My apologies if I sounded insensitive, Winter. You must understand that we are an agency that studies these creatures, and selkies have been rather uncooperative and elusive despite living right off our shores. Don't think this creature's death was in vain. We can learn a lot from it. We already have. Your dissection findings and her remains will be preserved for future study, and who knows what we may learn from them given weeks or months to do so."

Was she merely a specimen to them? Immanuel licked his lips before slowly meeting Judith's eager gaze. "Miss Elliott, I'm not certain how to phrase this, but do you—and the Interceptors—view selkies as human?"

For a long moment, Judith merely studied him, her brassy curls blazing gold in the afternoon sun. The tendrils of her mind fell away as she said, "Cryptids, creatures of that nature, are not my area of expertise, so I claim no intimate knowledge of selkies. The Interceptors are divided on what constitutes a human being or, for lack of a better word, personhood."

"I see."

Clearing her throat, Judith rose. "Well, Mr. Winter, if that will be all, we greatly appreciate your time and help in this matter. We will send someone to investigate the case, but if we need any more information, we will contact you. May I borrow your sketches to have photographs taken? It will only take a few moments."

"Yes, but—" As she reached for the doorknob, Immanuel opened his mouth twice, the words refusing to issue from his lips. He had to say something, for the selkie's sake if not his own. Finally he called, "Miss Elliott, I would like to continue investigating this case."

Judith stopped, her back ramrod straight as she looked back at the young man hunched before her desk. Despite her hard hazel gaze, Immanuel never wavered. She motioned for him to wait. Calling down the hall, Cassandra Ashwood appeared at the door. The dark-haired woman in her smart gown looked over Judith's shoulder and spotted Immanuel as she gave her instructions. With a wave and a wide grin to Immanuel, she took the sketchpad from Judith's hands and disappeared down the hall. When Judith turned back to Immanuel, her features were caught between annoyance and amity. Perching on the corner of the desk closest to him, Judith folded her arms across her chest and searched his face.

"So you want to join the Interceptors now. Why the sudden change in heart?"

Clasping his shaking hands in his lap, Immanuel fought to keep his eyes on hers. "I thought I could join unofficially for now. I would like to see if this is what I'm looking for before I agree to anything permanent."

"You cannot possibly think you can join un—"

"It was in the contract. Read it for yourself, and you'll see that I can be called upon to continue an investigation."

"At our discretion."

"At *your* discretion. You said it yourself that a scientist who is also a practioner isn't easy to come by."

"Yes, but we have everything we need from you. You finished the autopsy."

Immanuel's throat tightened. "I don't know why the Interceptors want me and Adam to join together, except that you said we were more powerful together. It sounds like we would be an asset to the organization, and if they want us as badly as you make it seem they do, I'm hoping they might be willing to work with my terms."

A faint laugh escaped Judith's rouged lips. "Does Mr. Fenice know about your proposition? I seem to recall he was a tad skeptical of magic."

"He has come around, but no, I haven't told him yet."

"That could backfire on you."

"I know." But both of them had so little to lose now.

"I'll tell you what, I will plead your case to my superiors and get a file together for you. They may not agree, but there have been several discussions about how to bring you around," she replied with a knife-sharp smile. "Now, you must know that a practioner doesn't simply join the Interceptors like one joins a club. There are certain protocols that must be followed, especially regarding your and Mr. Fenice's connection."

"But I thought you said the Interceptors were tolerant of…"

"Not an emotional connection, a magical one. We can discuss that later. In the meantime, I would suggest you start figuring out what you will say to Mr. Fenice should they agree to your proposal. While you have your strengths and unique abilities, they want you *and* Mr. Fenice. You won't get in by yourself."

"I don't mean to be forward, but why? What makes us so special together? Adam…" He paused for a moment, struggling with how to phrase it without coming off as insulting. "Adam isn't a practioner."

"Yes, but every practioner is better with their amplifier. Let me explain. You know that Cassandra is my partner in multiple ways, much like your Mr. Fenice, and she is a normal person. The reason why an Interceptor really needs a non-practioner partner is to ground us. They will see things we miss because we are too wrapped up in using our extranormal abilities. In your case and in mine, your partner is an amplifier, which means, as you have probably guessed, they can elevate your abilities by simply being in your presence. After the ceremony I mentioned before, Adam's connection to you will be even stronger."

"But what makes him an amplifier? Is it merely because we're companions?"

"Well, a bond is necessary, but his alignments are the opposite of yours. You know about batteries and magnets, Mr. Winter?"

"Yes."

"Then, you understand the power of opposite poles. What happens with extranormal abilities is that we tend to align with a specific element or pair of elements. In my case, mind-reading aligns with air while Cassandra's personality is very much grounded in earth. Therefore, we are opposites."

Immanuel fingered the stitching on his satchel thoughtfully. His mind reeled at the thought of the four ancient elements having any sway beside the growing periodic table. He wanted to reject the notion as superstition, but he had seen so much those past few months that sent his mind spinning yet it all proved true.

"What element is my ability? Air as well?"

"You," she paused, "you are a strange breed, Mr. Winter. You have two elements. Which two do you think are most needed for life?"

He blinked, hoping the answer on his lips wouldn't prove him to be a fool. "Water and air."

"Precisely. My theory is you were born with the ability to manipulate water since you mentioned your alchemical heritage, but after suffering through a series of traumas, your body took on air as a way to adapt to your needs. It's your *wyrd*."

"Excuse me?"

"Your *wyrd*. Your fate. Your trauma shaped your abilities. It's fascinating really. There are several known cases in ancient writings."

For a long moment, Immanuel merely glared at her through his clotted eye. He had never found his traumas to be *fascinating*. Did they see him as another exotic specimen like the selkie? Swallowing down the thought, he added, "So that would make Adam fire and earth?"

"Perhaps. Though, he only needs one opposite element to boost your abilities. It would be ironic, wouldn't it?" she said with a smirk. When he didn't respond, she continued, "Adam, the Biblical figure was born of clay, and the name itself has its origin in the color red, which is your Adam's most prominent feature." With a dismissive wave of her hand, she added, "The point is by having Mr. Fenice with you, he will amplify your already unusual abilities, and the Interceptors won't need to find you a partner. Trust me, Mr. Winter, you don't want to have to tell your partner that they have been replaced by your lover. Peregrine can attest to that."

Peregrine. Immanuel snapped open his pocket watch and nearly propelled out of his chair. "My apologies, Miss Elliott, but I have to go. I have an appointment with the director at the museum, and I didn't realize I had been here for so long. If I don't go—"

"Go on, then. We will be in touch about when the handfasting will be held, and I will have your sketchbook delivered to your address."

As Immanuel reached the threshold, he felt the familiar touch of Judith's powers knocking at the back of his skull. "Did I forget something? I really must go."

"No. I was merely wondering what you're planning to tell Sir William about the sideshow spectacle I brought him."

"That it isn't real, but the skin is. There's a seal somewhere missing a pelt, and it's possibly a breed I've never seen," he replied slowly as her hold nudged deeper despite his futile efforts to keep her out. "That way I can keep the body a while more."

"Very smart. You may want to start thinking of excuses for missing work."

Immanuel cocked his head.

"You'll need it if they agree to your terms, won't you?"

Chapter Six
Torschlusspanik

Shoving the front door shut behind him, Immanuel heard the familiar skitter of nails across the floor as Percy slunk in from the parlor and circled along the hem of his trousers. A tired smile crossed his lips as he ran his hand along Percy's spine, feeling the rub of his fangs against his hand with each nuzzle.

"Give me a moment, Percy," he murmured as he slipped his satchel off and hung it on its iron hook. Peeling off his coat, he ran a hand through his damp hair and listened to the whine of a door upstairs followed by Adam's familiar tread. At the sight of Adam coming down the stairs, Immanuel's body stirred. Dressed in his best suit with his henna hair pomaded and his irises bright against the brilliant blue of his waistcoat, Adam was a sight to behold. Raising his gaze to Immanuel's flushed cheeks, a wry smile quirked his lips.

"I thought that was you. I was about to have a bite, would you care to join me?"

As he reached his side, Immanuel searched for any sign that Adam had been drinking again, but to his relief, he appeared perfectly poised as if he hadn't awoken smelling like a gin bottle.

"Sure," Immanuel replied, slipping his arm into the crook of Adam's elbow and following him into the hall with Percy at their heels. "How did it go with Hadley and the earl?"

"I'll get to that in a minute, but first things first, you promised me something."

Adam stopped mid step and slipped his arms around Immanuel's waist. Pulling him close, he pressed his lips to his. Heat bloomed in Immanuel's core as his body flushed at the brush of Adam's hand on his neck while the other gently tugged the shirt from his trousers. All day his lover had been in the back of his mind, but Immanuel had banished the thought for fear of what he might find at home. He melted in Adam's grasp as he ran his hands along Immanuel's sides, sliding over old scars and healed bones before coming to rest on a familiar nick in his ribs. A low moan rose in Immanuel's throat at the skim of his lover's tongue against his own. Focusing on the rush of blood pounding through his body, Immanuel let the world fade into nothing more than heat and sensation. More than anything, he wanted to strip Adam's clothing away to reveal the body he still daydreamed about, but when he let his mind drift, he found the selkie's dead eyes staring through him, her body cavity empty. The confines of the workroom faded away until the cold darkness of his basement prison closed in around him. Immanuel broke from Adam's lips and grasped the edge of the hall table for support, his heart thundering as if he had nearly drowned. Holding him firm, Adam kept his gaze trained on Immanuel and waited until he could breathe again.

"Are you all right? We can wait."

"Yes, no, but I'll be fine," Immanuel replied breathlessly as Adam helped him straighten but didn't relinquish his hold. "I missed you."

"And I you." Leaning so close his breath set his hair on end, Adam whispered, "Let's get upstairs before I take you right here."

Immanuel's heart sputtered between anticipation and lingering fear as Adam urged him up the stairs. As they rounded the landing,

Adam caught Immanuel's lips and led him back toward the bedroom door. Immanuel glanced over Adam's shoulder between kisses to find the curtains already drawn against prying eyes and the bedsheets open and ready.

Following his gaze, Adam grinned as he reached for the front of Immanuel's grey jacket. "Without employment, I have a lot of time on my hands, so I figured I may as well be ready for when you came home."

The breath hitched in Immanuel's throat as Adam pressed his lips to his neck. Branding his skin with kisses, he wrapped his arms around Immanuel to capture every subtle jolt and silent moan. Every time Immanuel closed his eyes, the ghost of the selkie surfaced, but with each taste of Adam's skin or a whiff of the perfumed pomade in his hair, he grounded himself. Adam would be his anchor.

"Your skin is like ice," Adam breathed into the soft flesh of his collar as he drew a line down Immanuel's pale chest.

Biting back a cry, Immanuel closed his eyes at the brush of Adam's hand across his trousers. Before he could utter a word, Immanuel's jacket peeled away, followed by his belt as his hands frantically worked across Adam's buttons to keep up. Last time Adam had surprised him this way, he had received a bonus for helping to solve a money laundering case at work.

"Things went well, then?" Immanuel asked, pausing long enough to admire Adam's sturdy, henna-dusted chest as his shirt fell open.

Adam's hand closed over his while the other snaked around his waist. He swept Immanuel back in a swaggering waltz. Stopping at the edge of the bed, he brought his hand to Immanuel's cheek. The tip of his finger traced the curve of Immanuel's lips before coming to rest on the raised stripe of his scar.

"I would like to tell you, but I'd prefer it if my mouth was occupied with something much more interesting."

With a tug, Immanuel's trousers slid to his ankles in a rush of wool. The hunger in Adam's gaze as it glided over Immanuel's nearly naked body sent his blood pulsing. In three steps, Immanuel was in bed with

Adam straddling him as he yanked the heavy covers over them. Adam laughed, collapsing into Immanuel's waiting arms. When they had first started living together, Immanuel had feared this sort of intimacy. That the closeness would turn into claustrophobia, that it would resurrect his memories of torture and confinement, but he found with closeness came comfort. When the nightmares came—and they came often—Adam was there to hold him, and when reality slipped from his grasp, he could ground himself in the cinnamon and black tea of Adam's skin or the hum of Percy's bones. The breath hitched in Immanuel's throat at teeth grazing his earlobe and deft hands sneaking lower. It had been a year since he was kidnapped. The thought hit him so hard he opened his eyes. *Only a year.*

"Are you all right?" Adam asked, his eyes softened with concern as he leaned back. "Tell me if I'm crushing you with—"

"No, no, it isn't— it isn't that," Immanuel replied, running his hands over Adam's shoulders to keep him close. He opened his mouth, the words hanging in his throat as he met his lover's gaze. "It's nothing. I just realized it's been a year since I was taken by Lord Rose."

"Today?"

"No, but within the last week. I honestly don't remember the exact date. I didn't even think about it until now."

Adam watched him with the same look of concern he had seen so many times after waking from some dreadful memory. "I'm sorry. I didn't know."

Enveloped by a quilt, safe in a house with a man who loved him, that time seemed so impossibly long ago. Lacing his fingers with Adam's, he stared into his eyes. Adam's heartbeat radiated through Immanuel's ribs where they met. There was never a time he looked at Adam and saw Lord Rose. That was, until the day before. Adam kept the monsters at bay. He couldn't be one, too.

"Don't be. It feels strange to speak of it and not want to cry, so that's progress, I guess. In December, I'll have been free for a whole year. Adam, I need you to promise me something."

"Anything."

Immanuel's eyes burned as he blinked. "Don't do what you did yesterday again. I don't want to— I *can't* be afraid of you. I can't."

A stricken look passed across Adam's features, but it dissolved into the firm set of his jaw and the hurt look in his eyes as he nodded. "I promise. I love you, Immanuel. I hope you know that."

"I do."

With every ounce of fear and relief, Immanuel kissed him. When Adam issued a stifled moan, Immanuel locked his legs around him and twisted until Adam stared back at him, prone against the sheets. For a moment, Adam merely watched him. Even without touching him, Immanuel sensed the rush of his lover's heart at being held beneath him. Adam let his arms fall on either side of the pillow. Mental chains could be as strong as the real ones Immanuel refused to inflict upon his lover. Sensing him stir, a knowing smirk crossed Immanuel's lips. With the tip of his tongue, he slowly traced the trail of hair down Adam's chest until it reached the hem of his drawers. Kneading his sides, he locked gazes with his lover but lingered at his waist with his lips pressed to Adam's skin even as the fabric beneath his drawers tented and brushed against the aperture of his neck.

"Tell me your news, and you'll get what you want."

"Now?" Adam squeaked, his voice uncharacteristically tight.

"Hmm," he hummed into Adam's flesh as he hooked a finger beneath his waistband and pressed his knee between his legs to nudge them apart.

Adam released a hoarse laugh and hid his face in the pillow. "You're a horrible tease."

"I said, I'll stop for a price."

"Fine. Fine. You know how Lord Dorset's estate manager was murdered a few months ago? Well, he still hasn't found a suitable replacement, and Hadley told me they have been paying an exorbitant amount for a firm to take care of it for him. It was only supposed to be until they found someone else, but he forgot to keep looking."

Keeping his head down, Immanuel frowned into Adam's skin as his hand traveled lower. "They were taking advantage of him?"

Adam jerked. Biting his lip, he shot a look at Immanuel. "Hadley believed so. Before I could even say anything about what happened at work, she asked if I would be willing to look over the books to double-check their work if I wasn't too busy. I looked over his accounts and what Hadley had laying around and told her they were doing a good job as far as I could tell but they were overcharging him. Lord Dorset seemed relieved that I could make heads or tails of it at all, and he wanted me to visit again when he could get all of his papers together. When I said I had plenty of time to help him due to, you know, Lord Dorset asked if I would be willing to take it on full-time."

"So you didn't turn it down?"

"Strangely, no, but I haven't formally accepted yet. I told him I would think about it because I had a promising offer from someone else."

"Do you?" Immanuel asked, resting his head on Adam's thigh as he spoke.

"Not yet, but I don't want to leech off Lord Dorset. I pictured what I would say if he or Hadley offered some hand-out to keep us out of the gutter, but he is offering me a real position any accountant would covet. Being his estate agent would require me to go to Dorset a few days each month to see to his tenants and I would have to deal with his late-father's investments and companies. I do that with our family businesses already."

"It seems a small price to pay for security."

"I agree, and as an added perk, I would have more leisure time if I accepted it. An estate manager doesn't have to sit in an office every day, so it's a step up from being an accountant even if it is more work. Eilian may be oblivious, but if I do it, I have to prove that I can do a good job— an even better job than that firm. That—" Pausing as Immanuel massaged him with the heel of his palm, Adam released a contented shudder. "That will be the challenge. I would have cracked some champagne for us to celebrate this development, but it appears as though someone dumped it down the drain."

"That was all your doing, *mein Schätzchen*. We can get more later."

Immanuel's eyes brightened as he dragged Adam's drawers lower. "Luckily, I know other ways that we can celebrate."

Immanuel slipped beneath the covers as Adam closed his eyes. His hands crossed above his head, gripping the pillowcase. His hips bucked under breath and lips and the grip of unseen hands. Words and worries died away as the world extended no farther than the walls of their bedroom.

⁕

Adam lay with his eyes closed, listening to the steady tattoo of rain pattering against the glass and the clatter of steamers sloshing over the wet cobbles. His side vibrated as Percy purred between them and Immanuel released heavy, puffed breaths on the edge of sleep. Adam curled and stretched his toes in satisfaction. That was infinitely better than champagne. Wiggling closer to Immanuel, he kissed his forehead, eliciting a sweet, sleepy smile from the German as he nestled into his arm.

Just as Adam let his head sink into the pillow, his body jerked at the peel of the doorbell.

"Raid!" Immanuel cried in a strangled whisper as he scrambled up, blindly grabbing whatever clothing he could lay his hands on. Kicking off the sheets, Adam leapt to his feet and threw on his dressing gown as he crept toward the window.

"Go! Go hide!" Adam called, waving Immanuel out of the room. Pulling back the curtain, he kept his body flush against the wall. His labored breath fogged the glass as he looked up and down the street for any sign of grey police steamers. Below a woman in a maroon gown walked from their door into a cab. Relief washed over him as he fell back against the cool plaster to catch his breath.

"It was a false alarm, Immanuel," Adam said.

Turning, he found Immanuel standing in the hall, his chest heaving with hiccupped breaths as he struggled to button his shirt. Panic pulsed through his features as he murmured something in broken

German. His mismatched eyes stared sightlessly ahead while his fingers worked frantically.

"No one is there, Immanuel. You can stop."

When he didn't look up, Adam stepped closer until they nearly touched. Gently laying his hand on Immanuel's shoulder, his lover leapt back as if he had been struck. For a moment it was as if he didn't recognize him, but with a blink, his eyes cleared.

"No one is here."

"Are you certain?" he asked breathlessly, following Adam back into the room with halting steps.

"Very. There isn't a single police cab here and bobbies would be banging down the door. Besides, it was a woman who rang the bell. I watched her get into a cab and leave. A policewoman or anyone of importance wouldn't have left so quickly. She probably just went to the wrong house."

Immanuel dropped onto the mattress beside Adam, his legs sapped of their strength. His breath came in shallow, loud gasps that rocked his thin form. He wanted to stop. He wanted to get up, but his body stayed rooted in place as his mind spun with panic despite his best attempts to focus on the room around him. Adam was saying something he couldn't hear. Finally, he stopped and merely rubbed Immanuel's back. With a tremulous breath, Immanuel let his head fall against his companion's bare shoulder and closed his eyes.

A man was screaming, "*Aufstehen, Stück Scheiße!*" an inch from his ear. His clean-cut features contorted in fury had been burned into his mind for half a decade. The man had slapped manacles on his wrists and hauled him off to a cell after greeting his mother at mass the day before. Immanuel's body twitched as the cell's walls grew closer and filthier until all that remained was the voice echoing through the mortar loosely holding together his mind. Moisture collected at the edge of his eyes against his will.

A voice broke through the memory as Adam wrapped his arms around him. He spoke softly to him, reminding him to see and feel what was around him. Pushing down, the soles of his feet rocked against the cold boards, and if he breathed deep, he could smell Adam's cologne and the spice of his own skin on his lover's lips. Adam slowly rubbed Immanuel's shoulders until the tension released from his body and his panicked breath quieted.

"Deep breaths. Take deep breaths, Immanuel. You know I would never let any harm come to you."

"I know, but, if it *was* them, if it was the police—" He didn't want to think of it. Sitting up, Immanuel ran his hands over his clammy cheeks and up to his temples until he could string together a coherent thought. He swallowed and licked his dry lips. He needed to think of something else. "Was it was Miss Elliott at the door?"

"I don't think so. She's blonde, isn't she? But it could have been Miss Ashwood or Emmeline Jardine."

"I doubt it was her. I haven't heard from Emmeline in months."

Immanuel lay back on the bed, breathing in measured breaths until his heart slowed enough that he didn't hear its steady tide in his ears. Looking down, he found his shirt buttons askew and his trousers rumpled and cockeyed, only to realize they belonged to Adam. He released a silent sigh. If only he could keep a cool head like Adam, but his body reacted before his mind even registered what was going on.

"If it was Miss Ashwood, why would she come to call on us and then leave?" Adam asked, pulling the blanket out from under Percy and wrapping it around his waist as he fished through his wardrobe.

Unbuttoning his shirt, Immanuel tried again but his shaking fingers mismatched the holes once more. "Miss Ashwood may have been dropping off my sketchpad."

"The sketches from the dissection?"

Immanuel nodded. "I stopped to see Miss Elliott before I went to the museum. The Interceptors were interested in the specimen as well, so I let Miss Ashwood photograph my anatomical drawings for the Interceptors' records."

"Ah. Then, I'm fairly certain it was her, and we have nothing to worry about." The mattress dipped beneath Adam's weight as he knelt beside Immanuel. "Come on. Let's get dressed and have a bite to settle our nerves."

Adam kissed his forehead before collecting the clothing strewn across the rug. Slipping on fresh trousers, he retied his blue silk dressing gown and called for Immanuel to follow him downstairs. With the lingering stab of fear in his breast, Immanuel stayed a step behind. As he passed each window and door, he pictured the protection sigils drawn on every entrance in blood and oil and wondered if they could hold back a legion of policemen. Somehow he doubted magic could ever stop gross indecency charges.

At the bottom of the steps, Immanuel found his sketch book upended under the post slot with a large envelope lying beside it. As Adam disappeared into the kitchen, Immanuel dropped the book on the hall table and inspected the thick packet's seal. Emblazoned in iridescent plum wax was a strange beast. While it had the torso of a man, its head resembled a bird and its legs forked into a fish's tail. In its hands, it held a torch and shield, but when Immanuel squinted, he could see that surrounding the creature were the words, *Obscuris vera involvens*.

"Truth in darkness," he uttered under his breath, flipping the envelope over for any indication of who sent it. Making certain Adam was busy in the kitchen, Immanuel ripped it open and withdrew the first page.

Dear Mr. Winter and Mr. Fenice,

Miss Elliott has informed us that you have requested certain terms before joining Her Majesty's Interceptors. It is highly irregular for one to make demands of us, but we shall agree to your terms for a probationary period. Be warned that if you fail to handle this case to the best of your abilities, you will not be accepted into the rank of Her Majesty's Interceptors now or ever. All reading material from our library will be forbidden to you and any contact with other Interceptors will terminate immediately. That is the price you pay for your indecision and ambivalence.

In regards to your notes and drawings, we were very impressed with your findings, particularly the detail regarding the selkie specimen's internal mechanisms. Apply these skills during your investigation and you should succeed. If you decide to join fully now, we shall forego the probationary period. This will be your final chance to join without fear of repercussion.

Please fill out the accompanying paperwork and return it to Judith Elliott's office as soon as possible, as she will be acting as your liaison for this case. We are unsure if Mr. Fenice is aware of these proceedings as we have not seen him on the premises since the summer solstice. If he is not involved or refuses, consider your contract canceled and destroy the paperwork enclosed.

We look forward to having you both,
The Hierophant

The hierophant? Immanuel stared at the title before rereading the letter. A chill fell over him. He had never met anyone at the headquarters apart from Judith, Cassandra, and occasionally Peregrine, and he had most certainly never dealt with anything called a hierophant. *That is the price you pay.* Immanuel swallowed against the knot in his throat. Had he been disrespectful? That hadn't been his intention. He was merely afraid. He had hoped to bide a little time to think, yet somehow it seemed that he was in a power struggle he had never intended with someone he never met.

Eying the shelves of books in the parlor, Immanuel wondered if the dictionary might explain what it meant. While he had lived in England for four and a half years, his English only went so far without help. He reread it again slowly. Perhaps he had merely misunderstood their tone. Was it really now or never?

"Are you coming?" Adam called, ripping Immanuel's attention from the letter.

"I will be right there."

Immanuel stared past the page, his gaze trailing toward the yellow glow of the kitchen's lamps spilling into the hall. He had hoped for at least a day to ease Adam into the idea, but now... Immanuel chewed on his lip. Had he made a terrible mistake? Stuffing the letter back into the envelope, Immanuel tucked it under his sketchpad and left them on the hall table. Adam stood in his dressing gown, picking through odds and ends from the larder.

"Do you want actual food or would you settle for some of the trifle you made the other day?"

"The trifle is fine," Immanuel replied quietly as he gathered plates with his back to his companion.

"Was it Miss Ashwood with your sketchbook?"

"Yes, thankfully."

"Good. I never did ask about your day, did I? Was Sir William pleased with your report? More importantly, were you able to turn it in on time?"

Immanuel's mouth shifted into a lopsided frown as he heaped a spoonful of strawberry trifle onto a plate. "I did, but... I don't know how I feel about it. I lied right to Sir William's face, and the worst part is he bought it without question."

"That the creature is fake?"

Immanuel nodded and slid the dish across the table without looking to see if Adam caught it. Leaning against the counter, he closed his eyes and rubbed his brow. He couldn't believe how easy it had been. There had been no question or inquest. Sir William simply believed the specimen to be fake, and therefore it was no matter what reality dictated.

"At least it made for a quick meeting."

"I suppose, but I can't imagine what would have happened if I said it was real. Even if I presented him with the evidence and dissected her in front of him, he still wouldn't have believed me. He probably would have accused me of creating it myself. From the moment he showed it to me, he was so certain it was fake. There was not a shred of doubt in his mind."

You must admit the situation is rather queer. I didn't believe my eyes the first time I saw Percy."

"I know, but he's a man of science. People didn't think dinosaurs existed or that evolution was real, but they are and believe it now. He complains daily about how the curators and the public ignore evidence right in front of their noses, yet he does the same thing. A scientist should always play the skeptic, but they shouldn't wholly discount evidence when it's presented in logical detail." Immanuel crossed his arms and sank into the table. "It's horrible to know he would have rebuked me if I dared to question his judgment, even though I'm right."

"If it bothers you so much, why didn't you simply tell him? What's the worst that could happen besides getting laughed at? You would have had the last laugh in the end when you proved him wrong, wouldn't you?"

"Because he would have dismissed me on the spot or sent me to a lunatic asylum before I could even go into detail. I can't go into the museum director's office and claim to have discovered that mythological creatures are real."

Immanuel stared at the trifle warming on his plate with a sigh.

"What else is there? You have that look on your face that you make when you're upset about something."

Swallowing hard, Immanuel tried to push what he wanted to say from his mind. That he had complicated their lives again. "It's just that she was much more human than any of them thought."

"Human?"

"You saw the specimen when she was whole. It look like a seal. After I saw her death, I knew— I knew she was more than an animal. Her thoughts were like ours," Immanuel replied, his voice cracking against his will. "When I told Judith the truth, that she was real, she treated her like a creature, too. That's why I've done something. Something you may be very angry at me for."

Adam looked up, his blue eyes narrowing with suspicion as his hand hovered above his bowl. "What did you do?"

"Please don't be mad at me."

"That isn't exactly comforting, Immanuel."

"I— I decided to join the Interceptors."

For a moment, Adam merely stared at him across the table. "And?"

"I know we discussed that we wouldn't get involved with them because our lives were finally settling down, but with everything going on—you losing your job, the politics at the museum—I told Judith I would continue the investigation." Immanuel raked a hand into his hair before covering his eyes with it. He had caught a glimpse of Adam's expression, and he didn't want to see it again. "I couldn't help it. They didn't think she was a person. They acted like she was nothing more than a specimen. She was murdered, Adam. *Murdered.* And no one cares about her beyond her abilities."

Words hung on Immanuel's lips, refusing to leave his throat.

That could have been me.

"So what are you going to do? What about your job? Sir William isn't going to give you time off to go traveling. You'll end up sacked like me. Besides, you aren't a detective, Immanuel. How do they even expect you to figure this out on your own?"

Adam's mouth hung open at the realization of what he said while Immanuel merely stared up at him with red-rimmed eyes and a hopeful look.

"Oh, no. I'm an accountant—an estate agent even—but I am not a bloody detective. I have prospects, and I'm not going to ruin them by—"

"I know, I know, but when I agreed to this, I didn't think you would find something so quickly. You were so certain you would be out of work for ages, and I thought joining might make you feel better because they would pay us. You seemed excited about the idea of joining the Interceptors a few months ago."

"When I was running on adrenaline, it was great, but now I can see that it's dangerous. You said it yourself, we have a good life right now. Everything is falling into place, and besides, we aren't swashbucklers. You were just accepted into the Royal Zoological Society, I will be attending to Lord Dorset's estate, and we're happy now."

Immanuel chewed on his lip and stabbed at the trifle until the bits of strawberry bled out.

"Aren't we?"

"Most of the time, I am, but working at the museum isn't what I expected it to be. I thought I would be making discoveries or at least doing something I could be proud of. All I do is run errands and research things I don't even care about. I don't care about walruses or seals, and I most certainly don't care about meetings or how to best extort money from our benefactors." Releasing a frustrated huff, Immanuel's face fell but added, "I kept thinking it would get better. That once Sir William saw how dedicated I was to my work, he would give me more to do, but I have gotten nothing but the things he is too good to do. Do you know what I do at work, Adam?"

When the redhead merely shook his head, Immanuel released a ghost of a laugh.

"Magic. As soon as I know no one will bother me, I start working on my sigils. Honestly, I have been thinking about the Interceptors since two weeks after Lord Hale died. I wrote to Judith asking her for some books to further my studies. That's why I can manipulate tea and little things like that. At the museum all I do is sit behind a desk. With the Interceptors I thought maybe I can actually make a difference. This selkie was murdered and they seem to care more about my notes, but I know she was afraid for the rest of them. I *felt* it. If I can figure out who did it, her death wouldn't be in vain. Perhaps I can even give them closure and make up for what that person did to her. Why should I have extranormal abilities if I can't do some good with them?"

Squatting beside Immanuel's chair, Adam took his hands in his. Heat radiated from Adam's skin through Immanuel's icy palms as a circuit of energy coursed through them.

His voice and eyes softened as he said, "If you feel so passionately about it, then you should join. I don't want you to be unhappy, Immanuel. I don't want you to regret not trying this."

Adam of all people knew the gnawing nausea of unfulfilled

potential, of repressing for the good of someone else. He had done if for so many years before…

"I will. I want to, but the thing is, they want you, too. They said they would only take me if I brought you."

"Why would they want me? I don't have any extranormal abilities."

"I said that, but apparently if the two of us are together, you amplify my powers. It has something to do with elemental affinities that make us better than the sum of our parts. Without you, they won't let me in, and I'm already on thin ice with them as it is."

"Did you not think that was a bit odd? You weren't the least bit suspicious that they have been so adamant about both of us joining?"

"No. They have Judith and Cassandra, and no harm has come to them. Judith even said they would protect us. We would never have to worry about raids again."

"But what would they want with me? Am I just there to stand behind you and act like a human battery? How fair is that to me?"

Immanuel stared at him for a long moment, fear and sadness twisting into something that sent a wave of energy humming through his glass. Gripping his spoon until his knuckles turned white, Immanuel waited for the feeling to pass before speaking.

"If we agree to this, it would only be this one time. We could always decide after that we don't want to join permanently, but if we don't do it now or you don't agree to join with me, I won't be allowed to try again or speak with Judith and Cassandra anymore."

"So you're going to force my hand?" Adam scoffed.

"No, but they are because I'm forcing theirs."

"Did you ask Miss Elliott or Peregrine if this is normal?"

"Not yet, but if I don't, I lose them and my links to my…"

He shifted in his seat, the chain that held the vial of immortal forget-me-nots pulled the hair on the back of his neck. He had barely glimpsed beneath the surface of his magic, and they were already threatening to take it from him.

Adam shut his eyes at the tremble of Immanuel's hands within his.

Releasing a breath, he gently kissed Immanuel's cheek and brushed a loose golden curl from his scarred eye. "Tell me what I have to do, and I'll do it. For you."

Chapter Seven
Soul-binding

Adam had never filled out anything as intrusive and strange as what Miss Ashwood dropped off with the hierophant's letter. Something about the litany of questions got under his skin, but for Immanuel, he would fill them out as fully as he could manage at so late an hour. They asked about his relationship with his family, with Immanuel, if he had ever witnessed anything he couldn't explain, had he ever accidentally unleashed any extranormal abilities in times of stress, and other questions whose purpose he couldn't fathom. As they sat at the kitchen table writing into the wee hours of the morning, he would glance over at Immanuel and find him with his ears covered and his mouth silently working to puzzle out a question. A small smile crossed Adam's lips as he pictured Immanuel before he lost his vision and gained scars doing the same in some dreary library back at Oxford. He couldn't imagine how no one had taken a fancy to him then.

Not long before dawn, he and Immanuel wove their way through the halls and up the stairs to bed with bleary eyes and exhausted minds.

After sleeping far later than they intended, they took a steamer to the Inner Temple Gardens, but as Adam sat beside a half-dozing Immanuel, a question hung on his lips. Was he sure they should do this? What Immanuel told him the night before about the need to recruit them both nagged at his mind, but every time he wanted to ask, he saw the glint of promise in his companion's eye and let it drop. If Immanuel was hesitant, he didn't show it. When the steamer finally stopped, Adam's gaze wandered over the manicured lawns surrounding Interceptor Headquarters. It seemed so far from the tight, soot-coated buildings of the banking district, so much greener and grander. He wondered whether the lush space came as part of their land grant or if it had been conjured and maintained by the practioners within its walls. Following close behind Immanuel, Adam's stomach knotted and his hand tightened on the packet of papers as they entered the headquarters.

Adam's gaze swept over the marble floor carved with Roman numerals, the winding stairs, and the halls and wings that seemed impossible from the outside of the building. What surprised him were the people passing in every direction who seemed far more normal than he could have imagined. He had been there once, but it had been late at night, and after seeing a creature trapped in a human host, everything else seemed benign. By the time they reached Miss Elliott's door, Adam could feel sweat collecting in his armpits and an ache developing in jaw from clenching it too tightly. Stopping before the mottled glass, Immanuel threaded his fingers through Adam's even as his muscles tightened and his eyes darted for anyone who may have seen.

His companion gave him a reassuring smile. "I promise it will be fine. Are you ready?"

Adam readjusted the packet in his grip and straightened the fine fabric of his jacket. "As ready as I'll ever be."

Drawing in a fortifying breath, Immanuel knocked. The door swung open to reveal Cassandra Ashwood's petite form. Her gaze flickered between Adam and Immanuel's faces before returning to the papers in Adam's hand.

"I knew you would come around," she said, her features brightening as she stepped aside to let them in. "Let me take those from you."

"The letter says we are supposed to speak to Miss Elliott. Is she here?"

"I am now."

Adam and Immanuel turned to find Judith standing in the doorway in a red military jacket and a naginata in her hand. She carefully angled the pole against the wall behind the door and turned to the men with a measured grin.

"My apologies, I was practicing. I wasn't certain you would show."

Neither was I, Adam thought, keeping his attention on his feet for fear of Ashwood or Elliott calling attention to his hesitance.

"Let me make sure nothing is amiss."

Taking the envelope from her companion, Judith withdrew the papers with a furrowed brow. She flipped through the pages with little interest until she reached the letter. As she reached the final line, her mouth tensed for an instant before returning to her usual impassive mask.

"It seems that everything is in order, so we can get the process started. We can't keep the hierophant waiting, can we?"

Immanuel opened his mouth as she walked toward the door, but before the words could escape his lips, Adam asked, "What is a hierophant?" as if reading his mind.

"The hierophant is… it… *That* is a discussion for another day, once you're fully initiated. Just know that the ancients left us more than dusty relics and their word is law around here. It really doesn't matter right now." Clearing the air with a wave of her hand, she motioned for them to follow her. "Let me gather everyone together, and we can begin the handfasting. Cassandra, you can take Mr. Fenice, and I will take Mr. Winter."

Adam looked between Immanuel and the two women, his blood frantically pumping at the thought of being separated in this labyrinth. Turning to his companion, Adam found Immanuel's countenance brighter than he had seen it in months. Before Adam could speak, Immanuel and Judith were out the door and all that remained was the stab of fear in his breast. Cassandra stood at his side, giving him a small shrug and a reassuring smile.

"Once Judith knows what she's doing, there's no stopping her. It's go, go, go all the time." She shook her head and stepped through the threshold. "We had better follow them before she gets cross."

"She— she isn't going to do anything to him, is she?"

For a moment Cassandra merely stared up at him as if he had spoken nonsense.

"She isn't going to hurt him?"

"Oh, goodness, no. A handfasting isn't a blood ritual, it's a soul ritual. No one is harmed. Did no one tell you?"

He shook his head as Cassandra lingered with her hand on the knob. It seemed he knew even less than he thought.

"A handfasting is merely a ritual that bonds two people's energy together. It's semi-permanent."

"Like what happened with him and Emmeline?"

"Sort of. That's more permanent since it's a blood and soul bond. Technically, we aren't allowed to conduct those sorts of rituals on other people. They can only do that themselves, and even then, the legality is iffy at best."

Why? the question rose to his lips but was dashed away at the rattle of the door.

"Out you come. I can tell you more as we walk."

Closing the office door behind them, Cassandra took Adam in the opposite direction they had come, leading him down corridors lined with statues and paintings he wished he could stop to examine. From the corner of his eye, they seemed to shift and silently call to him. A boat bobbed on an oil tide while a woman across the hall in a gilded frame beckoned with a hooked finger, but he was afraid to look. He had already seen so much he thought only possible in nightmares or the minds of the mad, and that was plenty. As they passed, a little voice inside told him to look. Then again, his sanity felt like it was on thin ice every time he watched Immanuel spill tea with his mind or shoot a cup across the table without touching it. He still wasn't certain he could grow accustomed to magic.

As they walked, he tried to map the winding halls, but after traversing levels and following ramped passages, it was impossible. What if they had been lied to and they were taking them down into the depths to sacrifice them to some blood-starved pagan god? In a den of witches, anything could be possible. *Get a grip*, he snapped, passing a mustached man whose features seemed to grow sharper as they crossed. He had to remember Immanuel was one of them and he couldn't think of them as the corrupted crones of fairytales. Adam straightened his back and kept his eyes straight ahead. He had to trust Immanuel.

Clearing his throat, he began, "So what do you do for Miss Elliott as her partner? Immanuel says you aren't— you don't—"

"I'm not special?" she replied, her full lips curved in amusement.

"You could say that."

"I do quite a lot actually. I'm a secretary by trade, so I do a lot of secretarial work when we're not on assignment. With your accounting skills, we could certainly use you here."

"But what about when you are on assignment? What do you do then besides follow her around?"

Cassandra glanced at him. Something between annoyance and disappointment flashed across her features. "I investigate, just as she does. You don't need extra-normal abilities to think and observe. Many times we're even better at it than they are. I don't know about your Immanuel, but Judith gets so caught up in her abilities or the abilities of others that she can't see anything else. I have to remind her that not every problem can be solved or created with magic. Practioners alone on assignment can get themselves into a lot of trouble, especially if there are other extra-normal beings around. They can sense them, you know, but you and I pass as normal, boring humans. We are there to investigate, to keep them focused, and do whatever we must to help get the job done."

"So we're just glorified policemen?"

"We're much more than that. We're actors, sounding boards, errand boys, partners, whatever is necessary."

"I don't know if I want such a subordinate position."

"It's what you make of it, Mr. Fenice, though I doubt Mr. Winter would think of it that way. I certainly don't." Stopping before a bolt-studded iron door, Cassandra rested her hand on its massive ring. "This is where I will leave you. All you have to do for the handfasting is take a bath, change, and say 'yes' when the priestess asks. I promise you, it's easy and painless."

Adam opened his mouth to speak, his mind stumbling over what she had said. "Is this—? Can two men…?"

"Yes, and for centuries, no one batted an eye. Take solace that for more time than not, no one cared. The Interceptors live by the universe's rules. Not Her Majesty's, not the Papacy's, no one's but ours." She glanced toward a door further down the hall before turning back to him. "It seems Mr. Winter is already settled, so I will see you at the ceremony, Mr. Fenice."

ঔৎ৶ৎ৶

Adam drew in a slow, steady breath, the sweet taste of incense on his tongue. In his time with Immanuel, one thing he had mastered was breathing. He had spent so much time reminding his partner that using his lungs would keep him from passing out from panic or pain that he had begun to emulate his techniques. They were oddly effective, especially when standing naked in a strange bath before what felt like an execution. At least they had left him alone to take care of it by himself. Adam's eyes darted around the antechamber, lingering on the immaculate veined marble floor and the matching bare walls. Somehow it didn't feel austere despite the lack of paintings or tapestries. A presence hummed through the space, louder in the silence, though always there beneath the surface at the Interceptor's headquarters.

Without thinking, he laid his hand on the stone above the sunken pool. Immanuel was nearby. He could feel the resonance of his energy as clearly as he heard his heart beat each night. Adam released a short laugh. He was beginning to sound more and more like him every day. *Immanuel.* They had only lived together a few months and knew each other nearly a year, yet he had followed him here to get their souls strung together. It sounded like lunacy. He smiled to himself. His entire life had been lived as all or nothing, so why would his relationship with Immanuel be any different? He loved him. He loved him with all his being, and that felt far better than the years of nothing.

Carefully climbing out of the bath, Adam toweled off the dusting of herbs clinging to his skin before turning his attention to the silver tunic hanging near the door. His clothing sat neatly folded on a chair beneath it. He could easily go out in them instead, but was defiance worth it? Slipping on the drab tunic, he was pleased to find that it dusted the floor and covered everything, even if he did look like a dandified friar. As he took a hesitant step forward, Adam wondered if perhaps he should have slipped on his undergarments or stockings beneath it.

Opening the whining door, Adam's heart shot up his throat. He had expected to find a hall or another antechamber on the other side but instead found a souring chapel lined with stained glass windows. The scenes of knights, gods, and unidentifiable creatures glowed from an unseen source. His mind rushed over what he had seen on the way in, but he couldn't fathom where a cathedral could fit into the narrow lot. Entering the hall, his steps faltered as all eyes fell upon him. People in brightly colored robes and tunics lined the cathedral in a crowd four people thick except for the path leading to the altar. The occasional symbol was emblazoned over their hearts, and while Adam recognized a few from art or crests, he had no idea of their significance.

"Please, come forth," an elderly woman called as she stepped to the center of the dais. She was dressed in a pristine white robe, and while she appeared slight, frail even, her light eyes were keen and quick beneath her spectacles and her voice rang clearly through the chamber.

Adam's heart thundered in his chest as he took a hesitant step forward. The silence combined with the crowd and the dizzying pulse of energy emanating from every surface, hit him as an overwhelming sense of dread. As he grew closer to the dais, he could make out two younger women in purple on either side of the witch holding multicolored ropes that resembled drapery cords. He swallowed hard, speculating what purpose they might serve, but before he could form a guess, the breath caught in his throat as Immanuel locked eyes with him from across the platform. Immanuel's wide mismatched eyes flickered with the feverish glint of fear, but it quickly disappeared behind a warm smile. When they reached the stone altar together, the priestess's gaze traveled between them. Adam wanted to run. He wanted to disappear to avoid having a thousand eyes upon them, a thousand eyes knowing their secret, but Immanuel's resolute features held him in place.

The priestess cleared her throat. "Today we will be joining the energy and spirits of these two men through a fasting. May we welcome Immanuel Winter and Adam Fenice to Her Majesty's Interceptors. Before we begin, we shall call upon the four elements to bless this union of spirits."

From one of the women's hands, the priestess received a wand tipped in crustal. The crone stepped closer, her mouth working in a lilting chant as she drew a circle around their feet in one smooth sweep. As the circle closed around them, a hum echoed through the soles of Adam's feet. It was that same feeling he felt when Immanuel traced a sigil of protection over his heart: something between a palpitation and the visceral resonance of an incoming metro train.

"Today we call upon the cardinal elements and their wisdom of creation to bless Immanuel Winter and Adam Fenice. May these blessings bring success and strengthen your ties. Please join hands."

Adam resisted the urge to dig at his sore wrist. His eyes darted to the waiting crowd before rising to Immanuel's face. With a faint nod, Immanuel grasped Adam's hand, holding it without hesitation. Closing her eyes, the priestess whispered words in a contorted language Adam could not understand. The women on either side of her parted their lips and their voices harmonized into a siren's call. The air around them distorted until the crowd fell dark and the light from the high windows turned upon the five figures on the dais. Their voices reached a crescendo at the same time as the priestess held an ancient word. Immanuel's eyes widened as a patter of rain washed over them.

"To water, Lady of the West, we call upon you to bathe them in joy and wash away their sorrows.

"To fire, Gentleman of the South," she said as the water dispersed as steam over Adam and Immanuel's locked hands, "we call upon you to warm their souls and light their way in the darkness, even when all seems lost."

Murmurs fluttered through the crowd as a breeze stirred Immanuel's curls. The witch paused but quickly recovered as she continued, "Air, Mistress of the East, we call upon you for your gifts of purity and renewal. May the dust of the past be blown away."

Adam tightened his grip on Immanuel, knowing what would come next. The moment the word left the woman's lips, the ground trembled beneath their feet, nearly casting Immanuel into Adam's arms. The priestesses' harmony faltered.

"Earth, Master of the North, may you sustain them and enrich their lives. May you help to build them a stable home to which they will return."

Adam released a tense breath as the energy ebbed, pulled back like the tide. Shifting under the hundreds of eyes watching them in confusion and scrutiny while others merely stared in impassive curiosity, Adam tightened his grip on Immanuel's hand.

"Now, look at your partner."

Standing straighter, Adam stared into Immanuel's eyes. He tried to focus his gaze on the copper coin that bloomed in his left iris, but every nerve in his body cried for him to look away, even if those eyes bewitched him wholly. *Not in front of these people*, his mind screamed. The intimacy of a prolonged gaze could seal their doom, yet Immanuel stood there smiling tenderly at him, unafraid and unrepentant. Adam's stomach twisted at the curves of his lips and the softness in his eyes even after all he had been through. He loved him.

"Do you swear to respect your partner and never break that bond of trust?"

"Yes," they said in barely more than a whisper.

One of the women stepped forward and wrapped a blue cord around their hands.

"And so you are bound."

A twang of energy rang through their hands and into their bodies, following their blood until with a heartbeat, it dispersed. For a sharing of pain, a red cord was added, followed by a yellow for burdens, and finally a green for life, and with each, the burn in their veins intensified. The cloaked woman stepped forward once more and carefully tied the four cords together until neither man could move his palm apart. Energy hummed between them, and as Adam locked eyes with Immanuel, he could make out a faint glow trailing from his lover's body to his own.

"As your hands are bound, so are your souls in trust and power. May the stars lift you and the earth ground you."

Behind them, the crowd of Interceptors blurred, and the force of hundreds of practioners acknowledging their union with their power hit them. Adam's eyes burned with the flood of energy forcing its way through his form. His head swam at its magnitude and the indiscernible emotions traveling within it. Love, fear, awe. He turned his gaze from Immanuel in time to see the priestess step back to allow them to come closer. With their bound hand, Immanuel pulled Adam to his chest and held him tight with the other. His free hand cradled his neck and hugged his shoulder, even as he buried his face against it. Adam's mind faltered. He should shove him away or flee, but his body betrayed him, pulling Immanuel to him as best he could. Tears scalded his lids at the alien relief of holding Immanuel in public and not having to fear a beating or trip to the gaol.

Stepping back, Adam smoothed his robe and smothered the emotion from his features. The crowd slowly dispersed, leaving only small clumps of people at the periphery of the room. An occasional eye would stray upon them as they passed. Their probing, wary gazes were followed by whispered replies. Adam had heard their gasps during the handfasting and wished he understood what had shocked them, but with the remnants of euphoric power coursing through him, he didn't care. As they stepped off the dais, Immanuel gradually released his hand until all that held them together were the four ropes. Adam spied Judith and Cassandra over his shoulder as they cut through the remaining practioners.

"Mr. Fenice, Mr. Winter," Cassandra began as she and Judith stood shoulder to shoulder, "congratulations on taking your first step into the Interceptors. I'm so glad the ceremony worked for you. It doesn't always."

"And I was right about the dual alignment, wasn't I?" Judith replied, nudging a tutting Cassandra with her elbow. "Too bad we weren't taking bets; it isn't something we see very often. Now, I hate to cut the celebration short, but things have developed quicker than I anticipated and I must speak with you in private. Get dressed, and Cassandra will lead you back to my office."

Chapter Eight
The Exception

By the time Immanuel emerged from the marble bath, his hair had dried into horned curls at his temples and his clothing looked as if he had slept in it. A moment later Adam stepped out of the next door looking as neat and put together as when they arrived. As he drew closer, the fresh bond pulsed along Immanuel's skin until it drew into a fine thread and leapt across the gap to Adam. If he focused on it, he could feel it thicken and narrow with each step they took behind Miss Ashwood. Reaching Judith's office, they found her perusing a lengthy missive. Adam and Immanuel exchanged glances as they waited by the door. Finally, she put the parchment aside and motioned for them to take a seat.

"My apologies for rushing you, but this news has to do with your case. Since the hierophant apparently agreed to your terms, you will be sent to the Seolh-wiga Island to look for the selkie's killer. You will have exactly a week before we send another team out to finish the job. Our source at the landing fields confirmed that's where the specimen originated, which lines up with past selkie sightings. In this envelope, you will find train tickets to get to Scarborough along with tickets for the ferry to take you out to the island. We have also included our usual rate for a week's work and unseen expenditures. If you need any more money or want to back out early, you can send us a telegraph. The information for how to do that is in there as well. We have a contact who will meet you at the dock to get you settled."

Immanuel stared down at the packet, eyeing the strange purple seal he had seen on the previous letter. "I know I asked to follow-up on the selkie's murder, but if there is already someone on the island who can look into it, I don't want to cause any added expense or step on anyone's toes."

"Oh, he isn't an Interceptor. He is from the Special Branch of the Metropolitan Police. I'm not privy to what he was investigating, but the name I have been given is Will Jacobs. He offered to share his lodgings with you and assist you should the need arise."

When Adam and Immanuel regarded her warily, she straightened and added, "I wouldn't worry about him. Keep to yourselves, and you won't have a problem. We often share safe houses with the Metropolitan Police, but I wouldn't necessarily share my life story with him or the specifics of the case."

"But how did you know we would join?"

"I didn't. We have had ongoing contact with Mr. Jacobs for a fortnight, and his offer was open to whomever we sent. Your names will be telegraphed to him as soon as you leave."

Taking the packet from Immanuel's hands, Adam tore the seal and studied the train tickets inside. A crease formed between his henna brows as he asked, "These tickets are for tomorrow morning. Isn't that short notice?"

"What?" Immanuel cried, snatching the tickets from his hand. "I have work! I need more time to figure out what to say to Sir William. He'll— he'll sack me without a reference if I just disappear. And if I don't do this, I—"

Immanuel's mind spun through the hundreds of ways this could all go wrong. He could be giving up everything for nothing. His hands shook as he reached to push a stray hair hanging in his face. He opened his mouth, but before he could speak, Adam laid his hand on his arm and leaned forward.

"What do you suggest he do, Miss Elliott? Mr. Nichols apparently is able to get away with duping his employer. I'm certain you know a way it can be done on short notice."

"It's very simple: lie. And make it a convincing one. You could claim to be deathly ill or have a family member who needs tending to."

Lie. Immanuel stared down at his feet. Hadn't he done enough of that lately? Besides, he had been laying the groundwork for a different story. The pelt was supposed to have come from an undiscovered species of seal, and he would have to go to look for them, hopefully with the museum's blessing and at their expense. That wouldn't work now. Chewing his lip, Immanuel swallowed hard.

"Once we're there, what are we supposed to do?"

"There are several objectives. First figure out if the selkies are still nearby. We doubt they will interact with you, but perhaps you can find them amongst the other seals. More importantly, find the person who you believe killed the selkie. Listen for any rumors of conflicts between them and the locals, and report back. There is a telegraph on the island at your disposal. Remember, you are purely there to observe, investigate, and report back. You will not confront or arrest anyone. If you know who it is, Mr. Jacobs will assist you in that regard. Do you understand? You are to apply your knowledge and that is it."

"Yes, ma'am," Immanuel replied quietly. After what happened that summer, he couldn't blame them. The Interceptors had considered it a victory, but it had cost Lord Hale his life when he could have been spared had Immanuel not interfered.

"So what are the rules?" Adam asked, his arms folded across his chest. With his jaw set and his head high, he seemed as haughty as one would expect a dandy. "There have to be rules for magic. There always are, and if I'm supposed to trail around and keep tabs on him, I would like to know what they are. Or is that perhaps how your hierophant plans to keep him out?"

Judith's hazel gaze narrowed, hardening as she regarded Adam. The tendrils of her mind flickered out, sending aching pulses through his temples, but he refused to let it show.

"Watch your tone, Mr. Fenice. I'm doing you both a favor by sticking my neck out to let you have your way."

"Adam, please," Immanuel whispered, keeping his eyes down. "Don't start."

Leaning back in his chair, Adam waited expectantly with his arms barred across his breast.

"I would listen to him if I were you, Mr. Fenice. In terms of rules, you have already heard most of them. The main one being don't get caught using magic in front of people, unless you want to create another Inquisition, and don't make a mess of things. We won't always be there to clean it up for you. Our employer doesn't like a high body count unless absolutely necessary."

Meeting Adam's stony features, Judith held them for a long moment from across her desk. Immanuel's gaze flickered between them. Both had protected him, both had a ferocity few would expect, but in that moment, he wanted nothing more than to leave them to bicker by themselves. He rubbed his temples and closed his lids as his damaged eye throbbed with fatigue. Releasing a shuddering sigh, he looked up to find Judith and Adam watching him, one with pity and the other concern.

Before they could speak, Immanuel stood and took his coat from the rack by the door. He wouldn't let his infirmities of mind or body control him. He had to act. He had to do this right, with or without their help. "Let's go, Adam. If we leave now, I think I can catch Sir William before he finishes up at the museum."

Adam followed, slipping on his coat in a fluid motion. Immanuel ducked into the hall ahead of him, but as Adam opened the door to leave, Judith slipped in front of him. Putting her hand over his, she threw her weight back until the door clicked shut. Adam tried to jerk his hand out from under the small of her back, but she held his hand

and gaze firm.

"Remember, Mr. Fenice, we are here to guide you," she said, her voice unnervingly calm. "Whether you choose to take it is your choice, but once lost, our trust is rarely regained. You wouldn't want that for Immanuel, would you?"

"Is that a threat?"

"It's the truth."

⚬ල ⥁ల⚬

Walking up Cromwell Road toward the Natural History Museum, Immanuel kept his head down, though his mind's eye traced the familiar arches of the windows and the spires of the brick minarets. The bitter wet wind burst from the trees, snaking down his neck and under the collar of his wool coat. A shiver passed through his thin form despite several layers of clothing. He tugged the brim of his top hat lower and resisted the urge to fold in on himself to guard against the cold. As much as he didn't mind his position at the museum or the tedium that accompanied it, he hated going there on the weekend. It felt as if the entire city had emptied into the museum, spilling out onto the parks and galleries surrounding it until he could scarcely move without accidentally bumping into someone lurking in his blind spot. Between his own embarrassment and their nasty glares, he avoided the place as often as he could, but as he reached the iron and stone fence lining the lawn, he raised his gaze to the window he knew belonged to Sir William Henry Flower's office. The yellow haze of an electric light glowed dismally in the drizzle.

Taking a blind step forward, a hand clamped down on Immanuel's arm and yanked him back into the trees. He wheeled back, swinging his fist to dislodge his assailant but the man held firm. As Immanuel drew back with his other hand, the man raised his face. Relief washed over him at the realization that it was Peregrine Nichols digging his nails into his wrist. The short man glared up at him from under the brim of his bowler hat, his normally impish face grim. With a flick of

88

his hand, he released Immanuel, who quietly rubbed the spot on his wrist he was certain would be bruised by morning.

"Peregrine, what are you doing here?"

"Same thing you are, coming to see Sir William. I assume that's why you're here."

Immanuel nodded, leaning against the ivy-clad fence as he worked to slow his breath. "I didn't see you at headquarters. Mr. Fenice and I will be leaving tomorrow to go to investigate the specimen I received from the Interceptors. It's only a probationary case, but I need to give some excuse to Sir William as to why I have to leave. What do you tell him? I know it's short notice and— I—" Immanuel stopped short at the look darkening Peregrine's features. "What is it?"

The petite man shook his head and held firm to the fence's iron pike. He languidly eyed a pair of women strolling past in their Sunday best, waiting for them to cross the road before turning his attention back to Immanuel with renewed annoyance.

"I can't believe you still insist on doing this. Even before you had a clue what Lady Rose and Lord Hale were cooking up, I told you to stay away from the Interceptors, but here we are. Did that teach you nothing?"

"It's only an investigation for a week. It isn't like that."

"How do you know?" Peregrine hissed. "Lives are at stake, they always are, and you think you can just waltz in and start changing the rules. Do you not think the rules are there for a reason? Are you truly that arrogant?"

Immanuel blinked, opening and shutting his mouth several times when his voice refused to come. "I— I just thought since—"

"Don't you understand? Of course you don't. You're a scientist with a fancy pedigree, that's all. You are *not* an Interceptor, and the sooner you realize that, the better off you will be. Sure, you're a Lazarus and a Resurrectionist, but that means nothing if you have no training. You are not the exception, Winter. You're the rule. The best thing for you to do would be to go back to Elliott's office and tell her you've come to your bloody senses and will wait to go through the proper channels, like everyone else."

The breath seeped from Immanuel's lungs with each word until he thought his ribs would collapse in on themselves. Before disbelief and hurt settled in his chest, indignation consumed them. "Pardon me, but what cause have you to berate me? My dealings with Miss Elliott and the Interceptors are none of your business."

"Are they now?" Reaching into his breast pocket, Peregrine pulled out a leather case lined with capped vials and tossed it at Immanuel. "Do what you will with them. I didn't know who I was making them for, but either way, I've already been paid for my troubles."

"What are they?" Immanuel asked, pulling a vial out to reveal an opaque ointment peppered with bits of green.

"Figure it out yourself if you're so damn smart."

Peregrine's dark eyes trailed to Sir William's window. The light went out, and a stately shadow passed across the curtain as he reached for his hat and coat. In his mind, Immanuel could hear the director's echoing tread upon the stone steps as he left for the day.

"You had better hurry if you want to catch him, and you better have a good story ready. He was in a foul mood when I saw him. I can't imagine he would take kindly to your excuses." Turning back to Immanuel, Peregrine stared into his features, lingering on his scar a moment too long. "Good luck, Winter. I hope this doesn't backfire on you."

Pushing past him, Peregrine strode down the street. As he passed each tree, Immanuel swore the nearest branches bowed toward the curator as if reaching out to touch him. By the time he crossed the road and melded into the throngs of museum-goers, the trees had fallen silent once more. The glass bottles rattled in Immanuel's hand in time with his churning thoughts. Glancing up at the museum's ringed portal, Immanuel tucked the leather pouch into his pocket. Sir William Henry Flower would be out any minute, and he couldn't be caught if he wanted his plan to work.

Selkie Cove

Slipping into the foyer, Immanuel truly exhaled for the first time since leaving the museum. Beyond the honks and clatter of steamers on the other side of the door, Immanuel could make out the tap and scuff of Adam's footsteps above his head. Lingering at the coat rack, his gaze trailed into the living room where two shelves stood against the wall. Beside books on evolution, taxonomy, chemistry, and anatomy stood romances and novels from the continent and beyond. Shelved together, they served as the only public sign of his and Adam's intertwined life. Immanuel rubbed the top of his hand where the shadowy touch of the four cords still remained. The experience had been surreal. Never before had he been acknowledged like that before. Even though his uncles lived together as a couple, no one had done anything like that. No one had discussed a bond or given them vows. No one there had said they were abominations or against the seemingly inane rules of polite society.

A wistful smile crossed his lips as he touched the vase of carnations sitting before the hall mirror. Gently stroking their browning heads, Immanuel could see the look on Adam's face when the priestess stepped back. For a brief moment, he had seen that flash of vulnerability he so often missed. The brown edges of the carnations' petals stretched at his touch and melted back to their white flesh. Reaching into his pocket, he stroked the smooth braids of the cords. If only Johannes and Theodor had been able to experience something like that.

Climbing the steps, Immanuel found Adam with their suitcases open on the bed and piles of clothing and toiletries scattered on the dresser and nightstand. Upon hearing his approach, Adam looked over his shoulder at his lover and gave him a dashing grin that sent his blood humming.

"That was quick. How did it go with Sir William?" he asked as he carefully folded a pair of blue pinstripe trousers.

"Aren't those a little... bright?"

Adam looked between the trousers and Immanuel in his usual grey wool. "I didn't think so."

"If we're to investigate, shouldn't we try to blend in?"

"You mean, shouldn't *I* try to blend in?"

"Honestly, it's hard to miss either of us, but—"

"I understand. I wouldn't want to look like some haughty Londoner if we're going to be bumbling around in the middle of nowhere."

Tilting his head, Immanuel watched Adam unpack and repack his suitcase. "You found it on a map?"

"In an atlas, actually. Apparently the island several miles off the coast of Scarborough."

"Where is that?"

"The north-east coast."

Immanuel nodded and sank onto the edge of the bed, trying not to imagine how far or how long they would travel to get there. Leaning back, he ran his hand along the prominent spikes of Percy's spine as he lay sleeping in the lid of his suitcase. The skin-less Siamese picked up his head and stretched. His nails scratched against the luggage as he languidly stepped over it and climbed onto Immanuel's chest. A hum rang through his sternum as Percy settled into a loose ball. Sighing, he closed his eyes and let the rhythmic vibration lull him into a doze.

"What's wrong?" Adam asked. Even without looking, Immanuel could feel him standing inches from his knees, watching him. "Did something happen with Sir William?"

"No, I didn't even see him. At this rate, I should just call in dead tomorrow. I wouldn't have to worry about my job then, would I?"

The suitcase slid aside and Adam squeezed in beside him. Resting on his elbow, he regarded Immanuel with a thoughtful frown.

"Don't say that. It couldn't have been that bad."

"I never even talked to him. I ran into Peregrine, and I got so befuddled that I couldn't think of anything to say." He scrubbed at his face with the heel of his hands. "If I froze up in front of Sir William, I would be in worse trouble than I am now."

"So what are you going to do?"

"I will send in a note tomorrow morning saying that I'm gravely ill. If he presses the issue or asks why I never replied to his messages, I will just say I was in the hospital."

"It's worth a shot. He can't argue with an incapacitated man. What will it be? Typhus? Typhoid? Malaria? Something that makes you vomit is usually enough to assuage even the most tiresome employer."

Immanuel chuckled to himself as Percy wormed across him until his skull rested under Immanuel's chin. "Those may be a bit dramatic. I was thinking a bad cold, a wet one. Pneumonia at the worst."

"Ew. Well, it always worked for Austen." Fabric shuffled near Immanuel's ear as Adam sat up and carefully tucked a pile of clothing into his suitcase. A belt slithered out from under Immanuel's back, the cold metal catching his skin. Percy stretched a languid paw as Adam ran a hand over his side before landing on Immanuel's ribs. "So what are we going to do about our little friend?"

"We could just tell the housekeeper not to come for a week. It isn't like he needs to be fed."

"Could you imagine explaining *that* to Hadley?"

Immanuel could still picture the mouse massacre that had occurred a week after he brought Percy home. He had discovered a mouse's nest in the workroom, and when Adam came home from work, he was greeted by a skeletal cat flecked in blood and proudly carrying a carcass. Dropping the offering at Adam's feet, he trotted off to find another quarry. Being the less squeamish of the two, Immanuel had been the one to clean up Percy's messes. For a dead cat, he was quite the avid hunter.

"We could always contain him with a hatbox and a brick. That should hold him, don't you think?" Turning his head, Immanuel gave him a dirty look that elicited a laugh from his companion. "You know I'm joking. Is there anything you want to add to your bag? I think I packed everything."

He had nearly forgotten the pouch of vials was resting on the bed beside him. Staring at the ceiling, Immanuel focused on the hum of Percy's purr resonating through his chest. Should he tell him? Even he didn't understand Peregrine. He rarely did, but this time... this time something felt different. Adam had been cagey about what the Interceptors were planning, and now Peregrine said something to the same effect. Immanuel swallowed and shifted against the lumps in the mattress. If he told him what he said, would Adam change his mind about going?

"Immanuel?"

"No," the word escaped his lips before he could stop himself. "Wait, I will be right back. There's— there's something I forgot I needed downstairs."

Sliding Percy onto the coverlet, Immanuel trotted past Adam with his head down. The cat followed close at heel, nudging at his ankles when he could catch up. Immanuel paused at the bottom of the steps, his eyes following the motion of a steamer trailing down Baker Street. Laying his hand on the cool window, he closed his eyes. A hum of energy passed through his arm. If he cleared his mind, he could picture the web of protection symbols running around the perimeter of the house in a great chain. On a day like today, he needed to feel their reassuring pulse. He needed to know if he truly belonged with the Interceptors or if this magic was just another part of his life, a hobby discarded for the next interesting thing. Slowing his breathing, he felt the sigils beat in time with his heart.

It was as much in him as he was in it.

Chapter Nine
The Widow Larkin

While the train to Scarborough was emptier than Immanuel expected, he hated being trapped inside the cramped compartment. Adam couldn't convince him to take the Underground after his first experience with claustrophobia, but the cacophonous chugging and clanging of the locomotive grated on his already frayed nerves. Chewing on his lip, he tried to apply his mind to the dossier Judith had provided them. At first, he had thought all it contained were tickets and instructions for the telegraph, but as he sifted through the envelope on their way to the train station, he found a copy of the Interceptors' file on selkies, a drawing and description of their liaison, Will Jacobs, directions to the ferry in Scarborough, and a reiteration of their objectives. Staring at the file, the words blurred through his mind as quickly as the scenery outside the window. Beside him, Adam read the newspaper, the massive page blocking the dossier from view should a nosy passenger come by. Immanuel grumbled, stuffing the report into the envelope as he twisted toward the window. Resting his forehead on the cool glass, his stomach flipped and cramped mercilessly, churning his meager breakfast until he feared it would come back up.

"Are you all right?" Adam asked, folding his paper and setting it aside.

"I'm beginning to regret everything." Burping into his hand, he winced. "There's no way Sir William will believe that I'm ill and under Dr. Hawthorne's care. Do you think he'll inquire about it?"

"I doubt it."

"What did you tell Hadley?"

A smile quirked his pencil mustache. "That you got me mixed up in some haired-brained scheme, and that I should be back next week. Did I show you the article I found?" When Immanuel shook his head, Adam produced a piece of folded newsprint from his breast pocket. He opened it to reveal a drawing of a lighthouse. "I knew I had heard of the island before. It was in the paper last week. Someone hooked a generator to a lighthouse. Now the whole town runs on electricity made by the water. Imagine doing that in London. The power-mongers would have a fit."

"Imagine that," Immanuel murmured, closing his eyes.

The train vibrated beneath his cheek, traveling through his skull and down his neck until his discordant thoughts scrambled. Perhaps if he could dwell on it quietly for a little while, he could figure out what he should do when they arrived on the island. Before he could put a plan together, Adam shook his arm. Opening his eyes, Immanuel shot up at the squeal of the train grinding to a halt. He glanced out the window, his heart pounding in his throat when he realized he had slept through most of the journey. As he straightened in his seat, he pawed the moisture off his cheek and patted his chest and lap for the envelope.

"I have it. You dropped it when you nodded off," Adam said, pulling their bags from the rack above their heads.

"When? How long?" Immanuel rubbed his eyes with the heel of his hand. "I need to see the envelope again. I'm not certain where—"

"It's straight down the boardwalk at the end of the pier."

Before Immanuel could gather his wits or check his vivalabe, Adam shoved his suitcase into his hands and pulled him to his feet. Stepping onto the station platform, Immanuel drew in a long breath. His heart slowed at the taste of briny sea salt coating his lips and teeth as they walked along the promenade past tidy shops and nearly deserted beaches. Somehow this felt right. *Water and air*, a little voice whispered beneath the distant rumble of thunder. Immanuel swung his bag, his sleep-drunk mind lingering on the ashy clouds gathering in the sky above a magnificent hotel carved like a sandcastle in the town center. If he closed his eyes, he could smell the earthen perfume of petrichor and the sense the hum of energy in the air. Whether it was from the storm or a practioner nearby, he couldn't tell, but he let himself be engulfed until his entire body resonated with its power.

"There it is," Adam said.

Looking up, Immanuel found a set of massive wooden steps giving way to a long pier. Waves rocked against the wooden pilings, sending jolts through the boards below their feet. Immanuel clamped a hand on his top hat as the wind whipped off the sea. Shivering, Immanuel put his head down against the assault, his eyes roaming for anywhere they could seek shelter. While the town appeared to have every amenity, it was a holiday spot, and from the solitary pier, it was clear that very few in the off season needed to venture past the shore. On a bench near the final pair of rough pillars, Immanuel resisted the urge to huddle against Adam's side. The bitter damp seeped into his wool coat and put a sheen of moisture and salt across his cheeks. Beside him, Adam looked out to the water, the upturned collar of his coat accentuated the fine cut of his jaw. Across the pier near the rail, a woman sat with a basket perched on her knees.

"Can you see the boat?" Immanuel asked, his voice struggling against the wind.

Through the roiling clouds, a pale light flickered. Squinting, Adam could barely make out a hint of color, but the light never bobbed with the rhythm of the sea.

"I think it's only the lighthouse."

"It should be here soon."

Immanuel and Adam turned to find the woman watching them with an amused look. She gripped the railing and hauled herself to her feet. As she stood, she held her belly and released a puff of breath. Upon realizing she was with child, Adam trotted to her side and put out his arm for her. Thanking him under her breath, she looked past him to lock eyes with Immanuel. A ripple of familiarity passed through him, but he couldn't place her. Her cheeks were soft and her mouth and brows straight, lending her face a natural gravity. Her russet hair had been twisted into elaborate knots and braids that felt at odds with her simple dress and worn fur coat. There was something about her, perhaps it was the way she held herself or the faint hint of an accent, where she stressed her consonants a moment too long, that was so familiar.

Leaning against the rail, she still held Adam's arm but let her weight fall against the dock. "Where are you headed?"

"Seolh-wiga Island."

"Really? What for? You know the boat only goes out there twice a day on Mondays, so you'll be trapped until next week."

"Are you serious?" Adam asked, his henna brows knitting.

"You didn't know?"

"We're meeting someone there for a business meeting. It was short notice."

Immanuel's eyes darted between the woman and his lover, unsure how much he should divulge. "Thank you for the information, Mrs.— "

"Mrs.— Miss Larkin, Greta Larkin. I'm happy to be of help and have a spot of company. It isn't exactly a short trip."

"Where is everyone?"

"All the locals are in the pub. I'm surprised you didn't go there yourselves."

The German's cheeks pinkened. "We didn't know."

She nodded. "I'm not surprised. Visitors to the island have been few and far between lately, except for you two and that other fellow.

Not many live there to begin with, but…"

She shrugged and readjusted the wicker basket on her arm. Before Adam could ask her anything more, a foghorn tooted in the distance. Through the mist appeared the black helm of a small, antiquated model of steam ship Immanuel recognized as a cousin of the type he had seen used on the Rhine. From what he remembered, it was incredibly loud, very smoky, and rather slow. The red wheel at the back chopped at the water, kicking up murky surf until with a few dying whoops, it settled into relative calm. Smoke billowed out of the chimney stack, coating the dock in a grimy fog. With Britain being one of the wealthiest countries in the world, Immanuel wondered how they had yet to modernize their ferry service with a new boat, but then again he remembered Miss Larkin said it was only locals who used it.

At the sound of the horn blasting once more, voices rose on the wind as the rest of the passengers left the pub. As the boat slipped into the dock, a ruddy-faced man, his skin lined from years at sea, jumped out to tie the ropes to the dock and drop the ramp out for the ladies to use. With a nod, Miss Larkin released Adam and took the boatman's hand to step into the ferry.

Adam stared down at the bobbing gap between the boat and the dock. In the minute space where they didn't quite meet, he locked onto the roiling waves. Through their murky depths, he could make out the occasional shadow of a fish or the nonsensical image conjured up by his fearful mind, visions of faces or hands trapped beneath the surf. Immanuel and the rest of the villagers lingered over his shoulder, their eyes burning into the back of his head. Immanuel's hand stirred at his side, but he clasped them behind his back. Adam briefly wondered if it would had been a reassuring pat on the arm or a shove on the back. Swallowing hard, Adam hopped over the gap. His suitcase slapped against the cabin as he stumbled forward. The deckhand chuckled under his breath, catching Immanuel's eye as he easily stepped onto the deck. The ship was barely more than a long cabin lined with windows and four narrow pews. Adam went to offer Miss Larkin his arm to escort her inside when the boat jolted to life again. He lurched forward, but she and Immanuel caught him before he could pitch into the metal wall.

"Don't have sea legs, sir?" she asked with a knowing grin.

"I suppose not," Adam replied, though he wished his pride would let him say that he had never been on a boat or out at sea or anything past the shore. His stomach flipped with the seesaw of the deck beneath his feet. "Shall we—" He swallowed hard. "Shall we go inside?"

"You can, but I'm going to stay out here." Greta stared out at the water and the lighthouse in the distance. Her silhouette cut through the grey sky and removed all doubt from his mind that she could do without their support. "It will be too cold soon, and I don't want to waste the few days I have."

"But in your state, shouldn't you—"

Immanuel squeezed Adam's arm as the boat began its slow chug into the mist. "Shall we take your basket, Miss Larkin? We can store it with our luggage and keep it dry."

Murmuring her thanks, Greta handed over her heavy wicker basket without taking her eyes off the horizon. Adam stumbled toward the door to the narrow cabin, wrenching it open to let Immanuel pass through. A few people raised their gazes to them before returning back to their conversations. Near the door, they found an empty bench free from the prying ears of their fellow passengers. Carefully placing the basket between their suitcases to keep it from sliding, Immanuel motioned for his companion to take a seat. Adam sank into the wooden bench, flicking a piece of peeling white paint off the seat as he fought the urge to gag. Feeling himself green, he looked up to find Immanuel watching him with a cheeky grin.

"Don't give me that look," Adam snapped. "You are the odd one, not me. I don't know how you don't want to puke your guts out."

"Because I have been on a boat before. My father liked to take me and Johanna fishing."

Adam scoffed and shuddered at the thought.

As Adam drew in steady breaths and stared at the boards,

Immanuel watched as an island materialized through the fog. Near the dock were row after row of bright houses like the ones they had seen in town and behind them a centuries-old church towering in the distance. His mind meandered to their vacation in Dorset that summer, the hours spent at the water's edge until their skin began to peel and Adam's freckles disappeared beneath a haze of red. A bell clanged somewhere above them as one of the crew called out the name of their next stop. Immanuel's heart sank, realizing the picturesque village wasn't meant for them. He tucked his legs in as most of the passengers filed out before, with a lurch, the boat continued on its way. Leaning against the metal sill beneath the window, Immanuel watched Miss Larkin on the deck. She hadn't moved from where they left her, even after the mass exodus of passengers. Her body swayed in time with the water as if it was as natural as land.

"I wonder where her husband is," Immanuel whispered. "Women who are that far along don't usually go out unless they must. I hope he isn't negligent. She seems nice."

"I was thinking the same thing. Did you notice what she said before? She said misses, then corrected herself."

"A widow?"

Adam tipped forward as the boat pitched from side to side, a loud scraping emanating beneath their feet. Before he could hit the planks, Immanuel latched onto his arm and hauled him back. In an instant, the boat righted, turning Adam's face a deeper shade of sickly grey, and continued on its puttering course.

He swallowed hard. "I guess that is possible, though she wasn't wearing widow's weeds. Or she could…"

Turning back to get a better look at her, Immanuel found the deck behind them empty. "Where did she go?"

Before Adam could stand to look, Immanuel threw open the cabin door, letting it fall back against the wall with a clank. Adam darted out after him, grabbing whatever surface he could as he followed him around the perimeter of the pitching deck, but it was empty apart from them. As Adam turned his attention skyward toward the captain's perch, Immanuel gasped.

"There! Look!" he cried, pointing to a reddish shape bobbing in the water behind the boat. "Stop! Turn the boat!"

His voice died beneath the cacophonous roar of the engine and the wafts of smoke and wind. Immanuel looked between the shrinking figure and the upper deck. Whipping off his coat, Immanuel kicked off his shoes and climbed onto the rail when a hand clamped around his belt.

"Are you out of your bloody mind?" Adam cried. "That water is freezing!"

"Do you want her to freeze to death instead, Adam?"

His mouth tightened, but in one swift motion, he grabbed the life preserver off the side of the ship and shoved it into his lover's hand. "I will get the captain. Just don't— Be careful."

"I will. When I tug the rope, pull us back."

When Adam nodded, Immanuel jettisoned off the deck and plunged into the icy water. Immanuel surface with a rough gasp, the shock of the frigid water paralyzing him for a moment until he thought his heart would hammer out of his chest. Blinking the water from his eyes, he paddled forward blindly. With each dip of the water, he lost sight of her. The tide rushed against him, slowing his strokes and infiltrating every layer of clothing until he feared he would sink beneath their weight. Waiting, his muscles ached and his limbs shook, but the moment he saw her russet hair, he pressed on.

"Miss Larkin!" he cried as the rope on the life preserver grew taught. "Miss Larkin, come to me if you can!"

Her grey eyes widened as she spun toward him. The waves lapped against her face as she coughed, threatening to swallow her up with each crest. Struggling to paddle against her heavy fur coat, she lurched forward, her face ashen and her cheeks red.

"Greta, give me your hand," Immanuel call, as she released a cry that was cut off by the gurgle of water. "Adam will pull us back."

Her jaw chattered and her eyes went wide with each slow stroke forward, but as their hands nearly touched, the waves peaked and shoved her back.

She gagged, tears mingling with seawater. "I can't!"

The water. Immanuel stared at the water, his mind synchronizing with the rhythm of the waves. He had done it with the cup of tea at work, so maybe, he could do it here. He closed his eyes, giving in to the natural metronome until with a click, his mind snagged the energy. With an exhalation the water rose up over his head before dropping down far enough that Greta tumbled toward him. Gritting his teeth, Immanuel extended his arm as far as he could reach. His nose burned and his temple flared with pain as he pushed against the water with his mind. The moment their fingers laced, the energy ripped away with a gasp of breath. He pulled her closer, wrapping an aching arm around her thickened waist while desperately tugging on the ring. Her body shook against his side, her legs kicking futilely with his to keep them afloat. Immanuel's head swam as he tightened his grip on the life preserver. He had gotten to her, but his arms felt somewhere between lead and jelly while the world darkened and spotted. Watching the boat come into view, Immanuel pressed his forehead to the ring. His arm slipped on Miss Larkin, but she quickly tightened her grip on his neck.

As a wave crashed over them, Immanuel's hand slipped from the ring. His heart sputtered as he dove forward to catch it before it drifted from reach when something brushed against his hip. Grasping the life preserver, his eyes widened as a grey head peeked out of the waves. It's doe eyes regarded him before disappearing below the surface only to reappear a few feet away. It circled them, always staying little more than an arm's length away until they reached the barnacle-spotted hull.

Leaning over the rail, Adam and the deckhand grasped Miss Larkin by her cold limbs and hauled her aboard. Immanuel clung to the side of the ship, his frozen fingers barely holding onto the rope he could no longer feel. For a moment, he merely hovered there with his face pressed against the metal hull, drifting. Someone was speaking to him, but he could scarcely hear through his labored breath and the churn of the engine. Chattering his teeth, he stared up at the redheaded man. He knew him. Immanuel's mind wandered into a place as cold and blank as his limbs. The man above him stuck out a hand to pull him up as the captain yelled something, but it was so much easier to stay still. To let go.

Before he could drift, hands ripped him out of the water and threw him onto the deck like a fish. Gasping at the cold air rushing over his body, Immanuel curled in on himself, his body alight with pain. He stared down at his hands, which had turned bright red and blue at their tips. His head swam, the world blurring against his will as he sank to his knees. Taking a halting step forward, his foot slid, and his face and shoulder collided with the frigid boards. Pain should have rippled through him, but all he felt was nothing.

ACT TWO

"There is no folly of the
beasts of the earth which is
not infinitely outdone by the
madness of men."
-Herman Melville

Chapter Ten
Menhirs

Immanuel stirred, stretching his legs despite the weight of several heavy blankets stacked on top of them. As his mind surfaced, he could make out the crackling of a hearth nearby. Hesitantly opening one eye, he spotted a rickety bed less than an arm's length from his, shoved against the wall. The walls were roughly plastered and cracked, barely covering the beams and stone behind them, but as his gaze migrated to the ceiling, an ancient, rough beam hovered over his head with a series of wooden ribs hanging above it. Cocooned within the bed's enticing warmth, he considered just closing his eyes and drifting back to sleep when his foot brushed something hard. Adam perched on the iron foot rail. He sat rigid with the fireplace poker clutched in his hand. Shifting his grip, he stabbed at the crackling logs, his face a mask of calm that didn't quite reach his eyes. Immanuel watched him a moment, unable to pinpoint what lay behind the unnerving quiet. Had he done something wrong?

"Adam," Immanuel called softly, fighting off the thick layer of blankets to sit up. "What's wrong?"

Adam whipped around at the sound of his voice, his face blanching before breaking into a rare, unguarded smile. Setting the poker in its place, Adam came to his side and dropped onto the mattress beside him. He reached out to touch Immanuel's face, his hand hovering in the space between them as if he could go no further, but his gaze didn't falter when it met Immanuel's. It reached further to touch something so deep it sent a twang of energy through his bones. Closing his eyes against the sensation, Immanuel leaned into Adam's palm. Warmth radiated against his cheek, and for a moment, Adam didn't seem to breathe. He sat perfectly still with his hand outstretched and his eyes on Immanuel's form. Adam swallowed hard as Immanuel wrapped his hands around Adam's and kissed his palm. When Immanuel raised his gaze, he found slight bags had formed under his lover's eyes and his normally dazzling smile had fallen somewhere between pain and happiness.

"What's wrong?" Immanuel asked softly, pressing Adam's hand to his cheek.

Adam's free hand twitched, revealing an angry patch of skin growing on the inside of his wrist. "I can't believe you're really all right," he whispered. "I know you're extra-normal and more *durable* than most, but... But nothing is infallible."

Immanuel licked his peeling lips and tasted the lingering salt of the North Sea. His voice faltered as his mind finally cleared. "What happened to Miss Larkin? Is she all right?"

"Yes, at least I believe so. Despite being in the water for so long, she didn't seem as affected as you were. The captain thought it was due to her fur coat or even the baby. She shrugged us off at the dock and went home."

"Will... will it——?"

"I didn't want to pry. Miss Larkin seemed concerned but not as much as I would have been." Leaning closer, Adam kissed Immanuel's forehead and swept the stray hairs from his face. He sighed and regarded his companion, taking in each feature in turn. "You gave me such a fright. She was alert and talking, and you were limp." He opened his mouth, but the words refused to leave his lips. *I thought you were dead.* And all he could do was stand there, offering his assistance and tepid concern, when in his mind he was begging Immanuel to stay with him. He kept thinking if Immanuel died, he wouldn't be allowed to hold him once more. He wouldn't be allowed to grieve or lay claim to their life together. Squeezing the bridge of his nose, he fought back the burning behind his eyes. Even now, he couldn't say or do all he wanted. "Are you all right?"

"I think so, now that I have thawed. I'm sorry I gave you a fright. How long have I been sleeping?"

"Since we pulled you onto the boat yesterday. You were out cold until we reached the shore, but you have been in and out of consciousness most of the morning. Murmuring in German mostly. I thought you had gone into shock." Adam shook his head. "And there's no doctor in this blasted place."

Stretching his arms and legs, Immanuel curled his toes and then his fingers. Everything felt stiff, like his skin had shrunk a size too tight, but as he straightened, he winced at the pain in his temples. He should have expected a headache. His attempt to control the waves was too much too soon.

"You should lay with me," he murmured, the warmth and safety of the bed slowly pulling him back into sleep.

"You forget yourself. We're in the cottage we're supposed to be sharing with Mr. Jacobs, and I don't know when he will be back," he replied in a harsh whisper, though Immanuel could detect a hint of a smile in his voice. Glancing toward the door, Adam added, "Not that I wouldn't want to cuddle up to you when you're only in your skin."

Immanuel's eyes widened as he reached lower and found, at the brush of his palm against his bare thigh, that Adam had been right.

"What happened to my clothes?"

"They were drenched, so I dried them by the fire. The captain recommended warming you in a state of undress. Apparently it works better that way. He told me not to be squeamish about it."

"Little did he know," he replied with a laugh. Sighing, he stared up at his lover with a tired grin. "I'm just glad Miss Larkin is all right. We should call on her today. What is Mr. Jacobs like? Do you think we have to worry about him?"

"I haven't met him. The captain led me straight to the cottage when I told him where we were staying. He said he hadn't seen Jacobs, but he would probably be back by nightfall. He never showed."

"Did we go to the wrong place?"

"I don't think so. The captain did say Jacobs was investigating a disappearance, so he's probably busy. Besides, the door was unlocked and he was expecting us, so I can't imagine he would be upset to see us here. I was just surprised I didn't see him at the dock. That's where Miss Elliott said he was supposed to meet us, isn't it?"

"I believe so. Do you think he didn't get Judith's telegram or maybe he took the earlier ferry into town and we missed him?"

"I don't know, but the larder is very well stocked, so I don't think he went into town for groceries."

A pit formed in Immanuel's stomach. Something wasn't right. "Can you hand me some clothing? I would like to get up and have a bite. If you don't think he would mind us rummaging around."

"Are you strong enough?" Adam asked, his blue eyes tinged with worry.

Before Adam could react, Immanuel pulled him closer until their lips met. Between Immanuel's urgent movements and the arousal of fear and deprivation, Adam was soon on top of him. Keeping one ear on the door, his lips worked down the delicate flesh of Immanuel's neck. Immanuel's body locked, pressing against him beneath the layers of blankets. Adam could picture the shape of Immanuel's ribs beneath his pale flesh, the way his scars stood as starkly as tattoos. More than anything he wanted to have Immanuel beneath him, to see his body tense and relax with the rhythm of his movements. The taste of him on his tongue and the sensation of his skin burning like ice beneath his palms was all it took to set his nerves on edge. Immanuel ran his fingers down Adam's ear, returning to clasp the back of his head to his offered neck as his hips bucked beneath the blankets' weight. With a press of his hand, he directed Adam's mouth back to his lips. Drawing in a shared breath, Immanuel's tongue slipped into the hot part of Adam's mouth. Adam suppressed a moan at the feathered touch, but as Immanuel's hand slid down the front of his trousers to cup his growing erection, Adam shook his head.

Breaking free, Adam touched his lips and rasped, "We can't. We have to stop."

Falling back against the pillow breathlessly, Immanuel watched as Adam straightened and readjusted his clothing. "I think I have sufficiently proven that I have enough strength to command my body, but I would prefer to have some clothing before I get up. A union suit at least."

Adam regarded him with a sly smile. "If you insist." Crossing the room, he opened the top drawer of the shared dresser and pulled out his undergarments along with a shirt and trousers. "I took the liberty of unpacking your belongings. I needed a way to keep busy while I waited for you."

Catching the union suit Adam tossed to him, he slipped it on beneath the covers. "I greatly appreciate it. I would have lived out of that suitcase all week."

"I know, that's why I did it. So what do you propose we do first?"

A shiver passed through Immanuel's form as he threw off his covers and took the pile of clothing from Adam's arms. The tips of his fingers were still red and he wasn't certain he had full feeling in his toes, but it was good enough. Tucking his shirt into his trousers, Immanuel's eyes fell upon the window where the ocean's undulant light winked back at him through the curtains. By the height of the sun, he knew it had to be mid-morning at least, yet it felt as if he should have stepped off the ferry a moment before. He ran his hands over his cheeks before lightly slapping them, hoping he would perk up with time.

"I thought we might walk around and get our bearings."

"But your coat is still damp."

"I could just borrow one of yours."

Adam frowned before retrieving a spare black coat from the wardrobe. "It will be short on you."

"That's fine. I was thinking we could talk to the people who live here, ask about the local seal population. The selkies could hide with regular seals or they could have a colony all their own."

"Do you think the locals will really care about seals?"

"If they breed near the island, I assume they would notice. You can't exactly ignore a herd of barking beasts overtaking the beach every year." Immanuel paused, his lips parted as an odd thought crossed his mind.

"What? What is it?" Adam asked, straightening his companion's tie.

"No. No, it's nothing. I think I would like to look around."

Slipping past Adam into the hall, Immanuel wondered if it was possible for so many secrets to stay hidden on such a small island.

～◦§◟ ◞§◦～

The cottage was larger than Immanuel had imagined. He wasn't sure what he was expecting, but staying on an island that was only accessible once a week, he hadn't expected to find a house littered with ancient carved wood, an obscenely large, soot-caked hearth, ceilings that nearly grazed his head, and a bathroom in a shack outside. Well, the last one perhaps he had expected. The floor in which Immanuel awoke contained only one other bedroom that was smaller than their own but with only one bed that had yet to be turned down. While sparse, the rooms were hung with watercolor seascapes and decorated with motley quilts, which had all been unceremoniously dumped onto Immanuel's bed after his rescue, but what Immanuel loved most were how the rooms were illuminated by mullioned windows facing the beach.

With Adam following close behind, Immanuel trotted down the narrow steps into the common room. A massive hearth dominated the room along with an equally large table made of thick, wooden boards that a Londoner of refinement would have considered crude. Behind a broad, oaken door stood a cavernous kitchen where several crates of canned goods and dried meats lay waiting for its owner. The parlor had been appointed with worn, bowlegged chairs, but the fussy, outdated furniture gave the room an air of familiarity. A smile crossed his lips as he stroked the carved lintels above the fireplace. Through their looping knots appeared pop-eyed dragons and impossible plants. The carving was old, perhaps even far older than the house itself, and as Immanuel ran a finger along them, he swore he felt the vaguest twinge of something more.

"I didn't even notice this when we brought you in," Adam said, hooking his thumb toward a door at the far end of the parlor. It sat adjacent to the front door, neatly hidden should the door open.

"A cupboard?"

"One way to find out." Grasping the knob, Adam tried to turn it and then threw his weight into it. The door merely rattled in its hinges. "Do you think he could be in there?"

Immanuel knocked hard on the door. Assuming the man may have been asleep and hadn't heard them come in. "Mr. Jacobs? We were sent here by the Interceptors. Judith Elliott told us to contact you."

Stepping back, Adam waited but heard no response.

"I didn't see anyone else's things upstairs. The spare room was empty."

"This has to be his room." Adam stepped back, running his hand along the top of the door for a hidden key but came away with only dust. "If he works for the Special Branch, it would make sense for him to lock his door."

"I suppose."

"Well, let's go have a look around before it gets dark." As he reached for the door, he caught sight of Immanuel's pensive features. "If you wear a coat and gloves, you should be all right, but you have to promise you will tell me if you're cold."

He released a breath, his eyes running over the threadbare cottage.

"It isn't that. What if he comes back while we're gone?"

"He missed us, not the other way around. I'll leave him a note if you are worried."

Adam rifled through the drawers until he found a pad with a pencil tethered to it stashed in a kitchen drawer. Scribbling out a quick note, he tore the page off, folded it, and carefully placed it on the hearth's lintel where Mr. Jacobs couldn't miss it upon entering. Immanuel inclined his head toward the door, and with a sigh, Adam nodded and followed him out. He didn't like the idea of him out and about so quickly in the murky cold that clung to the island like a miasma, but he knew stopping him would be a pointless endeavor. There wasn't a doctor on Seolh-wiga Island, just a bunch of superstitious sailors, and if Immanuel's hypothermia turned into pneumonia or bronchitis, there would be nothing he could do.

As he tucked Immanuel's scarf tighter around his neck, his eyes ran over the house he had barely cast a glance at when they arrived. The slate and stone cottage sat atop a cliff overlooking the ocean with a dirt path winding away along the undulant green terrain. The house was broad like an upturned hull and covered in moss until it looked as if it had been shorn from the hillside rather than built. They walked only a few feet before it hit him: the silence. The only sounds were the crunch of their boots on the path, the mournful call of gulls, and the roar of the waves crashing into the beach below, as loud as the pulse in his temples. He had so rarely been out of London that the disconcerting absence of human noise set Adam on edge. Silence in London was quiet at best. This was *true* silence, a brief glimpse of what it was like before humans fell upon land as heaving, unrecognizable beings. Part of him wanted to speak to shatter the illusion, but something inside of him—equally awed and terrified—sought to submit to the nothingness he so often fought.

"What's wrong?" Immanuel asked at his elbow, his head tilted as he watched him.

Adam shrugged and shook his head, trying to unsuccessfully rid his ears of the pressing sensation. "Nothing. It's just so quiet."

A chuckle escaped Immanuel's lips. Taking a step down the path, he kicked up a spray of dirt. "And I think I'm a city boy. You should hear it in my head. This island is humming."

"What do you mean?"

"It's hard to explain, but when you're a practioner, you become attune to other extra-normal entities. It's like a dog-whistle or a tuning fork. It's barely perceivable most of the time, but it's there if I choose to notice or if there's a lot of it." His gaze flickered over the skeletal ruins of a church rotting beside row after row of makeshift headstones. "In London, I can only hear it if a person with extra-normal abilities is close. Here it's different. I feel it everywhere."

"Do you think it could be amplified from the handfasting?"

"Possibly, but I wish I knew where it was coming from."

Standing at Immanuel's side, Adam stared at the gaps in the ancient church's stone walls. It rose high above their heads, lichen-caked walls standing by sheer will while the roof and entrance had fallen away centuries ago. If he focused, he could picture where the altar must have been and the stained glass windows that muddied the view of the natural world in favor of god's light. Why anyone would build something so grand where so few would ever see it was beyond him.

As the hill rose before them, Adam paused at the apex. From there, he could make out the whole island. If they headed back toward the inn and continued down the path, they would arrive at the village. Thirty or so stone and slate houses clustered around the dock, stacked and staggered on top of each other like mushrooms jutting from the grass. On the beach, men and women clustered around a man he assumed to be a parson holding a baby. Taking a shell full of sea water, he poured it over the infant's head. When Adam turned to ask Immanuel about the strange baptism, he found him looking off toward a farm house surrounded by patches of mismatched land, but what drew Adam's eye was the towering light house on the opposite bluff.

It stood apart from the island, rising proudly from the sea on a pedestal of rock and foam. Its body had been constructed with layers of bone and blood brick. Atop it sat a glass and metal dome where a light cast its beam upon land and sea. Attached to the lighthouse's side was a large, squat house in a style closer to the beacon than the little houses littering the island's opposite shore. While he couldn't see its face, he assumed from its red brick and square roof that it was probably a Georgian building put in at the same time as the island's light. A smaller shed-like building sat at the bottom of the cliff, near the water's edge and beyond it a series of flat stones that turned with the motion of the sea. Adam watched as the undulant path of white stones leading from the mainland to the lighthouse was swallowed stone by stone into the sea. The tide rose, quickly covering any evidence of their connection.

"Immanuel, do you know what those wheels are?"

Adam's companion shook his head but pulled him along the path to where they could get a better look at the mechanical contraptions.

From far away, they could have been mistaken for the white spray of a cresting wave. Upon closer inspection, Adam could see they were large turbines submerged beneath the ocean. With the rhythm of the tide, they spun, cupping and spilling water with each rotation. Beneath the tumultuous rush of water, he could make out a faint mechanical growl. Adam's eyes brightened as he reached into his coat and withdrew a folded newspaper from his pocket. Flattening it against his leg, he revealed the drawing of a spiraled lighthouse.

"No wonder it seemed familiar," Adam said. "It's the lighthouse from the article, the one with the generators."

Immanuel stared down at the drawing, his eyes moving between the picture and the spire breaking through the blanket of fog. "Does it say anything more about what it can do?"

"No. All it says is the water wheels power the city and they even create a surplus of energy on good days."

"I don't know if we can call this a city."

"I think the author was trying to be kind. The article is more about whether or not this type of thing would work in London or Liverpool. There's very little about why it was created or who created it."

"But why have water generators here?"

Adam shrugged. "Perhaps it was too hard to string power lines from the mainland. Gas lamps and oil are so finicky. At least with electricity, you don't have to worry about blowing yourself up. Yet our lavatory is out in the yard," Adam murmured.

"We can't have everything." Immanuel bit back a laugh and sighed contently at the quiet. Staring out at the waves licking at the path at the base of the lighthouse, he wondered who could have envisioned such a clever invention on an island with so little. "What else does it say?"

Adam's eyes scanned the rest of the article for a third time. "There isn't much else. It mentions how the generator works and the economic implications. Oh, wait. It says that the creator was an eccentric who had lived in 'the city' his entire life."

"All scientists and inventors are eccentric. All that means is the person writing it doesn't approve of how he acts."

"My sister is an inventor," Adam replied sharply.

"And you don't think the other society ladies call her eccentric?"

"Touché."

Leaving the flooded path to the lighthouse behind, Adam and Immanuel passed through a sparse woods lining their path. Above them birds tangled through the trees, only pausing to watch them to pass. Sunlight filtered through the leaves despite the grey day, but as Adam strode toward the clearing with his mind on lunch and what shops the quaint village could hold, he suddenly found himself alone. He turned to find Immanuel at the edge of the bare earth where the path diverged, his toes barely brushing the grass, his pupils wide and transfixed.

"Immanuel?" Adam called as he slowly walked back to his side.

His companion never moved. Adam stood at Immanuel's shoulder and tried to align his gaze with Immanuel's. At first, it appeared that the lush oasis was empty apart from the foliage, but then his gaze fell upon a crooked rock he had initially mistaken for a tree trunk. It jutted from the earth at a strange angle, and as he followed it higher, his eye jumped to its nearly identical companion a few feet away. Thirteen stone trunks stood in a ring like a mouth of crooked teeth.

"Graves?"

Immanuel shook his head while the rest of his body stayed rooted in place. The moment Adam put a steadying hand on his shoulder, the clang of cathedral bells erupted in his ears and lightning raced across his vision. Clamping his hands to his ears, Immanuel staggered back. In that brief second of contact, he was certain he had seen lines and forms cutting across the ground in a twisted grid while the circle of stones had lit up with symbols as complex as those he traced in ink at the museum. Slowly returning to his senses, Immanuel blinked and felt the rough edges of the grass pressing into the heels of his palms. Adam was saying something, something he couldn't hear with the ringing in his ears, but as he reached to touch his back, Immanuel held his hand up to stop him.

"Magic," he murmured breathlessly as he rose to his knees. "It's concentrated here."

Swallowing against the taste of blood in his throat, he slowly stood. He ran his hand over his arm where Adam had touched him. The spot stung like a wound and the bottoms of his feet itched within his shoes as if the energy had passed through them like a bolt. Immanuel looked up to find Adam regarding him as much in concern as in confusion.

"I didn't mean to hurt you," Adam said softly, his hand flexing beside him as he resisted the urge to touch Immanuel. "What did I do?"

Immanuel took a step closer until their sleeves brushed. "I don't know. I could sense there was something here before you touched me, but when you did, it was as if everything grew very loud."

"An amplifier."

He nodded. "And a big one at that. I'm afraid to get any closer at this point. Would you be willing to go to the stones and tell me what you see?"

"Of course."

Adam flashed a debonair smile at his panting companion and

slowly turned toward the knoll in hopes that Immanuel wouldn't see the hint of fear in his eyes. As he took a step into the grass, he worried he, too, would be struck by whatever invisible force sent Immanuel crumpling, but luckily, he passed without incident. For once, he was pleased that he wasn't extra-normal, as Immanuel called it. He would hate to soil his knees with grass stains so early in the trip.

Drawing closer to the circle of stones, silence fell over him like a curtain. He stood less than a hundred feet from Immanuel, yet the faerie circle felt miles away, as if time and light had depressed around the clearing. The stones towered over his head, spinning away from the center. From the edge, he could barely make out another ring of smaller rocks, hidden amongst the long grasses. Adam was about to take a step into the inner ring when a figure appeared at the opposite end of the path.

"What do you think you're doing?" she cried.

Greta Larkin leered at each man in turn as she strode toward them with a teenaged girl who looked remarkably like her on her arm. A step behind them came a man whose features spoke of charcoal and steel. His stony gaze regarded Adam suspiciously before turning to Immanuel with something softer. He met Immanuel's mismatched, scarred eye at the same time that Adam noticed how he leaned on his walking stick more than the average gentleman. The silver handle had been bent crooked while the length of the cane had been crafted of sturdy wood that had become scuffed and scratched with age. Adam chanced a glance at the man's legs but was met with a reproachful scowl from Miss Larkin.

Stepping back onto the path, Adam put on his most effervescent smile. "Miss Larkin, I thought that was you. You look well after yesterday's excitement."

Her hard expression faltered but remained as a strain at the corners of her eyes.

"I'm so sorry if we were trespassing, Miss Larkin. We just wanted to see the monolith. I thought perhaps it might be prehistoric, like Stonehenge," Immanuel added, his gaze darting nervously toward

Adam.

"You are right about it being ancient, sir." The man's voice remained flat even as his eyes glinted with interest. "The standing stones are believed to have been created by—"

"The *menhirs* are sacred to us, and you really shouldn't traipse through," Greta snapped.

"We are very sorry. We meant no harm."

She nodded slowly, looking between Adam and Immanuel and the circle of stones. "I can see that. Just don't do it again, Mr.—?"

"Winter, and this is my— my associate, Mr. Fenice."

Adam gave a slight bow and extended his hand to Miss Larkin and then to her daughter and her male companion.

Her mouth quirked into an uncomfortable grin. "I never did properly thank you both for helping me yesterday after I lost my sea legs. It's good to see you alert now, Mr. Winter. It would have been a waste to dive in for another and not save yourself."

Swallowing against the knot in his throat, Immanuel nodded. "And are you and the child all right?"

"Oh, yes," she replied, a true smile brightening her features as she rested a hand on her protruding belly, "swimming away."

"What business do you have on the island?" the gentleman asked.

Greta shot him a reproachful look and released a huff. "Please pardon his abrupt nature. He doesn't mean to be rude. This is my nephew, Mr. Byron Durnure."

"Like the poet," Byron added, "and the knight."

Adam opened his mouth to speak, unsure how to respond. Her nephew looked old enough to be her brother, and there was something about him that vaguely reminded him of Lord Sorrell, a man with a demeanor at odds with a mind burdened by a library's worth of information.

"We are here to study seals. We work for the London Natural History Museum. I'm a curator and Mr. Fenice is a—" Immanuel paused, wishing they had worked out a story before they arrived.

"A humble journalist. Mr. Winter and I have been friends for some time, and when I heard he was headed out here, well, I jumped at the chance to join him. Perhaps, I could speak with you at another time about the history of the island or who created those generators by the lighthouse."

"Uncle Byron did that," the girl replied proudly.

Her mother shot her a look and tightened her grip on the girl's arm, but if she noticed, she didn't show it.

"That's quite an impressive device. Now, why did he do that?" Adam asked, giving her his full attention and charm.

Immanuel watched how his smile held her wholly, as if she were the only one on earth. The ability to make one feel as if they were the be-all and end-all of Adam's attention was a power Immanuel greatly admired, especially as it seemed to work regardless of sex, age, or station.

She gave him a conspiratorial grin and continued, "Well, they wanted to stop using our lighthouse because it was too hard to run electricity from the coast. That would make the island dangerous and we might have to leave if ships avoided it, but Uncle Byron said we didn't have to get electricity from Scarborough. We could take it straight from the water."

As Greta's mouth tightened in silent exasperation, a bashful grin crept across Byron's features. He shifted his hand on his cane and swept an invisible strand of charcoal hair from his forehead.

He kept his eyes on the ground and said, "Thank you, Clara. Magnets are the key. All you need is—"

"Byron, don't bore them with all your science."

"Actually, I'm a scientist myself. I would be very interested to know how they work," Immanuel replied, hoping to stop shame from overtaking Byron's muted pride.

"You are? I have never met a real scientist before, I mean not in person, just my friends I write to. I have a studio I work in. You should come there. I go every day from five until one. How long will you be on the island?"

"About a week. Where is your—"

"Byron, we need to go," Greta said sharply. "We need to get home and start dinner. Thank you, Mr. Fenice and Mr. Winter, for your assistance yesterday and I'm sorry Byron bothered you. Good-bye."

Before Greta could usher Byron and Clara out of sight, Clara called over her shoulder, "If you're looking for the seals, they live off the coast on an island by the guest cottage."

"Do any of you know where Mr. Jacobs is? We haven't seen him in some time," Immanuel asked, hoping his question wouldn't betray his story.

"Ask the lighthouse keeper. He rented him a room at the old inn," Greta replied curtly.

With a few reproachful glares and harsh words muttered under her breath, the three disappeared the way they came. Adam and Immanuel looked at each other, the unspoken phrases flowing between them only to be drowned out by a shiver passing through Immanuel's thin form. He hugged his arms against the cold and bit his lip.

"Shall we go to the cottage for a warm-up and then to the lighthouse?"

Adam nodded, knowing that even in the seclusion of the forest, he couldn't risk putting his arms around him to still the shivers. Instead, he let his hand fall.

Chapter Eleven
Dead Men's Tales

Adam and Immanuel hadn't intended to cut through the village proper on their way home, but even if they hadn't, they wouldn't have missed much. It had taken them walking half a mile past it before they realized they had gone through the village in its entirety. The houses that made up the settlement had been tacked onto the hillside along lopsided streets that followed the topography of the land rather than any sense or plan. Much like their own, they were a remnant of a forgotten era, only they seemed more careworn. Their roofs had missing slate shingles and the glass in the windows had been cracked or were missing all together, covered over with bits of paper or wood. Several of the houses reminded Adam of a rotting pumpkin, holding their shape but at any moment could collapse in on themselves. He had spent his entire life in London with fewer holidays than he would care to admit. For all he knew, that could have been the norm for a place so out of the way. Near the docks, the houses grew taller and closer to create a wall of shops. The only difference between them were the faded signs swinging from rusted or broken chains near the door. All appeared to be long empty.

A chill passed through him at the thought of the island dying, the generators and lighthouse its last fleeting gasp of life. In the distance, Adam could make out the bobbing sails of fishing boats, but from that far out, he couldn't tell if they were piloted by men or ghosts. He had heard of towns in the States that stood still as death, long abandoned when the well of wealth ran dry, but he had never imagined it in Britain. At the edge of town, he tried to imagine what the island had looked like in its prime, but all he could see were the embers of slate and stone.

As they followed the circular path that Adam hoped led back to the inn, he watched Immanuel stare off through the trees to where the glacial water trembled and rolled against the sky. His cheeks were red with the cold and his arms tightly wrapped around his middle, but he hadn't complained. Narrowing his eyes, a smile lit his features.

"Adam, Adam, look!" he cried, grabbing his lover's arm and pointing toward a flat, black rock jutting from the water.

Squinting, Adam realized the rocky outcropping was littered with at least forty plump grey seals sunning themselves. Adam couldn't help but grin at the gleeful glint in his companion's eyes. No matter how many times he saw Immanuel unabashedly delighted, it never failed to charm him. Sometimes it seemed as if Immanuel was seeing everything for the first time.

"I thought you didn't like seals."

"I..." The smile fell from Immanuel's cheeks only to reappear as a pup waddled across the jetty before sliding into the water. "I hate being the 'expert,' but I don't dislike them. They are quite adorable creatures for the most part. Do you think they're real seals or selkies?"

"Devil if I know. Maybe you can go down and ask them yourself. How do you intend to find out where the selkies are?"

Turning his back on the pinnipeds lounging on the rocks, Immanuel walked with his head bowed. A shadow fell across his features as he paced the edge of the cliff. "I don't know. Do you think I could simply ask someone about the legends?"

"Well, Mr. Durnure and Miss Larkin's daughter seemed eager to talk. If they know anything about the selkies, they may tell you. Miss Larkin, on the other hand, seems like a hard nut to crack."

"I wouldn't ask her unless I had to. Maybe the lighthouse keeper would know."

"Do you think he would let us go to the top of the lighthouse? You could probably see the whole island from there."

"I don't see why not. If we can reach it, that is. You saw how badly the island flooded before, but—"

The words dried in Adam's throat as Immanuel's eyes fix on something at the end of the bend and he started toward the edge of the cliff as if in a trance. Before Adam could reach his side, a gasp escaped his lips, and he clamped his hands over his mouth, staggering back into Adam's chest. He clenched his eyes shut for a moment before turning to Adam.

"Don't. Adam, don't move," he cried, his voice quavering as he raised his hands as if to catch Adam should he try to push past him.

His eyes glinted with moisture, but what scared Adam most was how the blue of his eye disappeared behind blown pupils. It was the look he had in the grips of night terrors.

"Immanuel, what is going on?"

He chewed on his lip, his eyes far away for a second before meeting Adam's steady gaze. His voice came in little more than a whisper as he said, "There's a dead man in the water."

"What?" He shook his head. He couldn't possibly have heard right, but with Immanuel's wild gaze and protective stance, he couldn't be sure if the man had been conjured by his mind. "Are you certain he's dead? Could it be a dead seal?"

"I— I don't think so. There's— there's a lot of blood and his head— it doesn't look right."

At the strain in his lover's voice, Adam knew to tread carefully. It was the precursor to seizing lungs, tense muscles, and his bichrome eyes staring blindly, lost in a vision of pain.

Slowing his pulse with a long breath, Adam held Immanuel's gaze as he replied calmly, "Let's go down and check. We could be wrong, and if the man is gravely hurt, we are wasting time when he needs help."

Immanuel stayed with his arms out, but he bit his lip as he turned the idea over in his mind. "I don't want you to see, Adam. I don't want to see…"

Glancing over Immanuel's shoulder, Adam averted his gaze upon seeing the figure slumped in the boat. No matter what he had said to Immanuel, he was certain of what he had seen. Adam gently rested his hands on Immanuel's shoulders, hoping to keep his eyes on him.

"*I* will go down to the beach. You're in no shape to deal with this. Let me—"

"No," Immanuel said, the word startling Adam with its finality. "I can't let you go alone. You've never dealt with dead bodies before."

He wanted to remind him of his older brother's passing or the dead opera singer in the Hawthornes' basement laboratory, but before he could say a word, Immanuel was walking toward the fork in the path that led to the beach below. Adam chased after him. By the time they reached the top of the stairs, they were in step. Sand shifted beneath their feet as they followed the rough-hewn stairs carved into the rock's face. At places the steps tilted at jarring angles, and whenever Adam took his mind off their descent to hazard a look at the man sprawled facedown in a boat near the water's edge, his foot would slip from the end of the tread and bring him back to the task at hand with a rushing heart. He pictured himself slipping between the uneven rails and tumbling down the cliff. If he smacked his head on one of the recycled beams serving as makeshift treads, he would surely end up with a concussion or far worse.

At the bottom, Adam released a relieved breath and stretched out the tension in his neck from the dangerous descent, but when he turned to speak to Immanuel, he found him sprinting down the beach, kicking up sand with each long stride. Adam bolted after him, his shoes slipping, nearly sending him to his knees. He grimaced as his loafers crunched across a crab he saw a moment too late. They would never be the same after this trip. Ambling closer, Adam could make out a battered rowboat wobbling with the lap of the waves, unable to dislodge itself from a pile of petrified tree branches and detritus near the shore. Seagulls stood on the lip of the boat, scattering with a shriek as Immanuel neared. It wasn't until Immanuel stopped running that Adam knew his eyes hadn't betrayed him.

A man slumped in the boat with his legs splayed, one arm reaching for an invisible foe while the other clutched loosely at his chest. Adam stepped closer until he could make out what had been the man's face. It was pressed into the boards of the boat, bloated and blackened beyond any hope of recognition. Water sloshed at the bottom, polluted with blood and the feculence that had leeched from the corpse. Vomit lurched in Adam's throat at the searing stench of putrefaction, but he swallowed it down and blinked away the burning in his nose. Pushing his nail into his wrist, he released a tense breath and turned to find Immanuel with his eyes closed and his hand clamped over his mouth.

For a moment, Adam feared his lover would vomit or cry until he swallowed and said softly, "We need to find a policeman or—"

"Or who, Immanuel? There's no one here."

Immanuel replied without opening his eyes, his voice hoarse, "I know. I know. But what are we going to do? We don't even know who he is." Glancing at the man's body, Immanuel released a ragged breath. "Adam, I think he was murdered too. Look."

Following the line of Immanuel's trembling hand, Adam could make out a hole in the fabric of the man's woolen jacket. His skin had been dented and torn by the beaks of seabirds, but this wound looked far deeper. It could have been a bullet hole or a stab wound, but it was impossible to tell with his jacket obscuring its size and Adam was in no hurry to remove it to check.

"How long do you think he's been dead?"

Immanuel shook his head, clasping his hands tightly under his armpits as he circled the boat. "Dr. Hawthorne told me the stages of decomposition, but I'm not sure. I don't want to touch him, but if he's loose, at least a day. Probably more." He swallowed hard. "His hands are just beginning to blister, and his skin is a greenish color."

"Please, no more, or I will be a greenish color," Adam said, watching the seals further out play in attempt to cleanse his mind of the man's corpse. "We need to find someone to deal with this."

"But what if he was murdered by the same person who killed the selkie? It could be anyone here."

Adam looked up at the bluff for any sign of passersby before dropping his voice. "Are you saying there could be a serial killer on the island?"

"Possibly. Well, maybe not a serial killer but someone willing to kill. I won't know for certain until I— until I—" He drew in a shuddering breath as he stared down at the man's prone body. "I don't want to."

"Want to what?"

"Touch him. See him die."

"Could you even do it with him in this state?"

"I could with Percy."

Adam sighed at the battle waging across Immanuel's features. Determination and fear struggled for control, but as Adam reached out to put a hand on his shoulder to steer him away from the boat, Immanuel dove forward and slammed his palm onto the back of the man's neck. The skin slipped unnaturally, sending a new wave of bitter bile knocking at Adam's esophagus, but what chased it back was the sudden blankness that fell over Immanuel's face. For a moment, it was as if he hung suspended on his feet. His body froze in place while his mind disappeared to a realm beyond Adam's sight. As if shot back into his body, Immanuel staggered forward. His hand caught the edge of the boat as he shuddered and stumbled to one knee. He moved to touch his chest but pulled his hand back, remembering the putrid flesh it had grazed a moment ago. His bichrome eyes watered as he stared at the shells and pebbles dotting the sand.

"Immanuel?"

Turning his gaze to Adam, Immanuel swallowed and slumped down until he sat in the sand with his hands shaking at his sides. "Same. It's the same."

"What is?"

"The murderer. I think. I couldn't see it. It was underwater. It happened so fast." His eyes went distant, the color of the sea settling over his blue irises. "It rocked the boat, and when— and when he went to see what it was, it grabbed the oar. It hit him with it, but the man pulled a gun. Then, it— it stabbed him with a stick or something."

Adam raised a henna brow. "A stick?"

"I don't know what you call it. A big metal stick."

"But he had a gun? You're certain?"

Staring at the body for a long moment, Immanuel nodded.

Adam rolled up his sleeve, held his breath, and carefully slipped his hand into the man's exposed pocket.

"What are you doing?" Immanuel hissed. "Someone will think you're stealing."

"You said it yourself, no one is here, and I have an idea of who he is."

Reaching into his coat pocket, Adam steeled himself against the ooze of congealed blood leeching into the fabric. At least, he told himself it was blood. Nestled deep in the pocket, his fingers brushed against a wad of paper. He carefully pulled it out and set it aside before moving to the man's other side to tug the edge of his coat out from under him. Fishing through that pocket, he withdrew a pocket watch before he found what he was looking for: a leather wallet. The leather was coated in a layer of offal, but with the edge of his nail, Adam pried it open with a yawning groan. A badge appeared below a paper license.

"Just as I thought; it's Mr. Jacobs."

"Jacobs? But—" Immanuel's eyes ran between the badge and the decomposing corpse slumped in the boat. "What are we going to do? He was our contact. He was supposed to help us. He— We need to contact the Interceptors. You have the telegraph information, don't you?"

Adam nodded. "Once we figure out what to do with him, we will telegraph them. Help me lift him, so I can reach his breast pockets."

Biting his lip, Immanuel averted his gaze as he slipped his hands under Jacobs' shoulders. His body gave beneath his grip, the skin sinking unnaturally with each touch. Immanuel focused on the solid bones of his clavicle, picturing the way they looked, labeling them in his mind in hopes that he could trick himself into thinking that it was merely a body and not a person. Personhood complicated everything.

"Got it," Adam said, sitting back on his heels. He dropped a few more scraps of paper onto the growing pile beside the boat along with a pocket watch and a small purse of coins. Adam stood to wash his hands in the ocean when he spotted something glinting beneath the seat in the boat. Holding his breath, he reached between the agent's legs, his fingers brushing against the icy metal of a gun. He gingerly dropped it beside the rest of his belongings before retreating to the water's edge with Immanuel in tow.

Adam released a breath, watching the cloud of mist dissolve into the aether. His hands burned with cold until he could no longer feel them, but at least the smell and offal was gone. A hesitant smile crossed his lips at the realization that *he* had figured it out. Somehow, they had even managed to keep it together. Perhaps he could be an Interceptor after all.

Before he could praise his companion, Immanuel wretched into the sand beside him. Rubbing his lover's back, Adam hovered beside him, listening as his silent sobs dissolved into the rhythmic ebb and flow of strained breaths. Almost together.

"Hey. Hey, look at me," Adam whispered at his ear. When Immanuel finally turned his red-rimmed eyes toward him, Adam wiped the tearstains from his cheeks and said, "It's all right. What we just saw was horrible. You were very brave to see his death. You didn't have to do that."

"I'm sorry," Immanuel cried, his voice cracking against his will as he splashed water over his hands. "If I had known what I was getting us into…"

"We can stop at any time. We don't have to go through with this. We could easily call Scotland Yard and hand this off to them."

"No, no, we can't. Not after all I've seen. I'm sorry, Adam."

Nodding, Adam released a tired sigh and helped Immanuel to his feet. Pulling a handkerchief from inside his coat, Adam carefully wrapped Jacobs' belongings in a neat bundle. When he turned back, Adam found Immanuel's eyes wide but far away. Adam touched his arm and watched as his lover surfaced again.

"Come on, we're going to put this in the house. Then we're going to find someone to help with the body, but when we speak to them, I don't want you to tell them it's Jacobs."

"But why? We have to get his body back to his family."

"I know, but think about it this way: why would someone want to kill him if he was a stranger on the island? He obviously wasn't robbed. You said he was set upon by the killer."

Immanuel licked his lips. As his mind quieted and Adam's words finally sunk in, he replied, "Either he wasn't a stranger or he found something."

"Exactly, and if we act like we know too much, that could be us. We can tell the Interceptors, but we can't tell the villagers."

Adam took a step forward, but turned back to find Immanuel standing locked beside the boat. "Should... should we just leave him here? What about seagulls?"

He didn't have the heart to tell him it wouldn't make much of a difference. "Well, I'd rather leave him than leave you. Unless you want to find someone and I can stay."

Immanuel shook his head and slowly walked to his lover's side, casting one more glance at the dead man. Climbing up the embankment, Adam's mind turned over the corpse in the boat. Had Jacobs ever gotten Judith's telegraph letting him know they were coming or had he died never knowing they would arrive? Adam stepped to the side to catch a glimpse of Immanuel's face, but he was as pale and drawn as he was on the beach. It was no use telling him now. It would only upset him.

At the top of the hill, on the edge of a ragged step, Immanuel stopped. For a moment, Adam feared he was teetering and was about to fall back on him, but when he put his hand on the small of his companion's back, he glanced back at Adam before turning his gaze back to the dirt path ringing the island.

"Someone is coming," he whispered.

Between the mist and the trees, a shadow condensed into the form of a man. Adam tightened his grip on the handkerchief-bound bundle. There was nowhere to hide it, no time to run back to the inn and toss it inside as he had hoped. The rocks surrounding the steps were crammed together like an overcrowded mouth, but beside a boulder near the steps, there was a crevice within arm's reach just large enough to shelter a parcel. Leaving Immanuel at the rail, Adam shoved the bundle into the gap in time to watch the figure round the bend. The man stiffened. His shoulders squared and for just a fraction of a second, he slowed before carrying on toward them with his head down. Adam shot Immanuel a silencing look before charging forward to meet the stranger. In his thick sweater and cap, he could have been a captain or sailor, but as Adam drew closer, he noticed his hands were far cleaner and smoother than the men who had pulled Immanuel aboard.

"Sir, sir, please help!" Adam cried, keeping his features open even as the gruff man glared at him over his hawkish nose.

"The island's a big circle. Just keep walking 'til you find whatever it is," he grumbled, pushing on.

"Sir, you don't understand. On the beach, there's a body."

The man's careworn face fell before snapping back to bother and indignation. He opened his mouth as if to speak when a shorter figure emerged from the other end of the path.

"What's all the shouting about?"

"Miss Larkin, oh thank god, it's you," Adam said, ignoring the man's protests even as Miss Larkin regarded him with a nearly identical expression. "There's a body on the beach. Is there a constable on the island?"

She looked between Adam and the grumbling man with a stern frown, but her gaze softened slightly upon seeing Immanuel's haunted features.

"Casper, what is he talking about?" she asked the grey-haired man.

"Hell if I know. I just got here."

"Well, you're the one always going on about being a deputized constable and a man of knowledge, do something about it."

"And the doctor and the lighthouse keeper and the resident everything you people need when it's convenient for you."

Miss Larkin leveled a glare at him that could have set him to stone, but he was already ambling down the rickety steps toward the beach, cursing under his breath. Miss Larkin took a step toward the edge when Immanuel cut in front of her.

"You shouldn't go down there. It isn't safe for… for…"

"For an invalid, like me? Trust me, I'm not foolish enough to attempt those bloody steps with a cannonball strapped to me. Casper will take care of it." Standing on tiptoe, she asked, "Is he a floater? We get the dregs from wrecks sometimes."

Immanuel shook his head as Adam motioned him to stay put. "He's in a boat."

"What's he look like?"

His hand instinctively moved toward the paper folded in his jacket pocket where Will Jacobs' face stared back at them. With a sudden stab of guilt, he regretted that he never took the time to commit Jacobs' to memory. "I don't know. He's already corrupting."

"A pity." Pausing, her gaze lingered on the pale pink scar standing starkly against Immanuel's ashen skin. "Is this your first time seeing a dead one?"

"No, just the first this far gone." Ignoring her probing look, Immanuel cleared his throat and asked, "Is there a telegraph or any way we could get in touch with the police in Scarborough?"

"You can either wait for the ship back to Scarborough and use the telegraph there or you can try to use the one at the lighthouse. It's finicky, but not as finicky as Casper. Mark my words, he'll say the matter is settled and you'll have a devil of a time convincing him to give it up to the mainlanders." Watching Adam and Quince move below, Greta absently ran a hand over her belly. "I hope he wasn't one of ours."

Chapter Twelve
Restraint

"It's all settled," Adam declared, shutting the inn's heavy door behind him.

Turning, his heart pounded in his throat as his eyes roamed over the parlor's faded chairs and the dark paneling lining the perimeter of the makeshift dining room. If he hadn't known how the place looked when they arrived, he wouldn't have noticed the subtle signs of disarray. The pillows sat askance on the sofa and the cushions had haphazardly been shoved back in the place while the drawers in the banquette had been left ajar. Worst of all, Immanuel was nowhere to be found. Just as Adam was about to bound up the steps to look for him, Immanuel slunk out of the kitchen carrying a kettle and two chipped china cups. Adam's shoulders sagged in relief as he carefully dropped the bundle of pilfered trinkets onto the nearest chair as he hung up his rain-dusted hat and coat. He hadn't wanted to send Immanuel home by himself, but when Casper Quince interrogated them on where they found the body, Adam saw the way he held his ribs, as much in cold as in fear. At least he could alleviate the former in trying to assuage the latter.

Lowering into the dining chair across from his companion, Adam kicked off his grit-filled loafers. More than anything he wished Immanuel would settle on his lap and wrap his arms around his neck as he did so often after dinner, his body familiar and warm with Percy purring by the hearth. Instead, he sat rigid in the hand-worked chair, his gaze locked on the steaming curling out of the kettle's spout.

"Quince is taking the body and the boat back to the lighthouse for safekeeping. Apparently the place has a basement where the body will stay cold long enough for reinforcements to get here. Not that it really matters with him looking the way he does. It doesn't sound very sanitary, does it?"

"So the police *are* coming?" Immanuel asked, his voice thin as he poured them each a cup of tea.

"Yes, but…"

His companion's eyes widened, pinning Adam with their silent plea before he could shrug.

"There's a storm coming that could disrupt the telegraph lines, so we would never know if they received the message. Quince thinks our best bet may be going directly to Scarborough."

"What you're saying is the authorities won't know about any of this until Monday?"

"It's only a few days."

"A few days on an island with no way off and a killer running free."

Adam sighed, resting his hand against the hot teacup to keep from working at the scab on his wrist. "Immanuel, you knew it could be dangerous when you got involved with the Interceptors. Did you forget what happened with Lady Rose?"

"I know, but—"

"But?"

But what? That he had no idea one murder would lead to more? That this was supposed to be a simple mission to gather facts? It all sounded so simple: find out if the selkies were still on the island, and *if* the murder was more than an accident, try to find who it was and then leave it up to Mr. Jacobs to deal with. But now there was no more Mr. Jacobs and there were two very real murders. Two corpses on his hands, two deaths he had lived but couldn't prevent, two families without a body or a word as to what happened to their loved ones. Immanuel's head pounded at the thought. He couldn't stop any of it.

"Gah! Immanuel! Immanuel, stop!"

Jerking from his thoughts, Immanuel looked up in time to see Adam run into the kitchen to fetch a towel as tea gurgled in thick gushes from the top and spout of the kettle. The moment his mind cleared enough to realize what he was looking at, the tin lid clanked shut, leaving only a growing pool of tea spreading across the table in an inky stain. Immanuel pawed at his pocket for his handkerchief only to find it in time to have the tea run off the side of the table in a shower of rivulets. He glared at the spreading liquid, furious that his mind or body or wherever magic resided had betrayed him. Drawing in a steadying breath, he stared at the tea, willing his mind to connect to it. With a twitch, it caught, and he pulled on the liquid until it slowed and finally stopped spreading. Holding tight to the invisible lattice, he raised it until the tea bubbled from the rug.

"What a bloody mess," Adam spat as he threw a towel on top of the spill. "What were you thinking?"

Immanuel gritted his teeth and rubbed the pain in his scalp as the headache bloomed anew and another shower of tea pattered onto the floor beside him. Dropping to his knees, Immanuel tried to mop it up with his handkerchief, but it was immediately saturated. He swallowed hard at the sound of Adam wringing the towel out over the kitchen sink. The dark paneled walls and patchy threadbare carpet tilted around him. Closing his eyes against the disorienting sensation, Immanuel sat back on his heels.

His voice cracked against his will as he finally replied, "I— I didn't mean to. I didn't do it on purpose."

"How does this happen by accident? Magic doesn't just *happen*. I thought you needed sigils and quiet," Adam said, disappearing into the kitchen with the offending teapot, which he dumped into the sink with a jarring clank that made Immanuel blench.

"When I'm upset, it just… happens."

"Explain to me how this just happens, Immanuel. You can't just let this happen. Do you not realize what could go wrong?"

Smacking his head on the lip of the table as he stood, Immanuel released an oath in German. He rubbed his scalp and tossed the soggy handkerchief where Adam had just finished cleaning. His lover gave him a defiant glare and batted it aside.

"Do you think I want to make a mess? I didn't even know I had done anything until you yelled at me!" Immanuel cried.

Adam rose and barred his arms across his violet waistcoat. "Then you need to learn to control yourself. What if you did that in front of someone else?"

"I'm sorry, but I'm scared." Immanuel stared into Adam's eyes and was met with the hard gaze he usually reserved for everyone but him. "I was thinking about the case. I was thinking about how we're going to figure this out when our only resource was killed by the same person who killed the selkie. It's hard to control your emotions when everything is going to hell."

"I have a very simple plan. We keep our heads down, stay inside the cabin, and wait for the ferry to come on Monday, so we can get out of here in one piece. The Interceptors can solve their own case."

"How can you say that? You know we have to find the selkies and— and find her—their—killer. We promised we would."

"*You* promised we would. I don't have to be a part of this."

"So you are going to leave me high and dry. Thanks, Adam. That's lovely of you."

Adam froze as a sooty breeze whipped down the chimney, flapping the lapels of his jacket. The leaded glass window rattled in its frame behind him while the oil seascape over the hearth clattered against the stone until it came down with a sickening crunch. At the sight of Immanuel's darkening gaze, Adam took a step back. The air seemed to suck out of the room, leaving them in a pocket of petrichor and soot. On either side of them, the chairs shook against the floorboards in time with the air rushing past Adam to collect around Immanuel's thin form.

"Just because you have nothing to lose, doesn't mean I do. Do you know what happens if I don't figure out who did this?"

Adam raised his hands in surrender as the electric globes on either end of the living room danced in their sockets.

"No more Judith. No more Peregrine. No more Interceptors. No more magic. No more help."

"Immanuel, I—"

"No, listen to me. Yes, I told Judith and the Interceptors that I would figure out whether the selkies were still on the island and who killed the selkie, but I promised the her I would find some way to do her justice. And I will. This isn't about doing some duty or solving a case. This is life or death for me, Adam. This is life or death for a lot of people."

Adam watched in horror as the wind stoked the flame in the hearth until it licked at the mantle, flaring with each seethed word.

"It certainly was for two people so far. How many more will die if we don't do something? Do you want to be responsible for that? Because I don't. I have enough on my conscience. And I don't know about you, but I want to be more than a curator or an accountant. I want to do something that matters," Immanuel cried, his voice breaking in time with the crack of glass behind him.

As the last word left his lips, the wind died, and the pressure that had built in the cramped sitting room fell away in an instant. Immanuel took a staggering step forward, the room turning on its side as the light faltered. His head pounded in his temples and eyes until he feared a vessel would burst to alleviate the mounting pressure. As he ran a trembling hand over his brows, Adam wrapped his arm around Immanuel's ribs. He held his lover firm as he took one hesitant step at a time toward the sofa. Gently lowering him onto the cushions, Adam released his arm and retreated into the kitchen once more. Immanuel rested his face against the back of the chair and shut his eyes. Even through his lids, he could feel the room tilt, but more worrying was the familiar metallic taste filling his mouth and the itch of moisture in his nose. His heart quickened and his chest tightened as he sat up in time to have Adam shove a handkerchief under his nose with one hand and hand him a cup of tea with the other.

"This is what I mean about controlling yourself," Adam said, his voice edged with concern boarding on fear. "Look what's happened. You gave yourself a bloody nose and you're shaking. That can't be good for you. You can't tell me that's a normal reaction to magic."

"Am I ever normal?" Immanuel murmured beneath the bloodstained handkerchief.

"No, but this certainly can't be good for you. Now, have something to eat before you pass out."

Taking a thin biscuit from the proffered tin, Immanuel choked it down, hoping it would soak up the coppery brine gathering at the back of his throat. Sitting next to him, Adam studied his face and body for any sign of illness or pain, lingering on his eyes before flitting over his chest and finally coming to rest on his quavering hands. Immanuel looked away, knowing dark circles were forming under his eyes faster than he could hope to replenish his strength. He flinched as Adam laid a gentle hand on his arm.

"I agree with you, by the way."

"What?" Immanuel turned to find Adam watching the bloodstain grow beneath his nose. "That I'm not normal? Because I'm well aware."

He rolled his eyes. "No, about helping people, doing something more than what's expected. I agree. It's just difficult." Adam released a bitter laugh. "I wish we could have adventures as long as those adventures didn't mean having to risk our skins to have them."

"That isn't how life works."

"I know, but I would like to see the case through, as long as we don't put ourselves in unnecessary dangers. As long as *you* don't put yourself in harm's way."

"Trust me, I have had enough bruises and cuts to last a life time," Immanuel said, setting the biscuits aside.

Adam cupped his hand around the back of Immanuel's head and tipped it forward until he stared at his feet. "Keep your head like this, and pinch your nose. It'll help slow the bleeding."

"How do you know this will work?" he asked, closing his eyes in hopes he could ignore the tickle of blood.

"We used to do it with George. Don't let go until I say so."

George. Adam so rarely spoke about his older brother that with his name came a hallowed chill. Immanuel had never met George as he had died months before he and Adam met, but he had noticed an unspoken tension surrounding him, especially where Hadley was involved. Neither twin wanted to speak of him, yet when they did, Hadley spoke of an ill-fortuned saint, a genius who died before his time. The mere mention of him sent Adam into his stiff, haughty bearing, as if he had to defend himself from his brother even beyond the grave. Immanuel couldn't understand it. His uncle had died years ago, but he hadn't pushed his memory away like that, even when his specter haunted his dreams. There was something Adam kept to himself, something perhaps he even hid from Hadley, but Immanuel was too afraid to ask if he could share that burden.

He swallowed down a wad of bloody snot, wishing he could rinse it away with a mouthful of tea. At least the flow appeared to be weakening. His stomach growled, and he wondered if it would be possible to hold his nose shut and eat at the same time. Opening one eye to find the remaining biscuits, he instead watched Adam pick up the fallen canvas and set it on its hook over the fireplace. Had he done that when they were fighting? He could vaguely recall the sensation of energy trailing from his skin, setting every hair on end, but he hadn't willed it or consciously commanded it. His head pulsed at the phantom sensation. At home, it had never happened to that extent. He had inadvertently revived a bee and took the wilt out of several vases of flowers, but it had never drained the life out of him like this. It felt as if someone had sucked the air from his lungs with a kiss, unaware of the strain until they pulled away.

"I think this lack of control is because of you," Immanuel peeped, his stomach churning at the sight of the blood soaked handkerchief dangling from his free hand. When Adam turned to him, his face darkened with skepticism, Immanuel continued, "It isn't on purpose, I think it's the handfasting. If my magic is feeding off both of our tempers, instead of just mine, that could be what's causing such an overreaction."

"That's possible, but I'm not nearly as—"

"I've caught you bothering at your wrist at least a dozen times since I woke up. You hide your worry better than I do, but that doesn't mean inside you aren't fearful. We both need to try to stay calm as best we can if we don't want to destroy the house."

Adam released a short laugh and slumped onto the chair beside him. "Thank god you aren't aligned with fire."

"Don't worry, I can still do plenty of damage without fire." Coughing, he asked, "Adam, can I please let go of my nose now?"

Glancing at his watch, Adam nodded, and Immanuel slowly released his nose. He sat back and took a hesitant sniff. While he could still smell and taste blood, it didn't appear to be flowing anymore. Licking the corner of the handkerchief, he carefully rubbed away the dried flecks affixed to his skin.

Taking the cloth from Immanuel's hand to clean a spot he missed, Adam said, "We have selkies, a dead man, and more magic than we can handle. What do we do?"

Immanuel sighed. He had been turning that question over since they found Jacobs' body, but most of the answers were impossible here. There was no coroner for an inquest, no one to call to help, no Emmeline to summon the deceased for a chat. His stomach knotted at the thought, but he pushed it away. Failure wasn't an idea he could afford to entertain.

"I'm thinking. Did you find anything of use in Mr. Jacobs' pockets?"

"Not really. Most of it was drenched in… something, and the ink had run badly. They were mostly notes, probably from one of his cases. Without a context, I have no idea what it all means, if anything. Do you want to take a look at them?"

Immanuel opened his mouth to speak when his eyes fell upon the nearly invisible door obscured by the coatrack. They had walked past it how many times that day, yet they hadn't tried to open it.

"Did you find a key in his pockets?"

"No, just his badge, his watch, and some coins. The gun, too, but that was in the bottom of the boat."

"You didn't see anything else there, did you?"

"No, but that means the key to his room may be somewhere in here."

"Or a seagull could have stolen it."

"Let's hope he left it here for safekeeping. Whatever he was investigating was important enough for him to lock it away; he couldn't chance losing it. Do you think that whatever case brought him to the island, also led to his murder?"

"Possibly, it was definitely the same person who killed the selkie. I know you can't see the visions, but it was the same figure. Do you think you can pick the lock?"

Adam frowned and cocked an incredulous henna brow. "Do I look like a common criminal to you?"

"I thought I'd ask. I could picture Hadley doing it."

"So could I," he grumbled. "But where do you think he would hide it?"

Running his eyes over the bulky table and the outdated buffet and china cabinet behind it, Immanuel sighed. "It could be anywhere down here. Somewhere close."

At the hearth, Adam felt around the bricks and wooden lintel for any sign of a hidden lever or loose stone while, behind him, Immanuel felt around the cushions of the armchair and sofa. While the house wasn't very large, there suddenly seemed to be an infinite number of places to hide something as small as a key. Each drawer was pulled away, its contents shuffled before being replaced until every knickknack had been upturned only to reveal piles of dust and the refuse of vermin. Before long, the parlor and dining room looked as if they had been ransacked from their repeated searches. As Adam disappeared into the kitchen to rifle through the pantry and cupboards, Immanuel surveyed the parlor with a keen eye.

Placing his hand on the locked door, he drew in a calming breath and let his finger trace the curve of the woodgrain. A little voice in the back of his mind called to him, *Make a sigil*, but he knew he was in no shape to do so. The taste of blood still lingered on his tongue, and with each movement, his body ached in protest. He had already done too much too soon. On top of that, he had never attempted to use a sigil to unlock anything. There was no guarantee that the expenditure of energy would result in anything but injury and aggravation.

Kneeling before the door, he put his eye to the keyhole. Through the narrow opening, he could make out light filtering across the bare wooden floor, rippling through the antique glass as if the room had been submerged beneath the sea. Contorting his neck, Immanuel could see what he thought might be a wooden desk or table. With his blurry eye and the odd angle, it was impossible to tell. If all else failed, they could break the window from the outside and shimmy in through the narrow opening. Immanuel wrung his hands and grimaced at the thought of having to endure cuts from the shards, as Adam would never fit. He was overdue for a bad infection, and he didn't want to tempt fate so far from Harley Street.

"Nothing," Adam called, patting a spot of what appeared to be flour from his jacket. "We could try to break down the door."

Immanuel straightened, giving Adam a doubtful look. The door appeared to be carved from solid—albeit ancient—wood, and neither Adam nor Immanuel were nearly as sturdy. Immanuel's hands itched. He was so tempted to use magic, just one more time, but when he looked up, he found Adam watching him with a deep frown.

"No. I know what you're thinking but no. I'd rather smash the front window and deal with a bill for the glass than have you hurt yourself."

Sighing, Immanuel pushed past his companion and sunk onto the lopsided couch cushions. He stared ahead, ignoring Adam as he gathered his coat and gloves from the stand. How could he be so weak? His damaged eye blurred with each blink. It all made him feel so powerless. Somehow he had expected that the further he got into magic, the stronger he would feel, yet a temper tantrum had left him drained. More than drained, though he would never admit it to Adam. It had begun to suck the life from him, one bloody drop at a time. Jumping at the pop of a log cracking in the hearth, Immanuel raised his gaze to the painting he had knocked off the wall.

The oil painting portrayed a fishing vessel hung suspended atop a wave, seconds from smashing into the rocks and jetties in the foreground. Why anyone on an island would want a constant reminder of the dangers they were in if they tried to leave, he couldn't imagine. Despite Adam carefully righting it, it already listed to one side, as if— Rising from his seat, Immanuel pulled the painting from its hooks and set it down on the sofa.

"Were you expecting a safe there?" Adam asked, dropping his shoes in favor of watching Immanuel.

"No, but something else seems to be behind it."

Feeling along the back of the frame, Immanuel traced the edge of the canvas with his fingertips. The paper lined back slid beneath his fingers, and as he reached the left side of the frame, he felt a bump. It was barely perceivable but it was unmistakable. He tilted the frame back until the light shown across the back of the canvas. Something rippled beneath the thick paper where the canvas met the wooden frame. Gripping the edge of the paper, he watched one of the tacks wiggle as he pulled. He carefully untacked the paper to reveal a long, narrow iron key dressed with curls of metal and a spattering of rust shoved between them. A high laugh escaped his lips

"Is that—?"

"It is," Immanuel said as darted toward the door.

His hand trembled as he tried to slip the black key into the lock. The key chattered against the metal until finally with a snick, its teeth engaged and the door clicked open. Pushing it aside, the air seeped from Immanuel's lungs.

Chapter Thirteen
Lost Lives

"What the devil?" Adam whispered, stepping past Immanuel into the darkened room.

The sun ducked behind the clouds as rain pattered against the glass, but even through the deep gloom, there was no mistaking row upon row of women's faces tacked to the wall. Half a dozen colored strings had been strung between them, crisscrossing to form a tangled web. Immanuel turned away from the wall, unable to face their stares. Turning to a camp desk behind him, Immanuel examined the layers of papers and journals littering its surface. His hand hovered over the pages. He feared that at any moment Mr. Jacobs would come barging in, demanding to know why they had broken into his room, but with the sudden weight of cold dread, he remembered the man slumped across the rowboat, facedown, his features blackening with decay.

Jacobs would never return, yet his room remained as a testament to his final thoughts, a final problem he would never solve. How many days had his words and belongings waited for him? Immanuel and

Adam stood elbow-to-elbow, afraid to take another step for fear of disturbing the quiet that settled like dust over Will Jacobs' room. Taking a hesitant step toward the desk, Immanuel carefully pushed the pages with the tip of his finger to reveal tide charts, captain's ledgers, and local histories beneath them. In the far corner near the mullioned window, the chaise's back had been draped with a rumpled blanket while a suitcase sat tucked beneath it.

"There are so many of them," Adam said, shaking his head.

Stepping back without taking his eyes off the chaise, Immanuel flipped on the lights, bathing the wall of paper in soft yellow light. Ninety-six women stared back at them from the plaster. The majority were crudely made sketches or merely names with ages and dates. A handful of drawings had been delineated by an artful hand and even fewer were photographs, their backings curling with the humidity. There was something about them, some unifying feature apart from sex that Immanuel could sense more than identify. He squinted at each face. Perhaps it was something about the roundness of the eyes or the fullness of the cheeks in respect to the nose. Then again, they could have been rendered by the same artist, which may have caused the pattern. Between some of them, strings had been pinned and tethered together with dyed yarn while the heads of the tacks pinning them to the wall had been brushed with paint. Immanuel's bichrome eyes followed the trail of red string from woman to woman but couldn't discern its meaning.

He swallowed hard. "Do— do you think we have a Ripper here or someone like Lord Rose?"

"I should hope not." The tightness in Adam's voice betrayed his calm demeanor. "I cannot imagine someone could get away with a hundred murders on an island this small. You would have no one left."

"What do you think we should do? Should we," Immanuel paused, eyeing the battered suitcase stuffed under Jacobs' makeshift bed, "go through his things?"

Adam followed Immanuel's gaze to the trunk and sighed. "May as well."

Watching his companion shift uncomfortably, Adam gently squeezed his arm. As he let go, Immanuel caught his hand, holding it close as he gave him a weary smile.

"You look over his notes. I will dig through his bag," Adam replied as he knelt down to retrieve the orphaned suitcase.

"Are you certain?"

"Very. If any of that is scientific, you would fair far better than I would. That and I have no qualms about rifling through his belongings."

I did it with George, and I can do it again. The words nearly slipped out, but Adam clamped his jaw shut and turned away in time to stop them. Clicking open the suitcase, he applied himself to sifting through its contents, but his mind slipped back to George. He had lost track of how long it had been since his older brother passed. Two years at least. It had been several months before Hadley and Lord Dorset became properly acquainted, that much he remembered. Eilian's first prosthetic had been the last thing George worked on but never finished. He had forgotten that.

Pulling out each article of clothing, Adam gave them a quick inspection and checked their pockets for anything of interest before carefully setting them aside. How many shirts and trousers had he folded when Hadley was too distraught to come out of the workroom? From the moment George passed, they had buried themselves in work. She focused on finishing the remaining orders while he arranged the funeral, took care of the will and financials, and moved George's things to the attic. He had been shocked by how many shirts were flecked with dried blood that hadn't come out in the wash, but what had disturbed him more were how large the cleaner shirts seemed. George had never been robust, and yet— He blinked, his eyes hot with a foreign feeling he hadn't indulged in years. Crumpling the shirt into a wad, he hurled it against the wall. Adam could picture himself standing in his brother's room, each breath heaving, caught on the sudden constriction in his chest. The hot lump of feeling that had been quietly building longed to escape, but he feared that more than anything. If he let it come, it may never stop. His hands curled into fists, then out into trembling claws.

Destruction. Blind destruction. That was all he could remember of that time.

Adam drew his hand back. Cradled between pairs of drawers was a gun. This time it was a revolver, and this one had not been lost to the corrosive kiss of the sea. The cold steel fell heavy in his hand as he snapped open the cylinder to confirm that it wasn't loaded. Back then, it had taken everything in his power not to tear the room apart, not to tear himself apart. A storm raged within him, beating against his mind until he could scarcely discern it from his own thoughts. But Hadley had kept him together. She hadn't known it, she still didn't, but she needed him and he knew losing her twin so soon after George would have dealt her a severe blow. No, he had to keep going to work for her sake. He told himself he had to keep moving forward because his stalwart sister was falling to pieces.

Hadley and George had been the ones keeping them afloat, and after his death, Adam had to lend his support until he could reprise his rightful role as the black sheep. He released a short laugh as he snapped the cylinder in place and spun it for good measure. Once Hadley seemed to be getting on with Lord Dorset, Adam imploded. His farcical relationship with Matilda Merriweather had been the first casualty. Then, briefly his sanity, his identity, his employment at the firm, and finally his relationship with Hadley, but thankfully, he managed to salvage those in time. Glancing over his shoulder, a wistful smile crept across his lips at Immanuel's knit brows as he poured over Jacobs' notes. It had all turned out for the best, hadn't it? He and Immanuel eventually found each other, and Miss Merriweather was now Mrs. Turnbull, which was far more than he ever could have offered her.

"Any luck?" he asked but Immanuel didn't stir from the page. Despite trying to touch him lightly, Immanuel jumped the moment Adam's hand made contact with his leg. "My apologies, darling, but did you find anything?"

Immanuel's gaze traveled back to the paper in his hand before trailing to the wall of faces. "I'm not certain. Mr. Jacobs didn't leave a key. I don't know if I'm reading too much into it, but I think the color of the pins represent how the women died."

"So they *were* murdered?" Adam asked, suddenly thankful to have the cold reassurance of the revolver in his grasp.

"Not necessarily." Immanuel stood before the wall, his hand moving from face-to-face with each flick of his gaze from the pile of pages. After a long moment, he stepped back. "If I have surmised this correctly from his notes, all of the women with black headed pins are listed as drownings in local records."

Abandoning the suitcase, Adam stood at Immanuel's side. While he hadn't noticed it when they first entered, he could now see that most of the dull metal tacks had been dabbed with ink. Black dotted most of the heads. He tallied the number before he registered he had been doing it.

"Sixty-seven drownings. That seems excessive, even out here. I mean, did a ship sink?"

"No, that's the strange part. Look at the dates at the bottom. The earliest date was nearly seventy years ago, but they go all the way up to this year. He has at least a page for each of them. Some more than others, and the black pins match with the deaths recorded as drownings."

"Even over seventy years, that seems like a very high number. Do they say if they're accidental or not?"

Immanuel shook his head.

"Well, what about the pins without paint and the red ones?"

"I'm not certain yet. I'm still picking through all of this. Some of the handwriting is really hard to read."

"I can imagine." With Immanuel's cramped, narrow handwriting, it was often so illegible that he had to make certain if he was reading German or English. "Did you see what I found?"

"Another one? Was Mr. Jacobs preparing for battle?"

"He was a policeman. I'm sure they didn't want to send him out to the wild unarmed. Honestly, two guns isn't exactly an arsenal. Now, I have a spare. I'd have a third if I didn't feel funny using the one from the boat."

Immanuel's face fell at the realization. "You brought your gun with you? What would possess you to do that?"

"Perhaps the fact that we were sent to deal with a murderer on an island with creatures that may or may not be human lurking about. You may have your magic, but steel is what makes me feel safe."

Frowning, Immanuel stared down at the mess of handwritten notes but found he couldn't focus on the words. Immanuel chewed his lip. His magic didn't make him feel safe. It was unpredictable energy he could wield with a thought, and that was what made it so dangerous. Magic had the potential to be an entire world for him to explore. It inspired all the promise and vigor science had when he first began his studies, but it never made him feel safe. Quieting his mind, Immanuel felt the pull of their bond between his ribs. Magic scared him far more than it provided comfort.

"So where are you keeping it?"

For a long moment, Adam merely stared at him with a raised brow as if trying to discern his meaning. "Why? Are you hoping to dash my Colt into the sea like you did with my champagne?"

"As tempting as it may be, I'm glad you brought it. We may need it, but I don't want to accidentally shoot myself. Tell me where you've stashed it."

Keeping his eyes locked on Immanuel's, Adam slowly unbuttoned his jacket and pulled it aside. Tucked against his hip was a black leather holster with only the butt of a gun sticking out. Immanuel swallowed hard. He hated knowing the gun was there, lurking against the familiar planes of Adam's form, but at least it was safely contained.

"Satisfied?" Adam asked, catching him staring at the line where metal met leather.

"Just don't take my head off if I get up during the night."

"I haven't yet, have I?"

A small smile crept across Immanuel's lips. As quickly as it appeared, it fell away when his attention returned to Jacobs' notes. "Adam, can you do me a favor?"

"Of course."

Immanuel's pulse quickened. Opening his mouth, he found his tongue tacky and thick. "I need you to write the information up on their posters as I read it. I may have found something, but I need to see it laid out."

♨ ♨

By the time Adam and Immanuel finished, it had taken several hours, two pots of tea, and a hell of a lot of shaking and cracking of Adam's hands to get out the cramps from writing on the wall in such careful script. Adam stepped back to admire their handiwork. Each face now had an approximate age, a location, a manner of death, offspring, and anything else relevant Immanuel discovered in the dead policeman's notes. Setting the onion paper aside, Immanuel stared at the wall of faces, his blonde brows knit in concentration. Adam watched him, wanting to speak, but he held his tongue even as he confirmed what they had already suspected regarding the black pins. All of them had drowned. A shiver passed through him at the thought of such a horrible death.

"The red pins are murders," Immanuel said suddenly, pointing to three flyers jabbed into the wall with red tipped pins. "See? This woman was murdered by her husband. Actually, all three were."

Adam took a step back, his eyes skimming to where silver pins jutted from the wall. He had wanted to pull them off the wall and rearrange them into groups, but Immanuel had refused for fear of disturbing some yet unknown pattern Jacobs had left behind. Following Immanuel's gaze from page to page, Adam felt the realization click in place.

"Black is drowning, like we thought, but unpainted is no cause. Look, none of them have causes of death."

Retrieving their respective pages from the pile, Immanuel's gaze flickered between the two papers. "You're right. That's strange, though. Statistically, many more people should have died from unknown causes than drowning. Maybe we switched them."

"Immanuel, you rattled off every line of notes to me. I know we have them labeled correctly." He stepped closer to the wall. "It is very strange though. Shouldn't we have a bunch of women who died of old age or in childbirth?"

"Age...," the word slipped from Immanuel's lips before he could stop it. His eyes went wide as he moved from picture to picture. The drowned women all had at least one child. "There are no old women or very young women. No children either. Their ages range from—"

"Twenty to fifty-five."

"But why? Why did Jacobs eliminate children and crones? Why focus on married women with children?"

Adam squinted, staring at the list of attributes beneath each name. "We're missing something they have in common, we have to be. We know they all lived on the islands within the last seventy years, they were all women, they all had children, we are to assume they were married, and they all died here."

"They all died here," Immanuel echoed, his voice hollow. "All of their deaths are suspicious. We have an absurd amount of drownings, several murders, and the rest are unknown. He didn't include women with natural deaths. That's why there aren't any old women or women who died in child birth or from illnesses."

"So Mr. Jacobs came to investigate the deaths of nearly a hundred women who died on the islands. He couldn't have thought they were all killed by the same person. That would be preposterous."

The words died in Immanuel's throat as the room fell into darkness with a shudder. For a moment, neither man moved. Beyond the cloaked window, Immanuel could make out the waft of waves on the beach below and the distant barks of seals beneath the patter of rain against the slate roof. How did light manage to block the world as well as a heavy curtain?

"Generators must be down," Adam murmured, trying the switch.

In the bleak evening light, it was hard for Immanuel to make out Adam's features, let alone the pages plastered to the wall. Releasing a tense breath, Immanuel sank onto the chaise. He closed his eyes and tried to recall what he had read, but all the faces blended into one. Even if he couldn't see or think straight, he had to try to solve this. He had to. A hand landed on his shoulder, sending him from his thoughts with a jolt. Even in the dark, he could sense the soft look he knew all too well.

"Perhaps this is our cue to have dinner. I'm sure we'll find some candles in the kitchen."

Immanuel opened his mouth to protest, but as he gestured toward the wall, his heavy limbs reminded him of the damage he had done earlier. Perhaps eating was for the best.

"All right, but we're going to talk over the case while we eat."

A rueful grin quirked Adam's mustache as he steered Immanuel out of the room. "I wouldn't have it any other way."

৵৹৩ ৩৹৵

Immanuel's heart thundered in his chest as a set of fine teeth appeared in the gloom, glinting like the Cheshire Cat's until a pair of amber eyes glowed above it. The man's smile cut him like a knife, pain welling in his breast at the thought of what he would do to him. Immanuel tried to close his eyes, but he was still there. A puff of hot breath laced with sulfur and cigarettes rolled from his mouth, scalding Immanuel's eyes. A strangled cry escaped his lips as the man pressed the knife into the hollow of his throat before running it torturously down his sternum and along his dented ribs. He wanted to move. He tried to will his body to flee, but fear held him fast. Wrenching his chin up, the man forced Immanuel to confront his amber eyes. That knife smile sliced across his lips.

"I told you, I would make you suffer, boy," Lord Rose said, sinking the knife deep into his heart.

Immanuel lurched awake. He kicked away the covers, pawing at his side and face. Patting his chest, he was relieved to find his body whole and his heart hammering beneath his ribs. Releasing a tremulous breath, Immanuel hung his head in his hands until his pulse slowed and the rhythmic puff of Adam's sleepy breaths anchored him in reality. They were on Seohl-wiga Island, far from London and Lord Rose's lead-sealed prison. Running a shaky hand through his hair, Immanuel wished they were in London, so he could visit Judith's office and ask after Lord Rose's vessel. No matter how many nightmares he had, he still feared one might be true.

Reaching across the bed to wake Adam, Immanuel was surprised to find the other side of the narrow mattress empty. He licked his lips and let his head rest against the heavy headboard. In his panic, he had forgotten Adam had insisted they take separate beds. It had taken a lot of convincing to even have Adam remain in the same room as him, but as he sat coated in cold sweat, Immanuel wished he had fought harder to keep Adam in his bed. After a nightmare, all he wanted was Adam. Wrapped in his arms, there was no room for monsters.

Rolling onto his back, Immanuel stared at the rough wooden beams bracing the ceiling and wished more than anything he could be home in his own bed with Adam and Percy curled up against his sides. Even if his cat would be the stuff of nightmares for those who didn't know him, Immanuel loved him, and so did Adam, eventually. When he awoke from a nightmare, he could always count on Percy to come nosing at him, as if sensing his distress. After running his hand along his spine and smooth head for a few minutes, his breath would fall into sync with Percy's silent purr. He missed that. As he slowly sat up and exhaled against the tightness in his chest, Immanuel tried to imagine what the cat was up to. Wreaking havoc, no doubt.

Running his clammy hands over his face, Immanuel watched Adam toss beneath his quilt just out of reach. In the scant moonlight, he could make out the hard line of his jaw and the faint peppering of henna stubble overlaying it. He could climb into bed with him and lay his head on his chest like he did at home. There Adam would instinctively pull him close even in slumber, but here— Immanuel sighed and quietly padded across the room to his suitcase where it sat on the dresser. Here, Adam would surely push him away. Sharing a bed in a strange place, even one far from prying eyes was too much of a risk, and he understood. He did, but that didn't mean he liked it. Immanuel rubbed his arms against the mid night chill before clicking open the latches of his suitcase as softly as he could manage.

He angled the open case toward the undulant beam of the lighthouse's beacon and caught the glint of the precious cargo he had hidden within. The handkerchiefs and rags he had wrapped around them had fallen away during their travels, but at least they were whole. He wasn't sure why he was so relieved to see his oil and mixing bowl. Adam would never throw them out, but somehow he had expected his companion to complain that Immanuel had brought them with him. He had found the palm-sized bowl in a cupboard in Hadley's old workroom. Unwrapping it, he turned it over in his palm as the moon and lighthouse beam caught its lustrous surface to reveal a cluster of faded forget-me-nots painted in its center. He had decanted the oil into an old perfume bottle, but somehow he doubted they would need it for its true purpose when Adam would barely look at him, let alone touch him, here. Carefully tipping a thimbleful of oil into the dish, Immanuel drew in a breath to clear his mind.

At home, he would have taken a nib or penknife and punctured his palm to add his blood to the oil, but after nearly freezing and having a wretched nosebleed from overstretching his powers, he knew he couldn't chance how much energy a blood spell might require. It was far more powerful and binding than anointing with oil or merely intent, but deep down, he didn't want a piece of him tied to this godawful island, even if it would keep them safer now. Standing before the window, he closed his eyes and let his mind fall into the familiar labyrinth of his protection sigil. His finger swept through the sigil's curves as he pictured bars locking, people walking past the house without paying it any mind, Adam's arms tightly wrapped around him. With a final tap, the sigil hummed to life, faintly resonating in the dark.

Moving from window to window, Immanuel traced the cruciform

flower. His bare feet barely made a creak as he walked through the house as if in a trance. With each sigil and twang of power, the Lord Rose shaped knot in his chest loosened until he found himself standing in what had been Mr. Jacobs' room. Immanuel stood in the doorway for a long moment. Even after he and Adam had spent hours poring over every picture and note, the air remained charged with expectation, as if it's owner would reappear at any moment. Placing the dish of oil on the desk, Immanuel wiped his slick finger on the edge of his pajamas and flipped on the lamps. The lights had come back on in the middle of their meager dinner, and though they had retired early, Immanuel's thoughts never left the sea of faces and names.

Who was Frieda Sewell? Or Kathleen March? Part of him wished he could lay his hand on the posters and see their final moments. While he hated the trauma of violent deaths, he wanted to know them. He wished he could separate them into individuals instead of statistics. Those last moments showed him who they were better than any file ever could. In those final seconds, their thoughts told of loves and regrets, of intimacy never shared aloud. Immanuel folded his arms to stave off the nighttime chill as he drew closer to the island's most recent victim.

Helene Balthazar. 1865-1892. Seohl-wiga Island. Blonde hair, hazel eyes. Unknown.

Attached to the paper was a blurry photograph of a woman sitting with her husband. Her lips were drawn straight and her eyes stared ahead, the corners tipped down while her husband held her hand and proudly sat for his portrait. There was something strange about her. The photographs appeared to be a wedding portrait, but she seemed resigned. Carefully unpinning the picture, Immanuel wondered if she had merely run away. If her husband had turned to drink or had beaten her, perhaps she had escaped in a boat or on the ferry while he was at sea. Perhaps in a fit of gin-fueled rage, he had killed her and dumped her body into the sea where she would fall to pieces before she could be found. Sailors surely knew the flow of the currents that would send a body to open water.

Tacking the photograph back on the wall, Immanuel stared at the red string running between three of the women. The names were different and they had lived on different islands within the chain, but they all had drowned and all had green eyes. Immanuel was about to move on when his eyes landed on the dates. Two out of three didn't have birthdates, but they had approximate ages: 36, 45, 57. Brown hair, brown hair, grey hair. Turning to the next set of strings, Immanuel traced its path. Once again, the women progressed in age, but the features remained the same.

"They're the same woman," Immanuel murmured breathlessly.

Each color string traced the life of one woman through her various incarnations. Somehow they had managed to hop between islands undetected, faking their deaths through drowning only to reappear again elsewhere. Their sixty-seven victims were truly fifty, and even then, there were a few he suspected may be repeats. But why had they done it? Why had they escaped their lives, often more than once? Helene's dower face flashed through Immanuel's mind. Had motherhood and wifely duties sent them barreling toward freedom by whatever means necessary?

"Immanuel, what are you doing up?"

Turning, Immanuel found Adam leaning against the doorway. He yawned and blinked in the bright light of the electric lamps. Against his will, Immanuel felt a yawn claw up his throat.

"I—" His gaze trailed to the dish of oil beside him. Adam still didn't understand his need to graffiti every surface to secure their safety. Magic still was something to be spoken of in hushed tones, so Immanuel said, "I was making sure the front door was locked, but I got distracted."

"Well, it's late. Come back to bed. We can figure this mess out tomorrow."

Eying the wall of women's faces one more time, Immanuel nodded and drifted to Adam's side. His companion snaked his arm around his waist and tugged him close as they turned to go up the steps. The house creaked with each tread, but as they reached the door to their shared room, Adam tightened his grip and steered Immanuel toward his bed. Immanuel looked between his companion and the sagging mattress uncertainly.

"We only have a few hours until sunrise. I think we can risk it." Staring into Immanuel's eyes, he brushed the hair from his forehead and cupped his cheek. "Especially if you warded the whole house."

Lifting the covers, Adam gestured for Immanuel to get in first before sliding in beside him. He stretched his arm beneath Immanuel's neck and around his shoulder to keep him close, even though Immanuel knew it would put Adam's arm to sleep. They shifted until finally their bodies fell into their natural grooves and Adam's thumb came to rest in the nick in his ribs. Immanuel closed his eyes and drew in slow breaths until all he could feel was the steady drum of his heart and the reassuring warmth of Adam's skin radiating through the thin fabric of his union suit.

Chapter Fourteen
The Lighthouse Keeper

Adam awoke relieved to find Immanuel sound asleep curled against his side. Unlike nights where Immanuel fell asleep an hour before he had to rise for work, there were no creases in his brow or signs of exhaustion, just blessed peace. Slowly turning onto his side, Adam studied his companion's lax features before gently kissing his forehead. When Immanuel didn't stir, Adam slipped out of bed, careful not to disturb him as he dressed in silence. Standing before the small mirror above the washbasin, Adam contemplated the auburn stubble sprouting along his jaw. Most days he sliced it off without a second thought, but this was a town where men worked with their hands and didn't take kindly to fussy dandies.

Creeping down to the kitchen, Adam lit and stoked the stove. He silently moved from cupboard to cupboard, gathering what he needed to make a palatable breakfast. For all the trouble Mr. Jacobs caused, at least he had the foresight to properly stock the larder. Cracking eggs into a battered pan, Adam listened as the boards whined overhead.

"Adam?" Immanuel called, his voice thin.

"Making breakfast."

That twinge of panic in his voice was what Adam hated about the rare occasions he awoke before Immanuel. Lord Rose had left behind more than poorly healed ribs and a scarred eye. Immanuel truly feared Adam would disappear one day, as if he had been nothing more than a figment of his mind. It had been hard to understand at first, but the previous night when he awoke to find Immanuel's bed open and empty, he felt that familiar pang of panic. He couldn't say what woke him. Normally Immanuel made enough noise that if Adam dared to sleep in, he would be up by the time Immanuel began to open and shut the drawers and wardrobe.

No, what had awoken him wasn't noise. It was the absence of his presence. For as long as he had known Immanuel, he had always felt there was something different about him. He had chalked it up to favoritism, but the more he spent time away from him, the more apparent his "otherness" became. He couldn't hear it, he couldn't see it. Hell, he couldn't even really describe it, but Immanuel had a loudness to his being, even when he desperately tried to make himself invisible. Strangers' eyes found their way to him in a crowded room despite his somber grey suits and his bichrome gaze locked on the ground or hidden under his hair. The night before there was a moment when the ringing in his head cleared, and Adam awoke from a sound sleep at the sudden quiet. Over the sizzle of bacon, he wondered if this static had been a byproduct of the handfasting or if it had always been this way, but after living with Immanuel for several months, he had finally begun to take notice.

By the time Adam had scraped eggs and bacon onto the scratched china and had the tea kettle whistling, Immanuel wandered down the steps, pausing at the bottom to stare into Jacobs' room for a long moment. Turning back to Adam as he ducked into the dining room, Immanuel broke into a wide grin.

"What happened to your face?" he asked, biting his lip to suppress a laugh.

"I decided to try a more rugged look. What do you think?"

Immanuel's eyes darted over his features. "Can I touch it?"

"Fine," he replied, rolling his eyes.

Standing before him, Immanuel cupped Adam's face. At first, he slowly ran his hands over the day's growth, but as he reached his jaw, a mischievous smile crossed his lips. Immanuel rubbed his hands across Adam's cheeks as if trying to create a spark. He pulled his face away, warding his lover off with the plates of food.

"That's enough, you silly git." Dropping the plates onto the table, Adam watched Immanuel hide a yawn. "How did you sleep?"

Immanuel shook his head and picked at his eggs. "Like I could sleep for another five hours. You should have awoken me earlier. I didn't mean to sleep this late."

"We have both had a rough week. I thought you might appreciate a little extra shut-eye."

"While I appreciate the thought, we're wasting time. We only have five days left to figure this out, and we're no closer to knowing who murdered the selkie or Mr. Jacobs. I don't even know where to start."

Frowning, Adam nudged Immanuel's arm as he absently poked holes in his breakfast with the tines of his fork. "You can start by eating your breakfast. I don't need you swooning on me." Raising his gaze, Adam caught the glint of sunlight off the glass beacon. "I was thinking I might go to the lighthouse and speak to the lighthouse keeper, what's his name?"

"Quill. No, Quince. That's not a bad idea. Miss Larkin did say he was the village… everything. He might know something."

"While I'm there, I thought you could go visit that strange chap, Byron. He seemed willing to chat with you."

"At the same time? We aren't going together?"

Adam released a short laugh and set his teacup aside. "Don't you think it would look odd if we went everywhere together? We told Byron and Miss Larkin that you are here to study seals and I'm a journalist who is tagging along. Do you think a journalist would have much interest in studying seals?"

A fitful frown crossed Immanuel's lips as he stared at a forkful of egg. "No, I guess not, but is it safe to split up?"

"I'm only going to speak to the man, not get into a boat with him. I had already planned to take my revolver with me when I went. Speaking of which, you should take Jacobs' gun with you."

Immanuel opened his mouth only to close it again. "I have never fired a gun. I have never even handled one."

"Really? You have never gone hunting?"

Shaking his head, Immanuel hesitantly choked down a bite of bacon and eggs. "No, my family never went. And with my abilities now, I try to stay as far away from corpses as I can. I really don't want to see myself shoot anything. It's hard enough to eat poultry as it is."

"Fine, but you still need to eat."

ᘔ ᘔ

By the time Adam managed to flush Immanuel out of the cottage, his companion had eaten approximately four bites of his breakfast and looked as sullen as he did after a bad day at the museum. Leaving him at the crossroads, Adam tried not to look back at Immanuel heading between the trees toward the village. If he did, he feared the worry he had suppressed all morning would overtake him and he would call Immanuel to tag along with him to the lighthouse. He had to be strong for him, he had to if they had any hope of becoming something more. Adam blinked. When did he suddenly get on board with this notion?

Turning his collar up against the damp chill, Adam stuffed his hands in his pockets and made certain to temper the fluidity of his gait. Through the scant trees and roiling fog, Adam could make out the deep red brick of the lighthouse rising from the grasses like the Tower of Babel. Attached at the beacon's hip was a matching building, squat and square. While it lacked the pretention of the red brick houses Adam was familiar with in London, the lighthouse keeper's home was more modern than any of the slate-rooved houses populating the island. As he followed the washed out dirt path where the sea segmented the island each day, Adam trailed into the sand-stained grass. Salt coated his lips and teeth, casting his body in an earthen crust as he stood staring at the distant, flickering forms of birds. Not far from shore, a dozen metal buoys bobbed in a curved line that paralleled the shape of the coast. If he hadn't seen the brick shed hugging the cliff and cables trailing into the water, he never would have guessed their ingenious purpose.

"Oy, what you think you're doing? Get away from the edge, you ruddy fool, before you fall in."

Adam turned to find the lighthouse keeper trudging toward him from the house, red-faced and puffing out plumes of breath. Taking a step back, Adam tipped his hat to Casper Quince and gave him his best company smile. "Just admiring your gorgeous views and unsightly generators. Nice to see you again, Mr. Quince."

When the other man released a chuckle, Adam relaxed a fraction. It was a calculated risk to say, but as Mr. Quince reached his side, he drew in a long breath and gave the bobbing generators a glare.

"You know I tried to stop them from dumping them out here, but I was overruled. Progress and all that. Electricity," Quince murmured, retrieving a pipe from his pocket. "What's wrong with gas lamps? You don't hear of gas lamps going out at all hours."

"It did interrupt my work last night. I must say it works a lot better in London."

"I suppose it does. You like it? People get sick from it?"

Adam narrowed his eyes. "No. Not unless they fall on a line or try to grab it, and that's more stupidity than sickness."

"They aren't that far off."

"Isn't that the truth. To answer your question, Mr. Quince, it works very well. It goes out during storms sometimes, but that's it."

He nodded thoughtfully, running a chapped hand over his whiskers. "You and the other bloke from London?"

"Yes, though Mr. Winter originally hails from Germany."

"I got family out that way," Quince said, more to the wind than to Adam as he filled his pipe and struggled to light it against the breeze.

"Haven't seen them since I was a lad."

"Mr. Quince, the reason I've come here is I am working on a piece about the history and lore of Seohl-wiga Island, and I was hoping you could help me."

"That right?" Quince ran his pale green eyes over Adam's form from shined boot to carefully brushed top hat. "What's a Londoner got to do with us?"

"I heard the island was struggling, despite the piece I saw in the paper about the lighthouse and generators. I would like to write something that will give people a reason to come here and visit, spend some money in town. Too many places like this are dying, and it's a damn shame."

Adam kept his eyes locked on the horizon, where sea and sky blended to form a line of sparkling grey. When you're an outsider, you let them come to you, Adam reminded himself as he waited. Adam knew how to bait the hook, how to subtly steal clients before they realized what he was up to.

"May as well come inside then. No sense catching our death out here."

Quince turned back to the house, pausing only long enough to cup his pipe and light it against the wicked wind. Leading Adam across the waving grasses and gravel, Quince tromped into the brick house, not even stopping to unlock the door. Adam blinked, reminding himself once more they were no longer in London.

The house was warmer than Adam expected. Seeing Casper Quince's drab figure skulking outside, he had expected a home closer to a cave than a seaside cottage. The inside of the house had been plastered and whitewashed to reflect the light pouring in through the elongated windows facing out toward the sea. The floorboards were rough and unstained but had been covered with rugs that, though careworn, were clean. Taking off his hat, Adam stared up at the white boards and exposed rafters jutting from the brick like ribs. The only tell-tale sign of its owner was the undertones of fish and muck.

At one end of the room a loft lined with bookshelves stood above a parted door where Adam could make out what looked like the shape of a trunk or dresser. The house was small, utilizing every foot efficiently. Even the rafters above the loft had been crammed with nets, rods, and other items Adam couldn't identify. The furniture was an eclectic mix of homemade pieces and those that had been hand-me-downs or even from passing ships. As Adam drifted toward the loft, straining to read the titles, Mr. Quince headed straight for a squat, latched cupboard beside a faded and patched armchair. The titles lining the shelf were familiar, some sat on their shared shelf at home. Others he couldn't place in a certain discipline, apart from science of some sort. Adam sniffed the air, his nose crinkling at the overwhelming stench of dried ocean somewhere nearby. *The tools*, he thought, his eyes trailing up to the rafters as he returned to the cluster of chairs.

In his home, Casper Quince appeared much less formidable. Outside he seemed large, swelling up with each breath despite being shorter than Adam, yet inside, he seemed to deflate and his cactal demeanor receded beneath layers of whiskers and wool. Lingering at the edge of the rug, Adam studied the lighthouse keeper. Casper Quince was comprised of varying shades of olive brown and grey. His skin had been deeply creased from years in the sun and wind while his mastiff jaw was firmly set into an impassive frown. It was strange to see a man who had sent a twinge of apprehension in his heart the day before putting on reading glasses in a tidy home. Somehow he had expected something far more... slovenly.

"Drink?" Quince barked without looking back.

"Yes, thank you. You have a lovely home, Mr. Quince."

Grunting an acknowledgement, Quince handed Adam a cloudy glass and sank into his armchair. Adam stared down at the chair across from his host. It was one of the seemingly homemade pieces that appeared half-finished and rough. Fearing he might get splinters in rather unpleasant places, Adam perched on the edge of his seat and took a sip of his drink. He grimaced and his eyes bulged at the astringent tang of bathtub gin. Catching Quince watching him from the corner of his eye, Adam suppressed the urge to cough and took a long swig. Immanuel would not be pleased.

"You read the article about the island?" Quince asked, watching the ribbon of smoke drift from the bowl of his pipe.

"Yes, I read about it in the London papers a few weeks ago. It was quite interesting."

"I sent that in myself," he replied, the faintest hint of pride curling the corner of his lip.

"Really now?" Adam couldn't picture Quince writing anything, let alone an article in a reputable city paper. "Well, it certainly piqued my interest and my editor's."

"At least someone in London took notice." Placing his glass on the side table, Quince slouched lower in his chair and folded his hands over his chest. "So what do you need to know?"

As the smell of sweet pipe tobacco hit his nose, Adam was glad he asked Immanuel to stay behind. Even if it didn't have the burn of cigarettes, the pipe would have set him on edge. Watching Quince blow the remnants of smoke from his nostrils, Adam reached into his breast pocket to find a small pad of paper and a pencil. At least looking the part of a reporter would save him the hassle of remembering every detail Immanuel would demand later.

"Tell me about the island itself. I know it's quiet now, but I'm sure it has quite the history."

Adam was immediately sorry he asked. For the better part of an hour, Quince spoke of pirates and Vikings and parts of history Adam had apparently slept through in school. By the time they reached King George III, Adam's head swam with drink. Setting his drink aside, Adam straightened and focused waited for a gap to speak as Quince's tail finally reached his lifetime.

"It's the smallest of the islands around here. Most people are fishermen or fishwives. Lots of men don't want to be fishermen anymore. They want bigger and better, so they go off to the city and never come back. We've been dwindling for generations. The weird ones are me and Byron Durnure. We've stuck around."

Adam nodded and replied before the other man could go on, "Do you know anything about the monolith in the middle of the island?"

"The monolith?" he asked, his gaze running over Adam suspiciously.

"The stone circle. Miss Larkin got very cross with us when we got too close."

He scoffed into his drink. "She would. They think the stones are sacred. That they can take you to the land of faes if you're made of the right stuff."

"The faes?"

"They don't call it that, but that's what it is. Faerie nonsense that should have died when reason reached the island. We got plenty of legends, changelings and fish people."

"Can you speak more about those legends?"

Mr. Quince shifted in his armchair. Adam followed his gaze to find it resting on an outcropping of rocks outside the window. Between the waves lapping and the considerable distance, it was impossible to tell if anything inhabited them besides sea birds, but somehow Adam felt there must have been seals sunbathing. When Quince turned to find Adam watching him, he ran a tired hand over his salt and pepper stubble.

"I don't want you writing this down. I don't want loonies coming here to see if it's true." He took a sip of his gin and waited until Adam set his pencil aside to say, "The locals believe that the seals can change into beautiful women. That sometimes they lure people to their deaths or fall in love with human men. It's just a sailors' folktales."

"So you don't believe it?"

"I don't take it as gospel like the ones who've never left."

"From the way Miss Larkin spoke of you, I thought you had always been on the island."

"I left to get some schooling. Thought I might become a university man. When my father died, he left me enough money from smuggling to study natural philosophy. He thought I could do better, get off the island for good." Casper's light eyes darkened, fading as he clutched his glass tighter. "Didn't come to pass. The island never lets you go.

Not without a fight."

"And what about your mother? Was she happy to see you back?"

"My mother," he replied, his voice sharpening. "She up and left before I could scarcely remember her. The last thing I remember is her patting my sister Hilda on the head and slipping out the front door without so much as a look back at me. She died not long after."

Staring down at his notepad, the word reverberated through his mind. At some time the day before, he and Immanuel had read the statistics of a faceless woman, never knowing she was Casper Quince's mother. Adam tapped the page with the end of his pencil and made a note between two lines to tell Immanuel.

"I'm sorry for your loss."

Quince grunted and took a long swig of his drink.

The words tumbled out of Adam's mouth before he could stop them. "I also lost my mother as a child. I don't think you ever get over it, even if you were young. Mine died of consumption the same year my father did. My older brother ended up raising me and my sister. He caught it and died a few years back."

"Consumption's a nasty business. Your sister still alive?"

Adam nodded.

"You're lucky."

The older man's jaw hardened as they lapsed into silence. Without asking Adam if he wanted anymore, Quince refilled his glass and downed most of it in one glug. His eyes trailed to the sea again before snapping back to Adam with a shake of his head. Clanking the glass on the side table, he settled back into his chair.

"What else you need for the paper? I need to get back to my rounds."

Staring down at his notes, Adam took a grimacing sip of liquor. "I won't include it in the article, but I'm curious about the legend you mentioned. It sounds familiar. For the life of me I can't remember the title, but my mother read it to me. Some Danish story about a mermaid. Is it the same thing?"

"They call them selkies."

"I must have been mistaken, then."

"Like I said, it's a bunch of hogwash. It's a nice excuse when your woman runs off and leaves you with a brood of brats and nothing else to show for it. The same story appears wherever the Vikings stopped."

"Really? That's curious."

"It's just a seaman's fantasy. You'll want to talk to Byron about the generators before you leave. That should be the draw to get people here."

Adam nodded, pretending to jot it down. "So have the selkies gone the way of the faeries in these parts?"

Smoke spilled from the bowl of Quince's pipe, twisting in on itself until it nearly formed the shape of a figure. Limbs danced in slow motion only to be dashed with a sudden exhalation as he raised his sea green eyes to meet Adam's. "One can only hope."

Chapter Fifteen
Skulls and Shells

Immanuel stood on the weather worn path, watching Adam as he disappeared down the fork in the road without looking back. His chest tightened as he waited for Adam to turn around or at least cast a glance in his direction, but he never did. Fiddling with the strap of his satchel, he realized he had forgotten to mention to Adam that he didn't know where Byron Durnure's laboratory actually was. He had never asked. The island was small enough that he could only circle for a few hours at most, but even if it was far simpler than London, it didn't mean he wasn't afraid of getting turned around.

The wind stirred, whipping his hair against his face and bringing with it the taste of the sea. The further Adam withdrew from him, the more certain Immanuel was that he could feel something deep within the island. It reminded him of what he felt when he tried to manipulate air or water. A web of energy just out of sight, that if viewed from the right angle glowed. Watching a rolling puff of breath disappear into the aether, Immanuel smiled at the thought. Magic truly was all around them. At that, a strange thought crossed Immanuel's mind.

Opening his satchel, Immanuel felt around the bottom until his fingers brushed against the cold, brassy surface of the vivalabe. Immanuel balanced the device in his palms, watching a beam of sunlight reflect off its coffered surface until it glowed. A pulse deep within the metal reverberated through Immanuel's hand with each tick, but he knew if he put the vivalabe to his ear, he would never hear the whirl of internal mechanisms. Whatever powered it, it didn't require winding or gears. *Magic*, his mind whispered. A series of concentric, crisscrossing lines encircled the outer surface like the face of an astrolabe. As Immanuel clicked the raised spot on the vivalabe's equator, the heavy lid fell back to reveal a more intricate surface lined with minute markings he still hadn't discerned. They seemed, to his limited knowledge, part alchemical, part astrological, and some with no known origin. He had nearly left it home, tucked in his dresser under a heap of handkerchiefs, but the thought of it being away from him was too much. Peregrine once told him it had chosen him. From the moment it rolled out of a broken flower pot, he had cherished it and its uncanny ability to make sense of a world he was only beginning to understand.

Balls of colored marble and stone the size of caviar ringed the perimeter of the dial. For a moment, the balls didn't move or change color. Immanuel eyed his piece, which always appeared as a piece of white quartz, when he spotted a stone he had never seen before transforming from a piece of red glass. It was a striated fleck of sandstone the color of a canyon at dusk. It had to be Adam. In Immanuel's hand the body of the vivalabe shuddered, and in an instant the rest of the balls began to transform. Pieces that had once been yellow or green morphed into varying shades of blue and teal, except for two, the white quartz and the orange sandstone. The blue and aqua balls raced across the surface of the dial as if they had been hit by a billiard cue. A gasp escaped his lips before he could stop it. There were so many of them. He was accustomed to seeing half a dozen on a good day in London to several dozen if he opened it at Interceptor's

Headquarters, but he had never seen it hone in on such a large area. Even at headquarters, it only focused on a hallway or wing of the building, so why had it focused on the entirety of Seohl-wiga Island?

Staring down at the vivalabe's face, he watched as several sapphire balls continued to move as if the people they represented paced or walked a beat while others bobbed in a dull line. Studying their position on the plane, Immanuel looked over his shoulder to the sea in the distance. If he squinted, he could just make out the dark shapes of boats on the horizon. Fishermen, they had to be. Turning back to the metal device resting in his palm, he watched how the brightest and most precious of the stones gathered together, gliding fluidly across the plane as one unit. Immanuel closed the lid before opening it a moment later only to find the vivalabe hadn't changed. His breath faltered as he gave the plane one last look before carefully tucking it back into his bag.

The vivalabe had only ever tracked those with magic or abilities. He had never seen it littered with so many stones of the same color, let alone that many clustered together. From what he knew of the vivalabe's power, the color usually represented the individual's abilities or personality. Having dozens of blue chips of marble and glass in such a small area would have to mean most, if not all, of the island's inhabitants had water-centric abilities.

With each step down the oak-lined path, Immanuel turned the idea over in his mind. He had never met a magical creature, apart from practioners, so it was possible that the vivalabe could pick up selkies, but even so, that would mean there were dozens or even over a hundred clustered in one island. No, that couldn't be. When Miss Larkin's daughter pointed out where the seals resided, he had only seen forty at most. No, this had to be something else, though dozens of practioners in such an isolated place still seemed unlikely. Then again, he came from a long line of alchemists turned scientists, and if magic ran in their blood, perhaps the islanders had interbred until magic became common place. But how had the Interceptors not noticed? They could have staffed an entire outpost with people from the islands, and that would certainly lighten their load and that of the Special Branch.

At the top of the hill, Immanuel opened the vivalabe once more, orienting himself against the clusters of practioners scattered nearby. Perhaps the Interceptors only cared about *cultured* city practioners, who spoke proper English and came from households of good name. The thought sent a flare of anger through his breast. He had seen enough of that at the museum to last a lifetime.

Following the winding path through the trees, Immanuel's thoughts slipped away at the disconcerting silence. Only a moment before he had been surrounded by waves crashing and the call of seabirds over the distant bells of boats, but it was as if he had stepped into a bubble, where he could hear only the crunch of his steps. As Immanuel hurried around the bend, his eyes fell upon a ring of grey stones jutting from the tall grass. Casting a glance the way he had come, Immanuel took a cautious step toward the circle. Even though no one was near to see him trespass, it felt as if a pair of eyes stared back from each tilted stone. Taking a step, he waited for the overwhelming rush of energy to paralyze him and send him scrambling for the path but nothing came. Adam must have been far enough away to no longer amplify his energy.

Crouching beside the nearest stone, Immanuel gently laid his hand upon its weathered face. A faint note rang through his mind as he felt along the stone's grain until he reached a slight indent. Narrowing his eyes, he could barely make out the shape of a letter or symbol carved so long ago that only a shadow remained. Immanuel didn't know why he wanted it or what he meant, yet it seemed right to move from stone to stone, repeating the process until he confirmed each stone had once had meaning. Miss Larkin had called it a sacred place, and in this bubble in time, he could understand why.

At a Sunday dinner, the Earl of Dorset had told him about great stone monuments scattered across the British Isles and around the world that followed the path of the sun or heavenly bodies, aligning at the proper moment to create a beam of light that would have dazzled the ancients. In the lush glen, Immanuel couldn't imagine the crooked stones aligning with— Clicking open the vivalabe, Immanuel tapped the invisible button again until the plane of balls disappeared. He had only seen the vivalabe used to align magic once, when Lady Rose had ripped it from his grasp and oriented her sigil against the device's readings. At the time, he had been too busy trying to stay alive and stop her ritual to pay attention to how she had achieved the alignment.

Stepping into the center of the stone circle, the symbols ringing the edge of the vivalabe appeared to sharpen. As he stared at them, ink darkened one symbol after another, jumping across the dial without warning. It was trying to tell him something he couldn't understand. Turning toward the sun, the symbols changed faster until suddenly they stopped. A gentle breeze blew across Immanuel's cheek and into his golden hair. He moved to step out of the circle, but instead of walking across the grass, Immanuel stepped through it. He looked down and did a double take. His foot was through the ground, swallowed up by grass and dirt, yet he wasn't falling. It was as if his feet rested on something he couldn't see just below the surface.

Immanuel's heart quickened. He couldn't see anything below his calf. Standing still, he waited for the initial shock to wear off. Easily lifting his foot, it reappeared through the grass without disturbing a single blade. It was an illusion. Feeling ahead with his toes, he found the edge where the step dropped off. Cautiously, he walked down until he had descended up to his neck. Below the surface, his hands shook. The air was colder and damper than that surrounding the standing stones, but at least it was air. Taking a deep breath, Immanuel plunged beneath the surface.

"No wonder she didn't want me here," Immanuel whispered in awe as he reached the final step.

Light streamed down through the veil. From the bottom of the step, Immanuel marveled at the standing stones surrounded by millions of roots stretching into the cavern along with the canopy blooming above them. Immanuel crept ahead, his eyes sweeping over the carved and pigmented murals lining the walls. Sand littered every crevice, catching the light to give the twisted dragons a twinkle in their eyes and the lolling tongues of beasts a phantom sheen. The patterns tangled overhead into a never ending briar of stone. At regular intervals, sconces of oil flickered. Following the hall of beasts past empty passages and rooms hidden by shade, Immanuel could smell the remnants of a cooking fire over the scent of fish and herbs. There was no fear of discovery, no race in his blood with the sense that someone would appear at any moment. If it hadn't been for fires blazing to light his way, he would have thought the hall had been abandoned long ago. Holding his breath, Immanuel listened for any sign of life and was met with the rhythmic pulse of the ocean rumbling faintly through the cavern. Sand crunched beneath the soles of Immanuel's shoes as he took a hesitant step toward the sound. As his footfalls reverberated off the stone walls, Immanuel wondered if some vagrant practioner had converted an ancient barrow into a home.

None of the walls appeared to have writing or symbols, but each carving had been carefully incised to link into intricate murals of life beyond the labyrinth. Some reminded him of wallpaper with twisting vines and knots repeating across the expanse of the wall while others depicted underwater scenes laden with fish and submerged flora of every conformation. Gently running his fingers over the tentacles of two braided squid, Immanuel marveled at how shells had been crushed and set into mortar to create a mural of fantastical beauty. He clenched his weakened eye shut and stared closely at a bright orange shell that formed one of the kraken's suckers. It wasn't a species native to the British Isles. It was too bright to be. During their holiday in Dorset, he and Adam had gone fossil and shell hunting near the tidal pools, and while their quest had uncovered several pretty cockles and an iridescent conch, none were this vibrant. Somehow this one had made its way from the tropics to the grotto. Stepping back, Immanuel's eyes widened as he tried to count how many shells didn't belong. With every surface coated in broken shells, there had to be thousands. But why? Why had anyone taken the time to gather foreign shells when they easily could have used glass or tiles or simply paint murals as they had the others?

Why go through all this trouble?

Careful to muffle the sound of his footsteps in to the cavern, Immanuel approached the threshold of the nearest room. The moment he reached the darkened entrance, his foot sank a hair into the stone below. Immanuel stumbled back, fearing he had triggered some long hidden trap. A hiss leaked out in the shadows only to be replaced with blazing light so bright it sent tears to his damaged eye. Four saucers of flaming oil ringed the expansive space, amplified by the mirrored glass sunk into every surface. The walls glowed with old Venetian mirrors broken into minute pieces beside shards of sea glass in every color, transforming the room into an otherworldly Versailles. In the center of the room stood a slab of solid white marble atop a dais served as an altar.

The word hit him as suddenly as the guilt and revulsion of his intrusion. *Sacred.* That beautiful space where light danced like the sea beneath waves was their sacred place. It didn't matter whose it was, it wasn't his. Religion or faith had been replaced early in Immanuel's life with mysticism and later by the heart-thrumming certainty that science would eventually yield any answer he sought. The pulse of the island pulled at him as if the walls deep of the cavern were closer to the island's heart. Now that magic had entered his life, he found he scoffed less at faith. Wasn't he merely closing his eyes and hoping something beyond his being would answer his call?

Backing out of the chapel with his head bowed, Immanuel returned to the fork in the maze and followed the other trail. It twisted past shell murals littered with spirals of lightning whelks and bright lion's paw scallops that formed stars floating amongst a sea of faceless mollusk husks. As he moved through the galaxy of shells, Immanuel noted how, as he passed stylized versions of the constellations, that the roar of the ocean grew louder. His steps slowed as his eyes fell upon a shock of white bone sunk into the mortar. Fighting his locking legs, Immanuel drew closer, careful to keep his hands at his sides, away from the femurs that mimicked the twisted lattice of the stone carvings. He followed their braids all the way to the vaulted arches in the ceiling and back to the floor. Their length suggested they were human, but the moment he turned, his fears were confirmed by a dozen grinning skulls staring back at him. Their sockets had been plugged with sea urchin shells while tiny cockles encircled the skulls like a hunter's trophy. The sound of the ocean dissolved beneath the tattoo of Immanuel's heart in his ears. Every fiber of his being screamed for him to run, to fly back through the labyrinth, return to the surface, and take Adam home. But he couldn't. There was no way he could find his way if he blindly ran, and he couldn't bear the thought of being trapped with whomever framed the heads of their dead. Swallowing down his fear, Immanuel kept his eyes on the sandy floor until a familiar heat kissed his cheek.

Sun flooded the room, and with it, the thunder of rain against the roof of the cavern. Ignoring the burning behind his eyes, Immanuel lingered on the massive whale skull jutting from the sand ahead of him to form the back of what he could only call a throne. It towered over him and nearly scraped the roof of the cave while its low seat was comprised of bones from animals he couldn't identify lashed together with taut strips of animal hide. At least he hoped they were from an animal.

The remainder of the throne room stood nearly empty. The walls were studded with murals of bones and shells to form what looked vaguely like a map. Immanuel drew closer, his blonde brows knitting in concentration as his eyes traced the shape of the islands and land masses. It was far too large to be just the islands surrounding Seohlwiga, but if he let his eyes blur, he swore he could make out the Faroe Islands near the top and possibly the coasts of Scandinavia. He stepped back, turning his attention to the missing wall behind him. Where there should have been stone and more tilework, there remained only a rounded mouth, hollowed out by the same hands that had squared and smoothed the system of tunnels. With each rock of the tide, water sloshed over the lip. Watching the water recede, Immanuel wondered if the room would soon be flooded by high tide. Shivering as a spray of seawater seeped beneath his coat, Immanuel wandered to the whale bone throne. While there was a coating of sandy grit across the seat, there weren't any cobwebs or layers of sediment to suggest the room hadn't been in use. A bubble of curiosity forced a small smile to Immanuel's lips. This place of skulls and shells gave him the same thrill he felt while playing with magic or uncovering the secrets of a new specimen. Someone had made this cave, and he would find out who.

He took in every feature of the throne room, hoping he could recall all he saw the next time he dined with Lord Dorset. He would appreciate the cave more than anyone. Perhaps he would even have some ideas as to who built it. Stepping around the throne, a niche appeared through the shadows, its opening blocked by the bulk of the whale's skull. Six trunks sat in the darkened hole, neatly laid out in a row. Immanuel ran his hand over the iron work and wooden planks of the closest trunk before pulling open the yawning hinge. He had expected to find it empty or filled with more bones and shells or even gold, as the old stories would have him believe. Instead he found a pile of fabric. Cautiously pulling the first bundle free, it tumbled out to reveal a simple gown. The style was a few decades out of fashion, but it had yet to be attacked by moths or vermin. As he went to replace it, the glitter of glass caught his eye.

Reaching deeper into the trunk, Immanuel fished blindly through the pile of dresses and women's undergarments until his hand brushed against something cold. In the dark, it was impossible to tell what it was, but it was solid and if Immanuel listened, he could hear the faint pulse of magic within it. He carefully closed the trunk and brought the treasure into the light of the throne room. It was a stone no bigger than his thumb hanging from a silver chain. Its surface sparkled and refracted light like broken glass, but within it, opalescent bits glittered beside flecks of orange and gold and the occasional speck of blue. Someone could have easily mistaken it for merely another pretty stone washed up from the sea floor, but as he closed his eyes and focused on its sleepy rhythm, Immanuel knew it was something more.

Running his mind over its smooth, glossy surface, the thin lines of power looped around it like gold thread. The clearer the lattice became, the quicker its pulse. Immanuel's breath slowed even as his own pulse quickened to match it. He was close, so close. With a final flick of his mind, he caught the string and the stone released an ear shattering cry. Immanuel stumbled back, clasping his ears as the stone bounced across the cave floor and came to rest within lapping distance of the water. Blinking away the pain, Immanuel cautiously slid the chain away from the edge before the next wave could steal it. Watching it twist in the breeze, Immanuel debated whether he should take it with him when he returned to the surface, but as he raised his gaze to the sun, all thoughts of leaving seeped from his mind.

A head appeared out of the water, followed by a dozen more. They bobbed in and out of the waves, swimming toward him at an alarming speed. Immanuel turned toward the hall, poised to run blindly through the cavern, but as they drew closer, he realized their heads were grey and littered with spots. He released a relieved laugh. *Seals*. How could he have gotten so panicked over seals? Clara had mentioned they roosted off the island's coast, and the cove easily could have been part of their mating or shedding grounds. Even with pups, if he gave them enough berth, they would leave him be.

For a moment, he merely watched from the throne room as they swam no more than thirty yards from where he stood. He marveled at how their bodies disappeared below the waves only to crest a few seconds later, glistening and sleek. After working in the museum, he had grown so accustomed to dealing with life secondhand through inky diagrams or alcohol-cured specimens that he had nearly forgotten that these creatures were real. That seals lived in the wild, existing without any need of him or his treatises on how they evolved. On land they seemed so clumsy, cute even, yet in the water, they were graceful predators. They had evolved perfectly for their surroundings. *If only the rest of us could be so lucky*, he thought taking a step back as the creatures approached the mouth of the cave.

Watching them warily, he had expected the seals to come to the mouth and swim away for the beaches or rocks further from the harbor, but when the first approached, he held his ground. Primal panic lanced through Immanuel's chest as the first seal turned its gaze to him.

Selkie Cove

Where there should have been glossy black eyes as round as billiard balls, he found their irises to be a cold blue. It laid its fins on the lip of the cave and hauled its body up. The sleek, tube of the seal's form widened and elongated into a pair of grey and pink legs as its fins folded out into arms with pointed nails. By the time the creature rose, her canine face had been replaced with a woman's features, as fierce as it was well formed. She glared at him, her glacial eyes never wavering as she approached. Her sealskin had nearly disappeared, retreating to the outer edges of her being. Grey markings curved over her arms and legs, leaving a gap of all too human flesh straight down her middle.

Immanuel opened his mouth to speak but closed it several times until his back hit the wall of the cave. His heart thundered in his throat. He hadn't even realized he was retreating until he found himself cornered as more woman rose from the sea. The woman nearest him reached into a niche in the throne and returned with a wicked blade. Swallowing hard, his attention flickered between the knife and her hardened gaze.

He was trapped.

Chapter Sixteen
The Den

Before he could speak, the last of the seals shed their animal forms. The frigid water slipped down their smooth, nearly naked flesh, but they didn't seem to notice even as Immanuel fought the shivers he knew were from as much the cold as the raw fear calling every nerve to attention. The women stood watching him, surprise barely masked behind distrust, if not strength. Two of the women exchanged words he couldn't understand. He thought he had caught a word or part of one in the guttural syllables that reminded him of his first attempts at English. They gestured toward the pendant in his hand before turning back to him. *The necklace.* Of course, its cry had called them to him.

"I wasn't going to take it. I just wanted to look at it," he explained, his voice high and strangled. "I swear, I'm not a thief. Please, take it back."

The nearest woman ducked as he held out his hand, letting the silver chain dangle from his outstretched fingers. He kept his gaze leveled on their faces, desperately trying not to venture lower for fear of angering or repulsing them by staring at the curves of their mostly-human forms. An umber-haired woman with sharp green eyes snatched the necklace from his hand and disappeared behind the bone throne. A murmur passed through them but was silenced by the slap and slosh of fins on the cave's floor. The women parted as a final selkie emerged from the sea. She effortlessly slipped from seal to full human with a swoop of her back as she stood. Silver hair tumbled down her back, covering a tattoo of swirls and lines just below her collar bone. Each of her movements denoted power in the grace of her limbs and the ripple of muscle hidden beneath padded curves. There was no mistaking that beneath a sculptural form, raw power lurked that would have swallowed any man who dared to trifle with her. Standing naked before him, he expected the women to seem vulnerable or ashamed as they would in London, but they stood firm and unapologetic. Somehow, *he* felt vulnerable and ashamed beneath his commonplace fear.

"How did you get in here?" she asked, her pale eyes boring into him, pinning him where he stood as Judith had done months ago. Her gaze locked onto his damaged eye and the scar running across it until a pressure began to build behind it as if she could somehow pry open the fissure. There would be no lying in her lair, not that he would dare to try.

"I stepped through the stone circle up on the island," he replied, fighting to keep his voice from faltering at a spark of pain in his socket. "I didn't intend to trespass. I had no idea it would lead here."

"But how did you get past the stones?"

Immanuel looked between the women watching him as if he were the dangerous creature. At his side, the vivalabe ticked as if murmuring an answer. "I'm not certain. I stood in the center, and when I stepped down, I found the stairs."

"We should offer him to the sea," one suggested, running her eyes over the length of his form. "I doubt he would come back then."

"Please don't," Immanuel peeped before he could stop himself. "I promise I will leave and never come back."

"Men are rarely worth the trouble of release. They always come back." Her lip curled in disgust. "He will come back for one of us."

"No, that's not why I'm—"

"He's familiar to me," a woman with a face awash in freckles said, stepping closer until her nose nearly brushed Immanuel's shoulder as she sniffed the air.

"A lover, perhaps? A seaman?" their leader asked, taking the knife from the glacial-eyed selkie.

"I only just arrived Monday with my companion." The small of Immanuel's back tightened as the women drew closer, inspecting him from all angles. "I came here to find out more about the selkies."

"Where did you hear that word?" the tattooed woman asked, the knife pressing against the soft flesh of his throat.

Immanuel resisted the urge to swallow at the feathery kiss of the knife. Tipping his head back, he pressed his skull into the salt-slicked mosaic. "I was sent from London to find you— to talk to you. I need to speak to you about a matter of great importance. The Interceptors— the Interceptors sent me."

"The Interceptors, you say?" She narrowed her eyes, focusing on a spot behind his brow. Taking a step back, she let the knife fall away. "Toss him."

The second he released a breath, relieved to have the knife far from his neck, the words hit him. His heart thundered in his chest as he turned to run, but before he could take more than a step, claws closed around him from all sides. He thrashed and tried to throw his weight, hoping his added height would somehow save him, but his boots slid across the sandy floor. Deceptively strong in a pack, the women dug their nails into him, holding him firm as they walked him to the edge of the cave.

"Please, please, don't," he cried, the toes of his shoes sliding across the slick stone. "I'm here to help you. I'm here to—"

Before Immanuel could finish, a hand shoved him in the back, sending him sailing through the air and crashing into the icy water below. He gasped, his mind reeling, but as he struggled to stay afloat, he realized he was hovering half in the water. Though his chest ached at the sudden cold and his legs grew numb, he hadn't been swept out with the current. Relief washed over him as he looked up to find the belt of his satchel hooked around a rough outcropping on the stone's face. Resting his head against the damp stone, Immanuel released something between a sob and a laugh. He wasn't certain if he could die but finding out was not something he wanted to do. And Adam. Oh god, Adam didn't even know where he was. If he had died… His morbid thoughts were interrupted by voices at the mouth of the cave. The selkies gathered at the lip. Murmurs passed through them, hushed tones of disbelief, anger, and a word he had heard not so long ago: *wyrd.* Fate.

"Cut him loose."

"Please, I can explain. I'm here from the Interceptors. I—" Gripping the strap tighter, tears welled in Immanuel's eyes as the silver-haired selkie reappeared with the obsidian knife. Meeting their leader's eye, Immanuel pleaded, "Please, don't. I have a life. I mean you no harm."

"Wait, Tara! I know where I recognize him," the freckled one called, pulling the dark-haired woman's hand back as she reached for the leather strap. "He's the one who dove in after Greta." She dropped her voice, "The *witega.*"

"Is that true, intruder?"

"Yes. I don't know what *witega* means, but I dove in after Miss Larkin when she fell overboard." Icy water wicked up his wool trousers, turning his legs to jelly. Tremors rocked his jaw with each word as he added, "Please just let me explain myself. If you don't like what I have to say, you can drown me."

The freckled woman gave Tara a tight smile and a nod. With a huff, Tara grabbed him by the arm and hauled him onto the gritty floor. Shivers wracked his body as he struggled to stand on numb legs but fell back to his knees. His toes burned and refused to move in his wet shoes and socks, yet the women around him stood bare as if it were the heat of summer. He squeezed the water from the hem of his coat and wished he could do the same to his trousers. How were they able to stand it?

Magic? Evolution? Neither seemed too far apart.

"If you're a *witega*, prove it," their silver leader said, watching him from her rightful place on the whalebone throne.

"I— I don't know what a *witega* is, ma'am."

"You will address me as Völva Hilde, witch. Now, show us your power."

Immanuel nodded and staggered to his feet. He wondered how they knew about Greta Larkin or that he had any ties to magic, but with Völva Hilde's gaze upon him, he didn't dare ask. His eyes traveled over the room, searching for anything he could use. There was nothing to bring back to life, apart from the skeletons embedded in the wall, but he had no desire to be saddled with whatever beast they came from as a pet. If they were human, it couldn't possibly be ethical. He could produce a breeze, but with the wind beating in through the cave's mouth, would they even notice? Immanuel shifted uncomfortably against the fabric clinging to his leg. That was it.

Kicking off his boots, Immanuel drew in a slow breath. He closed his eyes and hoped that, despite his shivers, he could put the cold and fear aside long enough to tap into the energy around him. A faint lattice beyond his vision slowly began to glow, dim as a dying coal. Magic pulsed across the darkened landscape as he reached for it until, with a twang, he hooked it. He pictured water pulling together on the surface of his trousers and socks, pooling until they were nearly dry. Releasing his breath, water droplets flung from his wet clothes, spraying at the selkies who had come closer to get a better view. Before the water could settle, he shot his energy forward and yanked. The water swung back to him like a bandalore, condensing on his outstretched palm. Without looking to see their reaction, Immanuel tried something he had only attempted a few times on tea. He stared at the undulating mass of water in his hand. As he sucked in his breath, a film of ice spread over the surface of the water until all the remained was a hollow ball of ice. Letting the ball roll off his hand and shatter on the cave floor, a pang of pain burst from his temple. He had forgotten how much harder he had to focus when Adam wasn't nearby.

When he finally raised his gaze to the woman on the throne, he found Hilde watching him with an amused look. "Not particularly impressive but entertaining, witega."

"Thank you, Völva Hilde. I'm only just learning to use my abilities," he replied, keeping his eyes on the floor where they were safe from offending anyone.

"Isa says you saved Greta's life by shifting the waves, so you could reach her. If that is so, then that is far from novice behavior."

Immanuel opened his mouth, his mind faltering over that moment. He could scarcely remember it. All he had wanted was to grab Miss Larkin's hand without losing his grip on the life preserver. He had felt the magic's resonance in the water, but in the chaos, he hadn't realized he even did anything.

"It wasn't intentional. Pardon my asking, but how do you know all of this?"

"We were there," Isa replied, the lines at the edges of her eyes betraying the youthful fullness of her freckled cheeks. "We felt our sister needed us."

"By the time we arrived to assist her, you were in the water with her. I thought of drowning you," Tara replied tartly.

His head swam as Isa added, "She thought you were hurting her."

"But you reached her when we could not. Why did you do it?"

Words died in his throat. Why? The answer suddenly seemed too simple. "Because she fell into the water." When they merely stared at him, he continued, "Because she's with child, and I didn't want her to freeze to death. I don't know why else anyone would do it. If you're looking for an ulterior motive, Völva Hilde, I don't have one."

Hilde narrowed her eyes. "Then how did you manipulate the sea when you can barely make ice? The sea doesn't bow to just anyone, especially a man using magic. It's unseemly."

Heat flushed Immanuel's cheeks as he eyed the ice melting on the rocky floor. Suddenly it didn't seem nearly as impressive. "It's hard to explain. It's as if I can see a net lying over the water, and if I focus, I can tap into it and manipulate it. It works much better when my companion is nearby."

"Companion?"

A barely perceivable look passed between the women, and for a moment, he swore he saw their weapons and guard lower a fraction. As soon as he saw it, it disappeared beneath scowls and hushed phrases. He swallowed against the knot in his throat. Clasping his hands in front of him, Immanuel resisted the urge to take the vivalabe from his bag and fidget with it. Even if he knew seeing a sea of blue stones would send his heart racing, at least he would know Adam was safe by the trajectory of the sandstone ball. The knife flashed in Hilde's hand as she handed it to an attendant, the lethal glint snapping him from his thoughts.

"Did your companion come from the city with you? Is she here of her own free will?" Hilde asked, her voice edged with consternation as she circled him in long, stalking steps.

"Of course, why wouldn't he be?" he spat, his voice rising.

"*He?* Your companion is a man?"

His tongue went dry. Opening his mouth to speak, Immanuel found his voice small as he looked between the powerful women staring him down. "Yes, my companion is a man. We were bonded by the Interceptors, and when he is around, my magic is more powerful."

"The Interceptors forced you to bond with him?"

Tears prickled the back of Immanuel's eyes. Honesty would either get him killed or set him free. Taking a steadying breath, he planted his trembling legs and replied, "No, we wanted to. We are companions." When the women looked to one another, he quietly added, "Mates."

A look of relief spread among the selkies while Immanuel's stomach knotted at the admission. Adam would be furious.

"You didn't come looking for a woman to bring back?" Tara asked.

Keeping his eyes on the ground, he hoped the wicked blade had disappeared for good and wouldn't reappear at his throat when they heard his answer. "No, ma'am. Neither Adam nor I need or want a wife."

Hilde studied his face. Stepping closer until she stood within a hand's breadth of him, she gripped his chin and tilted his face until they were eye-to-eye. Her firm grip lacked the roughness of Lady Rose, but in her gaze, he could feel the same pulse of power.

"Are you in want of a wife?" she asked, her voice level and low.

"No, Völva Hilde."

The invisible hand slipped into his mind by the time he finished saying her name. While Judith's mind forced through like a battering ram, Hilde's slunk into his consciousness with the grace of an eel. After a moment, she released his face and turned back to the women with a nod. In an instant, the air of fear and distrust had been replaced with wariness and hesitant curiosity. With a barked order, Hilde dismissed the other selkies. Tara and Isa remained nearby as the others disappeared down the labyrinth of passages or shifted back into seal form and slipped into the water. Tara glowered at Immanuel over Hilde's shoulder, the knife hanging loosely in her grip. Immanuel swallowed hard as Hilde returned to the throne and the other two women fell in on either side of her.

"What is your name?"

"Immanuel Winter."

"Winter, you said you came here by accident, but you also said you are here to help us. Explain yourself."

Immanuel licked his lips and straightened as best he could despite the damp weighing down his coat. "I had no idea your— your meeting place was beneath the stone circle. I merely went there to investigate, to see if there were any ruins or inscriptions." He opened his mouth but closed it. He had to be careful. "The reason my companion and I came to the island was to find you, the selkies. The Interceptors sent us because we received news that a selkie had been murdered here."

He had expected Hilde to stiffen or be shocked or even upset, but her face remained impassive. Beside her, Isa cast her eyes to the floor, her lips set in a tight line, while Tara scowled at no one in particular.

Though, he was beginning to suspect, that was just how she looked.

"And why did *they* decide to get involved this instance?"

"Someone, the person who murdered her, preserved her body and sent it to the Royal Zoological Society as proof of your existence. The Interceptors caught the box before it reached the society and sent it to me to confirm it—she—was authentic. I'm sorry to say she was very much real and certainly murdered." Recalling all he could, Immanuel described her markings and features.

"Berte," Tara stated.

Isa wrapped her arm around Tara's shoulders, but she shoved her away and with a tight breath, her face returned to its mask of arrogance.

"We can't say for certain it was her."

"Do— do women go missing often? Don't the men—"

"The men? The men are the reason they go missing," Tara snapped.

Immanuel looked between her and Hilde, hoping for an answer. When it appeared he would only receive silence and suspicion, he murmured, "I'm sorry, but I don't understand. Is there a kidnapper?"

"A selkie bride is prized in these parts and has been for centuries. Sailors want a sea wife. With a sea wife, your sons will be better fishermen and sailors, longer to tire and freeze."

"But what about selkie men? Don't they protect you?"

A sharp laugh broke from Tara's throat. "Why did they send *you* if you know nothing of our ways?"

"Tara, please," Isa murmured.

Immanuel's cheeks burned. He had been thinking the same since he arrived.

"There's no such thing as selkie men. Only women can change shape and live on land or sea. Half of the seals that live in these waters have selkie ancestors. If we breed with them, the women can shift, the males remain seals. If we breed with a man, our daughters can shift, but our sons remain on land."

"So why kidnap you?" Even as the words left his lips, Immanuel felt the gulf of naivety open within him. It was the same feeling that sunk in his gut during department meetings, that they were adults and he was still a precocious child out of his depth.

"You look old enough to know the answer, even if your appetite differs. We are hard to catch when we don't want to be, and the only way to keep us land bound is to steal our skins. Those of us who won't be courted are taken by force."

Horror hardened in Immanuel's throat. "Oh, I see. Then, you had good reason for trying to dispose of me."

"Why did they send you?" Tara demanded. "And what happened to Berte?"

"They sent me because I work at a museum in London where I'm considered something of a seal expert. That's the only reason I got involved in the first place. I became entangled with the Interceptors a few months ago, so when your friend's body turned up, they sent her to me to be studied. The Interceptors weren't certain if she was real or not."

"Of course they didn't," Hilde breathed between tented fingers. "We're nothing but a cabal of provincial monsters to them."

Before Immanuel could process what she said, the words were already tumbling out. "I was asked to study her body and determine its— her authenticity. They were going to hand the case over to someone more experienced, but I pestered them until they let me take over."

"Did you come to study us like your other creatures?" Tara asked, her voice hardened with a sneer.

"No, no, not at all." He held up his hands in surrender, fearing he would be tossed into the sea again. "I knew from the moment I saw her that she wasn't a seal or any sort of creature. Please understand, the Interceptors, they— they mean well, they wanted to find out what happened to Berte, but they still acted like you weren't real. I couldn't let someone who didn't see what I saw come here."

"And what exactly did you see, witega?"

Immanuel swallowed hard at the familiar nudge of Hilde's mind knocking to get into his. Closing his eyes, he let her in and drew up the last moments of Berte's life. The fear, the pain, the moment she knew it was all over. Hilde raised her eyes to his, her lips parted and her eyes hardened with grief. Pain rang through Immanuel's head as he closed his eyes and dropped his gaze to his feet.

"It was Berte. I heard her voice in my mind."

Before Immanuel could speak, Tara turned and made for the cove's entrance. A wave of nausea climbed up this throat at the sight of her body folding in on itself as she collapsed into a seal and slid into the water.

"I didn't mean to cause—"

"You didn't. We knew of Berte's disappearance, but we hoped she had merely been land bound or had made a secret love match. How did you come to possess her memories?"

"I have the ability to see a being's last moments. It isn't exactly the kind of ability I can show you, otherwise I would have said so earlier."

Straightening, Hilde motioned for Isa to give her space. "What do you intend to do? You certainly didn't come just to tell us this."

"I want to find out who killed her and keep them from hurting anyone else. I thought I might warn you or ask you for your help to find whoever did it, but if you aren't safe on land, I will do it myself. If I should find them, I will take them to the proper authorities for punishment."

As Immanuel spoke, Hilde whispered something into Isa's ear and the woman disappeared behind the throne into the niche. In a moment, she was back, clutching something between her clawed fingers. Crossing the sandy floor, she stood just far enough away for she and Immanuel to get a good look at each other. He let his eyes slip over her full, spotted hips and stomach before coming to rest on her mane of curly auburn hair. She ran an appraising eye over his form, lingering at his waist and his long neck before tracing his scar. Holding his hand, she turned his shaking palm up and let a caged pyramid of green fluorite on a rough chain drizzle into his palm. Her warm fingers closed around his, the faint scratch of fur and a web of tissue remaining even in her mostly human form. Giving him a careworn smile that revealed the points of her teeth, Isa returned to Hilde's side.

"Winter, we accept your help in finding Berte's killer, but let it be known that if you do not find whomever murdered our sister, *we* will find them. Should you cross us, know our justice will be far more swift than your Interceptors. Do you understand?"

Immanuel nodded despite the knot growing in his stomach. Judith had warned him that they wanted to avoid an interspecies incident, yet he found himself drawn deeper. Pushing the thought away, he focused on the rough, multicolored stone whispering in his palm.

"Yes, Völva Hilde."

"Very well. What you have in your hand is a calling stone. It's much like the one you found. If you need us, all you have to do is stand in the sea and activate the stone with your thoughts. We will be watching you." Leaning back in her throne, Hilde inclined her head to stare at the massive skull. Without taking her eyes off its sockets, she said, "Isa, take him up to the surface and make certain the circle holds this time."

Chapter Seventeen
To Live

Adam stared at the broken grandfather clock in the corner of the dining room. He had completed his third circuit around the house, tidying things that were no longer askew and fluffing pillows that had lost their shape years ago. Their makeshift dinner, a few jars of jam, some suspect butter, and coarse brown bread, waited on the table, but one thought refused to leave his mind, *Where was Immanuel?* After Adam had returned from the lighthouse with his head swimming in whatever swill Quince had served him, he had found the house empty. It hadn't alarmed him then. Byron Durnure seemed like the talkative type, the awkward kind of intellectual that Immanuel got along with swimmingly. It wasn't until after Adam had taken a walk through the village, chatting with any fisherman, housewife, or child who would give him the time of day, which wasn't many, that fear took root. Durnure had been in his workshop, unaware of Adam's presence until he tapped his shoulder to take his attention from the gadget he was tinkering with. The man had been covered in grease with a meticulously arranged toolbox open at his side. A look of unrestrained annoyance blistered his features as he spat that he hadn't seen Mr. Winter and returned to his work without another word.

He had never gotten there.

Rubbing his wrist, Adam hissed at the raw flesh before turning back to the lifeless clock. He had returned home in the rain, hoping beyond anything that Immanuel had merely been waylaid by a colony of seals or a local who wanted to chat. Had he gone looking for him at the lighthouse and become trapped there when that half of the island flooded with the tide?

More than anything, Adam wanted to leave and search for him. The thought of his body broken at the bottom of a treacherous staircase or floating among the waves terrified him, but he couldn't look too worried. Immanuel was supposed to be a colleague and nothing more, so why would he take it upon himself to turn the island upside down to find him? *Because he is more than that*, Adam thought bitterly.

Instead he busied himself with chores. At home, he would have gone over the books for Hadley's company or the ledgers from Lord Dorset's estate. Anything to take his mind away from the worst scenarios he could conjure. So he fluffed cushions, straightened picture frames, and hacked through an entire loaf of hard bread in hopes Immanuel would be home to eat it. *A tidy house is a tidy mind*, he repeated to himself. It might explain why Immanuel's office always looked like it had been ransacked while his appeared so clean that one might think it was unused. He learned early that when you had everything in order, few bothered to look deeper to find the cracks.

The kettle whistled on the stove, and the moment Adam disappeared into the dingy kitchen, the front door squealed open. Pulling the kettle off the stove, Adam dashed back into the living room to find a wide grin spreading across Immanuel's face even as rain ran from his hair into his water-limp collar. A lance of panic shot through Adam's breast at the sight of Immanuel's pale lips and his ashen skin glistening with moisture. With each breath, his cheeks flushed with color.

"Selkies! I saw selkies," he cried, his voice breaking with a laugh.

"You what?"

"I met them, Adam." He unwound his wet scarf and carelessly dropped his leather satchel onto the sofa. His frozen fingers fumbled over the buttons of his coat as he excitedly prattled on. "I should have been afraid. I should have, really. They were terrifying. They tried to kill me—twice—but Adam, I saw them. I spoke to them. I can't believe it."

Stepping forward, Adam undid Immanuel's coat and pulled it from his shoulders. "But how did you— Did you say they tried to kill you?"

"Yes, well, I can't blame them for that. They don't trust men, and for good reason. I told them about the murder, showed them my memories, and they want me to help find her killer. They actually want my help. I can't believe it, Adam."

The tale of his day poured from him. He recounted the sensation of stepping through the strange stones, the labyrinth beneath the island, and finally all that had passed in the selkies' den. When Immanuel finally finished, his face was awash with light. He was soaked to the bone, the water turning his linen shirt nearly translucent and his grey wool trousers black from the thigh down, yet he seemed more alive at that moment than he had for months in London. Adam swallowed down the oaths and reproaches lingering at the back of his throat and laid his hands on Immanuel's shoulders.

Adam looked over his form, the unrelenting fear constricting his throat. "You're all right? I mean, they didn't hurt you?"

"No, I'm— I can't think of the word, but oh, Adam, you should have seen them. It was terrifying. One minute they were seals swimming toward me, and the next, they were women or something in between. Naked as the day they were born. You think it would be odd, but it isn't. It's— it's—"

"Magical?"

"Yes," Immanuel replied breathlessly, deflating with a contented grin. "I have so much more I could tell you, but I don't know how to say it."

"Well, go change into something dry, and you can tell me all about it."

Looking down at his rain-soaked clothing as if he had only just noticed it, Immanuel nodded and dashed up the steps. The boards bounced beneath his buoyant tread. Adam released a tense breath and followed behind. By the time he reached their shared room, Immanuel had tossed his rumpled jacket and waistcoat onto the bed and was working at the buttons of his linen shirt. Adam snatched up his wet clothing and carefully laid them across the hearth grate. He was about to ask Immanuel for his soggy socks when he turned to find his companion staring at him with a wide grin.

"I want to show you a rather useful trick."

Drawing in a breath, Immanuel sucked the energy in the room into himself. The fire leaned toward him as beads of water appeared on the surface of his trousers and shirt. Immanuel held out his arms and let the droplets collect on his skin. With a flick of his hands, the water shot out. Adam turned in time to avoid most of the spatter only to hear the muted fire sputter and hiss as it died out, casting the room in shadow.

"Oops. I can fix that."

A narrow flame twitched within the pile of logs and paper. In the dark, Adam thought he could nearly see the energy crackling through the air like static. It stirred the hairs on his arm and sent a tingle over his skin that had nothing to do with the breeze Immanuel conjured to stoke the fire. The flame expanded in time with Immanuel's breath until it grew into a healthy blaze. A knot lodged in Adam's breast at the realization that Immanuel could do this without sigils or expending so much energy that he fainted. Somehow it had become normal.

"What do you think?" Immanuel asked, his eyes alight.

"It's... something. Aren't you tired?"

"No. These are just little tricks. When you're around, it's so much easier. I did the water trick with the selkies, but at the end, I turned it to ice. I don't know if I could do it if I were inside with the fire going.

At the time, it seemed impressive. I'll have to show you later."

As he pulled off his shirt, Adam traced the pale scars encircling Immanuel's ribs and dotting his shoulder blade with his eyes. Adam rubbed his sore wrist and perched on the edge of his mattress. He had worried so much when Immanuel didn't come home that he was certain he would return injured or exhausted, yet here he was, singing to himself and using his powers as if they were as natural as breathing. A part of him couldn't believe it to be true.

Something had to be amiss.

It had to be.

"You're very quiet. What are you thinking about?" Immanuel said, carefully lowering himself onto Adam's lap.

Wrapping his arms around Immanuel, Adam closed his eyes and stroked the damp, velveteen skin of his lover's side. He bit back the words threatening to spill from his mind. He had thought that something awful had befallen Immanuel, but he couldn't act. He couldn't bear to go looking for him and find him dead somewhere. The day George died, he had done the same thing. He knew he was dead by the quiet in the house. There were no wheezed breaths echoing through his door, no wet coughs, yet he couldn't bring himself to go in. Like a coward, he had let Hadley go first— no, he let her find him. He should have protected her. He should have protected Immanuel. The backs of his eyes prickled as he hid his face in Immanuel's flesh.

"Adam?"

"I was just thinking how talented you are," he replied in a strangled whisper. "You hardly need sigils anymore."

"A few of the books Miss Elliott lent me suggested all you needed was focus and intention. The sigils helped me focus, but the more I get accustomed to— to magic, the less I need them. Of course, having you nearby has helped with that tremendously." He breathed the last word into his ear, sending a wave of chills across Adam's cheek. His tongue flicked across his earlobe while his hands worked on the buttons of his jacket. "I wish you could have seen it, Adam."

Adam sucked in a breath. Opening his mouth to speak, he found he couldn't find any words to mask his fear. He couldn't shove Immanuel away and storm off in theatrical rage as he would with Hadley. He couldn't move, except to tighten his jaw and steady his shaking hand against Immanuel's thigh. How was he going to get out of this?

His lover's hand closed over his. Before he could pull away, Immanuel leaned back and ran his hand along Adam's cheek. He shut his eyes as Immanuel's nimble fingers combed through his hair. With his other hand, Immanuel tilted Adam's chin up until their gazes met. The excitement melted from Immanuel's face to reveal his thoughtful, soft-eyed expression. His copper and turquoise irises held Adam wholly as he traced his jaw in slow strokes. Every time he looked at him like that, Adam wondered what Immanuel saw that he didn't.

"Something's wrong," Immanuel whispered, as if reading his mind. "Did I do something wrong?"

"No, no. I— I was worried about you is all. After I visited Mr. Quince, I went to the workshop, and they said they hadn't seen you. I— I thought—"

Immanuel cupped the back of Adam's head, pinning his eyes on his. "You thought something happened to me."

Nodding, Adam averted his gaze. "After everything that's happened, I can't help it."

Silently sighing, the corner of his lip curled in a sad smile. "I'm sorry I worried you. I didn't mean to."

"I know."

"But, Adam, you don't have to worry about me. Despite how I look, I'm made of strong stuff. You have seen it yourself."

He wanted to cry that it may not work, that nothing worked all the time. That death loomed over them as the one cruel certainty of life. One day magic wouldn't save Immanuel, and Adam refused to put stock in something he couldn't see or even fully believe. No one had saved his parents or brother, and no matter how much he loved Immanuel, in the end, no one would save him.

"Adam," he said softly, his voice rousing him from his thoughts, "look at me. Am I whole? Am I safe?"

Tightening his grip on Immanuel's waist, Adam closed his eyes and stroked his side until his thumb found the groove in his rib. If he let his mind quiet, he could hear the steady thrum of Immanuel's heart. It had restarted three times before, but how many chances did he have left? There was no way he could be certain that death truly held no dominion over him. And it was foolish to hope it did.

"You don't have to protect me all the time." Immanuel's hands slid to the nape of Adam's neck. "That's why I keep practicing. I want to take care of us, and magic will help me do that. Don't you see? I found the selkies. That was half of what we needed to become Interceptors. All we need is to find the killer, and we can join. I'll learn more magic, you can bring that gun of yours, and we can fight the darkness together. All the people out there like Lord and Lady Rose, we can stop them."

"After all you've been through, all you've seen, why do you still want to go back to that world?" he asked, though he knew the answer before the words left Immanuel's lips.

"Because I want to live," he said, the words whispering across Adam's skin. He gripped Adam's face tighter until the redhead couldn't look away or didn't dare to. "I have spent so much of my life afraid. I can't do it anymore, Adam. I need to live, and when I was down there dangling from the strap of my bag, I knew I could drown; I was afraid. But it didn't feel like it did with Lord Rose. I chose to go there, I chose to do that, like I chose whom I would share my life with." The last he punctuated with a reverent kiss on Adam's brow. "I put Lord Rose away for good, and now, I want to put my other demons to rest one way or another. I can't do that at the museum. I need more. I need to know that there's a reason I'm still here."

Immanuel's lips twisted into a pained smile as he kissed Adam. Even with his eyes closed, Adam sensed the familiar twitch of his companion's mouth. It was the second before Adam knew to throw out his arms to catch him. When Immanuel pulled back, his eyes had reddened and watered at their edges. Apologies and platitudes hung uselessly on Adam's lips. With the edge of his hand, Adam cast Immanuel's escaped tear aside, feeling his own diminish. Immanuel held Adam's hand on his cheek, tilting his head into his warm grasp.

"Today was the first day I felt like myself in months. Seeing the selkies transform before my eyes and thinking of all the things I could learn from them, reminded me why I got into science and magic." He drew in a wet, crackling breath. "Because life is beautiful and strange and terrifying, and I don't want to waste a moment hiding from it because one man tried to break me. I won't be broken again, Adam."

If only he could be so brave.

Staring up at him, Adam's breath stuck in his chest until pain knifed through him and he released it with a shudder. He clasped his hand over his mouth and turned his face away as the sob leapt in his throat. Alien tears scalded his eyes and nose at the realization that his lover needed from him the thing he could never give himself. Pushing his knuckle into his lips, Adam stared at the floor.

"Adam, are—?"

"Promise you'll never leave me," he whispered, his broken voice foreign. "I can't bear to lose you, too."

"Lose me? Why would you lose me?"

Because that's what happened to everyone else he cared for. "Just promise me."

"I promise, *mein Schätzchen*. I promise." Immanuel's arms closed around him, pulling him tight to his breast. "I love you so much the devil himself would have to come collect me."

"Good."

The word fell desperate and heavy as Adam pressed his lips against Immanuel's. He needed him. He needed to feel every part of him to know for certain he was real, that he had returned to him in one piece. Despite the risk, despite every voice in his mind screaming, *Not here*, Adam tightened his grip on his lover's thigh when Immanuel threatened to pull away. Not now. He needed him now, no matter the consequences.

Immanuel unhooked the buttons of his waistcoat. His tongue

intertwined with his, sending waves of gooseflesh sweeping over Adam's arms and down his stomach until the front of his trousers strained at the thought of Immanuel's form so close and inviting. Adam fisted the quilt, resisting the urge to rip his lover's trousers from his narrow hips and pull him back onto his bed. Following his gaze, a smile crossed Immanuel's lips and with a flick of his hand, his trousers and drawers were on the floor. A protest rose in Adam's throat but quickly died when Immanuel pressed his weight against him until he sank back onto the mattress. Immanuel straddled his hips, his length brushing against Adam's stomach as he bent down to suck and nip at the delicate skin of his neck. Sensing Adam tense and turn his head away, Immanuel sat back with his hands resting on Adam's ribs and a lopsided frown on his lips.

"What's wrong? If you don't want me to…"

"I do," he said quicker than he intended.

His eyes trailed to the window behind him. The fog slid along the shore with the distant rumble of thunder, engulfing the lighthouse's beacon and diminishing it to a blinking star. Immanuel hopped off and yanked the curtains shut. Adam released a quavering breath and closed his eyes. He folded in on himself, imagining his body sinking deep into the mattress until nothing remained. If he could only get ahead of his mind and cut off his thoughts, then maybe he could pull himself together. The bed rocked beneath him. He opened his eyes to find Immanuel lying beside him, resting his head on his folded arm. Concern creased the German's brow as they locked gazes.

"Can you tell me what's the matter?"

Adam opened his mouth and closed it again, keeping his eyes on his folded hands. Words were more difficult for him than he cared to admit.

"Please, Adam. You do so much for me. Let me help you if I can. Do you not want to be an Interceptor? If you don't like this, I can tell Miss Elliott I changed my mind."

"That isn't it." He drew in a breath, hating the rasp of the words as he forced them from his throat. "I'm afraid."

"Of what? I told you, I can hold my own. I've made it this far, haven't I?"

"It— It isn't just you I'm afraid for."

Immanuel's bichrome eyes flashed with the realization as he clasped his hand over Adam's. "But you have your gun with you."

"Why do you think I bring it?" He lowered his eyes to his hand before raising his gaze to meet his lover's only to avert it again. Why was it so damn hard to speak? Staring at the plaster beside the curtains, he said, "I don't have magic like you. I'm human and nothing more. I'm very aware that if something should happen to me, that's it. I'm not like you, I only get one shot at this."

"Would it make you feel better if I said I had already thought of that?"

Adam turned to find Immanuel staring down at the chain hanging from his neck. At the end, a glass vial crisscrossed with silver and gold leaves hung, filled with perpetually blooming forget-me-nots. Ever since Emmeline returned it to him, Immanuel hadn't taken it off. He twirled the chain between his fingers, turning the vial in a lazy circle.

"I keep this with me just in case anything should happen. Whatever is in there is keeping the flowers alive, so there has to be some left."

"You would bind me to you like you did with Emmeline?"

"In a heartbeat. If that didn't work, I would use the sigil that brought Percy to life."

"You would do that for me? What if it's against Interceptor rules to bring someone back from the dead?"

"I don't care about the rules. I would bring you back no matter the consequences," he replied, the words sending heat down Adam's belly as Immanuel closed the gap between them. He rested his hand on his cheek and turned Adam's head until he held his attention. "If I knew how, I would have bound you to me long ago."

But what if you eventually no longer love me? Or what if I slowly waste away like my parents and brother? What if you're forced to watch me die for the remainder of your life? Adam wanted to ask, but the questions died on his lips at the press of Immanuel's hips on his own followed by the taste of his lips and the brush of his fingers laced through his henna hair. Kissing him deeply, Immanuel silenced his doubts with his easy command of Adam's body. Energy reverberated through his chest, building from practioner to amplifier and back until the air hummed. He kissed Adam once more, his fingers tracing a slow course over his heart. Power cinched around his lungs in invisible vines that buzzed like an electric wire. The current passed through him, eliciting a low moan as its heat spread through every inch of his body. Adam drew up to meet Immanuel's lips again only to find him marveling at the soft blue light hovering on Adam's skin where Immanuel had touched him.

He ran his hand along Adam's chest, dragging the trail of light until the ends connected. For a moment, Adam thought the spell would break and Immanuel would return to kissing his neck or collar until he drew back to hold Adam's gaze. He stared into his eyes, looking past his fear and need until his gaze settled upon something deeper, something that tightened its hold on him. In that moment Adam could see only him, and the world beyond those mismatched eyes fell away.

Tapping his finger over Adam's heart, the wires of light tightened as a wave of ecstasy burned through his form. Adam released a shuttering breath and saw a curl of blue escape his mouth. He should have panicked, he should have been afraid, but Immanuel's lips silenced him.

"My life is yours," he breathed, the light fading.

Chapter Eighteen
Damnatio Memoriae

Adam couldn't sleep. For hours he had stared at the ceiling while Immanuel slept soundly beside him. Every so often, his body twitched, waking Adam from the memories plaguing him only to have them fall back before his eyes the moment he settled. Slowly sitting up, Adam inched toward the edge of the mattress until he was certain he was far enough away that he wouldn't disturb Immanuel. Slipping out of bed, he pulled the covers over his lover's bare shoulders and smiled despite himself. Immanuel deserved a good night's sleep, and he would do everything in his power to ensure there were many more. Adam gathered the quilt from the other bed around his shoulders and sat at the foot of the bed where the dying embers warmed his stocking feet. Closing his eyes, Adam jerked as George's face flashed through his mind, young and whole but strained with rage. Before the dream could begin, Adam threw open the curtain and applied himself to studying the barren expanse of grass between them and the lighthouse.

What was it he always told Immanuel? *Breathe*. As he released a long breath, the glass fogged to reveal a flower traced in oil. During the evening, Immanuel had told him of the sigils warding the windows to keep outsiders from barging in, but that wasn't the reason he agreed to have an intimate night despite the voice in his head telling him it was madness so far from home. With each kiss, that voice sounded less like his own and more like George's, and that was when he knew he had to do it.

George. Why had he now come back to haunt him?

It had been two years since he died, and that morning when he heard blessed silence in the house, he felt—he pulled the blanket closer—relief, as if he had been holding in a breath for over a decade that he never realized he had been holding. There was no one left to meddle in his life, except Hadley, who seemed completely unconcerned with his affairs beyond the family business. It had been so easy at first; Hadley needed him, and he was good at being needed. George never needed him. He had made that abundantly clear.

Adam swallowed hard, wishing he had a bottle of something to dull the urge to share a memory he had never shared with anyone. He could have told Immanuel. He would have understood, but he could never tell Hadley. It would taint one of them, and if it was between him and George, the living would always lose. *A saint in life, a saint in death*, Adam thought bitterly. Dear old Saint George with his bloodied palms. He was the picture of a youthful martyr while Adam with his prideful, charismatic shell fell from grace faster than George could corrupt.

It had started innocently, sitting in George's workshop watching him reassemble a Japanese karakuri doll. Adam rested his elbows on the table, tipping the stool back as far as he could before clunking back into the table. George shot him a good-natured glare and lowered the jewelers loop over his eye. His school books rested on the corner of the table, abandoned the moment he found George alone. George had been born nearly a decade before him and Hadley, so surely he would know the answer to his question. Itching his wrist, Adam shifted on his stool until he managed to keep a leg off the ground.

"Do— do boys ever fancy other boys?" he asked quickly, his

stomach knotting at the thought of Peter Moore's laugh.

George opened his mouth to speak, the words cut short at the realization of what his brother had said. Raising the loop, he narrowed his gaze on Adam's reddening cheeks. "I beg your pardon."

"Well, there's a boy in school and— and I know he fancies a girl, but I fancy him, like she does, and—"

The blow came so fast that Adam hadn't known what hit him until he went crashing to the floor with the stool trapped around his legs. Adam scrambled back at the look in George's eyes as he stood over him, seething. He should run, he should leave, but his tangled, gangly legs and the fear crushing his thoughts kept him still. Before he could move, George hauled him up by the collar and released him with a shove into the workroom door.

"Listen here, you little molly. If you know what's good for you, you'll never say that again," he spat, his finger an inch from Adam's aching cheek.

Adam's gaze flitted over George's pale eyes, lingering on the bloody bolts that spread from the corners to match the veins rising on his neck and forehead. "But I— It's not normal but—"

"Damn right it's not normal. It's a sin, Adam. Do you want to go to Hell? Or do you want to go to prison for indecency? If anyone find out, that's where you'll go. You know they used to hang men like that. Is that what you want, Adam? To be some fucking Mary-Ann?"

"I…"

His lungs convulsed. How could that be when seeing Peter made him happy? He wanted to ask, but he shrank back, wishing he could disappear into the wood under George's burning stare. His brother raised his hand, and Adam braced for the punch he deserved. The blow came down hard beside his head, rattling the door in its frame and sending tears rushing to Adam's eyes. He dug his nail into his palm as George turned from him and stood at his workbench. His hands flexed dangerously against the tabletop.

When his brother finally spoke, his voice trembled with rage. "Get out of my sight. If I hear about this again, I *will* pitch you out. I won't have someone like that corrupting this house. You can be a rent boy if it pleases you, but it won't be here. You understand me?"

"Yes, sir," he whispered.

A cry climbed up his throat, but Adam bit it back as he struggled to open the door. Tumbling out the room, Adam quietly shut the door behind him and sank against it. Guilt and fear washed over him, drowning the thought of Peter's cupid's bow lips and infectious laugh until all that remained was a hollow pit. A seed had been planted that grew into blackened roots set deep into his heart and mind. In an afternoon, he had become a villain by his own treacherous heart. He hated George, he hated himself, he hated god for making him a way counter to nature. From that day on, George never asked Adam for help again and only spoke to him when necessary. Hell, he couldn't remember the last time George even said his name. Hadley was right, he was glad when George died.

Adam sighed, watching the sigil reappear with his breath. He never forgave him. When George's condition grew worse, it became easier for him to vent the pressure building inside. He purchased a few questionable books at first, then some bright clothing that drew attention to his frame, and near the end, he took the occasional trip to a club sympathetic to his needs where he lurked in corners, watching but never touching. Digging his nails into the angry patch of skin on his wrist, he pressed down until pain rang through his arm loud enough to break his thoughts. He didn't need to think of that now. George was dead, and he had almost everything he could have wanted.

Rising to return to Immanuel's side, Adam froze. A light trailed along the beach below. It bobbed and haltingly made its way along the rocks as if the walker used them for support. Unlatching the window, Adam grimaced at the hinges' shrill cry.

"Adam?" Immanuel called behind him, his voice crackling with sleep. "What's going on?"

"Ssshh." Never taking his eyes off the light, he whispered, "Someone is walking on the beach."

"At this hour?"

The mattress creaked as Immanuel joined Adam at the window. The figure cut through the lingering fog, disappearing and reappearing as a faceless ball of light. As the person drew closer, Immanuel leaned out the window with Adam's hand tight around the waist of his pajamas. A gust of wind cut through Immanuel's thin shirt and swirled the fog into the vague shapes of faces and beasts, but as the man drew nearer, he realized there was something familiar in his gate. It could have been the slide of sand beneath his feet or— Light flashed across the lacquered wood at his side.

"It's Byron Durnure. I can't see his face, but I'm fairly certain it's him," Immanuel whispered, teetering back.

"What could he possibly be doing out at this hour?"

"I don't know. Let's go down and follow him."

"Follow him?" Adam repeated, stepping back as Immanuel slipped on the jacket draped over the hearth grate.

"Think about it, Adam. He could be merely going for a walk or he could be going out to kill someone. If it's the former, then we go to bed with a clear conscience and sleep in, but if it's the latter, then we know who killed Jacobs and Berte."

"I suppose. Let's just hope he isn't heading for us." Watching Durnure disappear into the fog, Adam slipped a pair of trousers over his union suit along with his warmest coat. "Berte?"

"She was the selkie I autopsied. I forgot to tell you that Isa and Hilde confirmed she was one of their people."

Nodding absently, Adam grabbed his gun from the bedside table, clicked open the chamber to ensure Immanuel hadn't taken out the bullets, and slipped it into his coat pocket as he followed his companion down the stairs. Quietly tugging the door shut behind them, Immanuel crept toward the stones lining the edge of the cliff face. His eyes darted to the rickety steps leading down to the sand, but one look from Adam told him to stay put. *Keep the high ground*, Adam mouthed, kneeling between two mossy boulders. Leveling his gun on the inventor's form, he motioned for Immanuel to join him.

Below Byron stopped to watch the waves. In the distance, the lighthouse kept its vigil, as constant as the tide that powered the town. Placing the lantern on a petrified tree trunk, Durnure steadied himself on his walking stick as he plucked at his shoelaces. At first Adam thought he was merely removing his shoes and stockings, but within moments, the Londoners were thankful for the lack of moonlight. Byron Durnure stabbed his walking stick into the sand and limped toward the water until it lapped against his waist.

"Should we stop him? He'll freeze to death," Immanuel whispered, his mouth muffled by his scarf.

Adam motioned for silence as Durnure held up a thin chain ending in a pale purple crystal. In the flickering lantern, the disk flashed pink as he brought it to his lips. His mouth moved in a prayer, the sound lost beneath the gurgle of seawater, but as he let the pendant fall back to his chest, a note rang through the air. Adam's ribs vibrated with the eerie tone, sending a shudder through him. He turned to Immanuel ready to ask if he had felt it to find Immanuel staring rapt with his hand clasped over his heart. Rising from a crouch to get a better look, Adam caught Immanuel's arm and yanked him back down as a shadow darkened the sea, feet ahead of the inventor. The shape grow darker and smaller as it drew closer until it stood within arm's length.

The water rippled and parted to reveal a wide-eyed face and a head of curly blonde hair. As she stepped onto the shore, Adam could make out the faint outline of ashy swirls dotting her body. His heart thundered in his throat. It wasn't that he didn't believe Immanuel when he said selkies existed, he had seen the one in the workroom disarticulated into its distinct parts, but he had never imagined it *alive*. A smile blossomed on her lips as Durnure swept her up in his arms and drew her into a kiss as deep and passionate as any Adam had shared with Immanuel. Adam sank behind the boulder, averting his gaze from their intimate meeting.

"Immanuel," he hissed, "get down."

Casting a sidelong glance toward the couple, Immanuel crouched beside him. "Why? Do you see something?"

"No, but do you really think we should be spying on them? Unless you plan to study the mating habits of selkies, I highly doubt this will be of any use to your investigation."

"But what if it's all a ploy, and he plans to lure her and kill her like Berte. When he used his necklace, I felt the calling stone they gave me hum."

"Of course it hummed. She probably gave him the stone, so they could have midnight rendezvous away from his aunt." Adam peered over the rocks before turning back to Immanuel. "That doesn't look like a ploy to me."

"But what if he's acting?"

"Not every man is Lord Rose, Immanuel. You said it yourself, everyone on this blasted island has selkie blood, so why wouldn't he be involved with one of them?"

"I suppose."

In the dark, Adam couldn't see the look on Immanuel's face, but in his voice he could hear the flat note of resignation as he slid down beside him. His hand blindly brushed Adam's calf and hip before finding his hand. Adam laced his fingers through Immanuel's, holding them between his until the chill died away. Releasing a heavy breath, Adam rested his head against the boulder.

"Shall we go inside? I don't think they will leave for some time," Adam said softly, feeling Immanuel's sleep-heavy head on his shoulder. Anticipating his lover's response, he added, "I think we can still see them from the other bedroom if you're truly worried for her safety."

Slowly straightening, Immanuel stood and carefully padded back as he helped Adam to his feet. On the beach, the Durnure and selkie lingered in the red sand, illuminated by the flickering lantern light. Their voices barely rose above the wind and water, except for the occasional gust that would carry with it the lilt of woman's a laugh. At the sound, the knot loosened in Immanuel's chest, and without a word, he retreated to the inn.

The moment the door locked behind them, Immanuel took Adam's hand and led him to the spare bedroom. Pulling the chair from the corner, Immanuel settled near the window to continue his watch.

Adam reached for the light switch but caught himself. The ghosts of previous tenants clung to the dusty bedding folded at the foot of the mattress along with the must of moisture from too many nights spent with an empty hearth. The silence pressed on Adam's ears as he settled at the far end of the bed and traced the lazy path of a ship between swipes of the lighthouse's beam.

"How do you think he can stand water that cold?" Adam asked, his voice startlingly loud in the darkened room.

Immanuel kept his eyes on the beach, but as he spoke, his tone remained clinical. His museum voice, Adam called it. The one he used when he feared he would make mistakes, when he couldn't be Immanuel the German exile.

"I suspect it's a trait from his selkie bloodline. They don't seem to be affected by the cold water, whether or not they have full fur and blubber. Perhaps they simply don't feel it. They couldn't thrive here if they didn't have a tolerance."

"Do you think there are selkies other places? Tropical places?"

"I don't see why not. There are monk seals down in the Caribbean and in the Pacific, so I guess there could be selkies."

"Or mermaids."

"Or both. There's so much out there we don't know. We act like we know how everything works, and the things we don't, we call divine." Immanuel shifted, his body sighing into the chair while his eyes fixed on the forms below. He yawned. "Have you ever wondered when something stops being divine? Is it when we discover what it does or merely that it truly exists? Or is it when we think the mystery is gone?"

"I thought you didn't ascribe to any religion," Adam replied, his lips quirked with a grin.

Catching his expression, Immanuel returned a faint smile and let his head fall against the plaster. "I don't, but that doesn't mean I can't be awestruck. We take it for granted. We get the world handed to us in small pieces, disconnected from the rest. Surrounded by things of our creation, nature is a mystery to us. She doesn't follow human logic or order, but there most certainly is both. When you dissect and draw enough, you begin to see patterns."

"Patterns?"

"You know, similar shapes or conformations. Things repeat through species and time simply because they are the most efficient systems. Over time, we change to match nature, and end up better for it."

"And yet we go marching off to conquer it."

Immanuel scrubbed at his eyes and slid lower in his chair with his arms loosely crossed in his lap. "Do you ever wonder if we're making a mistake by doing that, Adam?"

"I hadn't before, but now…"

"It's like when you see a specimen in a jar, you can only think about it in isolation. It's drained of color and life, stopped from its natural processes."

"Conquered."

"Yes," he replied, turning to Adam with wide eyes. Catching himself, he quickly returned to the beach. "You don't think how it fits with everything else. Darwin talked about how when one thing is removed from nature, the whole system can crumble. Since I saw Berte's body, I keep thinking what people would do if they found out about selkies. Would they hunt them to extinction for sport or medicine or simply because they see them as something far more sinister than evolution at work. God help them if they ever found out about the werewolves."

Adam opened his mouth to speak when his mind caught up with his ears. "Werewolves?"

"Yes, well, I heard—" The words fell away as his eyes fixed on the sea. "She's leaving now."

Standing behind Immanuel, Adam watched as Byron and the selkie stood in the water face to face. Good-byes and final kisses were exchanged as the wind whipped up sand and sent the lantern's flame sputtering. The selkie backed away until she disappeared beneath the sea's inky surface. When the water stilled where she had stood, Byron hobbled back to retrieve his clothing. He dressed quickly, but for a long moment, he merely stared as if waiting for her to return. With a final look, he collected his walking stick and headed back the direction he had come.

⊙⊙ ⊙⊙

Adam lay with his eyes closed, his mind floating on the edge of thought just short of consciousness. While he couldn't move, he could sense Immanuel asleep on his cot and hear the gentle sigh of his breath. In the back of his mind, memories tumbled heavy. They swirled like smoke, threatening to blot out the trickle of sun creeping over the island. Turning his head, Adam scattered them and focused on the itch of stubble on his jaw and the sheets tangled around his ankles. He drew in a deep breath and shoved his face deeper into the pillow, wishing Immanuel hadn't fallen asleep on the other bed. His lover had been so peaceful that he didn't dare wake him or suggest he change out of his rumpled clothing. Darkness slid over Adam's mind again, inching its way into oblivion until he felt a jolt.

Adam sat up. For a second, he wasn't certain if it had been one of those dreams where he had nearly fallen off a precipice or if the ripple passing through the island like a shockwave had been real. Running a hand over his face, Adam looked over to find Immanuel with his lips parted and his brows knit as if in thought as he lay with his arm folded under his head. If it hadn't woken Immanuel, perhaps it had been in his mind after all. Adam consulted the pocket watch on the table between them and slipped out of bed to shave. *Never again*, he vowed, catching his scruffy reflection in the window. As he moved to take a step, Adam froze, pressing his foot back to the cold, rough boards to confirm he wasn't dreaming.

The lighthouse had gone out.

ACT THREE

"There is no fundamental difference between man and animals in their ability to feel pleasure and pain, happiness and misery."
-Charles Darwin

Chapter Nineteen
In the Blood

Immanuel stood before the wall of faces. A jumble of names and dates passed through his mind, all meaningless and useless. Stepping closer, he ran his finger along the blue yarn linking three women who had all drowned.

Drowned. He scoffed and took a few steps back until his shoulder brushed the wall. Adam was right, sometimes you can be too close to see the truth.

"Any progress?" Adam asked, carrying in a cup of tea for each of them.

Immanuel took his cup and drew in a long swig, relishing the soft heat running between his ribs. "They're selkies. All of them."

Adam stared at him, blinking twice before setting his tea on the desk. "And how do you figure that?"

"It was something Hilde said. She mentioned how human men would capture them and force them to marry. It stands to reason that if you were trying to get away from someone on an island and you have the ability to transform into a seal, wouldn't you run into the sea?"

"It makes sense, but all of them?"

Reaching into his pocket, Immanuel pulled out the vivalabe. He clicked it open and held it between them as the balls scattered across the top, turning blue before they could reach their destinations. Adam's eyes widened as he instinctively drew closer to touch its surface but pulled his hand back at the last moment.

He swallowed hard. "All of those blue ones are…?"

"I believe so. It seems when someone is the product of interbreeding with a selkie, they have an affinity for water or can possibly do very simple water magic."

"So how can we tell who is or isn't a selkie?"

"I think we can assume all of the women are selkies unless they came from the mainland. After centuries of interbreeding, you get a whole population that is at least partly selkie."

Adam's eyes ran over the papers pinned to the wall. "So Jacobs came here to investigate the high rate of disappearances reported on the island, but they weren't missing women, they were all selkies."

"Technically they're still women, but yes."

"But did he know they were selkies? Did he even know they existed?"

"I don't know. In his notes, he—"

Immanuel paused, darting for the pile of papers jumbled across the cramped desk. Flipping through the pages, he checked the dates carefully transcribed on the headers. His heart thudded against his ribs as he counted back from when he figured the investigator had been killed. He couldn't be certain, but—

He checked the dates once more. "There's a gap in his notes. The information about the women and the interviews with people from the other islands stop three or four days before he died. Where are the things from his pockets?"

Dragging Jacobs' suitcase out from under the chair, Adam dug out the pile of bloodied papers. Immanuel carefully opened each one, prying the half-melted pages apart as best he could without tearing them beyond salvation. Some were forgotten receipts from a life far from the island. Others were tickets or invoices, but as Immanuel flattened the next wad of paper, his throat convulsed. Blood had spread along the folds, casting fantastical shapes of bats and angels across the looped hand until it diluted and dissolved into fractured thoughts. Here and there, Immanuel caught something coherent in the blurred ink. *Islanders keep to themselves... No one willing to speak of disappearances... if part of life... legends state... met with... believes it to be familial madness and instability...* Immanuel frowned. So much of his notes had been dissolved by sea water from his pocket pressing on the wet bench or the offal leeching from his decomposing body that he couldn't make heads or tails of them without any context. *Madness.* If there was too much inbreeding, that was possible, but no one he met seemed mad or deficient in any way.

"Immanuel, look at this."

Tearing his mind away from the page, Immanuel's mouth hung open at what was in Adam's outstretched hand. In the center of his palm sat a jagged cube of translucent green stone wrapped in frayed twine. As Immanuel touched it, a faint pulse passed through the pendent in his pocket, as if it recognized the other.

"Where did you find it?"

Adam held up a tarnished silver pocket watch in his other hand. Its lid hung open to reveal an empty space inside where a face and internal workings should have been. "Jacobs' watch was hollow. I didn't even look at it when we found him."

With the stone in his hand, Immanuel tried to clear his mind for fear of inadvertently calling the selkies if his power flared. This stone had no metalwork or carvings, just the uneven polish from many years of the press of fingers. The magic within it felt as if the corners had worn smooth while the other in his pocket retained its intensity. Where could he have gotten his hands on a calling stone?

"Does this mean he could have been calling selkies?" Adam asked as he slowly took it from Immanuel's hand and returned it to the pocket watch.

His companion nodded before turning back to the pages strewn across the desk. "He found out something. He mentions legends and talking to villagers. Who knows how much he knew."

"Could the selkies have killed him for finding out?"

"The person who killed him didn't look like a selkie."

"A disguise, perhaps?"

"I highly doubt they anticipated someone would see his death. They were human. I can't explain it, but I can feel that. I need to go and talk to Miss Larkin and Mr. Durnure. He may have spoken to them."

Abandoning the desk, Immanuel grabbed his coat from the rack by the door. When he looked up from stuffing the vivalabe into his pocket, he found Adam beside him donning his jacket. Adam smiled at the look of surprise blossoming across his features. As Immanuel's hands stilled on his buttons, Adam slid his scarf from its hook and carefully wound it around his lover's neck. Adam tucked in the end of the flannel and leaned in to place a soft kiss on Immanuel's lips. The kiss sealed the words hanging on his lover's tongue with a twang of the invisible tether running between them.

Drawing back, Adam pressed his hand to Immanuel's cheek and whispered, "We're in this together."

⁘⁙⁘

Thunder grumbled overhead as Adam and Immanuel made their way down the weatherworn path with their heads bowed against the wind. The wind rolled with bullish force, popping Immanuel's ears and sending salt and sand into their eyes as they cleared the cemetery and fallen church. When the expanse of green gave way to tiered rows of houses overlooking the docks, Adam waved for Immanuel to follow him, his voice lost in the gust. Immanuel's eyes lingered on the darkened storefronts, but as they turned the corner, he found Byron Durnure's back silhouetted in the warm light of a shop window. The wooden placard swung wildly on a solitary chain. While it showed a worn painting of a butcher, the shop counter had been replaced with tables and stools. Instead of meat hanging from the hooks, it was a mechanical device as tall as a man.

Immanuel went to knock on the shop window, but Adam pulled him away to a small door, which had been painted long ago to look like part of the storefront. Rapping on the peeling wood, Adam stepped back and peered up at the light glowing dimly on the upper floor. A shadow moved to the window before disappearing back into the house. He went to tell Immanuel but found him watching Durnure with keen interest. Whatever device he was working on was simple for its size. Between Hadley, George, and their father, Adam had seen all of them create devices of porcelain and precious materials with pieces that outnumbered his bones. This invention lacked a semblance of that finesse and complexity. While large, it appeared to mostly consist of a turbine and a casement of clay or brick, yet he couldn't shake the feeling it was just as important as those precious pieces.

Adam and Immanuel snapped to attention as Greta Larkin appeared on the doorstep. Upon seeing them, her face fell as she released a huffed breath. Adam couldn't tell if it was from having to come all the way down or merely because it was them. *The latter*, he thought as she waved for them to follow her upstairs. The moment the door closed behind them, the stormed died down to a muffled roar even as the occasional gust sent menacing creaks through the cockeyed building.

At the top of the steps sat a sparse common room that was dwarfed by a sooty stone hearth flanked by two squat armchairs. Heat radiated through the room along with the smell of fish and vegetables cooking in the cast iron pot over the fire. As the men reached the top step, Clara popped out of the only other room with a book in hand and a broad smile on her face upon spotting their visitors.

"Go back inside," her mother barked before she could set foot in the common room.

The girl opened her mouth, her eyes running between the two men, but when she returned to her mother's stern countenance, she stepped back inside and slowly closed the door. Adam listened for her steps as Immanuel followed Miss Larkin to the wooden table, but Clara never moved from her perch near the door. He smiled to himself, knowing he would have done the same at her age.

"What is it you gentlemen need? I don't mean to be rude," Greta said as she eased into a low chair, "but I have supper to cook and wash to do."

Immanuel looked to Adam, eyes wide, silently asking if they should go on. Adam replied with a faint nod as they took a seat on the other side of the table.

"Miss Larkin, we have come to ask you a few questions."

Even as the last word left Immanuel's lips, Adam could see the woman's hackles rising.

"The thing is," the redhead interjected, "we were supposed to meet our associate when we arrived on the island. I think we spoke to you about him before, Mr. Jacobs. Frankly, we haven't seen heads or tails of him, and after finding the body on the beach, we are fairly certain he was the one to meet a rather untimely end."

Greta's face flickered with uncertainty.

"When we spoke on the ferry the other day, you seemed to be familiar with Mr. Jacobs or that you had at least met him. If he had a fight or falling out with someone, we thought you might know who."

"I'm sorry to hear about Mr. Jacobs, but if you think I know anything about his death, you're speaking to the wrong person. I doubt I can help you."

"Miss Larkin," Adam said, glancing at Immanuel to see if he was overstepping, and found his companion looked relieved to step aside, "did Jacobs speak to you? I know he wanted to interview people on the island."

Miss Larkin frowned thoughtfully, sweeping a few strands of greying brown hair from her forehead. She shrugged and replied, "He came around asking about some women who disappeared. I can't remember any names or anything, but I hadn't heard of them. They weren't too recent."

"Did he tell you he suspected the women were selkies?"

Immanuel and Miss Larkin's eyes widened in surprise, but Greta snuffed it out with a sniff and a shake of her head as she rose with the aid of the table. "I don't know what you're talking about. Selkies are an old sailors' legend. Now, if you can see yourselves out, I need to finish dinner."

"Miss Larkin, please listen to us a moment longer," Immanuel began softly, wringing his hands. "I have already spoken to Völva Hilde, and she has accepted my help in finding the person who killed a selkie woman named Berte."

Greta slowly turned back, her stormy eyes staring into Immanuel's face as if she hoped to discern something deeper.

"The only reason we've come is because we need help. We were supposed to meet Mr. Jacobs while we investigated Berte's death, but he appears to have been killed by the same person who killed her. I didn't know either victim, and I hoped you might tell us something about Berte or the selkies that could help us."

Lowering back into the chair, Miss Larkin leaned forward until her swollen belly disappeared below the table. She rested on her elbows with her attention leveled on Adam and Immanuel. Her eyes flared with the light of the hearth as she hissed, "How did two Londoners find out about selkies?"

Licking his lips, Immanuel replied, "We are working for the Interceptors. They're a group of practioners who are a bit like Scotland Yard, and they discovered someone had tried to mail a preserved selkie to the Royal Zoological Society. They wanted me to prove she was a real selkie and I discovered she had been killed."

"And why do you think your Mr. Jacobs and Berte were killed by the same person?"

Immanuel opened his mouth to speak only to find the words dissolving into visions of a hooked metal rod jutting from his chest. The sickening yank, the shocking disbelief and pain, the surreal sensation of his heart ineffectually squeezing around the rough metal an instant before it was yanked out. He jolted at the press of Adam's hand closing reassuringly over his.

"We also found this on Mr. Jacobs' person when we searched his body."

Swallowing, Immanuel forced his quickened breaths and pounding heart to slow as Adam drew the false-bottomed pocket watch from his coat. Tipping the calling stone into his palm, Adam held it out for Miss Larkin to examine. She twirled it by its fraying hemp cord. The stone spun lazily, glinting in the fire light.

"Can you tell us who could have given it to him or who made it?"

"No, they aren't made for a specific person. They can call anyone. Some create incantations to direct the call to one person."

"Intent," Immanuel said weakly, his face ashen.

"Yes, but that would only be known between the creator and her mate or child. This one looks old though, like something my grandmother would have made." When she noticed Adam's cocked brow, she added, "No selkie would give away a calling stone with an ugly bit of boat twine. It would reflect poorly on her line. A lot of the old ones look like this, though."

"Is it possible that Jacobs could have formed an attachment or had a rendezvous with a selkie woman?" Adam rubbed his wrist and released a cough to mask his discomfort. "We spotted your nephew on the beach with a selkie woman, so we thought perhaps Mr. Jacobs may have become entangled as well."

"Byron? You saw Byron on the beach with a woman?" Miss Larkin asked, her voice lined with the same steel she had used on her daughter.

"We don't mean to cause trouble. We're merely asking if it's possible that Jacobs and Berte or another selkie could have crossed paths."

"No. Berte wasn't much older than my Clara. She—"

Miss Larkin trailed off as the door below opened and shut with the rattle of glass and the low roll of thunder. Byron Durnure's dark mop of hair appeared through the rails, followed by his slow, clattering tread.

"Greta, I thought I heard someone come in. I wanted to make sure you were all right." Upon seeing Adam at the table, Byron stiffened before returning to his quiet intensity upon seeing Immanuel. "Mr. Winter, have you come to see my project?"

His aunt rolled her eyes, but before she could speak, Immanuel ambled over to him with an eager grin.

"I had hoped I would get a chance to speak to you. Your aunt said you were frightfully busy, but I would love to see it," Immanuel said to Byron, casting a meaningful glance back at Adam.

"Of course, follow me."

Adam waited until Immanuel and Byron cleared the front door to turn back to Miss Larkin. She regarded him with a smirk that unnerved him in how much it reminded him of Hadley.

"Your friend will be lucky to be out of there by nightfall. Byron's bright as they come, but he doesn't have the sense to know when to keep his mouth shut."

"That's all right. Immanuel will be happy to have someone as smart as he is to talk to." Adam cleared his throat. "I read an article about your nephew and his water-powered generators."

"That was Quince's doing," she spat. "He thought it would bring attention to the island, bring in some fresh blood. A fool's errand. No one's coming here unless they've already been here."

Adam nodded. "Your nephew is quite gifted. Has he ever thought of going to London or Edinburgh? He could study science or work for the electrical companies. I imagine he would do well for himself."

Greta released a rueful laugh that sank into a silent sigh. "He did live in Leeds for a time, but he had to come back. I know what you're thinking. The man he was apprenticing with was nice enough, seemed to like him despite the prattle. His eccentricities weren't the problem." She leveled her gaze at Adam, sadness crinkling the corners of her eyes. "Did Völva Hilde tell you about sea sickness?"

"I'm assuming you don't mean the shade of green I turned on the ferry."

"No, not that kind. There's a reason why no one leaves the islands for long. For selkies, we tend to follow the paths of our seal cousins through warmer and colder waters for breeding or shedding. It's instinct. Or we stay put when we're," she glanced down at her protruding stomach, "bogged down, which is also instinct. The men have a similar instinct."

"But I thought men couldn't be selkies."

"No matter whether they change or not, they still carry the selkie bloodline. Sea sickness begins and ends in the blood. Most of our sons grow up to be fishermen or sailors, merchants even. Some go off to live on the coast or other islands, but—"

"They can't stray from the sea."

"Right. I tried to tell Byron to find someone closer who could teach him about mechanics. Even London might have been better with the river so near, but he went inland. He didn't believe the stories of sea sickness. If Quince was around, he could have talked sense into him, but…" She drew in a loud breath and rested a steadying hand on her belly. "Our bodies crave the sea so much that it can destroy us."

"Is that what happened to his—?"

She nodded. "It nearly drove him mad. His leg wasn't always like that. They said he tried to jump off the roof of the shop. He went to the hospital and tried it again. Then he tried to cut the blood from his veins to cure himself of the ocean's pull, which didn't work any better than trying to off himself. We wrote letters begging them to send him home. He made it, barely, but we couldn't afford a doctor and he healed poorly. We thought he could at least have a chance at freedom, like Quince did. He at least got a few years by living close enough to the water to stave off the worst of it. But not Byron. He hasn't been the same since, Quince either." Her eyes darkened as a crash of thunder shook the house to its foundation. "We pay one way, the men pay another. Quince thought people might read about Byron in the papers and come to him. That if doctors found out about the men, maybe they could help them. But no one cares. Why should anyone care about us?"

"We came from London to see you."

"It's your job. Would you like tea or," she grimaced as she stood, "coffee?"

He wanted to protest that it wasn't their job at all. That Immanuel had gone beyond what was required of him because he cared about a dead selkie. Instead, he merely murmured, "No, thank you."

As Miss Larkin moved to fetch the kettle hanging in the hearth, Adam helped her back into her seat and retrieved the heavy metal contraption for her. She called out where the tea and sugar were kept, fatigue settling on her tired shoulders and careworn features. From what Immanuel said about the selkies in the cave, Adam had a difficult time imagining Miss Larkin gracefully sliding from seal to human and back again. With or without fur, she wasn't someone he would cross, but the allure of the selkie legend diminished under the strain of motherhood. Arranging her tea as she instructed, Adam gingerly placed it before her and returned to his seat.

He watched her take a sip, and the moment she had the cup to her lips, he asked, "What keeps you here?"

"What do you think?" Her eyes darted to her belly. When Adam merely looked at her, she added, "Selkies with child can't change. We're bound to one form until the child is weened, often longer if we aren't strong enough. I have been land bound for twelve years. Clara isn't old enough to shift, and I couldn't leave her behind by herself. Not that my husband wasn't a good man, but he made certain to have my skin enough that I couldn't even try to leave. Most of them didn't even make it a year." A bitter smile as painful and fragile as broken glass crossed her lips. "It's rather lucky. There was barely enough for us. We couldn't handle more mouths to feed, but he wouldn't let me go back."

Adam's ribs tightened. Immanuel had spoken of splendor below ground in the selkie's den with bits of shattered Venetian mirror and the foreign shells. Even the gems that made the calling stones could be of value. "The others couldn't help you?"

Greta's brown brows furrowed as she clunked the tea cup against the table. "Let's get one thing straight, when you come on land, you're on your own. You don't get any handouts, and I didn't expect any. Do you understand how risky it is for any of them to come on land?

Anyone could grab them off the beach and drag them off. The moment the deed has taken hold, they're land bound, and your world has very limited choices for us. I would rather starve than submit one of my sisters to my fate against her will."

"My apologies." Adam's hand trailed to his wrist, but he put them flat on the table in surrender. "It wasn't my intention to offend. I know nothing of—"

"That's obvious. What I'm curious about is how your partner got an audience with Völva Hilde. The Völva is sacred; no human is allowed near her. Did he court one of them or did he merely coerce them with threats of violation?" Greta spat, her dark eyes burning.

His pulse thundered in his neck as he ground his jaw. He couldn't yell at her, he couldn't do what he did when Hadley provoked him. He couldn't ruin Immanuel's investigation, he reminded himself as he released a slow breath.

"How dare you insinuate something so abhorrent," Adam growled. "He would do no such thing. He has faced captivity and violation himself, and he would *never* do that to another being. The way he met her was through wholly appropriate means."

"How do I know you aren't lying? That you aren't planning to snatch her or one of them with this pretend investigation."

"Because we have no reason to."

"But someone else could. You could kill her or drag her back to London and leave us to—"

Adam's hand came down harder on hers than he meant to, and she jumped beneath his touch. "Miss Larkin," he hissed under his breath, "we are no threat to you because we do not want your women."

Reading his meaning, Miss Larkin's expression froze between revulsion and disbelief. Her gaze ran over his face and form before trailing to the floor below where Immanuel sat with Byron. "How do I know you aren't lying?"

Dropping his voice, Adam ignored the throb of panic in his breast and replied, "Because you now know something that could put us in prison. If we cross you, you can use that information against us."

"I see. I will keep that in mind." Yanking her hand away from Adam's, she fiddled with the antiquated calling stone. "Let's get to the point. What is it you need to find who killed Berte?"

"Preferably, I would like to meet with the selkies and see if they could shed any light on what we've found. Could you arrange for them to meet at the house we're staying at? They could walk up from the beach and straight inside under the cover of night. I can stand guard and make sure no one comes near them. That much I can promise you."

"You will never get all of them to agree to this. There are far too many."

"Then, perhaps you can convince Völva Hilde and her court. I doubt they would agree if Immanuel or I asked, but you're one of them. Could you do that for us? You could use our calling stone if need be."

"I have my own." Raising her gaze, she narrowed her eyes and held out her hand. "You realize you're asking a lot."

Adam waited, but when she raised a frayed eyebrow, he pulled a few bills from the envelope Judith had given them and set them in her palm. "One meeting, that is all we ask."

Chapter Twenty
Defiance

Listening to Byron Durnure explain the intricacies of electricity and water-powered generators, Immanuel's head spun at the sheer amount of information and the speed at which it was delivered. Was this what it was like for Adam to listen to him ramble on about his specimens at work? It wasn't necessarily a bad thing. He caught enough information to understand the gist of his explanations, but it was clear he was out of his league in Durnure's presence. The inventor threw around theories and laws Immanuel barely remembered from his classes at Oxford along with names like Tesla, Hertz, and Edison, whom Immanuel recognized from journals but didn't really know.

The room reminded him of Hadley's studio, or at least how he imagined it to look before her marriage to Lord Dorset. His workbench was lined with old cans filled scraps of wires and screwdrivers and wrenches too small to drop in a toolbox. The surface of the desk had been cleaned and tidied before he left for the day. Tins of grease and oil sat beside turpentine and pots of paint in the far corner away from the smoking stove. Cogs, metal, and other pieces Immanuel couldn't name were grouped by size, shape, and material. Immanuel followed Byron's explanations, treading carefully through the junk-filled room with his elbows tucked close for fear of disturbing the monstrous engines propped on crates or the jagged hunks of metal salvaged from other machines.

"Does everyone bring you their broken things?" Immanuel asked when Byron took a breath, spying a cracked children's automata sitting on his workbench.

"If they can't fix it themselves. I also scavenge to get what I need. Do you want anything? Tea? Or bread? Greta always reminds me to ask, but I forget. Do forgive me for not asking sooner," Durnure said, tidying a pile of rusted rotor blades that had slid across the tabletop.

"No, thank you."

Immanuel watched the inventor pick up a screwdriver to start working on the engine propped beside his workbench when his hand faltered and froze an inch above it. Byron stared at it as if forcing his hand back to his side and dropped the tool on the table. Drawing in a breath, Immanuel bit back the urge to ask about the selkie he met on the beach or the ones he had encountered in the caverns beneath the island. His eyes ran over the incandescent bulbs resting on the counter near the window. If he dove in, Byron might turn him out. If a stranger had invaded his office to pester him, he certainly would, but he needed to know. He released a silent sigh. Adam was so much better at this than he was.

The whole reason he had left Adam with Greta was so he could avoid interrogating her. Somehow when Adam asked questions, it rarely felt as if he was coercing them, yet Immanuel felt about as subtle as a hammer. Adam had a way of leaning forward on his elbow and keeping his unflinching gaze on theirs. With a shift of his brow, he could relay his deepest sympathies or pleasure, but no matter what, you came away feeling as if you were the only person worthy of attention. Immanuel would have given anything to have his gift for diplomacy.

When the inventor took up a cloth to clean the tabletop,

Immanuel asked randomly, "Are you named after Lord Byron?"

"Yes. Durnure is coincidentally literary, but my mother had a soft spot for the romantics. She said it was the way they described nature, that it reminded her how she was connected to the sea and the land. Have you read Lord Byron's poem 'Childe Harold's Pilgrimage'?"

Immanuel shook his head, certain Adam would have recognized it.

"My mother used to recite it to me. It starts, 'There is pleasure in the pathless woods, there is rapture on the lonely shore, there is society where none intrudes, by the deep Sea, and music in its roar: I love not Man the less, but Nature more.'"

"That's beautiful."

His eyes drifted to a time left behind as his hand momentarily tightened on the cloth. "Yes. That's why she named me Byron. She loved nature more and she loved that poem." A wistful smile crossed his lips. "It makes me think of her, and why I stay, why I make all of these," he said, motioning to the half-finished motor resting on the table. "After the accident happened, that is."

"What accident?"

"When I was a boy, the island used to be powered by oil that they'd bring in on ships. They'd come too late and we'd have to go without gas lamps and use tallow candles." He wrinkled his nose. "We'd also run out of those. One day they sent the shipment, and it was dashed into the rocks and the oil spilled out. Fish and birds and," he opened his mouth but caught himself, "other things washed up on the shore for months after, all very dead. The oil did that. That's when I really started to care about electricity."

"That makes a lot of sense. Electricity is dangerous, but at least it isn't toxic."

"I figured if I died messing about with this, at least, it's just me."

Immanuel jumped at a crack of thunder so loud it could have torn the roof in two. Rain tinkled across the road. It beat on the panes, casting the room in undulant shadows. Byron raised his gaze to the sky, listening closely as if he was counting the seconds until the next strike.

In the glow of the electric lamps strung haphazardly across the makeshift studio, Byron seemed younger. Although his dark hair was sprinkled with grey, it was thick and lustrous. He had the pensive severity one could be attracted to if it belonged to the face of a brooding poet or nobleman, but combined with an expansive mind and obsessive habit, those features turned dismissive or intimidating. Immanuel could see how a selkie woman could look at Byron Durnure and see a handsome suitor rather than merely an eccentric or intellectual. He was probably no more than eight years Immanuel's senior. More men like Byron at the museum might have made his job more palatable. Men of intellect and action, who put theory into practice and actually *did* something. Learning was easy, Immanuel had always been good at that, but doing proved to be a far more precious skill.

"Mr. Durnure, how did you come to the idea of creating a generator that uses tidal power? Was the invention your own?"

"I improved upon a design by Mr. Tesla for an induction motor. It's essentially a bunch of submerged waterwheels hooked up to a giant generator. What I would really like to do is create a coil, like Mr. Tesla made, and pass the electricity through the air. But people are afraid of the idea, so water is the more practical option."

"Is the thing you mentioned—the coil—feasible?"

"Mr. Tesla has done it. He showed it off at the World's Fair, not that I could see it, but they said it lit up light bulbs feet away. The island isn't very large, but…"

"You can't afford to make it."

He nodded stiffly, his shoulders slouching a fraction. "It'll cost a lot to get all the parts onto the island. I have to order everything through catalogs and wait for the ferry to come on Mondays to deliver. Mr. Quince helped me write to investors and sell some patents to get the funds to construct the generators in the powerhouse. I can't sell them myself. It's too risky, but he can," Byron replied, fingering the handle of his walking stick. "Most of the others think I'm too stupid or…"

"After hearing you speak, I have no doubt that you know what you're talking about. There are professors at Oxford far less educated on the subject than you."

The inventor's cheeks flushed as he turned his face back to the nearest deconstructed machine. "That's very kind of you. You and Jenny are the only ones who think so."

"I work at a museum. Funds can be tight and science expensive. If you ever come to London, I would be happy to give you the grand tour of the Natural History Museum."

Byron ground his jaw, his wide gaze darting to the cane leaning against his misshapen leg. "No. I— I can't leave the island."

"I know you have responsibilities here, your aunt and your cousin, but one day, if you find yourself there, do stop by."

"Can we write instead?"

"Of course."

Twisting the stained rag between his fingers, he added, "Mr. Tesla and I exchange letters. They're infrequent. Sometimes they're nothing more than schematics or equations or corrections on the things from our last letter. He's a very busy man. Greta says I should be lucky to have someone so known pay me any mind."

"Your work has certainly earned his attention. You should be proud of what you've accomplished, especially considering all of the difficulties involved."

"Except it keeps shutting off." Byron kept his eyes on the ground, but his voice rose despite his obvious restraint. "I have run the calculations over and over, and it should be enough. Somehow even when the tide is at its highest, they shut off. Mr. Tesla has no idea. I have no idea, and I've stopped sending him questions for fear he'll think me more a failure or a fool. There's no reason for it. No reason."

"How about fish getting chopped to bits in the rotors or the ruddy things caking with mud?" a deep voice called behind them as the door swung open. "Could be that electricity was never meant to come out of water. It ain't natural. We should have kept the oil."

Casper Quince leaned against the open door, eying them with a sneer as rain dripped down his brow and trailed through the grizzly stubble lining his jaw. Immanuel stood still between the two men, watching as Byron clenched his fists and eyes. The inventor raised his hand before letting his fist drop with a soft rap on the table top.

"What he didn't tell you is that someone has to go and clean his little project every few weeks to keep them running," Quince called, shoving the door shut behind him with a clatter of loose glass. "I lost my outbuilding, too."

Setting his dripping hat on a box of wires and bulbs, Quince stepped toward the desk and swept Byron's stick to the floor. Byron kept his head down, mouthing, *Don't say anything*, to himself over and over as the man left a trail of muddy footprints in his wake. It was only when Quince grew closer that Immanuel realized what he was headed for. A pile of schematics sat across the far end of the table beside a metal tube wrapped in thin copper wire. Byron's eyes widened as Quince hovered over his papers, but he stayed rooted on his stool. Immanuel couldn't be sure if it was rage, indignation, or fear of falling that kept Byron in his place. There had been too many times at the museum when he found himself watching a confrontation happen from afar while his body stayed locked, preventing him from spewing exactly what he thought but would never dare say for fear of dismissal.

Quince chuckled, the bite of ethanol burning Immanuel's nose as the man passed. "Did he show you his scribblings? He wants to build a tower that spits lightning."

With each shake of his arm, rain sprayed from the sleeve of his great coat, but before they could hit the parchment, Immanuel's mind twanged as it caught the invisible threads. His energy flowed over the papers, hovering at the edges and catching the droplets like a net. Quince reached for the nearest page. His fingers skated over a film of air but never made contact, as if it had been coated in a layer of ice. He tried again, scratching at the edge to pry it up, but Immanuel's will held firm. Quince's brow furrowed as he let his hand linger a breath above the closest page. Raising his eyes, he met Immanuel's hardened gaze.

Quince set his jaw and stepped back from Byron's desk, ignoring the silent fury etched onto the dark-haired man's face. "You're friends with the fellow from the paper?"

"Yes," Immanuel said, never removing his eyes from the lighthouse keeper and his mind from the inked schematics.

"Where did you say you were from again?"

The moment Quince cleared the desk, Byron hobbled behind him to inspect the damage. Immanuel let the net of energy dissolve into the aether as Byron reached for his drawing.

"I didn't. We came from London," he replied, his German accent rising with steeled distain.

"No, no, I mean before that. Where that accent came from."

Immanuel stiffened despite himself, barring his arms defiantly across his chest and tucking his hands close to the dents in his ribs. "Berlin."

"That on the coast?"

"No, it's inland. Why do you ask?"

"I have family up on the coast. Thought you might be familiar with the area."

"My apologies, but I have never spent time on the coast, nor do I think I would have run into your family if I had. It's quite an expansive country."

Quince began to speak again but was cut short by a loud clang of metal behind the counter. From his rightful place at the desk, Byron stood with one hand on his battered cane and the other clutching a heavy wrench. He glared at the lighthouse keeper as he sank onto his stool and returned to his work.

His voice had been forced flat and nonplussed. "What is it you need Mr. Quince? I wouldn't want to keep you from your duties."

"What I need?" The grizzled man ran a hand over his grey stubble and said something Immanuel couldn't catch. Reaching into a tool box filled with drills of varying sizes, he held one up with a bit as thick as Immanuel's finger. "Needed my drill and my saw back."

"I already returned the saw."

Quince muttered under his breath, but as he headed for the door, he cast Immanuel a probing look over his shoulder. The German's anger flared so fast he feared his magic would inadvertently manifest. Drawing it in and letting the tense energy flow through his chest and out his limbs, Immanuel called the lighthouse keeper's name.

When he turned back to Immanuel with a raised eyebrow and an infuriatingly bemused grin, Immanuel asked, "Has the telegraph been fixed? I would really like to contact Scotland Yard and Mr. Jacobs' family if I am able."

"You never told me the telegraph was out again," Byron said, rising to his feet. "I can come up to the lighthouse right now and put it to rights."

For an instant, Immanuel was certain he saw Quince tighten his grip on the handle of the drill, but the older man quickly shook his head and reached for the door. "The thing's always going out. Don't trouble yourself, Byron. You know it'd only go out again in a storm like this."

Byron nodded thoughtfully. "All right, but I'll come by when the weather clears."

Donning his hat from the box of wires, Quince threw open the door and nearly ran into Adam. Quince stumbled back, looking up at the redhead as if he had seen a ghost before heading off into the village.

"My apologies, Mr. Durnure, but I need to borrow my companion."

"I understand."

Byron's shoulders twitched, his hands moving jerkily as he settled before the half-constructed engine. Shaking his head, he mouthed something to himself, his hand clenching and opening. Adam gave Immanuel a questioning look, but he cautiously stepped closer until Byron hesitantly raised his gaze nearly to his eyes.

"Mr. Durnure, I would love to see your generators when the weather is more hospitable," Immanuel said, fighting the urge to stay a few moments more. "I'm certain Mr. Fenice would as well. Despite what Quince said, I think your inventions are ingenious."

"Thank you. Mr. Quince isn't bad usually, just when he's had too much." His attention trailed back to the engine. "The engines are submerged and there's only one diving apparatus, but I can show you the powerhouse. There's a prototype there that you can look at."

"I look forward to it."

As Adam and Immanuel slipped into the downpour, Immanuel cast a glance at Byron. To his relief, Byron had his head down, his attention fixed on the papers before him and his pencil moving furiously. A small smile crept across Immanuel's lips despite the frigid gale sending rain deep into his hair and down his neck beneath the collar of his coat. He and Adam walked in silence until they reached the hill where the circle of crooked stones stood overlooking the town. Yellow squares of shining, wet light turned the tracks of dirt and gravel into undulant strokes of color. Adam paused, looking down at the rows of houses ringing the docks where fishing boats bobbed in the storm. Rain burned Immanuel's eyes and skin as he resisted the urge to pull Adam along toward the cottage. After a long moment, his lover turned from the lashing wind and squeezed Immanuel's arm.

"I have news for you," Adam said softly, leaning so close his breath brushed Immanuel's cheek with each word, "but you have to catch me to get it."

Giving his companion a wink, he dashed down the path, leaving Immanuel in his wake. Immanuel blinked before sprinting after him. For all his tailored clothing and pomaded hair, Adam was deceptively fast. They reached the house a second apart, tumbling into the door as Adam unlocked it before falling into the parlor, laughing breathlessly. Their trousers had been spattered with mud and they were soaked to the bone, but the rhythmic thrum of Adam's heart beating against his own as he held him, sent a soft sigh from Immanuel's throat. Adam kissed him gently and collapsed onto the sofa beside him. Immanuel's hand crept across the cushion until their fingers touched and tangled, settling into their familiar grooves.

"Well, give me your news."

Adam released a breathless chuckle. "Let me catch my breath. Tell me, were you able learn anything from Byron Durnure?"

"Besides the ins and outs of motors and generators? Not really. I never got the chance to ask him about his lover. Quince came barging in looking for one of his tools. I swear he was drunk. He stunk."

"What else is there to do on this island. The sea sickness probably drives him to it."

"Sea sickness?"

Ignoring the moisture settling deep into his clothing in the cool house, Adam told Immanuel all he had learned from Greta. When he reached the part where he had to reveal their secret to save Immanuel's honor, he had expected Immanuel to chastise him or at least seem upset, but he merely shrugged.

"You aren't angry? I've put us in danger."

"Perhaps, but I had to tell Völva Hilde to keep from being tossed into the sea. I wouldn't shout it from the rooftops or tell it to a man, but the selkies wouldn't trust us otherwise," Immanuel replied, squeezing Adam's fingers. "At least they don't seem like the type to involve the police."

"Thankfully. It was the only way I could convince Miss Larkin we had no ulterior motive, but at least we have a chance at having an audience with Völva Hilde here. Miss Larkin said she speak to them before dusk."

"You—" Immanuel's eyes bulged. "They could be coming here? Tonight?"

"Yes? Is that a problem?"

"No, but I need to prepare."

Chapter Twenty-One
Land and Sea

At half-past six, a knock sounded at the door. Adam hesitated, glancing toward the stairs for the gun he had stashed earlier, but when the rapping grew more insistent, he yanked the door open with a huff. Miss Larkin stood at the cottage door with her hair plastered to her face beneath the hood of her shaggy hide coat. She glared up at Adam, regarding his rumpled shirt sleeves and silk dressing gown with unrestrained disdain.

Before he could step aside to let her in, she said, "They will be here at ten. Apparently the Völva already agreed to a future meeting with your *friend*. You had better not be late, and don't even think of pulling anything or I'll eviscerate you myself. Got me?"

"I think I know how to handle myself," Adam replied, keeping one hand on the door and the other flared at his hip. In case she suddenly took it upon herself to barge in, he at least had a chance of stopping her.

"Not in front of them. Don't stare, don't make eye contact with the Völva, and don't speak to her unless spoken to. She is the leader of our people and will be treated as such. I'll be escorting them from the beach to make certain you don't do anything to jeopardize their safety." Dropping her voice, she added, "And trust me, I will use what you told me if you try anything."

Pulling her heavy coat closer, Miss Larkin gave him one last cutting scowl before returning to the path. Adam shook his head and blinked, not certain what had happened. After Immanuel saved her life and offered to find her compatriot's killer, she seemed to treat them more like monsters. With a pang of dread, he remembered what he had said.

Adam drew himself up, keeping his head high and his spine rigid as he retreated up the steps to get ready. He had lived by the rules of propriety and manners—to a point—his whole life; it had been the guide upon which he built a shell around the Adam who couldn't be. Purposefully, artfully, flouting certain rules, he had created the aesthetic that would at once shield him and act as a release valve for the part of him he thought he could never share. Adam smoothed his best waistcoat. If he could win over a dowager countess with his charms, surely he could make it through an hour with a few seal-women. He was accustomed to women being the most dangerous creatures in a room.

Immanuel, on the other hand, spent the better part of the evening moving from room to room in an ineffectual flurry of activity. He prattled on, half finishing one task and moving on to the next thing that caught his eye before he could finish the first. As always, Adam dutifully followed behind to deal with what his companion had missed. By the time dusk came, the inn appeared as clean and orderly as it had been when they arrived, and finally, Immanuel seemed to settle down somewhat. Even as he sat at the dining table with his autopsy notes and journal, he fidgeted, crossing and uncrossing his ankles. His eyes trailed from the door to his papers and back again so often that Adam could feel his gaze swipe across his neck like a knife.

"What are you so worried about? They agreed to your meeting," Adam said, not taking his eyes off his worn copy of *The Italian*.

"I know, but last time I ended up nearly drowned because they didn't like what I said. I don't want to ruin my chances with them. I'm coming to them for help."

"But *you* are helping to find out who murdered one of their own. You didn't have to do that, but you have. Now, try not to get anymore wound up."

Adam heard Immanuel make a sound of agreement, but within moments he felt his gaze slice along his skin again followed by the sound of his pen tapping against the table.

"Do you think I should run down to the docks and buy some fish? Would it be more hospitable for them if we had food for them to eat?" Immanuel asked, shifting in his seat.

"If the fishermen are smart, they're already inside. Besides, even if they were out, do we know for certain what fish selkies eat? I wouldn't want to offend her highness."

"Oh, I hadn't thought of that. If I get the chance, I must ask them about their eating habits," he replied over the scratch of the nib against paper.

And the house will stink like seabass and eels all night, Adam wanted to add but thought better of it. "I'm certain tea and Jacobs' leftover bread will suffice in terms of hospitality. What are you doing with your notes? Transcribing them in legible English?"

"Very funny. No, I'm trying to make sense of what I have learned with my findings from the autopsy. Some things line up, others leave me with more questions. I wish I could ask them, but I'm rather afraid to. Maybe when all of this is behind us and we bring the one who killed Berte to the Interceptors, they will trust us."

"You could ask Byron. He seems well acquainted with the selkies."

"I would rather ask them. At least now I can give the Interceptors more information on their mating patterns, how they transform, and more importantly, how the inheritance patterns seem to rely on the offspring's sex. If we could discover the mechanism behind this, it could open a whole new field of genetic studies. It's like birds. How the males are colorful and the females are subdued, but this is so much more complex." Immanuel's eyes brightened at the thought. "Perhaps I could study magic and the biological mechanisms behind transformative creatures with the Interceptors. That seems fairly safe."

"I thought you wanted something beyond safety, not that the selkies are particularly docile. What you're talking about sounds a lot like what you're trying to escape at the museum," Adam replied with a bemused grin as he watched his lover over the back of the sofa.

Setting his pen aside, he chewed his lip. "I— I know, but I want both. I want adventures like this on days when I can't stand the thought of being chained to my desk writing letters for Sir William. But after I've had too close an encounter with my mortality, then I crave a desk."

"Balance would be nice."

"Yes. I keep hoping the Interceptors might be the answer to that."

"That or you could join a gymnasium or sports club."

Immanuel released a muffled laugh and turned back to his papers.

"What are you snickering about?"

"Joining a gymnasium."

Adam cocked a henna brow. "I have a membership to one, you know."

"No, you don't."

"Yes, I do. How do you think I look like this?" Adam asked, gesturing to his chest. "Magic?"

Immanuel's eyes widened as they slid over Adam's form. "The same reason I can't seem to put on much weight: family trait. I've never even seen you go."

"Just because you don't see me, doesn't mean I don't. I go sometimes before or after work, especially when Sir William has you occupied at all hours. I started going when George got sick the last time." He fingered the frayed edge of his book. Exercise had helped to smother his thoughts. As George grew sicker, Adam spent more time working his back and lungs in hopes that he could strengthen his body enough that consumption couldn't touch him. What else could he do against an unseen assailant but prepare against the worst? "Since we started living together, I haven't gone as often."

"I wouldn't stop you."

"I know." He flashed a wide grin that revealed his straight, white teeth and shrugged. "But I would rather be home with you."

"I'm sure it was nice to see all those men half-dressed and sweaty," Immanuel added, punctuating the final word with a smothered snort.

"I suppose I can get that for free now, can't I? Still, if I'm to chase you all over god's creation, it might help to take up a sport again."

⁘

When the hands of his watch reached a quarter to ten, Immanuel had only written the description for half of the selkie caves. Sighing, he stretched until his back popped and his wrists cracked. At his motion, Adam roused from his doze and traded his dressing gown for his coat. At the door, Immanuel watched his companion check the chambers of his gun before slipping it into his pocket along with Mr. Jacobs' calling stone. Immanuel reached for the knob with a quavering hand when Adam caught his wrist. Slowly turning to him, Adam slipped his arm around Immanuel's waist and pulled him close. For a long moment, they merely stared into each other's eyes until Adam's fingers brushed along his cheek and he gently kissed him.

"Whatever happens with them tonight, I want you to know that you can do this. We can do this, with or without their help," Adam said softly, his voice rich and warm.

Immanuel swallowed hard, the cold metal of the empty pendent burning his neck. He hoped Adam was right because something felt off. He had spent the last few hours busying himself with his notes in hopes the answer would come. His stomach knotted. He was missing something; he had to be. Raising his gaze to Adam's face, Immanuel nodded and received another quick kiss. Adam opened the door, catching it as it flung to the wall with the force of the storm. Forcing it shut behind them, Adam cut across the lane to watch the beach from the ridge of boulders. Immanuel lingered at the door as a gale of miserable wind whipped through his clothing as if he were as naked as a selkie. Over the crack of thunder, a prickle of power trailed down his spine and dispersed across his skin.

"Should we go down to the beach?" Immanuel yelled over the wind.

"Better to keep the high ground. If anyone comes, we can hold them off better up here and give the selkies cover to get back to the water."

"Your friend is right."

Adam and Immanuel turned to find Greta Larkin standing in the shadows of the trees. Her face shifted in the stark shadows of her lantern's glare. Hanging from her elbow was a sewing basket overflowing with fabric.

"What's that for?" Adam asked, inclining his chin toward the basket.

"Dry cloaks for the Völva and priestesses."

"I thought they wore nothing more than their skins."

She curled her lip. "It's customary to wear clothing when the Völva has a formal meeting with a human."

"I'm going to go down and wait," Immanuel said, tugging at his collar as he looked uncomfortably between Greta and Adam.

The breeze whipped the edge of Adam's hair from its pomade, obscuring Immanuel's descent with ribbons of red. He crossed the sand and waited at the water's edge, the tips of his boots darkening where the tide lazily lapped the shore. Adam kept an eye on Immanuel a moment longer before turning his gaze to either side of the dirt road. Standing in the middle of the path, he half expected a steamer to come barreling down the lane, but this wasn't London and he hadn't seen a single motorcar since they left Scarborough. For what felt like an eternity, he stood at Greta's side with nothing but the wind and heavy silence between them. Occasionally Immanuel would cast a glance over his shoulder at them before turning his attention back to the sea. As Adam slowly shifted, a shadow caught his eye, but when he looked down the road with his gun trained ahead of him, he found only scant beams of moonlight and the occasional cry of a night bird. Greta eyed him suspiciously but said nothing.

Turning back to the sea, Adam saw movement in the water. A ripple broke followed by another and another, but before he could cry out to Immanuel, dark shapes rose from the inky depths. Through the moonlight and the scant glow of Immanuel's lantern, Adam could see what looked like the broad grey foreheads of three seals. Before Adam's mind could discern their bodies beneath the waves, the creatures began to transform. Their bodies stretched as they reared up on their hind fins. In front of his eyes, the fins stretched into legs, and where webbed paws had once been, graceful arms emerged. Gold glittered across their bodies, burning brighter in the flickering light as their grey seal skins melted into human flesh. Torcs encircled their necks while gleaming bands clung to their arms and ankles, catching the light with each step.

The breath caught in Adam's throat as his mind reeled at the sight. He had seen many things he never expected to see: a living skeletal cat, a beast from another world vying for dominance in a man's body, the dead return to life, but he had never seen a human slide between forms. On them it seemed so smooth and right, as if the human body had been born to break and bend and reform. He shuddered at the thought of their bones and ligaments stretching, aching, pain arcing as their bones cracked, but as the selkies strutted up the beach toward Immanuel, Adam couldn't fathom how they could subject themselves to such torture and shrug it off without so much as a grimace. Immanuel looked back at Adam as if unsure whether to give them space or lead the way. Adam watched the three women warily. The moment they drew close to Immanuel, Adam felt the subtle surge of otherworldly power burning across his skin and down his spine. Steadying his hand, he kept his gun at his side.

Standing before the silver-haired woman, Immanuel bowed low. He then did so for the redhead while the woman with inky hair did little more than glance at the gesture before stepping away. Immanuel raised his lantern and gestured toward the stairs. As the beam flashed across their flesh, Adam's heart crawled up his throat. They weren't truly naked, as Immanuel had said, that would have made sense. No, they were half human and half seal. He could see it on the silver-haired one's skin. A patch of pink flesh the width of a hand cut down their forms only to be swallowed up on either side by pale grey fur dotted with darker speckles. Their leader had a patch of fur near her collar that stood out. It had markings shaped like moons or swirls, and for a moment, Adam imagined what it would feel like to run his hand over them and feel the subtle changes of their skin from one form to the next. It would probably be the last thing he did.

As the women climbed the stairs with Immanuel behind them, Adam could guess what drew men like Byron to them. Besides a blood and familial connection, the selkies exuded power. He could never be sure if Immanuel felt it the way he did, but there was a pulse ringing through his body when he watched them. Even without magic, their limbs were defined and strong while their hips and breasts were padded with ample curves. A sculptural balance of softness and strength. Adam quickly turned his gaze to the ground as they approached but not before catching smears of kohl around their eyes and the flashes of gold ringing their bodies. Adam listened for any sign of intruders or spies as they reached the road. His gun hung limp in his fingers, the cold metal heavy in his hand.

At the top of the steps, Greta came forward. In front of the silver-haired woman, Greta bowed her head low, whispering a greeting in a soft, guttural language Adam couldn't understand. With a shake of fabric, the cape dropped out. The taller woman bent low enough that Greta could fasten the cape with a hat pin. She repeated her task with the other two women before the selkies turned toward Adam. Shockingly intelligent eyes swept over him, more probing than praising.

The silver tattooed woman stepped closer until their chests nearly touched. Adam slipped his gun into his pocket and bowed low as Immanuel had, keeping his eyes on the ground as the other women joined the Völva. Slowly rising, Adam met Immanuel's gaze as the women walked past them toward the house.

At the door, Völva Hilde stopped, her cape billowing across her pale fur like a shadow as she laid a hand on the rough wood and mossy stone on the inn's crooked face. Her mouth tightened. "Let's get on with it. I would prefer not to dwell here long."

Chapter Twenty-Two
Beholden

Adam stood near the door of Mr. Jacobs' room, watching Immanuel explain all they had uncovered. For Völva Hilde, Isa, and Tara, Immanuel translated the symbols and shorthand carefully inscribed on each missing woman's profile. The selkies nodded in acknowledgment, occasionally explaining or expanding upon something in English or to each other in their mother tongue. Immanuel patiently listened and answered their questions as best he could. Despite his initial pallor and anxiety, Immanuel moved through it all with a quiet competence Adam admired. A small smile crossed Adam's lips. This was what his uncle had seen in Immanuel back at Oxford when he felt invisible, and it was what Adam saw in Immanuel every day behind closed doors. So few had the chance to see him at his best. With each nod and confirmation from the selkies, Adam felt a swell of pride grow behind his heart. *If only Sir William could see him like this.*

Footsteps shuffled behind him in the front room. Adam glanced over his shoulder to find Miss Larkin standing at the table, her face ashen and her hand fisted against her stomach. He wanted to ask her if she was all right, but he feared speaking would anger the selkies or unsettle Immanuel. When they had come into the house, Völva Hilde made it clear that Greta was to stay in the front room while they met to discuss Berte's death. A flicker of anger crossed Miss Larkin's features at the dismissal, but she bowed her head and took her place on the sofa. When they finally came into the study, Adam had insisted on leaving the door open for security reasons and so Miss Larkin could listen in if she so chose.

"Now, what I want to know from you is if Berte had any entanglements, specifically a human man named Will Jacobs," Immanuel said, passing them Jacobs' likeness. "Or did she perhaps have any other suitors on the island, like one of the sailors or Byron Durnure."

"Durnure has a suitor, Jenny," Isa said when Hilde glanced at her for an answer.

"But did Berte have a lover or a captor, perhaps?"

"Not a lover. She chose to forgo mating to become a priestess. We assumed she had been captured when she disappeared. There was nothing to be done, then."

"Treacherous creatures," Tara murmured, her words and gaze falling heavy on Adam.

"Could she have been lured to the shore by family?"

Isa furrowed her brow as she tugged her cloak around her middle before shrugging it off at the elbows. "We all have families, in one way or another. I think Berte had brothers, but I'm fairly certain they were seals."

Adam's gaze flickered toward the narrow gap in the curtains behind the selkies. In the dim light, he thought he had seen a figure, but as thunder rumbled overhead and a crack of lightning lit the glass, all he could see were the boulders lining the road.

"The thing is, we found a calling stone in Mr. Jacobs' possession. Could they have been related through her mother? Perhaps from a different brood with a different father?"

Picking up the twine-strung calling stone, Immanuel carefully placed it in Völva Hilde's outstretched palm. She blanched and her eyes narrowed as she looked from the green stone to Immanuel's face.

"Where did you get this?" she demanded, her voice edged with a growl.

Immanuel swallowed hard, the moisture drying on his tongue. Opening his mouth, he measured his words carefully.

"We found it among Mr. Jacobs' possessions. When we discovered his body, we found a pocket watch with a hollow back. That stone was hidden inside it," Adam replied for him. "Do you recognize it?"

"It was my mother's," Hilde said in nearly a whisper.

"Your— your mother?" Immanuel stammered.

Panic rose in his breast at the look in the high priestess's eyes. Looking to Adam, he found his lover observing them carefully. He gave Immanuel a reassuring nod and straightened.

"Völva Hilde, is there any way Mr. Jacobs could have been in contact with your mother?" Adam asked, his voice level.

She turned to him, rising with a flourish of her cloak. "My mother has been dead since before my transformation. She's right here, among your many, many others."

In two strides, she stood at the wall. With the sharp hook of her finger nail, she jabbed through a poster above her head. Even from his place by the door, Adam could see the notation beside the sketch of her face: *Murdered.* The likeness wasn't very good, but he could see the curves of the dead woman's nose and lips in Hilde's.

"Then how did he get the stone?"

"That is what I should be asking you. Wasn't he one of your cronies?"

"We never met him," Adam stated coolly. "We never got the chance to because someone murdered him as well before we got here."

"My brother and I were the only ones who knew that stone existed. Our mother left it for us. Your Jacobs must have stolen it."

"Could you or your brother have simply lost it?" Immanuel asked quietly, shrinking under Völva Hilde's penetrating gaze.

"No, he would never lose something so precious."

Adam's henna brows furrowed. "Who is your—"

"Völva!" Shoving an elbow into Adam's ribs, Greta Larkin pushed into the room. "Völva Hilde, you need to see this."

Cold dread settled over Immanuel's form at the sight of his notes crushed in Greta's fist. Isa and Tara closed ranks around Greta and Hilde as they huddled over the crumpled pages. Immanuel opened his mouth, but no words worked from his lips as the women conversed in harsh whispers in their guttural tongue. Isa's hands trembled and her lips silently parted while Tara's scowl deepened. What scared Immanuel most was Völva Hilde's silence and how Adam had drew closer until he stood at his elbow. They exchanged a worried glance and waited. As Völva Hilde raised her eyes from the page to pin Immanuel where he stood, he blindly reached for Adam's hand. They're fingers intertwined, little fingers squeezing for a brief moment, before falling away.

"Explain yourself, *witega*," the Völva spat, shoving the balled pages into Immanuel's chest.

He tried to catch his notes, but they fell from his hands. The breath hitched in Immanuel's throat as his damaged eye burned. The papers fluttered to the floor and he dared not reach for them.

"I said explain," she growled, the force of her mind ramming his so hard his temples reverberated with pain.

"Those are the notes I made during Berte's autopsy. They're merely diagrams, drawings. I wanted to get a better understanding of selkie anatomy." When the selkies didn't move, he added, "I told you, her body arrived in London and the Interceptors wanted me to prove she was indeed a real selkie and not a well-made forgery. I told you that was the reason I came looking for you."

"You did not say you desecrated our sister. You have violated her in death as that monster did in life."

"No, I— I didn't violate anything. It was done with the utmost reverence, I can assure you. You must understand that autopsies are very common where we're from, especially when someone dies under mysterious circumstances."

"But you are a death seer, *witega*. None of this was necessary. You knew how she died. You saw her death. You needn't do more, but you did. You took away her dignity. You cut her into pieces and for what? You destroy to what? To learn? You learned nothing of value."

Immanuel's lungs convulsed. He gripped the papers tighter against the constriction of his ribs. His knees buckled, but Adam's grip on his shoulder kept him in place.

"What should we do with him, Völva? Should we tell him the punishment for violating a priestess?" Tara asked, her eyes glinting dangerously. Her features grew more grey and round, her teeth slowly elongating as her body curved in until she resembled something horrifically human yet unmistakably animal.

Isa shook her head, her orange curls scattering. She looked between the selkies and the men. Her eyes were glazed with fear and hurt, but her mouth betrayed her anger.

"No," Hilde declared, stepping away from Immanuel to the oil stained sigil on the window with a look of disgust. "He is already of the lowest breed. He is beneath our laws or punishments."

Adam released Immanuel's arm and darted from the room as the selkies made to leave, calling after them, "No matter what you think Immanuel did, he did it thinking he could help her."

"He did it to help *them*," Hilde spat.

"If he thought he was offending you, he never would have done it. Please, let him finish. We need your help to find who killed Berte and Mr. Jacobs. Someone on this island did it."

She curled her lip, the torc gleaming beneath the cords of her neck. "Why do you care? You knew neither of them."

"Because no one deserves to lose their life without having it avenged. If you help us, we can give you the killer and you can exact justice your way."

"We already plan to. Enough of our sisters have been desecrated.

Make no mistake, our justice will be swift. We will do what we should have done long ago."

Völva Hilde moved as if to grab the door handle but instead caught Adam's wrist. As her hand tightened on his, he flinched at the pressure of something prying at his senses. He resisted, closing his eyes and turning his head even as the spear drove deeper until his eyes burned. Pain burst across his brow like a pop of fireworks, but he gritted his teeth and swallowed it down with a grimace he hoped would pass as a smile. Her grip and gaze hardened the more he struggled against the prod of her powers.

"Why are you resisting? What have you to hide?" Völva Hilde demanded.

"I'm not hiding anything," Adam rasped as he raised his eyes to hers only to find hers nearly black.

"Then, let me in."

"Get out of my head."

"Why should I?"

"As you said, Immanuel isn't beholden to your laws," he replied through gritted teeth. "That means I'm not beholden to your will, either. Why should I have to turn my mind over to you?"

Her claws dug into his arm until pricks of blood dotted his freckled flesh and pain flashed across Adam's features. "I suggest you and the *witega* get off the island. I cannot promise my sisters will be merciful."

With a thrust of her arm, she threw him back and opened the door. Adam stumbled, cracking his head against the heavy wooden doorjamb. The room spun around him, his mind reeling at the sudden absence of her invasive presence. As he hauled himself up with the heavy knob, the only thing he could make out through the driving rain was the flapping of cloaks and the crack of muscle and bone. Releasing a deflated breath, Adam kicked the door shut and threw the bolt. There was no sense in chasing them now.

Wincing, Adam rubbed the back of his head and turned to find Immanuel where he left him in the middle of Jacobs' room. His heart sank at the sight of Immanuel's ribs trembling as he stared at where the selkies had once been, pages fluttering in his outstretched fingers. His lips twitched and his eyes clenched, but he didn't move. From the doorway, Adam watched, waiting for the impending implosion and wishing he knew what to say.

Adam quietly padded closer to Immanuel until they stood a hand's breadth apart. Immanuel bit his lip, keeping his burning eyes on the floor as Adam carefully pulled each paper from his shaking hands. With each page, Immanuel's breaths sharpened until they rattled his throat as a smothered wheeze. Bending down at his feet, Adam gingerly smoothed the last of his rumpled notes over his knee and set them aside. They had been bent and slightly torn, but they could be salvaged.

As Adam rose, Immanuel averted his gaze, his hands curled in loose fists over his heart. Adam wanted to beg him to look at him or at least breathe, but he felt it too. The cold dread that somehow the world was crumbling around them and it was all their fault.

"Immanuel," Adam said softly. He reached out to touch him but hesitated at the way his companion trembled. "Please look at me."

He shook his head. Forcing back the wave threatening to spill over him, he bit his lip and shut his eyes.

"Immanuel, you didn't do anything wrong."

Immanuel slowly raised his mismatched eyes to Adam's face. Tears gathered at the edge of his lids. He searched Adam's face as the first defiant tear broke from its mooring. Each word rasped out, punctuated by a sharp breath, "Yes, I did. I ruined everything."

Before Adam could reply, a sob leapt from Immanuel's throat. He covered his face with his hands as his voice collapsed into a string of convulsive breaths. He couldn't breathe, he couldn't think, all he could see was the look of disgust on Völva Hilde's face as she turned from him. Drawing in a strangled breath, his throat spasmed. His ribs ached with each wet cough and his nose burned, yet he didn't fight it. He deserved every second of pain after what he did. Sinking to the floor, he covered his face as if that could keep the pain or his troublesome powers in.

Somewhere outside of him, Adam unbuttoned the collar of his

shirt and managed to slip off his jacket. His companion spoke softly, telling him kind lies that only made him hate himself more because Adam wholly believed them— believed in him. Immanuel shook his head as words were beyond him, but the more he fought, the closer Adam held him. One arm encircled his flailing ribs while the other came to rest over his ear, pinning him against his lover's stalwart form. Adam gently stroked his cheek and brought his lips to Immanuel's forehead. Tipping Immanuel's head back, Adam met his gaze.

"Immanuel, you need to take a deep breath."

He shook his head again. How could he tell him he didn't want to? To breathe meant going on and he couldn't do that. Not yet. He had ruined all they had done since they left London. More than anything, he wished he would never have to breathe again, and when darkness finally enveloped him, there would be no worry of how to fix it or how to explain to Judith and the Interceptors how he had failed so utterly.

"I can't do this," he wheezed, staring down at his shaking hands. "I'm not cut out for this."

"Yes, you are. We... we just had a setback is all."

"A setback! They left! They— they— they wanted to punish us for an autopsy."

"Breathe," Adam said simply.

When Immanuel looked pleadingly into his eyes, Adam drew in a slow breath and watched as Immanuel struggled to mimic him through a string of raw coughs. Pulling him upright beside him, Adam wrapped his arm around his shoulder and let Immanuel's meager weight fall against him once more. His bony shoulders shuddered with each labored breath, his spine poking dangerously against Adam's side.

"We don't need them to figure this out, you know. Even if we never find out who killed Berte or Jacobs, on Monday we're going back to London. The Interceptors and Special Branch can sort it out."

"But what if they—"

"There is no way they could have expected you to handle this on your own without any formal training. You aren't even a full member yet."

Immanuel bit his lip and sniffed. "But what if I make a mistake again?"

"I'm certain you will. As much as you would prefer not to believe it, you're human." He carefully brushed a stray hair from Immanuel's forehead. "You know how often I make a mess of things, yet you still love me. I really don't think you made a mistake this time. There was no way for you to know how they would react," Adam replied, rubbing Immanuel's arm as his breath finally slowed to rhythmic puffs.

"But did I violate her? Hilde was right. I did see Berte's death. I didn't *have* to autopsy her, but I did. I don't even think I did it for the Interceptors or Sir William. *I* wanted to know how it all worked, how she could be so human and yet not. I needed to see where the lines blurred. Did I do the wrong thing?"

"It depends who you ask." Adam stared up at the thick timbers crossing to distract his mind from the hollow figure lurking in his memory. "Think about it this way. When you die, you stop being you. You have no use for your body. It's a shell as empty as one you would find on the shore, so no, I don't think you violated her. But when someone dies, those who love them don't see that body as a shell, at least not at first. They see the person they loved." His hand hovered over Immanuel's side. *It's only when they die piece by piece that you begin to see the edges of the shell.* "Do you think her autopsy was a waste of time?"

"No," he replied, with a shake of his head. "I learned a lot."

"More than if you merely relived her memories?"

"Of course. The information I gleaned from her death paled in comparison to studying an actual body. You saw how thorough my notes were. Miss Elliott said I added more information on their anatomy to their file than they had amassed since they first discovered selkies."

"See? You didn't harm anyone. The dissection may have offended them, but science offends plenty of people when they realize they are not above nature and her laws."

Straightening, Adam turned to Immanuel. His cheeks, lips, and eyes had reddened, making his eyes look shockingly vibrant and his scar almost white. In the silent house, his breath whistled in a steady rhythm, but the edge of anger and hurt had finally subsided into something far more thoughtful. Adam glanced toward the window for any sign of shadows or lingering selkies. When nothing appeared, Adam kissed Immanuel and rested his forehead against his.

"Promise me you won't throw away your chance to be an Interceptor unless you truly don't want to be one. I can't let you give up over this."

Nodding, Immanuel chewed on his lip pensively. While his outburst had drained him, his eyes seemed clearer. "Do you really think I can be a good Interceptor?"

"I have never been more sure of anything," Adam said, pressing his lips to the tip of Immanuel's scar.

Chapter Twenty-Three
Missed Signals

Immanuel wasn't so certain. In the few hours between when the selkies left and the sun rose, he lay in bed, wishing sleep would overtake him but knowing it never would. While Adam slept soundly in the other bed, Immanuel couldn't shake the lingering shame. Völva Hilde and the others believed he had done something unthinkable, and although, he didn't agree with them, he had committed a sin he detested. He had treated Berte as an thing rather than a person, just as Miss Elliott and the Interceptors had. He had let his curiosity and latent ambition take over, and—

Before Immanuel could finish the thought, he shoved off the covers and slipped out of bed. Washing and dressing in the dark, Immanuel quickly scrawled a note to Adam, in hopes he wouldn't give him too big of a fright when he awoke and found him gone. At the threshold, he lingered for a moment, watching Adam sleep before padding down the steps. He wished he could wake him and tell him himself, but he didn't want to talk. Through the warbled glass of the front windows, a dim ray inched across the rug. His notes waited on the dining room table where Adam had left them the night before, held down with their calling stone. Immanuel hesitated before stuffing the stone and folded papers into his trouser pocket. From his satchel, he retrieved his pencil and notebook. Thus far, it remained a rambling mess. Perhaps with solitude, he could put his thoughts in order or at least create the illusion of competence by returning to London with coherent notes.

Grabbing a coat from the rack, Immanuel carefully pulled the door shut behind him. The wind buffeted him, sending loose sand into his eyes and the collar of his coat flapping as he walked down the grass-lined path. In the distance, he could make out the faint sounds of fishermen and bells, the mournful cries of gulls mingling with lapping waves. As he reached the top of the steep embankment leading down to the beach, Immanuel thought the better of it and settled on one of the rough boulders lining the hill. From his vantage point, he could make out a little boat bobbing between him and the lighthouse and a few dark seals sleeping on a sandbar. Reaching into his coat pocket for the vivalabe, Immanuel ripped his hand away from the brush of cold steel. He swallowed hard as he carefully pulled the revolver out as if it might go off at the slightest provocation. For a moment he merely stared at it before putting it back and fishing into the inner lining of the coat. Stashed over his heart was the envelope Miss Elliott had given them when they left London. He had grabbed the wrong coat. In the dark, his and Adam's had been nearly identical. No matter, he would return it when he finished working.

Perched atop the boulder, Immanuel transcribed everything he could remember about the selkies. In his mind's eye, he could see them transform, sliding between seal and human with an ease only betrayed by the creak of bone and tear of skin reforming. Once he finished describing their physiology, he delineated what he could surmise about the social order of their colony and what he had seen in the labyrinth of tunnels. There were so many gaps, so many questions he wished he could ask them, but it was too late now. Perhaps he could return with

Berte's body as a peace offering. Then again, that could go very poorly for him. Sighing, Immanuel picked up the pencil only to catch the sound of a voice on the wind.

He turned, expecting to see Adam when, instead, he found Casper Quince ambling toward him. Immanuel slowly stood, hoping his added height would give the man pause should he decide to cause trouble again.

"Mr. Winter, you worked with Jacobs, right?" Quince asked, standing a good distance from him.

"Yes?"

"I don't know if Greta told you, but he came to speak with me the day he died. I think I have some information about the women that you might be interested in."

"Go on," Immanuel replied, slamming his hand on his notebook as the wind blew it open and sent his pencil skittering down the cliff face.

"Let's talk inside. I promise there will be some hot cider in it for you if you come."

Immanuel looked back at the cottage.

"It'll only be a few moments. Your pal won't miss you."

Stuffing his notebook into his pocket, Immanuel cast one last look at the darkened window and followed Quince to the lighthouse.

⚜

Immanuel paced across Quince's living room, fiddling with the strap of his satchel as the other man disappeared into the basement to fetch some cider. Every so often the other man's voice drifted up in a question about Immanuel's life, and even though Immanuel's jaw resisted each word like a trap, he managed to give him a flat, vague answer if it meant he could get a little closer to the killer. He lived in London. No, he didn't work on the water. No, he merely studied seals from specimens and the work of other scientists. Immanuel shifted uncomfortably as his eyes drifted to the squat clock sitting over the hearth. On the way over, he had watched the tide begin its march across the grass, slowly separating the lighthouse from the rest of the island. If he didn't leave soon, it would be impossible for him to get back until the tide receded. Unless he swam across… He batted the thought away. Adam would give him a well-deserved lecture if he so much as soaked his stockings in the sea. All he could hope was that Quince would be quick enough that he didn't have to worry about Adam waking to find the note.

Circling the parlor, Immanuel could see what Adam meant about the lighthouse keeper not matching his surroundings. He should have been at ease, but something nagged at his mind. Drifting over to the loft, Immanuel cast a glance toward the basement door before climbing halfway up the ladder until he could make out the books' spines. There were the expected volumes on tide cycles, atlases, ledgers, and texts on navigating the British Isles. Beside them, he found books on medicine, *Grey's Anatomy,* Huxley's manual on animal anatomy, along with several other relatively advanced tomes that one might find at a medical school, and a book on electrical currents. Immanuel furrowed his blonde brows. It was hard to imagine the man harassing Byron could be as bookish and knowledgeable on science as his library suggested.

Climbing down the ladder, Immanuel inched down the hall toward what he had assumed were bedrooms. As he turned his gaze, he froze at the beast staring back at him. His legs nearly buckled under him at the sight of its brown snout and giant glassy eyes peering up from a bedraggled pile of traps and crates. It was the head of the creature he had seen corner Berte and rise out of the murky water to skewer Mr. Jacobs. Drawing closer, Immanuel touched its brown head only to find yellow metal hidden behind a layer of mud. A hunk of metal had been blown out on the top by what looked like a bullet. He stepped back, blinking away the phantom images threatening to rush back to his eyes. Beneath the muck were several more openings and brass wingnuts around a flared collar. The beast had been a diving suit.

Immanuel's heart thundered in his throat. Casper Quince was the one to dive down to fix Byron's tidal generators when they became too encrusted with mud to work. It hadn't even crossed his mind that the generators would be fixed underwater. He hadn't seen one before, but he could see their flat tops peaking between the waves at the lighthouse's base. He had seen them before, hadn't he? In a nightmare where he found himself irresistibly drawn to them, to a sound at once horrible yet as nostalgic as a lullaby. Then that meant— His eyes widened at Quince's slow tread plodding up the stairs. How could he have been so blind? Immanuel looked over the shelves and furniture before landing on the gear stacked into the rafters. Above him hooks, rods, and oars of all sizes hung crusted in a film of sediment and gunk. Higher, running along the ceiling, Immanuel could make out a thick, black wire that disappeared above the door on the far end of the house.

Scrambling up the ladder, Immanuel grabbed an oar from the rafters, slid back to the floor, and ran the instant his soles hit the boards. He stumbled over the rug and reached the cellar door as Quince hit the third to last step. Their eyes met in surprise, Immanuel's gaze trailing to the hooked harpoon in the lighthouse keeper's hand. In one swift motion, Immanuel slammed the door shut, throwing his weight against it as he wedged the oar through the knob and into the frame. It wouldn't hold long with Quince battering against it, but it would give him time. Immanuel wrenched open the far door to reveal the dank interior of the lighthouse.

Water dripped somewhere in the distance, bathing the room in the stench of brackish water along with the tang of machine oil. Immanuel's footfalls echoed off the walls only to be drowned out by his rough breaths and thundering heart. Rounding the corner as he entered the main room of the lighthouse, his eyes fell upon a telegraph mounted on a table. Flipping the switch, he was relieved to hear the electric whir of its motor reawakening. He grabbed the envelope from the inside of his coat and pulled out the slip of paper with the Interceptor's information with shaking hands. His eyes darted over the square contraption beside the telegraph. Half a dozen copper-lined holes labeled with station codes covered its face, and in the top left a wired peg stuck out that connected with the rear of the telegraph. He scrambled over the numbers etched above each hole until he found the one that matched what had been carefully printed on the page. He stuffed the peg in, listening for any sign of Quince, only to hear the drum of wood thumping against wood. There wasn't much time.

He had only worked a telegraph a handful of times at the museum when the operator was unavailable or taking too long for Sir William's thin patience. It was simple enough, but as his hands shook and his mind tumbled ahead of him, he hoped he hadn't missed any steps. Luckily, it didn't seem as if Mr. Quince was particularly adept either, as a Morse code key sat beside the device. Immanuel drew in a calming breath and desperately tried to block out the thump of the cellar door behind him. With his eyes on the key, he entered in the code Judith had supplied him. He scanned the alphabet and quickly tapped out the most succinct message he could think of.

Short, short, short, short…short…short, long, short, short…short, long, long, short. *Help*.

Immanuel's mind reeled as he stared at the handle humming beneath his fingers. He had done it so fast that he couldn't recall if he had counted correctly or if he had even legibly spelled a word he had learned so well. Stepping away, Immanuel listened, only to hear the wind battering the brickwork and the patter of rain against the glass-domed beacon. He squinted down the hall but saw no sign of Quince. The lighthouse's only door stood less than ten feet away, and if Quince escaped the basement, he would have only seconds to get out before he was on him. He stared at the machine beneath his fingertips. What else could he say? What could he write that might make the Interceptors understand the gravity of his situation? Immanuel swallowed hard. If the harpoon was any indication, he could be dead long before they arrived.

Long, short, short… short… short, long… long, short, short.

As he began to type the next word, the door creaked open behind him. Immanuel froze, letting his hand down on the knob in a long, shrill note. The sound died away at the snap of the cord running over his head, and the device fell still. Slowly turning, Immanuel found

Casper Quince at the door with the hook of his harpoon tangled in the telegraph's wire. Rain dripped down his cropped hair and gathered in thick drops in his beard. His grey eyes burned as he leveled the weapon at Immanuel. Quince nodded for Immanuel to step away from the dead telegraph. As he moved, Immanuel's gaze traveled to the door standing open behind his captor. A breeze whistled in. laden with the taste of the sea. If he could catch it, he could knock Quince over or at least rid him of his weapon, but as he tried to focus enough to see the invisible threads, all he heard was his heart in his ears. For once, he was thankful to not feel the draw of Adam's energy nearby. Even if he couldn't use his powers, at least Adam was safe. Quince raised the harpoon until it hung inches from Immanuel's eyes.

"Let's go. We have some things to discuss, *merwif*," Quince said, nudging Immanuel back toward the main house.

With each step toward the cellar door, the dread deepened in Immanuel's gut. How long would it be before Adam awoke and went looking for him? How long before his love for him led him right into a trap? Immanuel swallowed against the lump in his throat as Quince kicked aside the oar wedged under the knob and nudged him forward with the tip of his blade. As his foot hit the first squealing board, a blow landed hard in the small of his back. Immanuel scrambled to grab the rail only to find the smooth, slick surface of stone. Pain bloomed across his back as he struck the first step. His elbow rang and head throbbed as he fell until the world passed in bursts of pain and blurs of grey. With a final crack, his poorly healed ribs bounced against the bottom steps and his legs crumpled under him.

Lying with his cheek pressed against the cool stones, Immanuel fought to keep his eyes open. His mind screamed for him to sit up, to run, to stay put and play dead until Quince left, but all he could do was listen as the door at the top of the steps creaked shut.

Chapter Twenty-Four
Unmoored

Adam groaned and pulled the pillow closer. What the hell was Immanuel doing to be so damn loud? he wondered, though not enough to move from the cocoon of his covers to find out. As the sound continued and his mind cleared, he could make out a voice outside the window accompanied by the pounding of a fist against the door. Adam bolted upright, his mind flashing to the police until he remembered where he was. Shaking off the remnants of sleep, he scanned the room for any sign of Immanuel, but as he rose, his eyes fell upon a piece of parchment left on the coverlet.

Gone to the beach to work. Didn't want to wake you. Feel free to eat without me. I.L.D.

Immanuel

Adam sighed and rubbed his eyes as the rapping continued. "Just a second!"

Grabbing a shirt and trousers from the wardrobe, Adam quickly donned them over his union suit and trotted down the creaky steps. He blinked with each stair, his mind on what he could scrounge up from the cupboard that might be palatable at such a wretched hour.

Opening the door, Adam quirked a henna brow at Byron Durnure waiting on the doorstep with his fist poised to knock. Byron leaned heavily against his scuffed walking stick, his breath labored as if he had attempted to run from the village to the cottage. Smudges of soot marred his forehead and cheek and his waistcoat had been torn across his breast to reveal a shallow scratch beneath.

Before Adam could speak, Byron blurted, "I need to speak to you and Mr. Winter straight away. Greta said I had to get you."

When the dark-haired man went to grab his arm, Adam ducked out of reach. "What are you talking about? What could be so pressing at this ungodly hour?"

Byron shifted, his grey eyes boring into Adam before darting toward the village. "The selkies are rebelling. Look."

Adam reached for his coat only to find Immanuel's hanging in its place. Releasing a breath out his nose, he slipped it on, feeling the narrow back tug with each movement. The damned selkies were the last thing he wanted to deal with, but the thought died as he followed Byron up the hill.

The village was in shambles. Through a haze of smoke, Adam could make out figures running toward the water, others moving through the streets from house to house as if searching. A house near the bay had been set ablaze while several around it smoldered as the embers ate their way through their ivy-clad roofs. The groan of a great crack drew his eye to the water where a ship bobbed wildly. Squinting, Adam could make out figures grappling on the fishing vessel. From that distance, he couldn't tell if they were selkies or men, but he could see bodies prone on the deck and dark forms floating in the water beside it.

The saliva dried in Adam's throat. "Why are they doing this?"

"Revenge," Byron said softly, "for all they have suffered. I couldn't find Jenny, but Greta said you might be able to stop them. She says you started this."

"*I* started it? I did nothing of— Never mind. We need to find Immanuel. He's down on the beach."

"No, he isn't." When Adam stared at him, Byron glanced at him nervously and added, "The main road runs parallel to the shore. I would have seen him if he was on this side of the island."

Adam rubbed his wrist, but as he moved his arm, he felt the weight of Immanuel's vivalabe in his pocket. "Stay right here, I'll be right back."

Shutting the cottage door behind him, Adam drew out the brass orb. Beneath his trembling hands, he could sense the stir of intellect within the metal. He clicked the front and the top fell away, but unlike every time Immanuel had used it, the balls didn't scatter; they didn't even appear. Adam released a breath and tried again. Staring at the contraption, Adam forced back the image of Immanuel being drowned or ripped apart by the selkies.

"Show me Immanuel," he whispered, opening his eyes only to find the stone balls hadn't moved from the perimeter of the plane. "Find Immanuel."

Gritting his teeth, Adam glared at the vivalabe and resisted the urge to hurl it at the wall. It ticked mockingly in time with his pulse. "Look, I know I'm not your master or owner or whatever Immanuel is, but he could be in danger right now. He and I are bonded, and if you don't help me, we may both lose something important to us. Please, show me Immanuel."

Adam stared the etched face of the vivalabe down as if willing the impossible parts inside of it to move. After a tense moment, a loud click resounded deep within the belly of the device as half a dozen balls slowly rolled across the plane, changing color as they went. A tiger's eye and a blue stone stood together while in the distance Immanuel's white quartz gleamed beside a chip of sapphire and a hunk of blue jade. He stared at the tiger's eye. In whatever logic the vivalabe used to discern bodies, it had decided to make him a striped, honeyed stone.

Adam followed the trajectory of the sliding stones and tried to imagine where on the island Immanuel might be. If the village sat somewhere behind his shoulder, then Immanuel couldn't be there or in the labyrinth beneath the island. The only things in that direction were the lighthouse, the powerhouse, and the sea.

"Thank you," Adam whispered to the vivalabe before snapping it shut and stuffing it into his coat pocket.

There were two people with Immanuel, and while he couldn't tell who they were, he hoped to god they were human. Byron's anxious knock sounded again. Adam took a step toward the stairs but stopped. Immanuel had his gun. Walking briskly into Mr. Jacobs' room, Adam snatched the dead man's gun, even though it wasn't loaded, and stormed past Byron.

"Where are you going? The village is the other way," Byron called after him.

Adam turned, locking gazes with Byron as he stood wide-eyed in the lane, and for an instant, he saw himself reflected in the other man's eyes, all fire blazing against the grim dawn.

"I have to go to the lighthouse. Mr. Winter is missing, and while I appreciate that all hell is breaking loose down there, I can't help you."

Byron's mouth fell open. "But Greta said to—"

"Greta started this mess. Let her deal with the consequences," Adam snapped, turning on heel.

"But what should I do? They're threatening to kill any who've wronged them."

"Then, if I was you, I would hope my conscience was clear."

Without waiting for Byron's reply, Adam marched down the path toward the lighthouse. Anger and fear bubbled up together, threatening to spew out, but he buried it deep, hardening it into cold resolve. His steps slowed against his will as he reached the dip in the path where the tide overtook the land. Water gushed over the hill in a powerful current. It was deep enough that Adam doubted he could attempt to cross it without being swept out to sea. Digging his nail deep into his palm, Adam steadied himself. He had to get to the lighthouse, but what would he do when he got there? Demand to see Immanuel? If nothing was amiss and he was merely speaking with Quince, he wasn't sure he could hide his relief. A good friend could still worry, couldn't he?

Something white bobbed at the edge of Adam's vision. Breaking from his thoughts, Adam spotted a rowboat beached against a hunk of driftwood. Adam's heart sank. The boat bobbed with the tide, revealing the dead man's ravaged form with each dip. As Adam scrambled over the rocks and dunes, the smell of rancid flesh hit him before he could fully see Jacobs' body. Holding his breath, Adam inched closer until he could make out the same frayed black coat and distorted face he had seen days earlier. Unlike their first encounter, his body had begun to leak a putrid liquid somewhere between blood and muck. His flesh had distended and fallen with gravity until his features resembled melted wax. Drawing as close as he dared, Adam noticed frayed gouges across Jacobs' body that he realized with sickening clarity had been caused by seabirds feasting on his corpse.

He swallowed down the bile climbing his throat. How had Jacobs gotten loose again? His body was supposed to have been stored in the cellar below the lighthouse. He had left Quince to deal with the body, but he hadn't thought to check that he did it. Had the tide swept into the basement during the storm and dragged the boat out to sea? Adam raised his eyes to the spiraling form of the lighthouse looming at the end of the precipice. Storm clouds darkened the horizon, blurring the world beyond the island into middling smears of grey and green. No, Jacobs' body had been released on purpose.

Adam kicked at the sand, releasing a string of curses. He should have told Immanuel his suspicions the night before, but he had been so upset by the selkies leaving that Adam had forgotten. *Quince.* Quince had killed Jacobs. Greta said she had seen them talking before he disappeared, but more importantly, Adam was certain Quince owned the calling stone they found in Jacobs' watch. Quince had said he had a sister named Hilda, and Hilde had a brother who had given away his stone to a stranger. Of course the moment he thought to ask, Miss Larkin had ruined any hope of getting help from the other selkies. Adam stared up at the lighthouse. Had he lied about the broken telegraph, too? Jacobs was dead and rotting, and as long as he was presumed missing, Quince's secret would be safe. But why? Why kill him and why kill the selkie in the first place? It didn't matter. Adam's ribs tightened, sucking the air from his lungs at the thought of Immanuel trapped with that man.

Resisting the urge to take a breath, Adam grabbed the side of the row boat and shoved it down. Immanuel's narrow-backed jacket strained as he tipped the boat on its side. Jacobs rolled against the boards with a wet slap, bits of flesh and offal spiraling at the soles of Adam's boots. *It's a shell and nothing more*, Adam repeated to himself as he shifted the boat further until it capsized on the sand. Carefully stepping over Mr. Jacobs' corpse, Adam slid the boat toward the water, stopping before it reached the water-soaked sand. He looked across the beach for anything he could use and found a twisted branch of petrified wood. The oars had been lost days ago when Quince had killed Mr. Jacobs, but if he could cross the stream before the current widened, he could stab and pull his way across like a gondolier.

Wiping his hands with his handkerchief, Adam checked the vivalabe one more time. He stared down at the brass markings surrounding the etched face, wishing he knew what they meant. Bits of uncolored stone lingered near the symbols, but they never moved. Adam banished the thought that perhaps its sudden silence was due to its owner's death. Shoving the brass device deep in his pocket, Adam grabbed a long branch of driftwood and pushed the boat against the wet sand until it hit the water with a rocking thump. The row boat bobbed uncertainly, threatening to tip him into the stream before he could gain his balance. Using the wood as a pole, Adam stabbed the land beneath the boat and dragged himself across the stream. Something—he told himself was water—sloshed into his shoes and drifted over the smell of the sea. He pushed all thoughts from his mind, except one: Immanuel needed him.

⚬⊚ ⊚⚬

Adam tumbled out of the rowboat and crashed into the grass, hauling himself up before the brackish water could wick up his trousers. Beads of sweat trailed down his back and loosened his pomade until locks of henna hair hung limp across his forehead. His arms ached from dragging himself across the water, and as he caught his breath on the shore, he cursed himself for not continuing his exercise regime more faithfully after Immanuel arrived. Rising to his feet, he turned in time to watch the boat bob away, swept up by the meandering tide. Adam reached for his tie before letting his hand drop as he remembered he left it back at the cottage. Instead he straightened the collar of his coat and smoothed his hair from his forehead before making his way up the hill.

The lighthouse seemed so much more imposing than it had the day he went to speak to Casper Quince. At the front door, Adam hesitated. His hand instinctively drifted to the gun in his pocket but remembered it was empty. Plastering on a neutral expression, he knocked and waited. When no one came, Adam peered through the window, but the whitewashed parlor appeared to be empty. Moving on to the lighthouse door, he knocked and once again found the building seemingly silent. Walking down the hill, Adam didn't know whether to feel relieved or ill. His eyes drifted to the outbuilding resting against the cliff side. The brick powerhouse thrummed with a rhythmic pulse that mimicked the ebb and flow of the sea. Drawing closer, Adam's skin prickled at the energy emanating through its walls. A crude sign hung on the door warning others of the dangers of electricity and barring entry to all but those who were responsible for its upkeep. Resisting the urge to train the gun ahead of him, Adam threw open the door and ducked inside. He stumbled in, moving behind the nearest generator for cover. Peering around it, Adam's heart sank. Empty.

Adam let his head fall back against the damp brick. His stomach

272

knotted at the thought of Immanuel trapped somewhere he couldn't reach him. That had happened to him once already; Adam saw its aftereffects in nightmares and delusions and irrational fears that he still couldn't puzzle out, and he wouldn't let it happen to him again. Adam was about to leave the powerhouse to head up to the main house with the intention to smash in a window when a voice carried above the generator's thrum. It had been so faint that he wasn't sure it hadn't originated in his mind, but it had been human. Biting back the urge to call for Immanuel, Adam slowly stepped out from behind the generator's massive steel wheel. He slid his hand into his pocket as he moved around the next wheel and found the cold metal of Jacobs' gun. As he trailed it ahead of him, he flicked his wrist at the foreign weight. It was too light, but Quince wouldn't know the difference.

Stepping around the last generator, Adam stared down the barrel of the gun at a metal door set into the bricks. Unlike the lighthouse, this knob turned easily in his hand. His relief died into dread at what waited on the other side. His heart scaled his throat at the brick barrel vaulted catacomb closing in around him. It wouldn't have reminded him of the underground rail stations back home, except for the shelves lining both walls as far as he could see in the dark. Light glinted off row upon row of jars filled with what Adam hoped were preserves but deep down knew were anything but food. He shuddered at an eye lazily spinning in its jar. Even in the dim light, he knew it to be human. The gorge rose in his throat as he spotted what appeared to be kidneys, lungs, and finally a heart submerged in alcohol. Bits of human and seal sat side by side, *objets d'art* in a mad man's studio. Adam crinkled his nose at how the smell left a faint tang on his tongue that reminded him of the awful swill Quince had given him. Adam's mind clung hopelessly to reason. It was possible that Quince or a past lighthouse keeper had procured some of the specimens through distributors in London or Edinburgh, but not humans. Immanuel had told him how the curators often lamented about the lack of human specimens available from reputable sources. Adam's mind flashed to the faceless women tacked to the wall of the study. Had they ended up disarticulated and jarred like livestock before anyone could realize they were gone?

He didn't want to think of a reason anyone would do it. Inching down the hall, Adam kept the gun ahead of him as he silenced his steps against the old brick. The tunnel above him grew to a semi-circular room with a ceiling high enough to dispel the wreak of the jars. Lingering on the threshold, Adam listened. The room was silent apart from the pounding of his heart in his ears and a faint whistling of breath. Adam reached along the wall until his hand brushed against a switch. In one quick motion, he threw on the lights and drew his gun.

The harsh electric lamps illuminated horrors far worse than any his mind could have conjured. Adam's hands dropped as he gasped but clamped his mouth shut before the sound could escape. The room could have been used for storage or smuggling; now, it lay somewhere between a dungeon and an operating theatre. Crates and trappings for fishing had been stacked in front of the door on the far wall to block anyone entering from seeing the long, stained butcher-block tables lining the other two walls. Bits of offal had dried onto the surface while what looked like a putrefied fruit sat in a pool of its own juices near the table's edge. A massive pot still loomed over Adam, but beside it were shelves and racks containing the lighthouse keeper's tools. Some Adam had seen in Hadley's workshop, but here they seemed made for disarticulation rather than creation. Beneath the smell of alcohol from the still, lingered the metallic tang of blood and rot mixed with sea water. A not quite human shape lay hidden under a sheet on the table. Adam willed his feet to move toward the figure, but his body stayed locked in the doorway.

It wasn't Immanuel. Adam knew that in the core of his being. If Immanuel had been decimated like that poor creature, he would have felt the tug of his soul crying out to his. He was sure of it. Perhaps it was the handfasting or maybe it was simply in his head, but he *knew* Immanuel's presence. This was one of Quince's victims, and he was too cowardly to look into the face of someone who had died because they didn't figure it out soon enough. As Adam reached the crates on the far side of the room, a faint breath whistled behind him. Adam froze, turning slowly with the gun pointed ahead. There was no one, no one but the shape beneath the dirty canvas. Swallowing hard, Adam inched toward the table and ripped the sheet away.

The gorge rose in his throat before he could stop it. Stifling bile-burned coughs, he wiped at his lips with his handkerchief and slowly walked back to her side. On the table lay a selkie. Her legs remained trapped in the smooth skin of a seal while her upper body was human, apart from her webbed fingers and the sleek grey fur covering her figure. A mass of sweat-matted curls clung to her face as she shuddered with each shallow breath. Adam's heart pounded in his ears as he caught sight of the deep wound bloodying her scalp. It slashed across her forehead, and Adam feared if she moved, he would see a flash of white bone. On the table beside her sat a hand drill and boning knife. Despite the coating of fur, her face shone with sweat and her hands fluttered against her arms as she hugged herself. Lightly brushing her hair from her lips, Adam realized he had seen her. Even though her face was fuller and more seal-like now, he recognized the swirls and dots decorating her arms and the blonde curls that had once been wild. It was Byron's companion, Jenny. *Byron.* A pang of guilt rang through Adam's gut. He had shrugged the man off without a second thought, yet the selkies had spared him in their massacre. He hadn't even thought to bring him.

"Jenny," Adam whispered to the place where her ear would have been in her more human form. "Jenny, wake up."

He gently rubbed her arm, but she barely stirred. Adam stood beside her, his eyes trailing to the hidden door. He had to find Immanuel, but he couldn't leave her. Immanuel would have shoved her into Adam's arms and sent him off to safety, and he would have been right to. As Adam lifted her shoulders, her head lolled against him, revealing a blackened bruise blooming across her temple. Grimacing, Adam slid his arms beneath her shoulders and fins. He hefted her to his chest, staggering back under her surprising weight. If he could get her through the tunnel and out to the sea, he could hand her over to the selkies. Even if they were rioting, perhaps they would come for their own. When Adam reached the door, he balanced her weight against his chest and fished in his pocket for Jacobs' watch. He let his head fall back against the rusted door; Immanuel had it. Jenny shuddered, releasing a not quite human cry. Hearing her breathing falter, Adam hoped she and Immanuel could hold on a little longer.

Adam reached for the door but tightened his grip on the selkie as a voice rang from the other side of the crates. His eyes flickered over the room for a place to hide, but he didn't dare put her back on the table. Darting into the hall of jars, Adam carefully lowered Jenny onto the floor behind the nearest shelf. He ripped off his jacket and stuck it under her head to ease her labored breath. Keeping his back flat to the wall, Adam slunk as deep into the shadow of the still as he could manage and waited for whatever walked through the door.

Chapter Twenty-Five
Where Magic Lies

Immanuel groaned, cautiously rolling onto his back and clenching his eyes shut against the pain blooming in his bones. Daggers lanced through his spine and hips where they had struck the stone steps on the way down while the rest of his body ached. Immanuel slowly opened his eyes, the pain in his temple flaring as black spots danced in his damaged eye. The electric lights glaring in a crooked line down the hall brought tears to his eyes, but even through the dim side of his vision, he could make out a brick tunnel looming over his head and a rusted metal door not far down the hall. He rose into a low crouch, grimacing as his knee slid into place with a sickening crack. The corner of his lip itched, and when Immanuel touched it, he found blood staining his fingers and crusted to his cheek.

Taking slow breaths, Immanuel fended back the panic threatening to overtake his senses. Each flare of pain sent him closer to the edge, and for a moment, he feared losing his connection to reality more than the man who had caused it. What was it Adam told him? *Feel.* He pressed his palms into the cold brick, running his finger along the nicks and imperfections. *Hear.* A steady pulse rang through the stone, like the repetitious chug of a locomotive and somewhere far closer, the scuff of steps. *See.* Immanuel turned to find Quince standing before a stack of old ropes and what looked like oversized crab pots. In his hand, he hefted the harpoon, its tip taking on a lethal gleam in the lamp light. Immanuel stood perfectly still as the lighthouse keeper closed the distance between them.

"I thought maybe I did you in. I expected *merwifs* to be more durable than that. Then again, you are city stock."

Immanuel's chest ached as he swallowed against the knot in his throat. "What do you want with me?"

"Answers and a bit more."

More? With a flick of Quince's wrist, the tip of the harpoon jabbed Immanuel's side hard enough to make him hiss the words through his teeth. "What sort of answers?"

"The kind that will save this island and you, if you play your cards right."

Immanuel's pulse pounded in his temples as he blinked in hopes it would clear the damaged side of his eye. The lighthouse keeper circled him slowly with the harpoon only inches from Immanuel's waist. At each glint or flick, Immanuel blenched only to receive a satisfied huff from Quince. His eyes surveyed Immanuel's form, lingering on his hands and finally on his scar.

Anger bubbled deep in his chest at the man's probing eye. "I— I telegraphed my employers. They will be here shortly to deal with Jacobs' murderer. If any harm comes to me, they will know it was you."

"It will take days for them to get here. You would be amazed how easily a body can disappear in a place like this. Help me, and we can discuss your release."

Immanuel's hands shook, but he clasped the them behind his back and stood. "Go on."

"All right. My first question is if you're a *merwif*, then how are you able to live away from the water without getting the sea sickness?"

"I don't know what a *merwif* is, but I don't think I am what you think I am."

"A selkie, a sea wife. There's no word for what we are, but there's never been a man who could get away without suffering for it. Some go so mad they throw themselves to their deaths rather than be apart from the water. Do you get an itch in your brain when you're away from it? Do you dream of the sea until you awake to find yourself drowning?"

"No," Immanuel said, his voice faltering against his will.

"You said you're from Germany. My mother told me there were tribes of selkies up that way. They shared a lot, them and our selkies, but maybe not sea sickness. I couldn't get out to those parts when I went away, but you could. I want to know what makes you different from us."

"I'm— I'm not a selkie," he whispered, hoping it wouldn't be the last thing he ever said.

Without looking at him, Immanuel could sense Quince's probing gaze upon him as if searching for something. The harpoon grazed his back. "A liar, like all the rest of them."

"I am not," Immanuel cried. Oh god, not here, not in this horrid place. He had promised Adam. "I'm—"

Quince ducked as the electric bulb over his head blew out in a shower of glass. Scrambling to catch the magic, three more bulbs burst in rapid succession before the last fizzled in its socket and blinked out. As the hall fell into shadow, Immanuel released a tremulous breath. Quince brushed the glass from his shoulders, his nicked hand leaving a thin trail of blood over his jacket and neck.

"Then, how can you do that? I saw what you did at Byron's shop. It certainly ain't natural, stopping water with your mind."

What could he say to make him believe or even understand when he could scarcely convince Adam of his powers? *Adam.* The idea that he was back at the cottage worrying about him stung worse than any injury he sustained in the fall. Why had he gotten them into this? Immanuel silently prayed to any god that would listen that Adam stayed out of harm's way.

"Well?" Quince prodded him with the blunt side of the harpoon.

"They call me a *witega*. I can manipulate energy, but that's it. I'm not a selkie."

"Then, I guess we're done talking."

As Quince raised the harpoon, Immanuel cried, "Wait, wait! Maybe if you tell me what you want, I can help you."

"I want to cure the sea sickness."

In Quince's voice, Immanuel thought he heard a hint of desperation, and desperate men were sometimes willing to listen. He swallowed hard. "All right. I can try."

"We need to take out where the devilry lies."

Immanuel stiffened at the word.

"I have tried to find it myself, but I couldn't." Quince's eyes flashed like a knife in the dim light. "I've tried so long."

"Is that why you have all of those books?"

"Yes, but they didn't help. I thought going to a university would teach me enough, but I couldn't stand it," he said, his hand instinctively reaching for his head. "I kept hearing the sea like a bloody siren song. When I ignored it, the whole world felt hopeless and dim, but that's how it feels here! We're all trapped on these blasted islands while *they* go off and leave us behind."

"Have— have you thought of going to the mainland in search of a wife? There is a theory that we inherit all of our traits from our parents. Perhaps, a mainland woman wouldn't give sea sickness to her children."

"I tried. I took out ads for a wife, but not even penniless spinsters want to come out here. That's why I wrote to the papers about Byron's inventions. I thought people would hear of them and come flocking to see, but no one cares about us out here. No one. We may as well be a different species to people like you. I even sent a *merwif* to some royal something or other society. People came flocking to see that Fiji Mermaid, but they couldn't care less when a real one turns up on their doorstep. They sent you, didn't they? And the other one?"

"He merely came to write an article. He has nothing to do with the selkie."

"But you studied her when she arrived at the society."

The breath hitched in Immanuel's throat before he could stop himself.

A smug smile crossed Quince's lips. "I heard your conversation with Hilda last night. You have notes, and I want them."

"I have them here," Immanuel peeped, reaching into his pocket. His fingertips brushed cold steel and parchment.

Quince snatched the papers from his outstretched hand and stared down at the anatomical drawings and tight lines of notes. His eyes darted between Immanuel as he flipped through each page, his face darkening until finally he folded the papers into his pocket.

"Let's go," he ordered, gesturing toward the door behind Immanuel with the tip of his blade.

"But I gave you all—"

"I want you to find the magic for me. I don't care how long it takes. You will do it."

Immanuel raised his hands, his breath tight in his throat as the tip of the harpoon angled toward the soft flesh of his neck. "I— I don't know where it is. No one does."

"Then you had better find it now. I have one of them ready for you. I nearly did it myself, but after seeing you with them yesterday, I had other ideas." At Immanuel's sudden pallor, he snapped, "That a problem for you?"

He shook his head as the bulbs down the hall flickered.

"And don't try anything funny, or you'll be next."

Immanuel's throat thickened at the thought of what awaited him. An autopsy could only last so long, and when he couldn't find the magic or soul of the creature, Quince would kill him. Immanuel desperately tried to cobble together a plan, but his head ached and his mind lagged unbearably. When the metal door creaked open, the wreak of decomposition and alcohol sent a wave of bile up his throat. Clinging to the doorway, Immanuel vomited over Quince's oaths as the other man dragged him inside. Immanuel coughed and wiped the tears from his eyes, immediately regretting it when he saw the studio of death. Following at Quince's heels, Immanuel stared at the man's back in hopes of blocking out the horrors in the periphery of his vision.

The lighthouse keeper stopped at a wooden bench, turning on heel and looking between the stacks of junk. "Where… where is she? I—"

As Quince ducked between the tables, Immanuel caught a flash of red in the shadows of the still. Pressed into the narrow gap between the vat and the wall, Adam Fenice watched him. Relief and nausea broke over Immanuel as a smile died on his lips before it could bloom. Their eyes locked and the twang of the bond echoed between them. Adam tipped his chin toward the door, but Immanuel gave a quick shake of his head and mouthed, *Get help*. Slowly reaching into his pocket, Immanuel kept an eye on Quince and pulled out the calling stone. Throwing the chain toward Adam, Quince turned at the sound but Immanuel loudly wretched, grabbing the edge of the table for balance to block Quince from walking in Adam's direction. When Immanuel looked up, Adam was gone and the knot in his chest loosened a fraction.

His voice low with anger and disbelief, Quince muttered, "I could have sworn I— No matter, I'll get another."

"No."

When Quince turned, he stared into the barrel of a revolver. Immanuel's hand shook as he held the gun aloft. He wanted to keep it's alien heft as far away as possible, but his muscles trembled under its weight. The lighthouse keeper looked between Immanuel's mismatched eyes and the gun, his hands tightening on the harpoon's handle.

"Please don't make me use it," Immanuel whispered. What would his brave Adam do in this situation? He kept the gun trained on Quince's face and narrowed his eyes as he pulled back the hammer with a satisfying click. "Back out slowly."

Adam hurtled down the hall, heedless of the echo his pounding feet left in their wake. Wrapping his arms around Jenny's prone form, he hefted her higher and ran as fast as he could without tripping over the uneven bricks lining the floor. He had to get back to Immanuel. Quince had killed Jacobs and how many other selkies. Hell, he could have murdered half the women on the wall after seeing his collection of specimens. The calling stone bounced in his grip, a whisper cloying at his mind. Eying the woman half-conscious in his arms, Adam knew what he had to do.

As he hurried past the thundering engines and out the powerhouse door, Jenny lifted her head. Her eyes had lost their sheen and the wound on her forehead bled freely into her mop of hair until it matted against the crook of his arm. Adam ran over the dunes to the shore, his feet sliding in the wet sand, nearly sending him and Jenny face-first into the tide. Dropping to his knees in the surf, Adam held her in front of him with his arms tight across her middle to keep her from toppling over. Her breathing had become labored, and as he tried to put the calling stone into her hand, she hissed and blindly nipped at his arm.

"Jenny, I need you to call the others," Adam said, putting the stone into her cold hand and wrapping his over it to keep it in place. "Call them to help you. They'll listen to you."

Her head lolled to the side, revealing a shock of white. A word escaped her lips Adam couldn't understand. For a moment, Adam feared he had lost her at her sudden stillness, but then her hand closed around the stone. A vibration passed through his arm and into his chest. It rumbled through him like the metro, but this struck something far deeper and older within him. The sensation grew stronger until it ceased, leaving him hollow. Jenny slumped in Adam's grip. While her face had turned a sickly grey, breath still whistled in her throat.

Adam released a relieved breath when a shot rang out.

Chapter Twenty-Six
Creatures and Monsters

Immanuel barely saw the blow coming. The moment he stepped through the laboratory door, Quince swung. At the last second, Immanuel caught the motion in the darkened side of his eye and ducked back. The harpoon's heavy shaft whacked Immanuel's arm instead, sending the Colt skittering across the cobblestone floor. Pain rang through Immanuel's arm as he scrambled for the gun, but when his fingers brushed the pearl handle, Quince knocked it away with the blade of the harpoon. Immanuel stumbled, falling to his knees and sending waves of pain through his bruised arms. Quince snatched the gun from the floor and pointed it at Immanuel's head. His heart thrummed as he waited for the fatal blow. He had survived so much that he secretly hoped he possessed some semblance of immortality, but when the bullet aligned with his temple, he realized how foolish he had been.

"Get up."

Swallowing hard, Immanuel tried to suppress the tremor in his voice. "I can still—"

"Get up."

Immanuel rose slowly, keeping his eyes low. Seizing him by the shoulder, Quince shoved him up the steps toward the surface. His body ached with each step, and as he dragged his feet up the narrow stairs, his mind never left the intermittent press of the gun on the small of his back. At the top of the basement stairs, Immanuel paused, his gaze lingering on the front door. Could he outrun— But before he could finish the thought, the muzzle of the gun pressed into his spine. Immanuel shut his eyes against the sound of the shot and the possibility that the pain wouldn't even register.

"Up," Quince commanded, urging him down the hall to the lighthouse.

Immanuel's stomach lurched as his footfalls rang against the spiraling metal stairs. He had to get out. He had to do something, anything. As they reached the third story, he pictured himself shoving Quince down the steps as he had done to him earlier, but he would only have one shot at that and Quince would have been a fool not to put a bullet in him the moment he turned. By the time they reached the hatch on the uppermost landing, Immanuel's calves burned and his chest constricted with fear as the lighthouse keeper opened the hatch and motioned for Immanuel to climb. Immanuel froze on the ladder as the wind sent a pebble from the floor above soaring past him. It disappeared into the abyss before landing seconds later with an echoing clunk. If he died, would Adam come home to a dead cat too? The thought sickened him, but he banished the vision of Adam's face falling.

At the top, Immanuel kept his hand firmly on the glass enclosing the beacon. He closed his eyes against a wave of nausea at the sudden sensation of gravity dragging him back to earth. He had never been so high. Slowly turning, he found the whole of Seohl-wiga Island laid out before him with its verdant hills and curling waves and, somewhere beyond it, the dim suggestion of land. If he had gone up with Adam, the limitless sky would have been beautiful. They would have stood there for hours taking in the view. Hands, maybe even lips, touching far from prying eyes. *Adam*. He had promised to never leave him. Immanuel hung his head. More than anything he hoped Adam had gotten somewhere safe, yet a little piece of him still hoped he would appear at the hatch to save him.

Quince's deep set eyes gleamed in the rising light as he twitched the gun toward the door leading to the narrow catwalk. Stepping onto the rickety metal lip, Immanuel bit back tears. Wind whipped his hair into his eyes and snapped his coat until his pounding pulse was drowned beneath the wail of air sailing past his ears. Clutching the rail, Immanuel turned to face his captor.

"Jump," Quince commanded, keeping the gun pointed at Immanuel's chest. "You can do it yourself or I can blow you over."

"But I—" Immanuel had forced the thought from his mind the entire march up the steps, but as he looked over the side at the rocks and grass below, he knew he had nowhere to go. Wind cupped his cheek and swept over his hands. "I can't. They'll know I was pushed. I wouldn't—"

"Lots of men do it. You wouldn't be the first."

He needed to think. He needed time. "May— may I say a prayer first?" Immanuel asked.

Quince's face twitched and his hand dropped a fraction. "Fine, make your peace and get on with it."

Keeping his head bowed as if in prayer, Immanuel knelt before the rail and closed his eyes. It couldn't end this way. It had been a year since his abduction, and he refused to squander his life by going quietly. Perhaps, once or twice in fleeting desperation, he would have considered dashing himself into the rocks, but since he had been freed, he learned things got better. Pain faded, he made peace with his scars, even the remaining memories of his captivity were slowly being pushed out by holidays and late nights with Adam. A tear slipped from his eye and spattered on the metal beside his hand. Life only grew brighter, and he wouldn't let someone steal the light from him again. With the next gust, the panes of glass enclosing the lantern rattled in their frames.

Wind.

Without Adam at his side, the magic would be harder to maintain. Immanuel exhaled slowly. He had to focus. His little finger worked frantically against the metal, twisting his stray tear into a convoluted sigil until his mind caught the unseen lattice. Gripping the railing, Immanuel gathered the wind. The air grew heavy with salt and sea until the energy grew taught as a bowstring. In the space of a heartbeat, the breeze transformed into a missile of air. It sailed over Immanuel's head, forcing him down as it rammed into the glass. Bracing his head against the rail, Immanuel clenched his jaw at the force of the air bearing down. The metal groaned beneath his feet until the glass at his back cracked like ice and shattered inward.

Heedless of the glass jutting from the metal frame, Immanuel scrambled over the low wall and made for the hatch. A shot rang out an instant before the beacon exploded in a hail of shards. Immanuel flinched and sucked in a breath at the seer of hot glass piercing through his coat, but he couldn't stop. Forcing open the hatch, he jumped down the ladder and ran. His lungs seized and his head pounded with each step, but he couldn't stop. As he hit the first landing, a bullet hit the wall over his head by the time his mind registered the shot. Immanuel stumbled forward, gripping the hand rail tighter for fear of falling over the side.

He staggered back, ripping his hand from the rail as a bullet blasted through it and embedded in the bricks at his side. Rising to his feet, a shot whizzed past his head, coming within a hand's breadth from his nose. Quince's footsteps echoed through the silent lighthouse as Immanuel's eyes swept behind him, catching a flash of grey and brown. Taking the remaining steps three at a time, Immanuel sprinted as fast as his long legs would carry him.

As he rounded the final flight, Immanuel froze as a man stepped from the shadows. He raised his gaze only to have the air squeeze from his lungs. Adam dropped his weapon and trotted toward him with open arms.

"Oh, thank god, you're all right," Adam cried. "I heard gunshots and…"

Before he could finish, Immanuel grabbed Adam by the arm and forced him to a run. They pounded down the hall. As they reached the front door, the corner of the crate at Immanuel's side erupted in a shower of splinters. Immanuel frantically tried to unlock the door, his bloodied fingers futilely slipped over the mechanisms. Adam crashed into him, pushing Immanuel aside in time to force the door open and drag him out as another bullet lodged in the frame where he had just been.

"The selkies are down at the beach," Adam said through rough breaths as he dragged Immanuel to the hill leading down to the powerhouse.

Immanuel's head throbbed as he staggered after his companion through the wet grass. The tide flooded over the bank, cutting off any hopes he had of locking himself in the cottage until the ferry came. His lungs burned and seized, but he resisted the urge to cough as Quince's footsteps pounded behind them. At any moment Immanuel feared a harpoon or bullet would whiz by, mercilessly slicing through Adam's jacket as it had Jacobs'. He shuddered at the thought as Adam shoved him over a dune without daring to look back. Sliding down the wet sand, Immanuel wished he could stop or lie down or at least breathe, but he knew the moment he stopped, he would be hard-pressed to keep on. Before he could catch his breath, Adam hauled him up by the arm.

At the edge of the waves, Völva Hilde stood upon seeing them crest the hill. On the flat rocks of the jetty, Isa and Tara tended to a wounded selkie. The gorge rose in Immanuel's throat at the blood clotting her hair.

"He's followed us," Adam called to Hilde, "the one who hurt Jenny and the others."

"You know it was him?"

"Yes," he and Immanuel replied in unison as they reached her side.

As Immanuel turned to the bleeding woman, he froze at the click of an empty chamber misfiring. Quince's chest heaved as he tossed the gun aside and slid down the sand, but upon seeing the selkies, he narrowed his eyes and set his shoulders. Völva Hilde snarled as Tara left Jenny and Isa, her fingers elongating into razor-tipped claws. Snapping at Tara, Hilde strode closer until she and Quince stood eye-to-eye. Immanuel's gaze swept between the matching looks of fury and recognition.

"*You,*" she spat, shaking her head as she stalked between him and the others. "My own brother... Tell me you aren't this monster, Casper. Tell me they're wrong."

His face blotched red. "Me, a monster? Look at you! You're one of them. You chose to become an animal, like mother."

"And you chose to become a monster like papa. I never thought you'd take one after what happened to her." Her mouth worked and after a moment, she rasped, "Why would you take so many?"

"To end it. This isn't right. We're half-breeds. It's against nature."

"He needs to be punished for what he's done," Tara growled.

Without taking her eyes from Quince's face, Völva Hilde replied, "Take Jenny back to the den. He's my kin. He's my responsibility."

With the yawn of bone, Tara slipped into her half-seal form with Jenny resting in her arms. As the next wave crashed in, they disappeared beneath the surf. Immanuel's vision spotted, but Adam caught his arm before he staggered. Fatigue fell over him as he sank into the sand, but he forced his eyes open.

Hilde and Casper locked gazes. Even through her thin seal pelt, Immanuel could see a faint resemblance in the curve of their lips and the hard set of their jaws. What must have it been like to see your blood in the thing you loathed? The tips of Hilde's fingers webbed together and her nails extended as she approached Quince. When Immanuel took a step forward, Adam dragged him back toward the jetty where Isa watched rapt.

"What's happening?" Adam asked as the siblings circled like two predators.

"The punishment."

"What?"

"The punishment for a blood-traitor is death."

Hilde lunged. Immanuel clutched Adam's arm as the siblings fell to the sand, tumbling across the beach in a blur of grey wool and fur. Barks and muffled curses rang against the wind only to be drowned beneath the thud of bone on flesh. Blood flashed, though from whom, they couldn't say. Casper rolled, pinning Hilde long enough to reach for his hip.

"No!" Immanuel cried, but by the time the word left his lips, the knife had sunk between the Völva's ribs.

With a roar, she tore it free, dashing it into the sea. Rolling over to face him, Hilde looked into Quince's eyes and drew her hand across his throat. Immanuel turned his face away at the sucking gag of blood clogging his throat. As he collapsed into the sand, Isa scrambled from the rocks and ran to Hilde's side. It was only when Adam's hand tightened around Immanuel's that he dared to raise his gaze.

Isa stood at their feet, her round eyes glossy with tears and her hands cupped over her mouth. Casper and Hilde lay side-by-side. Quince had fallen onto his side, the blood pooling beneath his neck and shoulders the only evidence of the violence they had witnessed. His eyes stared blankly ahead at his sister. A gash marred the sleek fur of her ribs, bisecting a dark whirl with a lazy flow of blood.

Their blood trailed across the sand, pooling together until it was impossible to tell where selkie ended and man began.

Chapter Twenty-Seven
Wyrd

For the first time in days, Immanuel Winter slept soundly. The fire crackled in the hearth, warming his feet as he dozed in the armchair with Percy purring on his lap and a damp handkerchief clasped in his hand. Adam smiled to himself as he watched him from the parlor door. Between cleaning out the stores of body parts in the lighthouse basement, burying the dead in the pounding rain, and expending far too much energy during his escape, Immanuel found himself at the mercy of a terrible cold. By the time a small battalion of Interceptors showed up on the morning ferry, the island had already begun to quiet. As he and Immanuel walked them through the village explaining what had transpired, they found bruised and scratched men patching broken windows or mending the damage done to their ships. Whispers told of women who had disappeared during the fray, some with their daughters, others had left behind those too young to shift. Men had returned home to find their sons waiting with strange stones around their necks and final notes from their mother. Many others stayed, though few took notice.

Immanuel jolted awake at a loud pop from the fireplace. Before he could blindly rise, his eyes watered and he released a series of hard sneezes that made Adam cringe. Percy leapt from his lap, casting a dirty look over his bony shoulder as he sat on the edge of the carpet and licked where Immanuel had touched him with an invisible tongue. Adam leaned against the doorway, watching Immanuel with a tender look as heat flooded Immanuel's cheeks. Turning from his lover's gaze, he blew his nose and coughed. Adam resisted laughing. Somehow, even in a state of snot and perpetual fatigue, he still found Immanuel oddly adorable.

"Did I wake you?" Adam asked, carefully setting a cloth-covered bowl and a paper-wrapped package on the end table.

Glancing at the clock on the mantle, Immanuel replied, "It's for the best. Miss Elliott sent a note saying she would be coming by with someone from the Interceptors to pick up Berte's remains."

"Did she say anything about…?"

Immanuel shook his head and sank back into the armchair.

"Well, I would ask her when she arrives, but I'm sure you got in."

Immanuel closed his tired eyes again as Adam disappeared down the hall. A few moments later, he returned with a spoon and a cup of tea. Setting it on the end table, he handed the spoon along with the bowl to Immanuel who stared up at him with a raised brow and a red nose.

"I stopped to speak to Hadley and Lord Dorset. When he heard you were sick, he had Mrs. Negi pack you some of whatever they had for lunch. I couldn't tell you the name even if I wanted to, but Lord Dorset said it would help your cold. It smells as if it could strip paint."

Untying the cloth, Immanuel's mouth watered at the hunks of mutton, potatoes, and rice bathed in a thick brown gravy peppered with bits of red and orange. He drew in a deep breath and could barely smell anything but the burn of spices.

"That was very kind of him. I'll have to send him a note to thank him later."

"I wouldn't thank him until you've eaten it. I left you some bread and tea in case you need to extinguish your mouth."

Adam watched with a slight smirk as Immanuel dug into his meal. With each bite, his face grew redder until it matched his nose and he blinked back tears. Drawing in a long sniff, Immanuel snatched up the teacup.

"*Das ist würzig,*" he croaked. Immanuel downed his tea and released a tense breath. "I forgot to ask, why did you go to see Lord Dorset again? You said something when you left, but I don't remember what."

"I decided to take up Lord Dorset's offer and act as his London agent."

"Really?" Immanuel dabbed at his nose between bites. "But I thought you—"

Adam waved dismissively. "I did, but this is a far superior position to being an underling in some office. Working for a gentleman will afford me more freedom and clothes, both of which I think I'll need if I'm to follow you on more adventures. I can't be a clerk and an Interceptor, but I don't think Lord Dorset would mind the occasional absence."

A smile bloomed across Immanuel's lips despite the burning on his tongue. Before he could remind Adam that nothing was official yet, the doorbell rang. Setting the bowl down, Immanuel grabbed Percy and apologized as he closed him in the hall closet. When Immanuel was ready, Adam opened the door. Judith Elliott gave them each a stately nod and stepped inside, her eyes sweeping over Immanuel's sore features.

"I hope I haven't come at a bad time, Winter. I didn't realize you were still ill," she said, her brows softening slightly with concern.

"I'm all right. I just decided to lend some authenticity to my excuse for missing work. May I take your coat?"

"No, thank you. I won't be long. Do you have the body ready? I have a man waiting outside to take care of it."

Immanuel nodded and resisted the urge to sniff. From the corner of his eye, he could see Adam giving him a pointed look, but he didn't dare work the words up for fear that the answer would extinguish his last hope. At least if he never asked, there would always be the possibility that she could still tell him they made it.

"Winter."

Immanuel turned mid-step to find Miss Elliott watching him with a keen eye.

"You know you're in, right?"

His heart pounded in his throat. Swallowing against the knot, he shook his head.

"You did what we asked of you. *More* than what we asked." Taking a book from their shared shelf, she checked the title and returned it to its place. "No one is pleased about the minor massacre, but you have no control over creatures."

Immanuel flinched at the word.

"We've spun it into a freak storm for the press, but we were quite impressed with how you both handled it, considering the circumstances." She cleared her throat, giving Immanuel a wide berth. "When you're recovered, we will get you set-up at headquarters and begin your training. Trust me, you'll need your strength."

A wide smile broke across Immanuel's face. Turning to Adam, he found his excitement mirrored in his lover's quiet glow of pride. Adam clasped his shoulder, his fingers lingering as if he wished to do more.

"I told you, you would make it," Adam said, giving Judith a knowing look.

"We both made it, didn't we?" Immanuel asked, a quaver of panic tinging his voice.

"Of course. That was the deal, Winter. We needed both of you."

"Good, very good," he replied breathlessly, his eyes lingering on Adam's mouth. "Let me get Berte for you."

Immanuel ducked into the workroom as the cabby stepped in at Judith's knock. The moment he was out of sight, his smile deepened until it hurt his cheeks. They got in. His scarred eye blurred, but he blinked it away. Now was not the time for tears when he still had one thing to do before they could celebrate.

In the center of the workroom sat a wooden crate and within the crate, a coffin. Hours after returning home, Immanuel set to work repairing the damage he had done during Berte's autopsy. One by one, he carefully loaded her organs back into her body, laying her heart in its rightful place beneath her sternum and her eyes in their sockets. He stitched her skin as neatly as he could manage and brushed the snarls from her hair. The smell of Quince's homemade swill turned his stomach, but he had to do it. He promised himself on the way home that he would atone for what he had done. Smoothing the carefully written label, Immanuel double-checked that he had spelled Byron Durnure's name correctly. He had to make certain Berte could return to the sea one more time.

The man hefted the heavy crate out to the cab without a word. When the door closed behind him, Judith pulled an envelope from her clutch and handed it to Adam. Turning it over, he found it had the same seal as their first letter with a chimera-like creature and the motto *Obscuris vera involvens* scrawled in purple wax.

"Congratulations, Mr. Winter and Mr. Fenice. I hope to see you both as soon as you're up to it." She smiled, her rouged lips sharp. "You're a more valuable asset to us than you could know."

With a quick good-bye, she let herself out, leaving the men in silence. For a long moment, they merely stared at the letter until the closet door rattled on its hinges. Percy burst out the instant Immanuel turned the knob, meowing soundlessly at Adam in complaint. Laughing, Immanuel scooped the cat into his arms and held him until he squirmed out of his grasp. Percy gave him a sullen look before slinking back to his spot by the fire.

"You did it," Adam said, drawing Immanuel into his arms, his fingers weaving through his hair and the across the nape of his neck.

"*We* did it." Pulling the letter from Adam's grip, he set it on the hall table and buried his face in his lover's shoulder. Immanuel closed his tired eyes, relishing the scent of Adam's pomade and cologne and the steady drum of his heart against his cheek. He coughed and whispered, "Are you certain you want to do this? There would be a lot of magic and strange things in our lives."

"There are already plenty of magic and strange things in my life. What's a few more?" he replied as he drew Immanuel in for a kiss.

A year ago he had thought his life over, but as he and Immanuel stood intertwined with lips and hands expressing what words could never convey, he found a seedling of hope growing against all odds. So much had been torn from him, yet he found it remerging from the ashes bit by bit. Somethings had been deformed into a shape he scarcely recognized, but with time, he thought they, too, might heal. Staring into Adam's eyes and seeing a depth of love he had never expected, he knew that even at the worst of times, it had all been worth it. Adam's hands trailed across the buttons of his companion's waistcoat as Immanuel released a moan into his lips.

A year ago, he never would have thought that after all that had happened, all he had seen, all he had lost, that life had more to give him. Most importantly, it had given him Adam.

About the Author

Kara Jorgensen is an anachronistic oddball with a penchant for all things antiquated, morbid, or just plain strange. While in college, she realized she no longer wanted to be Victor Frankenstein but instead wanted to write like Mary Shelley and thus abandoned her future career in science for writing. She melds her passions through her books and received an MFA in Creative and Professional Writing in 2016. When not writing, she can be found hanging out with her dogs watching period dramas or trying to convince her students to cite their sources.

For more info, please visit KaraJorgensen.com or subscribe to her newsletter, **Her Ladyship's Missive**, to receive a *free short story*, news about releases and sales as well as future projects.

Join her Facebook group, **Lady Jorgensen's Interceptors**, to chat with other fans, indulge in Victorian goodies, and get news before anyone else.

Also by the Author
The Ingenious Mechanical Devices

The Earl of Brass (IMD#1)

The Gentleman Devil (IMD#2)

"An Oxford Holiday: An Ingenious Mechanical Devices Companion Short
Story"

The Earl and the Artificer (IMD#3)

"The Errant Earl: An Ingenious Mechanical Devices Companion Short
Story"

Dead Magic (IMD#4)

Selkie Cove (IMD#5)

www.ingramcontent.com/pod-product-compliance
Lightning Source LLC
Chambersburg PA
CBHW030316200626
46816CB00006BA/1814